Praise for *Augusta Locke*

Finalist for the Mountain and Plains Booksellers Association Award

"Emotions on a human scale—love and loss, hope and longing—seem small things when set against Wyoming's expansive vistas. But when William Haywood Henderson brings life and landscape together, human spirit is not dwarfed by the harsh beauty surrounding it. Instead, in Henderson's new novel, the forces of tenacity, courage, and sorrow are brought into sharp relief by the spare landscape. . . . Henderson captures the feel of the land with lyric prose."
—*The Denver Post*

"Henderson's novel is an extraordinarily beautiful creation . . . told in languorous prose virtually encrusted with the details of nature—very reminiscent of Annie Dillard. . . . Gussie is truly her own kind of woman, and her own kind of mother. As much a story of lineage and the meaning of family as it is a story of nature, this novel covers a lot of ground in greater detail than one would imagine possible in some four hundred pages. Read slowly, and enjoy this raw and haunting tale."
—*Booklist* (starred review)

"As we move through Gussie's life, the landscape of the American West comes across as a living thing. Meanwhile, the characters who pass through her life are well-drawn, memorable."
—*The Philadelphia Inquirer*

"Like the many life-hardened pioneers who have come before her, Gussie Locke is tough . . . a woman who is achingly human in her unquenchable longing for something of life that is more tangible, more meaningful."
—*Rocky Mountain News*

"Henderson's astonishing talents as a descriptive, fluent writer are everywhere evident in *Augusta Locke*, which, though long, reads quickly and gracefully."
—*The Bloomsbury Review*

"Henderson's novel explores the losses inherent in a country where migration is the only constant. What makes a family beyond the blood ties that don't always bind? Some might say that Gussie is a woman ahead of her time, making choices that run counter to the status quo of the period, but she is a woman who is very much a part of the landscape of the open spaces of the West, the places most emigrants bypassed on their way to move fertile ground." —*Billings Gazette*

"Haunting . . . the book's particular strengths are its unfolding of a unique woman's life and its depiction of places where the natural world awakens the senses and commands respect, evoking wonder and awe." —*Library Journal*

"A near-epic saga . . . Beginning in 1903, the tale spans the century, and [Henderson] evokes period detail with relish, from the sputter of early motor coaches to the parched throats of ranchers during Prohibition. The evocative, the lyrical, the descriptive, in fact, is his keynote." —*Kirkus Reviews*

"Against the enormous beauty of the American [West] depicted in Henderson's third novel, people cast small but significant shadows while tending to families as fragile as fallen leaves. . . . Saturated with details of the natural [West], Henderson's work etches in high relief the image of a solitary life among scenic riches." —*Publishers Weekly*

PENGUIN BOOKS

AUGUSTA LOCKE

William Haywood Henderson was a Wallace Stegner
Fellow in creative writing at Stanford. He is the author
of two novels, *The Rest of the Earth* and *Native*. He grew
up in Colorado and Wyoming, and currently lives in
Denver, where he teaches at a nonprofit creative writing
school, Lighthouse Writers Workshop.

To request Penguin Readers Guides by mail
(while supplies last), please call (800) 778-6425
or e-mail reading@us.penguingroup.com.
To access Penguin Readers Guides online,
visit our Web site at www.penguin.com.

AUGUSTA LOCKE

WILLIAM HAYWOOD HENDERSON

PENGUIN BOOKS

PENGUIN BOOKS

Published by the Penguin Group

Penguin Group (USA) Inc., 375 Hudson Street, New York, New York 10014, U.S.A.
Penguin Group (Canada), 90 Eglinton Avenue East, Suite 700, Toronto, Ontario, Canada
M4P 2Y3 (a division of Pearson Penguin Canada Inc.) • Penguin Books Ltd, 80 Strand, London WC2R 0RL, England • Penguin Ireland, 25 St Stephen's Green, Dublin 2, Ireland (a di-
vision of Penguin Books Ltd) • Penguin Group (Australia), 250 Camberwell Road,
Camberwell, Victoria 3124, Australia (a division of Pearson Australia Group Pty Ltd) • Pen-
guin Books India Pvt Ltd, 11 Community Centre, Panchsheel Park, New Delhi – 110 017,
India • Penguin Group (NZ), 67 Apollo Drive, Mairangi Bay, Auckland 1311, New Zealand
(a division of Pearson New Zealand Ltd) • Penguin Books (South Africa) (Pty) Ltd, 24
Sturdee Avenue, Rosebank, Johannesburg 2196, South Africa

Penguin Books Ltd, Registered Offices:
80 Strand, London WC2R 0RL, England

First published in the United States of America by Viking Penguin,
a member of Penguin Group (USA) Inc. 2006
Published in Penguin Books 2007

10 9 8 7 6 5 4 3 2 1

PUBLISHER'S NOTE
This is a work of fiction. Names, characters, places, and incidents either are the product of
the author's imagination or are used fictitiously, and any resemblance to actual persons, living or dead, business establishments, events, or locales is entirely coincidental.

ISBN 0-670-03491-6 (hc.)
ISBN 978-0-14-303829-0 (pbk.)
CIP data available

Printed in the United States of America
Set in Iowan
Designed by Carla Bolte

FOR RITA GABIS

ONE

Bomber Basin

Alone in the granite scoop of Bomber Basin, together on a soft patch of alpine sedges, Gussie Locke and her grandson, Hayden, and her great-granddaughter, Laurel, waited for Jack Fisher. They gathered the remains of their lunch, wrapped up the bread and salami. The orange peels had curled into hard little bowls. The afternoon sounds were sharp and clear, carried on the unfiltered sunlight, the reflections from lake and cliffs, ten thousand feet high in the Wind River Range.

Gussie inhaled, held the afternoon in her lungs. Her cells consumed the air, forced the day's heat out along the trails of her veins. She had been drawn back to Bomber Basin by the pristine scent of the summer snowfields, by the rare altitude, by the memory of Jack Fisher riding into the basin, into the smoky light of the fire. She felt almost hale. In a few hours, Jack would arrive.

She had telephoned Jack, invited him to join her in Bomber Basin. She'd reminded him of the nesting finches, the odd color of the barren lake, the sun on the cliffs. She'd reminded him of the morning ice at the shore, the way the ice grew around the stones, a stitching of long crystals. She'd reminded him of the echoes in the basin, the amphitheater of the cliffs and the broken steps. And she'd told him there would be strangers he would want to meet, these two travelers who had found her cabin in its stand of aspen, in its unmarked acres far toward the end of the DuNoir road.

With a glance at his watch, Hayden climbed to his feet. "You ladies enjoy the sun," he said. "I'll get us settled."

Gussie squinted at his shape dark against the sun and the mass of Spider Peak. Hayden was slight, almost delicate, and she could see in him her own lean shoulders, her own blunt jaw and unruly hair. He must have had a rough time of it, so clearly steeped in her blood. "I could help you," Gussie said, though she didn't want to move. The sun was too warm, her muscles cramped by the ride up along East Torrey Creek. They'd left the broad view behind, passed Bomber Falls, followed the intermittent trail, the miles through the canyon, through marshes and meadows and dark forest, into the basin. Hayden had led the packhorses himself, and she'd expected him to be jerked from his saddle at any moment, his hand too often tangled in the rope, but she'd kept quiet. And now she knew that she'd only hover at his shoulder as he tried to organize the gear, that she'd have to refrain from pointing and suggesting. "I'm not going to help you, sweetheart."

"That's fine. How could I accept your help?" He carried the lunch supplies back toward the camp, leaving a trace where he'd sat on the sedges, a silvery patch of pressed stems. Gussie ran her fingers across that trace, felt the essence of the plants, felt the heat of Hayden's body, heat of the sun, and the cold earth beneath. In the shelter of whitebark pine, Hayden stooped at the panniers, started to arrange the goods they would need for the next week. The horses shuffled at the limits of their pickets, tearing the frail grasses from the roots.

Laurel lay back, closed her eyes. "He doesn't have a clue what he's doing," she said. "We'll be sleeping in a tarp and eating raw flour."

"He's on his own," Gussie said.

"That's not very nice."

"Nothing I can teach him that he can't learn himself."

The air gleamed, pressed light against Laurel's skin. Gussie looked at the girl's twitching eyelids, the dryness of her lips. Laurel was still a child, slim and bony, nearly thirteen. After a long still minute, Gussie almost thought she could hear Laurel's pulse, the quiver at her wrists where her sleeves exposed the white. Gussie's own skin was dry brown. It seemed impossible that Laurel would ever age, ever diminish, yet somewhere in the girl's long lines was Gussie's blood.

Apple flesh, Gussie thought. Laurel had brought apples from California. What a treat they had been, apples in December. They had unloaded Hayden's car, snow falling so fast that their tracks had filled before they could return for a final load, but the apples were all safely into the shelter of Gussie's pantry. *Porter, Northern Spy, Blue Pearmain,* Laurel had said, freeing each apple from its wrap of tissue paper. The red blush, the pale green, the slice of the knife. Huddled in the kitchen, they had shared a few, compared the sweetness, the snap of the skin, Gussie and these two strangers who'd emerged from the storm. *All from my grandmother's orchard,* Laurel had said, and that grandmother would be Anne, Gussie's own daughter, long gone from Wyoming, long lost to Gussie. *Anne,* Gussie thought. *Apple flesh.*

Apple flesh, the men had said, nearly seventy years ago, leaning close over the infant Anne, not yet a year old. And Gussie had centered herself in the hotel parlor, held Anne up into the light, folded back the corner of the blanket. The chandelier's radiance circled deep in Anne's blue eyes, and the shadows of the men also crowded in the blue, and Gussie's own shadow was an awkward form. *I'm not delicate,* Gussie had thought. The men were around her, around her daughter, heating the air with their breath. *Apple. Angel.* Then Gussie saw Anne's skin, the lucent white, the subtle veins—this was her daughter, her own flesh.

Gussie had been drawn to the infant Anne, drawn the same as all the others, men and women alike, drawn by the surprise of such a child in the Wyoming desert. Gussie had never quite been sure of Anne's weight in her arms, never sure of the girl's smile. It was not Gussie's smile. It might have been Jack Fisher's smile, but Gussie hadn't been able to remember Jack Fisher clearly enough to judge if the smile was his—unlikely that such a delicate turn of the lips could come from a man. Gussie had known Jack only a single day—he could have been dead, for all she knew, could have been moldering in the ground of some battlefield, the French countryside gray with rain, the Great War rolling far beyond his final steps. But Gussie had kept studying her daughter, looking at the curve of her ear, the hollow of her nostrils, the set of her shoulders, looking for Jack, looking for herself.

And here was Laurel, great-granddaughter, far toward the end of the century, dozing, the blades of the sedges pressing against her shoulders, her cheeks, the leaves of the wildflowers crowding the gaps between her fingers, her legs, the blooms abrupt and fiery in the brief summer. To Gussie this girl was remarkably strange, remarkably dear. There were years between them, whole continents of regret. Laurel had lost her mother, Ruth—an accident. Gussie had lost her daughter, Anne—abandoned. How many layers between Gussie and Laurel, how many people that Gussie would never know, how many seasons? Why hadn't Gussie known Laurel since her birth? Why hadn't Gussie held Laurel to the light, tipped back the edge of the blanket, opened her to the sun and sky? Gussie looked closer, but she couldn't find herself in the girl's pale form.

Gussie turned away from Laurel, squinted to focus the afternoon. Water ran everywhere in the basin. Up against the spine of the Wind River Range, even in July, snowfields held to the cliffs. Black rosy finches flew against the snow—Gussie heard their constant chatter, their bickering, feeding, sounds of endless years, of high country, low country, freeze and thaw.

Through long winters, from her cabin on the DuNoir road, for decades, with the glare of snow at the window, Gussie had watched the black rosy finches mob her feeders. The birds fluffed themselves against the cold, moved on through the aspen. And each spring, the finches didn't wait for the valley heat but scattered right off into the face of the Wind River Range. They dodged a Clark's nutcracker, ascended through clouds of newborn gnats, and then they reached the highest basins. They paired again, hunted out the old nests. Perhaps it was the cold the finches loved, and the memory of ice at the edge of a lake.

Gussie listened to each small sound—the chatter, the breeze, the rustle of canvas as Hayden dragged the tent behind him, ready to raise it in a spot they'd chosen among the pines. Gussie didn't want to watch him—it was her tent, but raising it was beyond her strength. She knew the smell of the tent—it was thick with decades of woodsmoke—knew the weight of the canvas, the wind it would take to disturb the heavy walls, how the canvas filtered sound. Over the years, she had lain in the tent at dawn and heard the shift of boots on gravel so clearly that she thought she could picture the scene perfectly, picture the gait of the man moving through the chill, but then the echo threw the action farther from camp or much closer than she had expected, and for a moment she'd felt blind and alone.

Hayden had the canvas spread out. He sorted through the stakes, worked to untangle the ropes. Gussie turned to Laurel. "Let's go, sweetheart. I can't wait here."

Laurel roused directly to her feet, helped Gussie up. "Where are we going?"

"To look for nests." Gussie stretched the long ride out of her tendons, moved on, taking the girl with her.

"Don't you want your binoculars?"

"You can't find a nest with binoculars."

They traced the lakeshore. Bomber Lake, a half-mile long, was an unnatural scoured blue. Above, water had leached from the fissures of the cliffs, streaking the granite with darkness. Following the fishermen's trail around the end of the lake, Gussie moved slowly enough to keep her heartbeat contained. Laurel held to Gussie's arm, balanced her. Gussie pointed to the mats of kinnikinnick, the pink flowers, red fruit, and the silky scorpionweed. She wouldn't find any wild bergamot, not at this altitude, but she could use it—a tea to clear her lungs, calm her belly, dissolve the gas that bubbled, or she could just pack the minty leaves around her aching teeth.

They passed the last of the trees, worked their way up the slope. Far above, a pair of finches dove among the rocks, fed at the edge of the snow. The finches went on. Gussie lost them.

"You should stop," Laurel said. "We'll sit until you can breathe." Laurel found a spot where soil had gathered, where grass had started, and she lowered Gussie onto the softness. Gussie held herself as still as her blood would allow.

Gussie felt her pulse at her temples. Her blood's passage hissed through her ears. She knew her blood moved in great circuits, found the heart, and then forced its way again onto the narrowing pathways. The finest veins threaded toward the surface and the blood cooled and caught the hint of daylight, then drew deep inside again. Her heart prattled in her veins. There was nothing to do about it except follow her doctor's orders and stop if she heard her heartbeat centered between her ears.

Across the lake, Hayden had finished with the tent. The spine of the roof sagged—it would collect water, pool and soak, drip on them, but only if it rained. It might not rain. He tied open the flaps, placed three cots in there, laid out the sleeping bags and pillows. There was room for a fourth cot, but Jack Fisher would have his own tent. Hayden sat on a cot, elbows on his knees, chin in hands, looking at the other cots. There would be no getting away from each other.

The finches chattered. Gussie turned, saw them again. She would have to get closer to the snow. "I'm fine now," Gussie said. "Let's go." She stood, pulled Laurel upright with her.

"Back to camp?" Laurel said, taking a step down the slope.

Gussie held steady. "We only just started."

"You've done enough for one day."

"We're going up." She turned, and Laurel came around with her. Gussie let the girl support her.

They moved into the scree slope, that steep pile of shattered stone, ascended the slabs of granite, broke through the spiderwebs that seemed the only substance holding the slope against gravity. Gussie kept her eyes on her steps, listened to her soles grind and slip. She heard her belt creak, her joints pop. Through a gradual half hour, avoiding the purple sky pilots, noting the pika trails and caches of dry grass, they rose from the lake, and, finally, with her hand clasped tight in Laurel's, Gussie found herself at the fringe of a snowfield.

And here the black rosy finches fed where the snow melted. They flashed. They came and went. Slowly, Gussie found the focus of all that nervous movement—the base of the cliff, just above, where the snow had shrunk back a few inches from the reflected glare, the heated stone.

"You see where they're going into the stone, Laurel?"

"Yes. I can see it."

"That's where we'll look."

Gussie made her way along the margin of the snowfield, and Laurel came behind, reaching up to Gussie's elbow or hip to steady her. They moved through the high sounds of falling water, stepped through the rivulets, up to the cliff face—cracks and deep-rooted weight.

To trace along the base of the cliff, to thread that gap of open stone and avoid pitching backward into the snow and sliding away, they had to press themselves to the wall and shuffle sideways. The going was narrow. Gussie's fingers shook. Her nails scraped. And then she reached a crevice, a pure cut, slender but tall. She gripped Laurel tight around the shoulders, held her, brought her close.

"Here we are, sweetheart."

They looked into the crevice, deep into the sound of finches in darkness. After a long while Gussie was sure she could distinguish the ruffling of wings, could hear the birds working at the weave of grass, stems, moss. No way to reach into that narrow gap. No way to prove she'd found a black rosy finch nest after half a life of looking.

"You have those thin arms, Laurel. Those long bones." She took hold of Laurel's wrist and placed her hand at the crevice, tried to feed the girl's fingers into darkness. "Reach in, Laurel. See what you feel."

Laurel held back. "No."

"For me, Laurel. I want to see the nest."

"Ruin it?"

"We'll put it back."

Laurel pulled herself free from Gussie's grip. "They'll peck me. I won't do it." Abruptly, she turned around, and Gussie turned with her. The snowfield pitched away below them. They caught themselves back against the wall. Laurel contorted her arms behind her, threaded her fingers into the crevice, took hold of the rock, and Gussie held to Laurel's arm.

Gussie exhaled. She was pinned by the brightness of the sun off the snow, pinned to Laurel's side, and through that brilliant haze she saw the whole valley below, the whole undersurface of the lake exposed, the bed diving to a dim fold. And the patterns of boulder and green spread all around, like a puzzled dream, a lunatic map. And the horses, their hooves clattering. And Hayden, dear boy, working away, deep inside the light, beyond the snow.

"I'm sorry," Laurel said.

"That's okay. Too late to find a nest, maybe. Or whatever's in there."

They were balanced high above the lake. It would be a dangerous descent. The light was as she remembered it. In a few hours, the lake would darken toward evening. The sky would detach above the cliffs, separated by a line of night, and the light in the basin would seem almost subterranean, as if the granite had collected light through the day, as if the basin lit the sky.

Gussie waited for the sound of Jack Fisher's spurs, the steel stars, his *halloo*, his *git-git* to his horse. Forty-three years ago she'd found Jack here in Bomber Basin, when she thought she'd lost him forever. Now, soon, he would arrive, and she would look to him, follow his approach. And Hayden and Laurel would also look to him, see the man, a stranger, their blood.

TWO

Ravenglass

"She's not the child I expected," Brud Tornig said when Gussie was three years old. "She's all forehead. Scares me, almost, the way she looks at me."

He cleared a small mirror with his sleeve, stood at the window in the northern Minnesota light, tried to capture his own profile, his eyes straining to the side. Scrounging in a drawer, he found another mirror, and with two mirrors he worked the angles, arms outstretched, until he settled himself. He was a striking fellow, the hint of Scandinavian blondness encased in Ojibwa. He brought Leota and Gussie, mother and daughter, close to his sides, worked the three faces together in the mirrors. Gussie watched their profiles swing and merge.

"She's not my daughter," Brud said.

"No question she's your daughter," Leota said.

"Hard to believe."

"The girl will change, given time. She might grow into the image of you. Or she might look like me."

Brud turned a mirror, held it squarely in front of Leota. "Look at yourself."

"I know what I look like." She ran a finger across her cheek, brushed at her skin, leaned closer to the glass, as if scanning for a blemish, a shadow imperfection. "What of it?"

"Don't tell me this is our child. She has nothing of us."

"She has our blood. She has our love. Doesn't she?"

"Sure. Sure she has."

Over the years, Gussie watched for the change, waited for her hair to gloss like Brud's, her eyes to pale like Leota's, something, anything, but she remained an odd muddle, floundering along in the wake of her beautiful parents.

◆ ◆ ◆

Often, during the early years, Brud returned home with a trifle for Gussie—a handful of silk flowers to weave into her hair, or lace for her cuffs, or ribbon. He came in from the roads and trails, from trading, from working the odd labor, and he dropped his pack on the bed, brought out a crumpled parcel.

"This is for your girl," he said to Leota. "I saw it in a window, in moonlight—it looked silver, like in a dream, but in the morning, when I returned to buy it, it looked different. It still looked pretty, but not the same. Never the same in daylight."

It was a length of deep blue crepe. Gussie was four years old. She remembered that May morning, remembered the dark blue crepe dress, Leota's creation, remembered sitting down in the dress in the brightness of the season's first heat, turning her face to the sun, her eyes closed. She lolled her head, and the crepe whispered, layer against layer, the petals of the sleeves, the overlapping skirts. She heard Leota say, "I think she has already ruined it. She has no sense of what to do with a dress like that."

Gussie could have sat there for hours, locked to the sun, waiting for a passing shadow to move her. The crepe was like warm air settled on her shoulders, drifting along her legs. She spread her arms, and the cloth opened out and caught more heat. She felt light enough to float up out of that clearing, up across the soft rolling surface of the Minnesota woods, where the lakes came and went in the green, where the marshes bubbled in tangled sweeps. She had never flown any higher than her father's shoulders. In winter, Brud carried her above the sedges, the strands thick white with frost and combed over by the wind. She let the sedges jag along her trailing palms, and she knew her skin was tough.

"This is the last," Leota said. "I'm not putting her in anything fancy again. We have to work with her nature. She collects all those scraps—sticks and thorns and insects."

"You're giving up on her?" Brud said.

"I'm not an alchemist."

So Gussie wore wool and cotton in brown and green and plaid. Leota pulled the shirts square on Gussie's shoulders or offered a patch for the knee, a white kerchief, a sturdier belt. Leota chose clothes that slid comfortably onto her girl's arms and legs, that withstood a rocky scramble or a slog through brush, and she offered up a gift of winter-wool pants, mimicked her daughter's smile.

"Try on these trousers, Gussie. Mr. Baxter told me a pair like this did his son fine through a blizzard. The poor boy was caught in a four-day bivouac without fuel."

◆ ◆ ◆

Gussie roamed the Minnesota trails toward town, where fences strung the last shadows of forest and each house shaped a unique desire. She looked for the ladies with their lemon hair and tough pink nails. The ladies greeted her with delicate voices. "Little one," they said. "You're lost, I think. Where's your mother? Where's that lovely girl, poor thing? Alone out there?"

Gussie tested her voice against their soft tones, flattened her syllables into a single breathless note. "My mother is at her work."

"What work is that?"

"She's making me a beautiful baby doll." A lie, but she enjoyed the strange melancholy that flickered across the ladies' faces.

"Oh, sweetheart . . . you simple child . . . that's so . . ." They handed her a drop of sugar candy. And then they continued along the street, went about their appointments, entered the shops, the curtained spaces of Ravenglass.

Gussie looked for the gentlemen with their black hats and rough-shaved chins. She liked the way they spit, adjusted their heavy trousers, complained. "Got too much to do before sunset," they said. "Never had a day in my life when the Lord wasn't after me, getting me down to business. My foot hurts. My back is nearly broke." And when they noticed her watching, they said, "Jesus Christ but she gave me a start. Quiet as a hunter. Got a bit of the old world in her. Like Brud."

"My daddy?" she said, smiling, advancing.

They turned away, as if they hadn't heard her, as if they didn't want to hear her. "That Brud is a man to be watched. To be watched out for. An attractive form, without a doubt. Cold as night."

Gussie kept after them. "My daddy," she said. "You know him?" And then the thrill as those tall men turned on her, glowered.

"Run on, little girl," they said. "Back to the woods. Back to your nest." They left her, but she heard them. "That daddy of hers came in from the trails north. He could keep going if he wanted, back to whatever fen or quag gave him rise. I'm not at ease with the looks the ladies give him. Don't care for the brute."

She knew it was wrong for them to speak this way, almost cursing her father, knew it from their blush, their bluster, their silence as they hurried back to their shovels, saws, ledgers, horses. But she wanted to hear them, wanted their words jangling in her ears, wanted the men's focus, wanted to hear her parents' names, wanted to know how her parents were known.

She moved on through the lanes that gave out to the wooded eaves, where the trails started again. She took a long circuit through the wilds, but she always returned to Ravenglass. She haunted the windows for the chatter and endearments. She followed the children, her schoolmates, traced their escapes around trees, through gates. She loved their high songs and the blushed pale of them all.

They spied her, chased her, drove her into a bank of lilacs. The dry inner branches scratched her skin, drew tiny beads of blood. She looked out through the dark leaves, the purple eruptions of blossom. All those small faces searched the shadows, timid now that their quarry was cornered, obscured.

"Come out, Gussie."

"Come in," she said, and she grabbed a branch, shook it. Pollen rained. Petals spiraled down.

The children sneezed, brushed at their cheeks, backed away a step. "You don't belong in there. This is someone's yard. Don't you know that?"

"I know."

"This isn't a place where you can come and go as you please."

Gussie let loose with the nasty squawk of a raven, the sound so close to real that she surprised herself, gave herself a shiver. The children scattered, screeching, glancing back. They found a safe vantage from which to watch, and toward evening they waited for Gussie to give up her sanctuary and emerge onto the lawn, exposed, ready for a new chase, but the mothers called, the bells were rung, and Gussie was left alone. She came out with the fireflies, into the dusky smoke, the bloodless sunset. She counted the lit windows, made her way from house to house.

One day or another, she would peer in at a windowpane, catch herself there, a frown in a cloud of curls, and then another face would appear in hers. Once it was the girl with the stung lips, another time it was the feebleminded boy, always a softer shape with blue eyes wide as dawn and the delicate little mouth shaping a silent howl. She aligned her eyes with those other eyes, opened her mouth in reflection. Her brown eyes eclipsed the blue, but her mouth could never shape such perfect terror. She rapped her knuckles on the glass and leapt away.

She heard the children talk. "Brud Tornig made Gussie out of scraps of hides his daddy, Einar, trapped. Old Einar pretty much killed everything within a day's walk, way back in the last century. She's all that's left."

◆ ◆ ◆

Brud and his father, Einar, had built the cabin in the red pines, a sheltered mile from the bounds of Ravenglass. They had chipped the shingles for the roof, whitewashed the cabin inside and out, settled onto the straight-backed bachelor chairs, late in the nineteenth century.

Gussie listened until the last sound of Brud's footsteps faded, submerged beneath the damp blanket of night. She couldn't know where he headed. There were trails, marshes, stone cases for lost lakes. He might parallel the farmers' open fields, continue past the white cedars, their roots gripping the dry rocks, past the maple beside a sluggish pond, the paper birch in its pure white skin. All a part of his blood, that slow pulse.

When Brud was gone, the house was silent, unless Leota didn't sleep, and then Gussie heard the clatter of china, the metal snip of scissors, rustle of magazine leaves, small flame in a hurricane glass. Leota's restless sounds pushed at the walls, crossed and tangled with themselves. And then Brud returned. His sleeping breath was like the quaver of loose leaves, the outside hush of night settled inside.

Leota had transformed the old bachelor cabin into a house with parlor. The trees were cleared to beyond the new fence. Honeysuckle screened the path far down the front yard to the gate, where white-painted stones edged the dirt road. With the seasons, Leota adjusted the furniture to the angle of the sun. Leota liked the way the sunlight diffused off the surface of her mother's table, brought to these woods in the dowry wagon from Duluth, liked the way it lit her face, as reflected in her mother's silver bowls. She studied the sterling curve of her chin, the faint blush. She tipped the chair a bit to the left, moved the table closer to the window, removed a doily from the cherrywood to clear the way. And from down at the front gate, Gussie often saw her mother far up at that window, saw the illuminated face, a startling white delicacy, with the dark pine eaves looming beyond.

When a man paused at the gate, looking up at Leota's bright face for long minutes, Leota emerged onto the front step with a broom in hand, made a show of sweeping the immaculate stoop, made a show of noticing the man as he waited, unmoving, shading his eyes for clarity, to be sure of what he saw.

"It's a lovely spot, ma'am," the man said.

Leota came down the steps to the path and said, "I've put my elbows to the place, but I'm just getting started." And then she wended among the honeysuckle until she could see the man clearly, stopped and went no farther, didn't make it to the gate. The man wasn't half the measure of Brud—no man who paused at the gate ever was.

Leota and Gussie bathed together. In the kitchen, in the dimness of the north-facing window, they filled the tub with the plash of hot water from the kettle, crumbled rose petals, inhaled the earthy steam. Gussie was nine years old, still small, still unsettled in appearance, her features shadowed beneath Leota's slender height. Together they stood in the tub, stooped and dunked sponges, washed each other. They turned, brushed elbow to shoulder, chin to rib. Gussie worked over her mother's skin, turning the white to pink with her pressure. Leota slogged her sponge through the water, wrung it out above her daughter's head, dabbed at the girl. Gussie cleared the water from her eyes, attended to the crease beneath her mother's weighted breasts, the faint hairs beneath her arms, the recesses behind her knees. A seamless expanse. A sublime translucence.

"Why do men look at you?" Gussie said, unable to look away.

"Because I deserve it."

◆ ◆ ◆

Alone before dawn, Gussie learned that if she listened long enough there were sounds to the darkness, sounds that circled against the coming sun. And then the swoop above the clearing, a raven alone in the first high gray, or a pair of ravens scanning the ground, a black gaze, cutting beyond the pines. She didn't know where the ravens traveled or how they found their way.

The ravens' calls slid across winter ice, drove deep into summer evenings through the insect buzz. And their calls sometimes took on the shape of other sounds—a mimic of dogs, other birds, voices, machines—a game, a ruse. She practiced her mimic of the ravens, tried to feel the meaning of their calls on her tongue.

She saw ravens like dark ash buffeted by the wind, high against the clouds. She saw them far across a field, mobbing a carcass. Brud told her that ravens would recruit a wolf to crack a newfound carcass and expose the yellow fat and the meat. Ravens gave her a tremor—the razor of their bills, their plummeting mirror courtship from a great height, the way they seemed to hold to each other headlong and then catch the air just above the ground.

Brud told her stories. When he was a child her age, eight years old, he and Einar trapped by scent as much as by sign. Blocking off the sky in huge cold sheets, the northern lights rose far beyond the reach of the small fire where Brud and Einar circled their camp, where they waited through the deepest snows in a bower of paper birch, the gold leaves dangling like Christmas from the ceiling. He told her of the ravens, how they roosted sometimes in huge numbers, a thousand or more, how a great horned owl might swoop through the darkness and snatch one with its talons. Would the ravens know that one of their kin was missing when there were so many others? She understood that ravens were dark like her father, sleek and smart, that they were vulnerable. He told her of his first view of Ravenglass, how it seemed a crowded roost, those big bundled wooden houses crackling full of life, and she understood.

She wandered farther from home. She found veins of open air in the pine forest, lay there and watched the sky. For hours, only clouds passed, only sounds from some other quarter, and then a whisper drew through the air, the sharp call of a bird, and a raven passed above that bright cleft of the pines, and in that flash Gussie saw the bird scan the ground, saw how it focused on her lying there, how quickly it judged her dangerous or worthless and moved on. She ran after the raven—she wanted to see again how it looked at the earth—but she ran into a black explosion, ravens rising all around, their voices loud and close, broad wings in the air, nothing she could follow. She was left there. A deer lay exposed to the heat, eyes pecked to murky pools, bottleflies making a green buzz.

That night, Gussie dreamed.

A raven skimmed the treetops. With his speed, the vantages shifted and fell away, but still he knew what each gap in the canopy held—good fortune, ripened seeds, death, meat to cache. And there was a small figure running, no more than a girl. He moved on. He might return one day to taunt her, to draw her along until she leaped, frustrated, trying to follow up onto his trails, but she was bound by her weight, her stupid clumsy stumbles. She couldn't see the world, the sky, the full hot course of the sun.

◆ ◆ ◆

Gussie stole a large mottled green egg from a raven's nest, took the long slide down the pine trunk. The black parents called harshly, snapped twigs from the branches with sharp moves of their bills, and the twigs fell twenty feet to the ground. Gussie kept the egg against her warmth. For a week it nestled inside her shirt or in the hollow of her neck when she slept. She listened to its tiny sounds, tested its fragile weight. And when it was ready, she peeled away the green shards and dried the creature on her palm, blowing softly.

She chopped food for it, dropped morsels into the gaping bill with the white edge. She fed it chicken eggs and shells, frogs, insects, fat, and it took whatever she offered. She watched its eyes move beneath the pink skin. It made a terrible scream when it was hungry. Its stubby wings twitched. She wanted to hug it but couldn't, feeling the bones inside its skin.

Within a week, the pinfeathers tipped from the wings. The skin showed the black shadows of feathers beneath the surface. She watched him—he might already know the paths across the plain of the world. When he had bulked, when he was glossy black, she carried him near to his nest, watched the ravens come and go, feed and preen. She sat there with him in her lap, and as the young ravens squawked in the nest he raised his head and listened, looked up at her, agitated his wings, waited for her to speak. She had no idea what to say to calm him. He flew, rose up into the pine woods. He called. She didn't understand. Such beautiful strokes taking him higher, impossible trails she'd have to learn for herself.

+ · +

Gussie traced Brud's trails. She followed him through a grove of paper birch, but he was already gone. A cold breeze rattled the peeling sheets of white bark, curled the pages back from the underbelly of the trunks.

She followed him to the edge of town, but he dove in through the fenced gardens and scented brush, and she lost him. She crouched there and watched lights drift through dusk. Silence settled on Ravenglass in gradual steps, with someone at a lit window looking into the darkness, retreating, extinguishing the flame, and then the lights all faded, and the sounds all lost their shape and died away, and the woodsmoke lay in a thin layer above the ground and dissipated.

She saw Brud walk out on a hot morning and stop beside a lake. A wall of gray stone caught the south-swinging sun and intensified its heat. He hung a small mirror on a tree, laid out a straight razor and a tin pan filled with lake water. Frogs peeped along the marshy edges, jays screamed at each other and moved on, but Brud paid no mind. For an hour he tested the water in the pan until he flinched from the hot metal. He removed his shirt, splashed the warm water on his face and neck, and with a cake of soap he lathered his skin, cleared the soap from his lips with the tip of a finger. Slowly he drew the razor across his skin, shook the gritty soap onto the ground, continued. He washed himself clean, flung the rest of the water onto the ground. Then he took the mirror, sat against the gray stones, pulled his knees up, and looked at himself. He tipped the mirror left and right, squinted as the reflected sun swung across his face—he was twice illuminated, by the direct sun and by the reflection he controlled. He inspected beneath his chin, around his nose, dug into the corners of his eyes. He scratched at the sparse hair on his chest, tugged at the hair beneath his arms, dug grit from his navel. It was a long process, this preening. She knew the smoothness of his shaved chin, knew the tight, dry feeling of the skin, from when he'd kissed her or carried her, when she was younger. She thought of how his white skin was shadowed by the buried whiskers. She thought of the newborn raven, of its slack pink skin and the shadow of feathers waiting, and then the first black fuzz that emerged and only made him look more cold and hopeless, and then the long black feathers that lifted him away.

She saw Brud strip off his clothes, roll with a woman in a bog, past the last fence. Gussie circled. Brud and the woman sank into the patterned light and fronds, until Gussie saw only a shoulder, a foot. She sat and waited, knew she shouldn't approach, knew she shouldn't hear the strange cadences they built, wouldn't try those sounds in her own throat, sounds she'd heard in the darkness of the house in the red pines, Brud and Leota alone.

The woman was left with pale ferns stuck to her arms and bottom. She brushed the boggy remnants from her skin and slogged about looking for shoes and blouse, plucking belt and stocking from the briars. She was a graceless woman, Charlotte from Ravenglass, schoolmarm, mother, wife, swatting at the cloud of gnats, her skin mottled and flushed. Hardly even a woman, Gussie thought, judged against Leota.

Brud moved on, clothes slung over his arm, his whiteness and dark patches a camouflage in the birches. Charlotte couldn't follow him. The distance was layered solid with white trunks, green shimmer.

+ + +

Gussie waited in darkness at the back gate, waited for hours until Brud approached, waited to ask him something, though she didn't know the words, knew only what she had seen, what he had done. He passed her, didn't see her—she was no more than a vague shift. She caught at his trousers, his pocket, held on, and he stumbled, turned on her, she felt him above her, the vital bulk, the quick hiss as he snatched her from the ground, seemed to smell her, test her weight, and then he whistled, a musty note against her ear, a velvet heat. "Little girl," he said, seating her on the top rail of the fence. "I might've broke your neck."

"Where've you been?"

"Working lumber."

"You weren't. You were in the bog, in the white trees."

"You didn't see me," he said calmly, close to her. He took hold of her shoulder, tipped her back, just to the verge of falling.

Her hand came up under his outstretched arm, but she couldn't twist her hand to take hold—he had her whole shoulder pinched. "I saw you," she said.

"Worked lumber all day. Got the pains to prove it." He tipped her farther, and she slipped, caught the rail behind her knees.

She saw the stars, the outlines of the trees like black clouds. Her face was hot. She couldn't swallow. "Leota is a woman," she said.

"Don't you call her *Leota*," he said, and he released her suddenly as if she'd sparked him. She fell, thumped on her shoulder, rolled. She was crying—tears on her hot cheeks, tears in the dewy grass. Brud was tall now across the fence, against the stars. "She's your mother. I worked lumber all day. Leota is your mother. Don't hurt her. You'll never know how I love her, how she needs me."

He took the back yard in a few bounding strides, and then the doorway brightened, a brilliant light cleanly cut from the night, and Leota was there. "I've been waiting for you," she said. As he pressed her there in the doorway, she tipped her head back and rose onto her toes to take his kiss, and her fingers drummed on his elbow and the small of his back. Brud glanced toward the gate, a sharp squint, moved Leota on into the light, and the door shut. Gussie pulled herself upright against the fence. Her bones throbbed. She wouldn't forget.

◆ ◆ ◆

She watched a raven, saw how it listened, where it focused, and she turned the same direction and pulled in a sound. Some sounds were pure heat, the forest expanding and steaming. Some had the shape of action, a shrill song, tapping. She guessed at the paths the sounds took—shuffling through groves, quick across water, as far as sound could carry—and she guessed at what gave rise to each sound, and what the sound meant for her, small girl alone. She waited at the center to catch it all.

And at night, she moved inside the house, looking for a better vantage. She listened, tried to hear. The walls were no more than thin slices of forest whitewashed, papered with ranks of hothouse orchids. The rooms betrayed her movements and breathing too easily.

Outside, she circled the house. The foundation was tight—no entry. The sumac had branched as high as the eaves, rising beside the windows, and the branches held her weight, swayed and creaked, settled, steady in her grip. Brud and Leota's window held the reflected sliver of moon falling through the highest spikes of the pines, held the stars as they followed the moon. The window was open slightly to the cooling night. Gussie held on to the sumac. She heard nothing for a long while. Then she heard the silence of an owl's wings overhead, a powerful silence taking the darkness, skimming a black shadow through the stars, across the Milky Way, and she made herself smaller, and she held tighter to the branch, and she thought of those saucer eyes that had already seen her, and she thought of those talons and their mortal splay and grasp. But the owl was gone, searching other prey. And she was alone.

Another night, after countless nights beside the open window, she heard Brud enter the house, the dark room. She could see nothing from outside, from the branches of the sumac, nothing but the moon again in the windowpane, no lantern or candle to illuminate the room and the bed where Leota lay waiting. Gussie heard his boots drop and skid, his trousers drape the footboard, his buttons pop open. And then the shift of the quilt, the groan of the springs. They were settled there, Leota and Brud, his breathing gradually slowing. Gussie heard how they moved together that night, how they rolled beneath the wedding-ring quilt, the endlessly interlocked pattern of blue circles, turning their perfect curves in on themselves. And then their low voices, their lips barely parted enough for sound, the words muffled against some obstruction—neck or shoulder or ear. Like a song they knew, their words went on without pause.

"I love you, Brud, I love you, you're handsome, my husband, always more beautiful, but this isn't enough, I want you to . . ."

"We can't."

"I want another child, another chance, I love you, your black eyes, your arms, your fingers, your chest, your beautiful face, handsome, more than handsome, I want that beauty inside me, I want another child, a beautiful child . . ."

"We have Gussie. I've said it. She's the end."

"I want a beautiful child."

"We have Gussie. That's what comes of you. You're more beautiful than any woman, but something inside you brought us Gussie. Not the child I expected . . ."

And Gussie loosened her grip, slid down from the sumac. And she watched the moon leave the window, the stars swirl. And she tried the words, tried them on her tongue, to see if the words would fit the shape of her mouth. "We have Gussie . . . That's what comes of you . . ." And she looked out into the night, climbed the fence, walked among the red pines. "We have Gussie . . . Beautiful child . . ." And the farther she walked, the louder she spoke, shaping Leota's tone, accent. The pines in the darkness held out their dead lower branches—the sharp fingers caught her arms, her neck, her eyes closed to the night. She ran, cut by the pines, far beyond the house. "Beautiful child," she said. Leota's own voice. "I want a beautiful child."

She took the miles fast, burst from the red pines, into the watery maze, looking only for distance, to lose herself. She'd seen what happened when a child was lost—she was still a child herself, thirteen years old—she'd seen the town gather together in a hush, seen how they all held tight and looked out into the woods as if they expected an apparition of the lost child to float down from the eaves. The men would break into teams, head out. Gussie had helped track the Andersen girl, whom they found, leash in hand, searching for her dog ten miles from home. She was a dull girl, following a dumb animal. And Gussie had helped track the Folke boy, whom they never found. The Folkes moved away after that, couldn't face the sound of the wind.

Gussie ran on north. Something would happen once the men all got moving, once Brud and Leota were drawn from the house, out onto the trails.

After two days, she heard her name called, far off. She kept going, looped around. The trees rattled like sticks in the pale sun. She nestled in a bed of reindeer moss, at the edge of a stand of cedar. An hour before dawn, when the sky began to give up its darkness, she saw that the cedars above her were full of ravens, big weighty birds tucked into sleep. She remembered what Brud had said of roosting ravens—"Those are the youngsters in a mob. None of them has found a mate, or else they'd be off in their pairs. These are the lonely ones. They've got the wrong scent or look or no smarts. You'll see."

After four days, she heard her name called again. She headed toward the voices. Men moved through late night, calling her name. In with one group, Leota held a lantern, the bright light on her neck and white throat. "Augusta," she called. "Gussie." Farther on, Brud was in with another group. "She's not in any trouble," he said. "She's never in any trouble. She's got a sense about the world. Four days is nothing for a girl like her."

Gussie remembered that night, the long wander she took, following Brud's search party as they zigged to where the going was easiest. Night had settled thick against the ground, and the stars drifted. The leaves dampened the voices.

"That girl is a haunt."

"She's a girl, she's just a girl."

"She could be right next to us."

"How would we know?"

"Where's the fellow with the bloodhound?"

"He's coming out to meet Leota and her searchers."

"We ain't going to find anything without a hound of our own."

"Whole thing's useless."

Gussie stood still. Brud's group didn't seem to move far, they seemed to be taking a long turn, moving back across their progress, starting north again and backing away. She waited. Someone approached, moving fast, nearly silent. She knew it was Brud—she knew how he moved through darkness, knew how he could leave something behind, quick, head for something of more possibility, an opportunity or distraction. She paced him through the starlit clearings, toward the other voices.

He called out. "Leota? That you? Anyone there?"

And now Gussie had a plan—she'd known it would come to her. She ran ahead. "I'm here, Brud," Gussie called, shaping Leota's voice, the perfect tones, and she accelerated toward town. "I'm here."

He came along fast, tracking the voice. "Leota. Where? Where's your light?"

"It's gone," Gussie said. "Lost it."

"Stop."

"I'm here."

"Leota. I don't see you."

"Brud," Gussie said. There were lights ahead—Ravenglass. Woodsmoke on the air. And far off again the sound of shouts and, nearer, the baying of a hound on the scent, *her* scent. "Brud. Gussie's not your girl," Gussie said, and she leapt from the woods, climbed the first fence. "She isn't yours."

Brud vaulted the rails. "Leota. Stop."

Gussie skidded through soft leaves, gardens. "I'll send her away. When we find her. If we find her." She swung through a long string of stair-stepping yards, along the edge of Ravenglass. "We can't have her with us. She's not yours."

"Leota." He was closing. "Send her away. Just us, alone."

Gussie saw her goal, a lit window, said, "Here, Brud," crossed through the maze of fences. Finally, the yard. She stayed to the darkness. Plunged into a bank of hydrangea. A final shout. "Tell Charlotte you don't love her. Then we're alone."

And there he was, suddenly beside her, so close she could smell him, the bitter scent of velocity. He spun, stopped, recognized the house. And she saw his profile etched with the window light, her father, the line of his brow, the unearthly form, exhausted, frightened. "Leota," he said. "Leota . . ." And he took the last strides, banged on the door, and the woman opened him to the yellow light, and he said, "Charlotte, Charlotte," unable to catch his breath, unable to say any more, turning to look back into the night. "A phantom," he gasped. "Leota," he gasped. And Charlotte stepped past him, scanned the night, turned and shoved him inside, slammed the door. The two of them. Gussie stepped into the grid of window light on the lawn.

The hound bayed, the gates swung open, one after the other, two houses away, one house away, lights ablaze, children at the windows, the dogs of Ravenglass now all in a chorus, in a pack. The lanterns swarmed through the trees and into the yard. Gussie jumped to the stoop, rattled the knob, shouted, "I'm here, I'm here,

I'm here." There was Leota with her lantern. The door swung open. Charlotte pushed Brud out into the clamor of dogs and men, and Charlotte yelled, "He's a beast. Take him."

Gussie leapt from under Brud's feet, found Leota as the crowd hemmed them in. And Gussie said, "Mother. I'm here." And Leota dropped the lantern in a burst of flame, took her child, held her fiercely, said, "Beautiful girl, beautiful girl . . ."

And the dogs and the men surged past, tracked a new prey, into the forest, onto the trails carved more by animal than by man. But the trails were known to Brud, the miles were a simple map to him, simple as language—he knew each lake, each creek that drew a low passage among the ridges, the craggy rocks that drew rain from the clouds. Brud was fast. He was easy across the northern miles. He left the hunters behind. They never saw him again.

+ + +

Leota and Gussie cried a long time. The sounds extinguished in distance, in time, deep into memory. They looked up. The women of Ravenglass watched them in silence from the brink of the yard, watched the two together in the red light of the fallen lantern, watched the beauty uncontrolled in sorrow and relief, watched the child they'd given up for dead, the child who had drawn them all to scandal, who had nearly calmed herself already, an oddity, a miracle, a strong child, holding like a vise to her mother's pale hand.

+ + +

Leota and Gussie boarded the next steamer. The small boat skimmed along the shore of Lake Superior, brought up the humblest ports and dismissed them astern. Gussie watched the range of the world—hills rose and fell in waves of farm and forest and lumbered stubble and wet roads. And then they hit Duluth, the piling on of wonders, but they didn't stop. They traveled as far as time and money would allow. They were on a train, and the forest burned away into wheat, bright altitude, endless miles where the surface of the world was held direct to the sky. And their tickets ran out. And they rode on in a freight wagon, up against the Rocky Mountains. They caught on the rough edge of Greeley, Colorado. Leota and Gussie closed into a small room together. Mother. Daughter. Alone.

Longs Peak

Gussie was nearly fifteen years old the day she met Jack Fisher. A Sunday in May 1917. Greeley. She sat square in the corner of the back seat of an automobile, dust settling on her white lap and the black leather seat. It was a slow drive from the wheat fields toward the fresh green trees along the river. Behind, dust muddied the sunrise. Gussie watched the sun reflected in the windows, watched her mother, Leota, and her mother's new husband, Frank Locke, watched Leota's exquisite neck and Frank's jaw with its stubble scraped beneath the red surface and the muscles tensing. Gussie would be baptized with his surname today—*Augusta Locke*. Frank's jacket was sleek black, iridescent, the fine early colors of the day reflected deep within. His collar cut a white crease across his meaty neck.

The automobile passed in through a gate. Far ahead, automobiles and wagons lined the edge of cottonwoods, and the mountains took the horizon high into blue, with Longs Peak like a dream of a white pyramid.

Before dawn that morning, Gussie had awoken at the sound of her mother's approach, looked toward the door. Leota entered the room, perched on the edge of the bed, pulled Gussie from beneath the blankets and sat her up. She held Gussie's face in her hands, studied her, leaned close, released her. "I finished the dress. I showed it to Frank. You'll be fine." When Leota had first come home with the bolt of linen, she'd said, "You'll be layered in white, Gussie. Brilliant. I'm capable of delicate stitches, always have been." And she'd told Gussie of her own childhood in Duluth, before the years in Ravenglass, of her own fine dresses, the tightness of the bodice that had made her feel upright, the flow of the skirts that had caught around her progress and slowed her. She'd rambled on about her childhood lately, new stories of boys and gentlemen, courting, kindnesses, attentions.

Somewhere below, Frank moved through the house, out into the chill darkness, looking for the farm manager, asking after the kind of minor assignment that might convince a man like himself, a banker, a gentleman farmer, that he is the soul of his acres, that he hears the bubbling of the aquifer far below, that he can cock his head like a robin and hear the seeds germinate and push toward the sun. This morning, for a few minutes, he might oil the gears of a planter, sort nails into cans.

Leota led Gussie down the hall to the front bedroom. Frank's scent was still damp on the air—tobacco, pomade. She sat the girl on the edge of the high iron bed, on the wedding-ring quilt, the pattern of interlocking blue rings. Leota sat beside Gussie, handed her a small silver dish, the usual routine, and Gussie held the dish on her lap. With a brush, Leota pulled through Gussie's tangles, extracted scraps of leaf, dry tendril, insect wing. She dropped the takings into the silver dish, and Gussie fingered through them, pinched a section of beetle carapace, inspected the dull horns and crenulations of the armor, tested its lightness, so airy that it might have been no more than a hollow black reflection. Leota secured Gussie's hair with ribbons and mother-of-pearl combs.

Leota dressed Gussie in white drawers and a muslin shift, brought from the closet the linen dress gleaming from the iron. "Let's slip this on and see what we've got." Gussie looked at her mother's fragile smile, dutifully raised her arms and took on the cold white linen, felt the tight fit about her shoulders. She shrugged and the dress rustled, the cuffs tugged at her wrists. Reaching down, she took hold of the hem, raised the skirt up, and inspected the fabric—tiny pale violets scattered wide. Gussie tried to see the structure of the flowers, but the stamens were no more than a loop of thread, and the petals no more than three loops each.

Leota stepped back. "You're my sweetheart," she said. "You're my dear little girl."

"Not hardly."

"You are today, especially. Look at you. Just plain beautiful."

Gussie stood there in the new dress, weeks of Leota's planning and work. She could step from the outfit and run, she could drop the ribbons and go wild, but she held still and displayed herself. Leota nodded and clicked her tongue, pressed softly at Gussie's back to urge her toward the mirror. In the lamplight, with the window just starting to go silver, she saw her shape in the looking glass, the scowl of her features, and her hair an uncertain color— pure black on the surface, but woven with shadows of red, hints of gold and ruined blond.

Leota brought the light closer, tilted the mirror for a more perfect image. Gussie studied Leota's handiwork, the collar a soft scallop. Leota helped her on with the narrow boots, tugged at the skirts to settle the flow. The tiny violets floated like early spring in a snowfield. Gussie could not remember ever being this well set. She inhaled deeply and judged the garment's bind—it strapped her, tugged at her flat breasts, forced her to follow the seams, the elegant lines—not altogether unpleasant. She held herself as still and steady as possible, inched toward the bed, sat and waited for Leota to ready herself, waited to see where this dress might take her.

Leota removed her nightgown. She was a small woman, the structure of her bones like wire in gossamer, her spine a faint line of shadow. Leota's dark blue dress covered her soft skin, the tracery of her veins. She took Gussie's hand and raised her from the bed.

"Let's go. We'll find your father."

"Your husband."

"We'll find Frank."

Gussie shadowed Leota through the halls of that tall house, a house without years enough for shade trees. All her life, Gussie had watched Leota walk ahead, watched how her steps always seemed to find the high ground, stir no dust, how she kept her hands planted forward at her hips as if she had no need for balance. They came to the top of the stairs, their hands on the banister, paused at the sound of the automobile approaching from the barn. A deep backfire rolled across the fields—pure distance in every direction.

Slowly down the stairs, Gussie held her skirts free from her steps. She and Leota paused again when the automobile stopped outside the front door. The engine cut off. Frank came in through the door, didn't look up to see them there, said loudly, "Leota, I'm ready when you're ready." He kept moving toward his study, saying, "Could've done this ceremony private." With the latch of the door, he shut himself in.

Leota glanced back up at Gussie. "We don't want to be late, do we? Can't keep God waiting. I'd like to be on his good side." She kept on down the stairs, a smooth glide, reached the floor, turned toward the kitchen. "Just a quick bite before we go. How does that sound?"

Step after step, descending, Gussie attempted Leota's glide. Somehow it seemed that the effort it took to hold herself erect and keep her skirts clear and count out an even tempo without looking down at her footfalls and slide her hand along the banister with her wrist at a loose angle and her fingers splayed, somehow it seemed that that effort overwhelmed her other senses, that she could hear nothing but a warm hiss only vaguely disturbed by actual sound, could see nothing but a light that refracted just above the surface of objects, could think of nothing but her feet tight in the slick-soled boots and her chest restrained. She alighted and turned, following Leota. If this was the effect of beautiful clothes and straight posture, then perhaps Leota never really saw this house with its dark wood, never really heard the empty afternoons or saw the meadowlarks on the fenceposts—to Leota a bird might be no more than another tumbling scrap of glass in a kaleidoscope, another lovely shape reflecting itself through the days and weeks. For this single minute, as she made her way in Leota's wake, Gussie felt that she might understand the comfort of beauty.

In the pantry, in the blue light from the small window, Gussie found Leota, the light adrift on the swirl of her pinned hair. Leota drew down a tin from a middle shelf, pried away the lid, removed a strip of candied fruit, placed it on her tongue, slowly chewed.

"I'd like to be pretty," Gussie said, although what she'd meant to say was, "How can you breathe in a dress like this?"

Leota dusted the sugar from her fingers, reached for Gussie, drew her close, patted her hand. "Of course, we'd all like to be pretty. But you are. Look." She held the lid of the tin. They peered into the dim sheet of metal. The skew of the fine lines of Leota's face. Leota's cold, pale eyes—Gussie thought of the skin of ice that locks the colors of a pool. Gussie's own face was square, solid, unaffected by the tin.

"You want to make Frank proud," Leota said. "That's good. He can make things easier for you. He worries. Each time you run off, he thinks you're gone for good."

"He'd think good riddance."

"You came with me to this house, and you're staying with me."

"If you're staying."

"Ridiculous." She replaced the lid, slid the tin onto the shelf, led Gussie through the halls, found Frank in his study.

Frank looked up from his papers. "Well," he said, "the dress is successful, I think. You look nice, young lady. A triumph of tailoring."

"Thank you, Mr. Locke."

Leota pushed Gussie forward a step. "She wants to take her place here with me. Isn't that right, Augusta?"

Frank pushed back from the desk, rose slowly, and his eyes made the tour of the dress. Gussie tried to exhale completely, to deflate, but she stood for him, waited. Beyond him, the window framed a long reach of plowed field and a newly planted windbreak of frail olive trees. Those olive trees might shelter a grasshopper, but they could do nothing to protect a real-size girl, nothing against the great miles of exposure that swept the county from Greeley through the washed-out creeks and rivers and the scattered farmhouses each hooked to the grid of section roads, each hooked to the First Bank of Weld, hooked to Frank Locke. "Sure," she said, sure only that she wanted to break his stare. "I'm part of this family."

"That pleases me," he said. "This dress is a good start, and we'll see how the baptism goes, knock wood, and then we have a whole list of options to consider."

He waved Gussie forward, stood with her at the window, the view still gray, early mist on the fields. "We'll be alright now, Leota," he said, without looking back. "Could you fetch my pocket watch?"

"Which one?" Leota said. Already her footsteps left the soft Persian rug, entered the hallway.

"The new one," he said. "Wouldn't be without it."

The sound of Leota on the stairs, then passing overhead.

Frank laid his arm across Gussie's shoulders. "Your mother bought me that watch. But, of course, you know that, don't you? It's Swiss. Keeps excellent time. She knows what's best for me."

"What's best?"

He turned away, fumbled in the desk a moment, came back. Taking up her hand, he gently pried her fist open, pressed a roll of banknotes onto her palm, closed her fingers again. "For a new wardrobe," he said. "We can't have you wearing trousers. You could buy clothes for a whole year with this. Think about what you want."

Gussie rolled the notes into the sleeve of the white dress and backed away.

◆ ◆ ◆

They drove toward the river and its band of cottonwoods, where automobiles lined in black ranks beside the wagons and buggies and grazing horses. A clutch of children in baptism white ran among the long shadows of the trees, and the others in Sunday dark watched from beside the tables at the edge of the open field, the tables mounded with baskets, platters of food, cut flowers.

Frank parked, switched off the engine. They climbed out and stood together, the crowd's voices in the distance, the river rumbling deep in the trees. The minister looked their way, gave them a high, loose wave.

Leota tugged at Gussie's waist, patted the girl's hair, said, "You're lovely."

"We'll see how well it holds together," Frank said. He inhaled deeply, settled his coat. "Let's proceed."

Frank and Leota strode away. Gussie held back. "I'll be a minute." A few men waited for Frank, dried their palms on the flaps of their coats, reached for his hand, moved in around Frank and Leota, and Leota was blocked, just a glimpse of her blue skirts among the trouser legs.

Gussie leaned against the fender and raised the hem of her dress. The black boots were knotted with her joints, wouldn't last through a single good hike. She bent down and adjusted the latchets, brushed the dirt from the sheen, stood and closed her eyes and let the early sun press her against the metal. She heard the stillness of the air, the high banks of leaves waiting for heat, the river moving along.

Someone called her name. The children had been gathered, and everyone headed toward the river, through the cottonwood grove. Gussie angled to meet them. In the cool shadows, the green light, she came in among the children, all white-clad, hanging together, silent, walking nervous. The children moved around her, glanced up at her, as if she knew something. She let them brush against her, buffer her. As they entered the willow scrub, down the riverbank, the minister said, "Welcome, Augusta."

The water was fast. At the center of the channel the sun had found an opening. Gnats rose and fell in fluttering clouds. It was mountain water, but from here in the floodplain the mountains were invisible.

The minister continued across the roots and mud, out into the water, sloshing and wavering, thrusting his arms for balance. Almost to the sunlight, he stopped and turned, and now his wide-flung arms beckoned them. The children held to each other and to Gussie, leaned forward as a group and looked down into the water. The riverbed was slick and dark. "Nice day for a drowning," Gussie said, a whisper to the children, and they all shivered and stepped forward.

Like a water spider, all legs and arms and white body, they made their way against the current, with Gussie's head looming above the white, scanning ahead to keep them on course. The minister reached to take them, rent them each from each, started his chant, "I baptize, I baptize," dunking left and right, a confusion of gasps and cries, the children climbing each other to escape the cold, trying to gain Gussie's elbows and shoulders, and finally the minister cut Gussie from the rest and plunged her beneath the water.

She heard the grind of river rock, heard, "I baptize Augusta Locke . . ." *Augusta Tornig,* she thought, a name she'd loved, a name she'd lost, a name she'd never deserved. The slender legs scattered around her, the white fabric billowed and flowed, the blue sky was far above, the water like a cold vise screwing down on her heart and lungs. The minister's hand covered her forehead, held her still and deep, the cold as cold as Minnesota winter, where a black spruce held night in its branches long after dawn, where whole groves of night rattled in the wind, far below the sky.

She was lifted up. The minister was soaked, his face blue with cold. She gained square footing and held his arm and guided him toward the shore. The children were ahead, on their own, fighting their way toward the waiting towels and blankets.

"Thank you, Miss Locke," the minister said, his breath in shallow gasps, and his arm came around her shoulders, his hand gripped her chest. "Those mountains must be a cold place. My hands are numb. I couldn't feel a living thing."

His hand kept twitching, and she felt the soaked cloth work against her skin. An odd feeling that brought warmth—his hand, his slender hand, his fingers barely formed into the shape of a man's—he was searching for something, she thought. She looked down and saw how she was exposed, how her dark places rose through the linen. "You just hold on, sir." He was a young man, skinny and frail. She slogged along, her knees shaking. She saw his jaw, a bloodless jut of bone with smooth skin and a silken shave, saw the dainty point of his nose, felt a new shiver to accompany the cold, a new warmth centered deep, a tightening of her skin. She hadn't known this before—the pressure of a man.

"This is an act of beauty, Miss Locke. Do you feel the beauty in your heart?"

"You're going to have to move your legs, sir. I can't carry you."

"Beauty within." A whisper, his chin on her shoulder. "Beauty deep within. Feel it?"

A few strides from the shore, she saw them all waiting, she blushed, this man on her, private, and she dropped him. He fell to his knees. Men sloshed past her, to the rescue. She dragged herself out of the river, heavy and chilled, up across the crumbling bank, into the trees. There was no real sun here, just the openings through the leaves.

Leota pulled at the wet cling of Gussie's dress. She took her in a blanket, knelt and loosened the latchets of the soaked boots. "How do you feel, sweetheart?"

"Graceful as an ox."

"A swan."

"Right."

"Do you feel different?"

"I'm wide awake now, if I wasn't before."

"The girl's got river grass in her hair," Frank said.

Leota rubbed Gussie's shoulders. "Really, Frank," she said, "that's beside the point, isn't it?"

"Nothing is ever beside the point. Clean her up. We have the breakfast now." He tugged at Gussie's collar, chucked her under the chin. "You're my daughter now, Augusta. Obedience, girl." He wandered away toward the sun and the tables of food.

Gussie pulled the combs and ribbons from her hair, dragged her fingers through to find the blades of river grass—long thin veins, pliable, cold. The water soaked the blanket. Leota busied herself, shaping the girl's hair again, pressing it with the blanket, angling the combs. The children raced past, their thin, wispy hair already drying, and in their excitement they tried to pull her along, but she stayed with Leota. They ran on, white blurs through the cottonwoods, away from the river toward the sun, in the general flow of their parents. And there was Frank, just entering the full sun. And here was Leota, the intensity of her attentions, her beauty muted by the shade.

"My girl," Leota said, her voice a sad whisper. "Miss Locke." Leota licked her thumb, rubbed at the freckles on Gussie's cheeks.

Gussie felt her skin stretch across her flat cheekbones. She tried the name *Locke* in her thoughts, but it seemed plain, unsteady. She replaced it with *Tornig,* and she remembered what Brud had told her of Einar Tornig, her grandfather.

Far north in the boundary waters, Einar Tornig found empty cities on the shores of frozen lakes. He stayed to the oldest creeks, the sad portages where the water was slow, where the air lay like blue felt, and he found an Indian lodge, a patch of cultivated ground, and he heard the voices skim a lake at sunset. A loon fluttered there, trying to take to the sky, trying to rise up and find fresher water, but it wouldn't fly, it spread its black wings and glided to a stop. The woods along the ridge held the last pink clouds. Einar camped there, beside that backwater, watched and listened through the night. Einar built a craft—peeled bark on a ribbed form—and in later years he and Brud skimmed

*the lakes together and ran the most shallow streams, tipped the canoe on shore
and lived beneath it through long rains. The wide silence, the months without
a human sound past Einar's breathing.*

Gussie understood now what he had meant, the way she heard
Leota's breathing from a distance, even when the day was full of
other sounds. She wanted to take Leota in a tight hug. She wanted
to hold her there in the shade, to let the day move on, move away,
the sounds fade.

How did Leota remember Brud, if she remembered him at all, if
she allowed it? Perhaps an image of Brud holding Gussie as an
infant—he is so much larger than the girl, engulfing her tiny head in
his palm, the fold of his strong arms, the girl's heart beating against
his own heart. As if he wants to decipher her, he studies the girl.
The girl returns his stare.

More likely Leota kept Gussie separate from Brud in her memory, and Brud moved alone, there at the deepest recesses of the
yard, through the goldenrod, the primrose, the sandreed in warm
summer waves. He might tell her a story of black spruce shattered
by storm, sphagnum soft as sleep—it was all he knew, the passages
north, perhaps all Leota knew of him now, his stories, his presence,
his world, his touch. He might hold her small waist, might pin her
in a quag of tiny-leaf ferns, and the cool distillation of the earth
welled up around their weight and stained her hands, his hands, the
side of her face, his hip, and a fern impressed her shoulder, left a
veined etch that roughed up her innocence. Or Leota saw the iron
bed where she lay watching the moonlit view—the light seemed
soft and slow, the woods flat, depthless. Brud came into the room,
passed against the moonlight, dropped his clothes and climbed in
beside her. He had been running—Leota couldn't see him, but she
smelled the sweat, the sweet briar scent that had caught on his
skin.

Gussie tried to follow the path of such memories down through
her own veins, to feel within herself what Leota must have felt for
Brud, what she might still feel. She felt her blood heating her limbs.

She felt the after-touch of the minister's hand on her chest—maybe that man's touch was the map, but she couldn't follow it beneath the surface of her skin, and the sensation seemed to have faded already to nothing but a chafe.

Gussie remembered circling the darkened house, finding the only lit window, and she braved the needling thorns of the wild rose and climbed to the view. Leota busied herself at the stove, shook the teakettle to judge the level of the water. Brud took her wrist and turned her, held her and managed to catch the lantern overhead, twist the wick to the barest orange glow, and the light settled like warmth on Leota's sharp nose and the white nape where her blouse was falling away. Leota's eyes left him a moment, they squeezed tight and lines sprang like ice cracking across her skin, and he kissed her temples and brow. Would Leota still know this? Would she have forgotten it for the sake of her daughter?

Gussie shrugged the wet blanket from her shoulders, turned to face Leota. "You're all right, Mother? You've settled on Frank?"

"Settled *with* Frank."

"He's the best, you think?"

Leota took her girl by the arm and started toward the gathered congregation. "Each evening, I like to watch for Frank's automobile. I can see him from a mile away. And then he stays with me. I don't need anything else."

"Does he need anything else?"

"He just needs a little order. Just wants a little beauty. Simple enough."

"Simple for you." Gussie pulled her arm back from Leota's grasp, and they entered into the bright sunlight. She followed Leota's drift among the tables, smiles and greetings on all sides. They each gathered food onto plates—pastries, preserves, boiled eggs. The minister, ruddy now with a teapot clenched in his white hands, blessed the food, presented the baptized. Each child nodded as his or her name was said, and Gussie turned half away at *Augusta Locke*, the murmur of approval as dry as chalk, and she swallowed, and her plate tipped, and the boiled egg slid among the sweet biscuits. She stomped a foot to free her dress from its cling to her thighs, and the egg escaped the plate, bounced in the grass. She didn't look up but took a casual step, pressed her heel down on the egg, mashed it into the dirt and roots.

Frank caught her elbow, took her plate, said, "I'll take this, if you're not ready to eat. Let me introduce you to a few people. Is that something you can do for me?"

"If I have to," she said, "but I'm still wet. Let me dry off a bit first?"

He looked at her dress where it bunched at the knees and dripped onto her boots. "All right. Track me down when you're ready. We'll take it easy at first. I'll make just one introduction, to get us started. You have to want to do this, Augusta. Things will change for the better. You'll see. You'll do as I say." He moved on, taking Leota with him.

Alone, hands at her sides, Gussie started a slow wander among the groups of adults, listened to the chatter about curtains, clapboard, vaults, machines. It made her tired. It seemed that they might go on, the day might go on, with an endless circling of the sun, as if the horizon had lost its power.

The girls close to Gussie's age had found a fallen cottonwood at the edge of the grove, and they all sat there on the silver trunk, balanced plates on their knees with the tip of a finger, the folds of their Sunday dresses opening only at the crossed ankles. The girls were neat, powdered—they had all been baptized years ago, at the proper age, the ceremony beyond their memory or interest. Laughter moved the girls all one way, shoulder to shoulder, and then they pushed off from each other, dabbed with napkins, settled back into conversation.

They watched a single boy who stood in with the men, the only boy near to their age who had made this excursion into the May morning, the other boys all shipped out to war, or still sleeping, dreaming of motors or a horse tangled in harness or miles of work folded across this soft landscape. The boy was fragile, beautiful, his hair razored softly about his skull, skin so pale it seemed his thoughts shone through, blushed his cheeks with the silly awfulness of what he couldn't help but think, being a boy so finely made on a morning so clearly building toward heat. Gussie knew the talk of those girls, their nostrils whistling with their dry calculations. They could crush that boy. He wouldn't stand a chance. But they didn't move from their perch. They bent at the waist, laid their plates on the grass, soft girls, hands moving without notice to flatten the skirts over their knees.

Gussie singled out the boy's voice from the rest, heard him say, "—found a nest in the reeds, in the marsh. The bird's song is like the water gurgling. I don't know how those birds fly through those stands of reed. The marsh is such a sluggish place, all that rot. The male is black except for the red wing like a flash—"

The banks of new cottonwood leaves hinged lightly against the breeze, and the warm sunlight started to dry the soaking Gussie had taken, decreased the weight of the dress. She felt the fresh tightness of her arms and belly beneath the linen—she felt almost delicate, something she could barely remember from when she was a child and could pass unseen.

She moved on around. There was Frank Locke, sugar on his chin. "—to supply the war effort," he said. He gestured wide, his pink hand flying. Farms were scattered across the cloudless distance, and windmills awaited the day's full power, and magpies scared up from a plowed field. Fences carved squares by the mile. Frank was a large man, bow chested, booming, his face tight with expression, flushed and shiny. "Dug deep into this county. Colorado. Solid success." And beside him, Leota Locke, his new wife.

Leota took Frank Locke's empty plate and slid it beneath her own. He dusted his hands clean, no pause in his speech. Leota would carry for him, answer him. And when they returned home that morning, Frank would lock himself back into his work, on through evening, and Leota would sit at a table in the parlor and read aloud to herself. Did she love the sound of her own voice? It had a certain luster. Gussie loved her. Leota was beautiful. She'd lift a page with a gentle pinch of her fingers, turn it, lay open the next horizon, the next event, without fear, without a moment's pause, her voice going on as if the lovely shaping of her lips were the whole act, as if it was all music without meaning. Gussie thought she understood the way beauty springs from beauty.

Leota reached for Frank, brushed his chin. Sugar fell to the grass in a sparkling rain.

◆ ◆ ◆

Gussie angled off through the cottonwood grove, slowed through each shaft of light. The white dress had dried enough to flow and tangle again. She swayed as she walked, let the skirt dance around her ankles. The sun, so much hotter than the air, laid bare her nerves. She felt her bones heat at the backs of her hands, felt the cartilage of her ears and nose, as if she were not quite formed, still taking shape, a slide between past and future.

Leota had spent weeks on the dress, the only time since the childhood crepe dress that she'd worked a plan like this for Gussie, that she'd sat in the parlor and measured out the image, her scissors carving panels and buffers. And Gussie couldn't argue with the beauty of this linen dress—it gave her a shadow with edges that preceded her, followed her, hid her steps, smoothed her gait. And the inspiration of the tiny violets, their wide spacing, just enough color to catch the eye, to force a moment of close focus. The eye trailed down the linen from speck to speck until the blooms became clear, and then the eye simply studied the tiny stitches and the delicacy and the fine whiteness of the cloth. Leota's fingers had pinched the needle, had drawn up and stabbed through again, secured each loop. And Leota had displayed each phase of the sewing to Frank, and Frank had approved.

Gussie looked back through the confusion of cottonwood trunks and green shade and bursts of sun and slivers of distance—a head-

light and tire, a child in full white somersault, a man with an arm-
load of lilacs, a young woman pausing to hold her hand to her neck
as if testing the warmth of her blood. Gussie walked on. Here in the
middle ground she heard the small echoes her boots scuffed up—
stone, soil, crush of weed and fallen leaf. Then the roar of the river
took over.

She found a path upriver. She thought of the source of all that
cold water, the long, high winter buried in silence. During the first
brief hours of spring, flies hover at the fringe of melting snow, feed
on the white reflection.

Gussie had never traveled up into the Rocky Mountains during
her nearly two years in Greeley. When Gussie and Leota had first
entered Colorado on the final miles of their road from Minnesota,
Gussie had seen a storm approaching from the west, but then she'd
realized that she'd been mistaken, that the dark line of clouds was
actually the mountains, not flying rain and lightning, just the earth
piled higher than any storm she'd ever imagined. In Minnesota, the
mountains had been no more than old ripples, the storms scudding
through the treetops. She couldn't believe the towering walls of the
granite peaks. She thought the peaks would catch the sun as it fell,
and fire would cascade the canyons, flood the plain. They would
burn up, mother and daughter. The rest of the way along the Platte
River road, she feared they were headed toward danger. They pulled
into Greeley, stepped down with their luggage. They moved
through the dry summer heat, the sunset flaring red. They would
hold on in that town, Gussie thought, only until some small moment caught up with them and dropped them into the fire. Or
dropped Gussie.

Leota took a position at a mercantile, her first employment in
her thirty years. Gussie started school in September, found that no
one cared who she was or where she came from, no one asked
about her heavy trousers and work shirts, no one knew that she had
lived in a country of remnant lakes, wolves, black spruce, that she
could still travel all those northern trails if she took a moment,

closed her eyes, held still, let her thoughts wander. She made no real friends—she couldn't figure how to maintain a conversation, how to sit with a girl and discuss colors or magazines or desire, how to duck from the rain as if it would somehow harm her.

Gussie and Leota lived in a series of side-street hotels, finally settled in a rooming house. From one window they watched the clouds reflect the green plain or the gray winter. From the other window they watched the western horizon throw the mountains high or press them flat, depending on the angle of the light. Leota washed the day's work from her hands and arms, her white skin restored, drew on her dressing gown and cinched it tight at her narrow waist, brushed her hair out long, touched scented water to the hollow of her neck. Leota was settled into the room for the night. She sat in the corner chair beside the lamp. Gussie curled on the bed.

Leota had spent the day selling cones of dark sugar, bolts of cloth, nails. The stock was dusty. The flour puffed from the barrel, filled the small lines around her eyes. On one evening or another, Leota strolled with a gentleman, took an early supper. Gussie saw them from afar, these gentlemen and Leota, turning a corner into honeysuckle shade, taking the raised walkway beside the creek, a pause at the bench with the western view. Gussie wouldn't approach, barely dared to breathe, as the man hooked Leota's arm.

But most evenings Leota sat in the corner and reached for a book, and Gussie breathed deeply in the closeness of beeswax, talc, balsam. Leota opened the book, pulled from the marked page a wedding photo, Brud's handsome face vaguely immortal or charmed. Leota began to read, not really to Gussie, it seemed, but more to fill the room—walls flocked with beige bouquets, the louvered blinds frozen with a quarter century of steam and high-altitude sun, the lightbulb with its spider lace—to fill the room with a steady rhythm, a lyric constant. In his formal stance in the photo, slid into the book, Brud pressed against the patterns of sound, the paragraphs of memory and fantasy and desire.

Leota slept, rolled against the wall. On into the dark, Gussie listened. The rooming house sailed through the westerly wind. Doors opened and closed, someone hissed at a cat, the stairs creaked down to the landing and stopped.

◆ ◆ ◆

This was a habit Gussie couldn't break—wandering off. She imagined what Frank might say when he saw that she had escaped. "That girl is doing this to me deliberately. No respect." And Leota would make excuses—"She's not a social girl, not like this"—her hand rubbing the back of his neck, leading him toward the automobile and the drive home. Then the afternoon with the wide empty view in every direction, and Leota on the porch long after dark, the cloud of insects around the light, the sounds of the plain—air moving through barn slats, fenceposts, sprouting wheat, alfalfa—the lights of Greeley like a dull mirage, and the stars working down into the eroded pathways of the mountains.

Leota will turn finally, when the night chill has arrested all sound, and she'll climb the stairs, find Frank asleep beneath the quilt. She'll join him, still listen for the night, for the door. She'll curl with Frank, and in the morning she'll awake and watch Frank dress for his day. She'll enjoy the close stuffiness of the room, enjoy the sound of the bureau drawers, the jingle of coins in the pewter dish, and she'll rise, pull on her house coat, go downstairs to the kitchen. No sign yet of Gussie. But the girl will return. She always returns.

Gussie always had returned, had never left for more than a day or two, here on the plain. Their first months in Greeley, she'd tested the edges of town, counted her way across the county sections, and more than once she walked too far and slept against a barn wall, returned to find Leota back at her job at the mercantile, watching the street, waiting for her.

But later Gussie veered off on the trail of Leota's gentlemen, looking for their homes, their friends, their jaunts into darkness. She never found much worth reporting, and even when she found an ill-fed pet or a broken-down house she didn't speak—she wanted to keep a secret, she wanted to leave Leota to her own desires, she wanted to see Leota reach for a man and run her finger along the line of his jaw. Frank Locke was not the man Gussie had imagined.

Gussie followed Frank to his lodge meetings, followed the cigar smoke into the night. She followed him to the fields where he constructed his new house, and she heard him say, "I'll have a bride in February—Leota Tornig. This has to be perfect. She's more beautiful than I can say."

Gussie followed Leota on a summer evening, when the bats were skimming the dusk and the air was warm, still, rich with the scent of mown hay and honeysuckle, followed her to the town square where the trees were huge arching shapes in the first stars. Leota passed beneath the lamps, passed through the thickening darkness. Frank Locke met her where the brick paths intersected, and they stood close to each other beside the fountain. They talked softly as the city sounds gradually sank away. Before he escorted her toward her room and her child, he took her hand and held it to his chest for a long minute, silent, and then he released her hand and took her arm and they moved on.

Gussie knew that Frank wasn't Brud. There was nothing she could do. She couldn't fix it. She would only ruin it.

◆ ◆ ◆

Gussie took the trail along the river. The trail was intermittent, halfheartedly carved by fishermen and deer and errant cattle, broken each time it encountered a fallen tree or a gully. She climbed through each tangle, felt the stones through the soles of those delicate boots. She paused to pull burrs from the hem of the white linen dress. Across the river, a boy was fishing, his line snaking with the whip of his fishing rod, and then he laid the line on the surface of the water, and it drifted with the flow. He waved to her, held a finger to his lips, pointed at the water, as if so much as a whispered "good morning" would wreck his chances.

After less than a mile, the trail improved. There were tin cans in the brush, a broken bedstead half covered with fallen leaves, and then the shapes of rooflines and fences and porches floated high into the cottonwood leaves, up on the lip of the floodplain. She came to a bridge, its underside crowded with swallows' nests, a muddy community stuck to planks and metal. She climbed the bank, up onto the bridge.

She turned toward town, left the bridge and the river behind. The houses stood bright in the morning sun. The road was still rutted and pocked from the spring rains. She kept to the grassy margin, held her skirt up just enough to keep the linen clean. She saw herself pass in windowpanes, in the fenders of automobiles, and her general shape was soft, elegant. People passed on their way to church, people she'd seen a hundred times, and they looked her up and down, and she said, "Hello," and they still weren't sure. The linen was barely wrinkled—the weight of the water and the complete dryness of the air had smoothed it, and Leota had managed to control her hair with the combs. Gussie pulled the banknotes from her sleeve, peeled them apart carefully, shook them out and counted. It was a great deal of money. She thought of breakfast. She thought of a train or a motor coach. She passed the old rooming house, straight on to the center of town.

The town square was empty except for a young man who rode a bicycle from corner to corner, turning back on himself and crossing again. He was no one she recognized. He held his hat on with one hand, looked straight up at the sky, wobbled along. Gussie made for the fountain to wash the trail dust from the backs of her hands, to dab her neck with cool water, as she'd seen Leota do, to look down into the water and see more clearly the shape of her hair as it puffed against the sky. The young man saw her, made an elaborate show of not seeing her, and he rode in her direction, weaving across the bricks, whistling, aiming as if he would accidentally run her down, but she gave no ground, playing his game, and he veered, fell, and she kept walking. She washed her hands in the fountain. She saw the glint of the mother-of-pearl combs. She heard the bicycle approach again and stop behind her.

"You scared of me?" the young man said.

"No." She touched the cold water to the back of her neck and felt a shiver.

"You think you should be scared?"

"Can't say."

"You're a strong girl. Could probably toss me, if you had to. I ain't much to be scared of."

"I believe you." She shook the water from her hands, leaned again over the water and patted at her hair, no idea of what the patting accomplished, but she'd seen it done. She turned to face him, sat on the edge of the fountain, crossed her ankles. There was mud on her boots, but that was no surprise.

He stood in front of her, straddling his bicycle. He removed his hat and squinted. He was her age or a year or two older. He was maybe seventeen or eighteen. Green light in his eyes. His face with just enough flesh to work the jaw, a nervous grind. His brown felt hat, pinched in his hand, looked stained from years of travel. His brow was stark white—the hat had kept the sun and storms and world off him. He crushed the hat to his chest, stepped out from over his tipping bicycle and let it fall. His shadow was on her hands, on her legs.

"I'm Jack Fisher," he said.

"Pleased." She smiled. "You may call me Gussie, if you'd like." She didn't know where her formal tone came from, some memory, almost Leota's voice, but she let it stay.

He sat beside her. They looked at the fine morning.

"I found this bicycle on a porch," he said. "I'm just taking a little tour, having a little fun. I'll return it when I'm through. Do you think anyone would grudge me that?"

"The owner of the bicycle might grudge you, but I don't really care one way or the other."

"I don't want to get caught. I got other worries. Tomorrow afternoon I got to start my way back east to volunteer for the war. I just came out west for a last chance. 'Go west,' you know. Greeley and all. Got here yesterday. I ain't getting any farther west. I'm low on funds. I'm low on time. I'll come back when I get a chance—I love the dry of this country. I would've liked to go up into those mountains."

"That's where I would go, too, if this was my last day before something terrible." Gussie pointed west, direct across the miles to Longs Peak, a sharp white jut above the distant foothills. How many times had she seen the sun go huge and red on the spike of that mountain? She'd always feared it, all her time in Greeley. She had held on in that town, paired with Leota, and now Leota was paired with Frank.

This young man did not seem dangerous enough to be a real danger, but he was sure to get her into some trouble if she let him, trouble enough just by leaving town with him, and any extra trouble would be a blessing, make it harder to return. "I used to be scared of those mountains, but I think I'm done with that," she said. "I'm going. Will you come with me? I'll pay your ticket. My patriotic duty."

"Well," he said, "that's mighty cute of you, Gussie. Are you trying to add to my crimes? Bicycle thief. Transporting young ladies."

"I'm going to the mountains. No crime in that. Follow or don't."

She stood up, straightened the dress around her waist. Truly a remarkable garment, the way it held up, the way it was so blinding white in the sun.

◆ ◆ ◆

Gussie and Jack dropped the bicycle in a ditch. They swung by Miss Rita's for Jack's duffle, no idea where he'd end up staying the night. "Gives me options," he said. Gussie waited out front by the lilacs, rubbed her shoulder against the giant purple clusters, studied the pungent dust. Jack came out of the gate, nearly running, his face flushed. "I liked that room," he said. "It's like you're sleeping in the view. You see this nice yard and the street and mountains. I can't believe it—going to the mountains!"

They made it just in time for the morning run to Estes Park. She paid their tickets. They were alone with the driver. The motor coach skidded west, hit the hills, shifted through the grades, the day as dry as the forest, the softened cliffs looming. Gussie watched the jostling of Jack's knees, his slim hands cupped in his lap. His trousers were pale brown, a bit worn. She folded her hands on her lap—the tough darkness of her skin. She tried to sit straight, to sway smoothly with the jolts.

She remembered what Frank had told her—"The first time I laid eyes on your mother, she was carrying a small satchel bound with string, and she'd hooked the string with a finger, and it seemed that the satchel must have been empty, the way it flew about. And I remember seeing you, Gussie, far beyond her, planted hard in the shade." And if Jack Fisher were to remember this morning, what would he say? "I found a bicycle. I found a girl. I think she was a pretty thing. All in white."

The May heat worked to take hold of the day. They rose beyond the steep canyon. There were waxy yellow cactus blooms on the south-facing slopes. Aspen spread in wide bands in the evergreens, and beside the road the Big Thompson River dug white through rapids, the meadows crowded with dandelions and fireweed. The thickly wooded north-facing slopes waited for the sun to swing higher.

They crested a final ridge and the ground opened flat for a distance, and the fields were scattered with a fuzz of sparse green in the battered brown. The town of Estes Park was far in the pines, and Longs Peak above, solid snow in the blue. "There it is," she said. They entered the streets, passed the shuttered holiday storefronts.

The coach pulled to a stop and they disembarked. A few couples and families wandered the streets, looking for open restaurants and the first tourist shops to unlock the till. Windows full of wooden clocks, plates and teacups, flags. It was early afternoon, but it could have been another day, another month, far removed from the spring dawn beside the baptism river. They looked up at the granite in the clear sky. From somewhere, the sound of water flowed, the sound of air through the black forest.

Gussie tugged at the seams of her white dress, squared it on her shoulders. She was not prepared for the cold edge to the air, for the feeling that her lungs were small and empty. Her head buzzed, and her arms were gooseflesh. She toed Jack's duffle lying at her feet. "Would you have something I could put around my shoulders?" she said, and she touched his arm.

"I might," he said, "but nothing as fine as you'd need."

"Don't worry about that." She bent slightly, smoothed the linen against her thighs, the tiny violets in delicate ranks. "This dress isn't anything special."

"If you say so."

He dragged his duffle off the sidewalk, into a doorway, knelt and loosened the drawstrings, pulled out stacks of clothing, smaller bags of gear. She knelt beside him. He sorted through the shirts and sweaters, paused with each on his flat palms as if weighing it, testing it. There were heavy work shirts, and a cable-knit that would keep the wind out, and some lighter shirts. Gussie pushed on the stack of trousers, felt the nice density of the fabric. She saw where he tried to secrete his white drawers back into the duffle, his fingers slim and nervous. He decided on a pale gray wool shirt.

"This will be alright," he said. "It won't ruin your getup too much."

He stood, and she stood with him. She held her arms back, and he drew the shirt up onto her shoulders. They both looked at her in the glass of the shop door. From her throat, the white linen ran a narrow path and flared at her hips. The gray hung loose and comfortable. She smelled the laundry soap, the bleach, but she also smelled the duffle and the crowding of his other clothes and smoke and faded sweat, mild and familiar.

"It feels good," she said, rubbing her arms. "Thank you."

She bought them box lunches, hired a ride up into Rocky Mountain National Park. The motor coach left them at the farthest point before the snow closed the road, and the driver promised to return in a few hours. They climbed down over boulders, found a spot of heat facing south, ate their lunch.

They could see nothing of road or trail, just the clearings through the forest, high into the cirques, the white ledges, the shimmering melt. Only a few hours above the plain. She could follow the water back down, if she wanted. She felt the thin air in her lungs, that air born fresh from the mountains.

They napped. Awoke to small, distant sounds.

"Listen to that," Jack said. The rattle of a dislodged rock, the chatter of a ground squirrel. He stretched his legs out straight, whistled a long, dying note. "I came out of Hanover, in Illinois," he said, as if she would want to know. "I'm the last of ten children, Gussie. I got the last of everything, so I left. I've been all over. I drained myself all the way down to Mississippi. That's a low place. Can't burn off the damp. Not like this. I got out of that place, left the voodoo and the Mississippi behind."

The heat had built against the rocks where they sat. Gussie felt the heat try to push her back toward sleep. Jack stretched his arms up, held his hands against the sun, squinted. He unbuttoned his shirt, untucked it, held it open, his pale skin in the sun. "The heat feels good," he said. "If you don't mind."

"Why would I mind?" She wanted to open herself to the sun also, but the most she did was flap the gray shirt, taste the small breeze on her lips. The silver granite surrounded them with sunlight. She looked at his belly, the flat smooth bands. Nothing like Brud. Even she had more muscle than this boy.

"So I signed on to a summer of forest fires, up north," Jack continued. "Those old skinny spruces go like matches. Fierce. There wasn't nothing we could do. We just knocked down some trees, tried to make a firebreak, and waited for the wind to shift. Watched that fire close off the whole view. And then it was just red and leaping orange, and the sun was buried in the smoke. The fire takes the air right out of your lungs—you can feel it happen. The sounds were something like today—the fire took the sounds up faster than a guy could hear, up to the sun.

"We were small," he said. "We just watched the fire. We couldn't speak. There was nothing left to do, nothing left nowhere else, nothing to remember, just the heat and the waiting. Like today."

"You think you've left it all behind," she said.

"You can hope so, can't you?"

"That's right."

"You must have a fine house, Gussie, or a husband waiting for you."

"Oh, yes."

"You got a husband?"

"Sure. Why not?"

"What's he gonna think, you being away all day?"

"I don't know. I ain't met him yet."

He laughed. He understood. "What's he like?" he said.

"I guess he's more handsome than you."

"That's good."

They sat up and watched the afternoon. Jack removed his shirt completely, draped it over a rock. The sleeves hung loose, fluttered in the breeze. Gussie removed her gray shirt, flung it to the rock, where it covered Jack's shirt. They seemed stuck to the granite, the shirts, as if the roughness of the rock and the intensity of the sun acted as some sort of glue. Gussie stretched her arm, her white linen sleeve, and pressed a finger firmly against Jack's belly, testing his skin for sunburn.

"You're taking a little sun already, Mr. Fisher." She pulled back, rubbed her fingertip against her thumb, touched the finger to her cheek. "You got a wife waiting for you, Jack?"

"Sure I do."

"What's she look like? Is she adequate, like my husband?"

"She ain't clear in my head."

"You must've had a hundred sweethearts, a man like you, in all the miles you been traveling around. What were your sweethearts like?"

"I wouldn't say I got sweethearts, but I got ladies I've been thinking about."

"Alright, then. Do me a painting of these ladies." She closed her eyes. She listened. She waited to judge the shape of her own arms, her legs, her brow.

"In Illinois," he started, "there was a little thing of a girl when I was just a boy, and she'd taunt me till I walked her off through the fields toward the river . . ." The river languished at the bend, far below the bluffs. The girl dangled at the long whip ends of a willow tree, kicked her legs, a small fry hooked. Nothing to remember but her bruised ankles, her spectacles gold and bent, her jagged freckles, her skirts billowing, flying around her bloomers. And then schoolgirls, so many schoolgirls, all a blur of new shapely blouses and oily hair pulled taut in tails, their new downy calves, their delicate ears and napes, the dry surface of their lips as insubstantial as chaff. A girl with a black fleck in the open blue plate of her left iris. A girl with a voice like wet gravel, a rainstorm, leaves falling, sticking to the skin.

He moved on down the Mississippi. He worked at docks, loading and unloading the smooth-running river traffic, worked the rich black fields of farms, dredged the catfish ponds, got to know the scents of different flowers, the touch of dogwood, the strange drapery of Spanish moss. He watched the adventures of the young ladies, the proper lace of their Sunday gloves, the heat glistening on their brows, their blush at any startle. A young lady with dill on her lips from a cucumber sandwich. A young lady with bramble tearing her hem, mosquitoes drawing blood.

There was a bayou girl who drew a knife down the belly of a two-foot-long alligator. The pearly guts spilled, and she scooped them away, dressed the meat, peeled those little reptile fingers. She assembled a stew of that gray meat with okra and rice, and it bubbled at the back of the stove. They waited at the table, the girl and Jack, and they drank tart lemonade, ate gingersnaps. She was not a good girl, but he hadn't figured it out until later when he remembered the scrape and shuffle of her chair as she circled the end of the table and came close to his legs, and he moved away, the heat stifling, and he remembered how she gently followed the drops of perspiration with the tip of a finger, tracing down her sharp nose, along her jaw, down her neck, into the gap of her blouse.

"She could've been your sweetheart, a girl like that, no question," Gussie said.

"I'm sort of slow, I guess."

"You're a gentleman. All gentlemen should be shot." She heard the boldness in her voice, felt the joke was someone else's joke.

He laughed, scratched fiercely at the bony center of his chest. He went on, told Gussie how he'd caught a long line of barges, plowed slowly north into cooler air. The river narrowed. He moved on. The land was pocked with lakes. The black spruce bristled.

"I know that country," she said.

There was a northern girl, he told her, who cleaned the rooms where he stayed. Each day, she arrived before lunch, and she carried the breakfast dishes from the parlor, ran a rag slowly up the banister, straightened the paper tiger lilies in the vase on the landing, reached overhead for cobwebs. She was slow about her work. She checked the view from each window, leaning at the pane. She might have been counting leaves. She might have been watching for someone. If her forehead touched the glass, she breathed on the oily mark, wiped away the moisture. He wanted to know what she thought, how she filled her head. She was plain. Her eyes were sleepy, pale green. Her shape was slim and taut inside her garments. She was partial to oversize white shirts, long wrinkled skirts the color of fallen leaves.

He followed that girl one evening, when the heat was smooth and close to the ground. She trailed along the edge of town, kept to the twilight beneath the cedar eaves, and there from the dusty ends of streets other girls joined her, spoke in whispers, and they kept on, a slow meander until they reached a dark house, tall windows, and they entered, sat in the front parlor in the falling darkness with the windows open to the night. He came up into the shrubs where he could see their gray shapes. The other girls, her friends, sat around her. They waited as the evening air stirred the sheer curtains, and, out in the last light, heavy footsteps echoed and turned a corner, a flock of birds sighed with each wingbeat as they flew to roost, a fiddle started—no, it was a rusty hinge—no, it was a boy calling, cut short. The girls laughed. They settled back on the settee, on the chair, and breathed deeply. He never forgot the candle they lit, the tall glasses of beer they drank, the way his girl leaned out the window with the billow of the sheers, so close to him, and said, softly, "I could wait forever, damnit, if I knew what I was waiting for." He never talked to her, just thought of her wrists, her eyelashes, her shoulders.

Gussie might have been that northern girl, if she had remained in Minnesota. She might have been a girl that a boy would follow. She knew all about following. But no one had ever followed her, not that she'd noticed. She'd followed others as they followed others. Brud taking the miles, taking the old drift through the cedar break, and he came to where the sills were open to evening. In against a window, he rose up and peered in.

Gussie turned to Jack. A pink burn on his skin, a few hairs scattered in hopeless wings toward his collarbones, his nipples small, stubby. His chest expanded, deflated, and she counted his ribs, watched the quiver his heart sent through his bones.

She thought of how she might touch him again, what she might say. She looked at her hands—they were as flat and strong as Brud's. She'd seen Brud place his hand on a woman's shoulder, on her neck, cup the side of her face. She looked closely at Jack's face—there was the palest shadow of a beard, just a golden glimmer of stubble. His neck was corded with tendon and muscle, the lump of his Adam's apple. His arms were narrow, the muscles clearly delineated, the skin holding tight.

She said, "You've got to get yourself a sweetheart," and she heard Brud's accent laid over her own, the voice from far in the northern climes, but she was nothing like Brud—no one would ever look at her the way they looked at that handsome man. She reached, she laid her hand flat on Jack's shoulder, left it there, felt the warmth of the sun deep in his muscles.

Jack said, "I've almost run out of time—my train's gone in the morning," and his arm crossed his chest, and his hand landed on her hand, held her there against the pulse of his blood. A long while.

The light started to angle. Gussie saw how the clouds at first seemed to exhale themselves out of nothing, rolling and shredding and growing in a bank above the highest ridge. Were the clouds pinned there by gravity, by the weight of the peaks? And then there was a cold multiplication, and the crags and canyons suddenly ran with mist and pale gray light, and above it all the sky built in complexities of lace, blazing white shims. A late spring storm. They drew on their shirts, gathered their goods, made their way up to the road. Soon the snow would reach them and the gray would blanket the sun. There would be no red sunset, no flash of last light swallowed by the next horizon, burning away.

The motor coach arrived. Wrapped in blankets, they descended, pursued by the final edge of winter. The town was silent in early evening. Tire tracks and footprints in the drifting snow. A churning nimbus around each streetlight.

◆ ◆ ◆

There was a hall, nearly empty, a high ceiling, electric lights suspended in the gloom. Gussie gave Jack a coin, and he started a piano-roll song. She stood up, held out her hand, and Jack led her from the table, from the plates of chicken and corn, from the bottle of syrupy red wine. The other patrons were too far off through the hall to take notice. Out at the center of the floor, Gussie stood with Jack, deep beneath the ceiling, almost too deep for the light to reach, surrounded by the tables, the silent couples, the red-and-blue bunting, the black-eyed animal heads, the huge clock face lit from behind, as thick and white as ice.

The music centered in her head, and she had to think the music to the surface, the steady chords half sour, cranking, and then she felt the music on her skin and let it move her muscles. Jack turned her, and she took the momentum, spun in crazy loops. He had hold of her waist, trying to keep up, and her dress had hold of her legs, two forces pulling opposite. They couldn't sustain more than four steps in any one direction before they started off on a new step. They didn't stop when the piano's mechanism retracted the roll and filed it away—they moved on, Gussie taking Jack with her, Jack holding to Gussie's waist, to her hand, his fingers white in her grip. Their soles beat on that huge floor—the endless strips of pine, the sliding clap of their boots.

"We ain't got any music," he said.

"We drank enough wine for a whole band."

"It's got me sleepy."

"We must look a fright."

"No. No. We look fine. Just fine."

He slipped, he lurched, she caught him, and they stomped harder, louder, swirled at the center of that tall, empty space.

◆ ◆ ◆

They found an inn on a side street, at the back end of town. She tried to see in through the windows, but all she saw was herself in the snowy streetlight, a costumed girl, and Jack with his duffle large against his back.

"If you was my wife, we could get one room," he said.

"I'm not proud. I'll be Mrs. Fisher to save a dollar."

She handed him some money, and they went inside. The clerk,

roused from sleep, barely glanced as Jack signed the register. The key was large and tarnished, attached to a burgundy tassel.

Their room perched high at the back of the inn, buried in late night. The large white snowflakes slowly melted from their hair, leaving them both damp. Jack found a towel, patted them dry, stood there with the towel loose around Gussie's face. "You can have the bed, if you want," he said. "Anything you want."

"We can both have the bed."

They took off their boots and climbed onto the bed with a clamor of springs. They settled back against the headboard. From up through the grate in the floor, where heat should have flowed, they heard a man and woman—*seventeen miles for the boy . . . you can't blame them for that*—and Gussie thought she might find the rhyme to those words, but they ended. For a long time they sat there. Then Jack climbed from the bed and turned off the overhead light, climbed back beside her. Slowly, from the darkness, the dim hallway light spread in a thin layer across the floor, and the window grew silver with the drifting storm.

Gussie wasn't sure that Jack would move again. "I don't know about you," she said, very softly, "but I'm not comfortable." She took off the gray shirt and began to release the buttons at the side of her dress, at the sleeves. The dress lost its shape. She fought her way down through the dress, emerged from the hem, draped the dress on the footboard, and rolled beneath the covers. "These are good blankets," she said. "Warm."

He joined her, fully dressed, noisy, the rustle of his clothes in the sheets, the coins in his pocket. Then he was quiet.

Maybe ten minutes passed. Maybe half an hour. She found his sleeve, freed the buttons, found his collar, worked him out of his shirt, tangling her own arms in the sleeves. They began to laugh, soundlessly, and their hands forced through a cuff, and his trousers caught at her undergarments, and it seemed that they had bound themselves in a pant leg, and then they were free, and the bed had heated.

"Mrs. Fisher," he said.

She laughed.

The aftertaste of soap on his skin. The starched sheets.

She worked at pressing her mouth to his. He held his lips taut, no gap, a thin line.

"I think I'm a criminal," he said, holding back a moment.

"Sweetheart," she said, and she found him and centered him and pulled him in.

It seemed like nothing, no pain, the way they moved together. Leota had said, once, late at night, "It's like a rasp at first, Augusta, a frightening rasp, full of odd music and other sounds, and then you learn it, you love it." But Gussie wasn't frightened—she'd seen it. Twisting for vantage, she bettered Jack's moves, pressed the air from his lungs. The tall room amplified every sound—the awful grind of teeth and bone like some comic collapse, always falling, never to rest. And even in a moment of silence, she thought their sounds continued through the inn and found a place to lie. Days later, someone would pass the end of the hall and stir up the stray guttural.

She rolled with Jack. She'd seen how Brud took a woman in the softness behind her knee and manipulated her leg. She found the soft backsides of Jack's legs. She'd seen how Brud talked constantly to a woman, a long song. She whispered to Jack, and he did what she asked. Jack was beneath her in the storm light from the window, in the creeping lamplight from the hallway. He was whispering back at her now, *Sweetheart, Sweetheart,* his teeth chattering, as if he were cold. And then she thought of the white women in the marshy reaches. And she thought of the moldering dampness of early spring. And she thought of the startle of her father, and the crowd upon him, after him, fast—who could wish harm to such a beautiful creature?—and the women crying, left behind, and the whole tumult moving far away.

◆ ◆ ◆

Jack Fisher was locked into sleep on the bed, exposed to the cold light. Gussie stood at the window, felt the icy air in the casement.

She was still warm. She brushed at the blood on her thighs—it flaked away, smelled of iron.

Slowly the snow stopped falling, the sky cleared, the stars and a small moon came in among the peaks. Moonlight drifted in white patches, pooled in gray shadow. The view opened out across a black creek, snow on boulders like marble steps across the water. There were aspens beyond, snow on the new leaves, and then dark pines. The mountains seemed too steep and white to be stone.

Somewhere beyond the pines, a light opened, square and yellow. Perhaps someone in that square moved through another life, listened for a child, fed kindling into a stove. The light extinguished, left no hint of the structure that contained the window, if it had been a window, left only the shadow light falling across the depths of her eyes, back in against her thoughts.

She didn't know if Brud had brought Leota home from Duluth by lake steamer or by the gravel road. She didn't know if they'd stayed their first night at an inn or if they'd just traveled, in a hurry to shut themselves into their own. She didn't know if they'd conceived her in the house in the red pines, or if there had been an excursion north, onto the trails, and she'd been born of bloodroot and liverleaf and boughs glazed with pitch and the small fingers of fern and a northern white cedar's slow capillaries. She'd always thought there was a touch of raven in her dark eyes. Now she had run wild. She was Brud's child. She was unwanting and unworthy of the Locke name, but she knew she'd keep the name for a while, just to see what she could do to it, maybe rough it up a bit.

In the snowlight and the moon, she stooped at Jack's duffle, pulled out all the clothes and sorted them, tried to determine color, fabric, warmth. She took a pair of socks thin enough to slide between her foot and her tight boots. Her own undergarments were soiled, so she took a pair of his white drawers, tested the stretch of the weave. She kept the gray shirt he'd lent her. And she tried on a few pairs of trousers, found a pair that was slim enough to set on her hips, and to fix the length she could roll the cuffs. She placed the clothes she'd chosen into the bottom drawer of the bureau. Jack would be in a rush, leaving before dawn to catch a ride to Denver. He would be gone before she dressed.

She lifted the linen dress from the footboard, held it square to her shoulders, and let it sway about her ankles. She stood in front of the looking glass. The white linen was silver in the moonlight, beautiful, a dream that would never look as good again under any sun. Carefully, she folded the dress up from the hem, tucked it in on itself, until she was left with a compact square that would hold its shape, the collar on top, the white linen invisibly marked by the soil of her skin. She ran her fingertips across the linen, the tiny nubs of the violet flowers like Leota's private Braille. She placed the dress deep down in the bottom of Jack's duffle, layered his clothes and gear on top of it. She smiled to think of when he would find it, the jokes if someone saw it, and his explanations. He would be far away, into Kansas by nightfall, down through the dark creases of the country, and finally to the coast and the Atlantic.

What Jack feared of the coming months and the war, if he feared, if he dreamed the miles to be traveled in the morning, she couldn't know. His ribbed chest held the only sound, the flow of heated air and blood, moving on.

Virginia Dale

Augusta Locke buttoned Jack Fisher's shirt against her throat and went out into the street. All altitude and cold air, the morning light skimmed across the melting snow, but Gussie could feel the spring heat on her skin, the sun burning through the last shock of winter. Down into the middle of Estes Park, she made her way, hopped the rivulets. Slush wicked into the worthless seams of her boots. She checked her pockets, counted the money, made her calculations—she had paid for the drive to Estes Park, for the hotel, sandwiches, bottles of wine, but still there was plenty. As long as she didn't give in to any more extravagances, the money should last her at least a few weeks.

She stopped, turned slowly, looked up at the peaks. She was surrounded, every horizon looming. She felt the ache of starved lungs, thought of the valleys hidden in the granite folds, the old cabins buried to the stovepipe in snow, the roads and trails rising slowly out of ice. One day, she might return to hike the rocky passes, look up at the close undersides of clouds, see the earth reflected, the swift storms layered miles high. But for now, she would descend again to the plains, the budded green, and the simpler roads.

She bought herself a khaki version of Jack's hat minus the stain of travel. She bought herself heavy brown boots. When she got the chance, she would darken the boots with bacon grease—she liked the way dirt accumulated on the tiny ridges of the grease like patterns on a riverbed. She bought a sturdy knife in a leather scabbard and a belt to secure it at her hip. She bought a few rolls, a stick of hard salami, filled her pockets, drank a cherry phosphate, and tipped her hat to the clerks trapped deep behind the counters.

Flattening Jack's trousers against her hips, she looked down at herself. She wasn't as crisp as she might have hoped, but there was quality in the cloth. Her shirt cuffs hung softly about her wrists. The rolled-up trousers cut nicely across her new boots. She had seen photographs of women in tight trousers, high on the backs of thoroughbreds, and she'd loved the way the trousers exposed the shape of their legs, no baffles of fabric. She thought of how Leota might look in trousers, the length of her legs revealed, her soft hips molded by the touch of khaki.

In the mirror beside the readymade dresses, Gussie was sturdy, boyish. With the flick of a finger, she adjusted the brim of her hat, gave it a sidelong angle across her forehead. She might almost have been Jack, skewed by a funhouse glass. She fluttered her hands, let her knees sink, took a loose turn or two—she would never have Leota's grace, never have Jack's lightness. But if she moved quickly enough, if she let her steps tease the ground, she might pass for a youngster with skill, purpose, a touch of guts or wile. She squared Jack's shirt on her shoulders. She was small inside the cloth.

◆ ◆ ◆

She rode the motor coach back down from Estes Park, climbed off when the mountains gave out. The rocky hillsides rose, brittle in the morning light. She looked toward the plain. Ten miles out, home lay in the hayfields, Frank Locke's home. She looked at her hands, the skin rough at the knuckles, looked at her trousers. She thought of the pink glaze to Frank's nails, the scent of his black wool trousers, the way he slid his hands around the steering wheel in his automobile, taking slow, perfect turns.

To the south, the foothills shrank toward Denver. She had walked south more than once, she had caught rides, she had smelled the coal smoke. In that direction the roads angled against themselves, and the buildings stacked high. Echoes died in the false canyons, music from alley doors, shards of bottle glass in the dark pools.

To the north, the hogback paralleled the foothills, funneling the view. The roads thinned out toward Wyoming. She imagined nothing but towns set far in the empty.

She started on the road north—a few miles of solitude. She tested her boots, took long strides, felt the spring of her muscles, got to thinking that she could chew up all the miles she desired without looking back. There was something new about her, but she wasn't sure what. Maybe she was happy. Maybe she was scared. She inhaled deeply, gave herself a few sharp thumps on the belly and breastbone, heard the sound, both hollow and solid. Then she was running. Her heart was pounding. She wasn't going to stop.

She heard a vehicle coming along behind. Slowly it caught up, and she increased her strides, took to the grassy margin. The truck pulled alongside, and the driver, an older man crabbed at the wheel, looked her over, moved on ahead. The bed of the truck came even. A boy stood at the rail, looked down at her, looked at the empty distance north and south, ducked forward and spoke to the driver through the back window. The driver slowed again, leaned toward her, one eye on the road, and shouted, "We got a little more speed going than you do. Climb in back."

Speed. Yes. Without breaking stride, she swerved from the grass to the road, took hold of the rail, swung herself aboard. The engine roared, sputtered.

She crouched in the bed of the truck, let her heart calm. The boy was red from the sun, a stunned smile on his face. The man drove on, weaving the ruts. The boy shifted beside her, jolted her knees, stared. He smelled of cat's breath, barnyard milk, his upper lip as pale-fuzzed as an insect's abdomen, fingers taut and ready for action. He dug into her sides, twisted her skin. "What!" she said, shying from the driver's backward glance.

The boy shied, too, sank down against her side, whispered, "You got a job, brother?"

She grabbed his hand from her side, gave it a fierce squeeze. He yelped, backed off. "I'm not ever going to be your brother," she said.

"No harm," he said, smiling again, staring.

A lifetime of the same taunt, children calling her "boy" or "brother," and she'd always left the bastards behind, but now she faced this boy, made her face as blank as beauty. She was a woman.

"You feeling okay?" he said. "You're looking a little off."

"I'm lovely, thank you. I'm lovely, as you can see—full of love."

"Oh, yes. Full. That's good. Listen, buddy, I'm looking for a boy to put a few years between me and an early grave. My own brothers all gone off, abandoned the farm and me. You could sign on. You could get food and a wage. What harm?"

"No harm. I'm not your buddy."

"Not my buddy? Ain't I told my daddy to give you a lift?"

"Yes."

"Ain't I told you I'd get you a job?"

"Yes."

"And you ain't much of a prize calf, neither, so I guess I'm your buddy, brother."

"Not your brother. Not even a boy, for heaven's sake. What kind of bull kicked you stupid?"

"Shucks . . ." he said, smiling, but the smile faded as he looked her over. And then he seemed to come to some sort of conclusion, lunged at her again, tackled her.

He wasn't hardly a challenge, his muscles good only for gallivanting and minor chores. She rolled him to his back, found his thigh, slid her hand up until she caught hold of the bit of padding at his crotch, left her grip there. For a long rough minute the boy didn't move, barely breathed, as his daddy drove north at an unsteady clip. Then the boy seemed to catch up with his thoughts again, and he hissed, *"Brother,"* wrestled free, punched her around—she felt his stick-fingers ball and fist into her breasts, force the tendons and muscle of her neck, the breath knocked from her pipes—and then she lashed back, felt his skin peel beneath the arc of her nail, and he was going at her pants, tugging at the pockets, and then of a sudden she was lying on the road, the truck steadily kicking dust north, no glance back from the driver, the boy dancing in the bed, straw flying, a fist held high, Gussie's cash woven in the boy's fingers. He whooped. The engine roared, fired, faded.

◆ ◆ ◆

Miles past Fort Collins, toward Wyoming, a man dropped her off, turned west, and was soon lost to sight, into the mountains. The road was bad gravel and corduroy, the hills a confusion of short grass, brush, and spikes of mullein. Pines dotted the rocky fists and upthrusts, the stone softened by ten thousand seasons of wind and ice and sun. No windmills turning. No cattle or crops.

She waited in the cottonwood shade beside a creek. The water sluiced along in its cut banks. A lonely afternoon, here in the band of sky between the hogback and the mountains. No traffic on the road. For all she knew, no one would pass for the rest of the day, or for days to come. Maybe she was on her own road now. She reached into her pockets again, but her money was gone.

Another chance, she thought, and I'd throw that boy over. She flexed her hands, pulled her fingers into fists, laughed. It was a matter of smarts, of course, not strength. She thought of his slender arms, his ankles too skinny for the neck of his boots, his eyes as beady and dry as a chicken's. Where he'd punched her on the neck and chest, all that remained was a little heat at the surface of her skin, and even the heat might've been no more than embarrassment. She knew better, knew how to watch out for herself, or at least she'd know from now on. Good for him—he'd given better than he'd gotten.

She thought again of the risk, unsure of why she'd done it, taking the boy quick between the legs, feeling the shapeless shape submerged there. No secret, that—she'd worked with Jack Fisher at trying to control that unruly protrusion—but it was the control that the thing itself exerted that intrigued her. She'd taken hold of the boy, and she might as well have taken hold of his heart and lungs and squeezed, shut him down. She tried to think her way into the boy's nerves and veins, tried to figure how it all attached, how that grip of hers could place him in a trance. She'd heard of carnival men who said a word and sent a man to sleep, or sent a man dancing or crying or singing foolish songs, but this wasn't a word she'd used, even though, she supposed, it was possible that the boy's trance had simply been a moment of listening. What did he hope to hear—endearments, music? No—he felt her, he was afraid. She saw the rigor of his mouth, the flare of his tiny flat nose. He felt the shape of himself inside her touch. He felt how easily she could bring him pain. He felt the spark of his nerves, felt his hollow lungs and his fine fingers and the ducts of his tears and the clench of his toes. And then he made it stop—he took his thoughts back and robbed her, left her.

She walked north along the creek. A few Barrow's goldeneyes cruised upstream, against the current. She followed. In against the banks, the ducks skimmed the pools, wove the drapery of roots and willows, dunked after larvae, worms, came up with a quick shake, and motored ahead. These were male goldeneyes. The gray females were farther upstream, at the reach of the view, small against the sky-tinted water. The males were boldly marked—a line of white slashes along their black wings like the windows of a town far in night, and the night itself was glossed purple on the males' heads, the eye a star flanked by a white crescent, as if the evening star, Venus, rode the sky, cupped by a horned moon.

Gussie knew the moon well, its crescent and decrescent, its half shadows fingering through fences, groves, limbs. From a nighttime treetop or barren hill, she had placed her own eye close to the moon and let her sight trace down the line of the light, had seen her shape splayed, elongated, etched far below, a mystery shifting on the vague earth. Of Venus, she knew only its surprising brightness, constancy, sharpness, and quick flight.

Still no traffic on the road. She moved on upstream, pushing the goldeneyes. The males kept a casual distance, paddling, feeding. The females were still far ahead. She made goldeneye sounds, a swallowed croak, to soothe them. They didn't answer, intent on their progress. After a while, the rocky hills loomed on either side, and pines tunneled green above, and the road perched above the creekside trail. The sounds were closer now, the flowing water like the flow of a vein, close to the ear.

And then the male goldeneyes scattered—wings snapped out, webbed feet ran the water, and they skittered into the dark under-bank. And at the same moment (so much the same moment that she thought her movement might have scattered the goldeneyes, but that couldn't be), Gussie startled from a huge black shadow that struck and passed her in a silent wingbeat, a golden eagle fast up the creek, catching all the moment's sound in the broad scoop of its wings. And the females ran the water and launched themselves. The eagle was faster. Those dull, sad ducks, midbeat. The eagle slashed one from the air, dipped with the weight of the catch, and veered beyond the creek.

From across the creek, Gussie watched the eagle in its landing of grass and thistles, the yellow buds of the mullein ready to flower on the stalks. The eagle spread its wings, lifted itself with an unbalanced beat, settled again with a better grip of its talons. It looked at Gussie across the water, and Gussie felt the severe focus, felt her edges defined, judged. She was no match for the raptor. She shrank inside Jack's shirt, tipped her brim down to the limit of her view. The eagle cocked its head, seemed to take the measure of its own massive bill, and began to tear away the gray feathers, the white collar, until strings of the duck's flesh stretched from beneath. Gradually, the shape of the duck hollowed, leaving bones and weightless clues to what it had been: a Barrow's goldeneye, female, taking a spring afternoon up a creek toward Wyoming. Gussie left that ruined goldeneye, left the raptor's dark wings, the bill hooked with blood.

◆ ◆ ◆

The road passed on toward Virginia Dale through a whole range of horizons, thin lines of red, stripes of white, smooth fields rising, pine scrub along the water. Gussie ate the rolls from her pocket, drew her new knife and sliced chunks of the hard salami. She licked the grease from the blade, dried it on her trousers, buried it in the scabbard.

She would need to find herself a job. She had done little in her life. She could wash a dish, scrub a pan. She could sweep a stoop. She could not tend to customers, she was sure—she didn't have the language for it. She could not cook, not well enough for anyone but family, but she could dress meat, skin a deer, render bone.

She had trailed with Brud on his hunts, she had climbed a tree and spotted game for him, she had slid down the tree after the rifle shot and helped gut the beast. After the belly was slit, she pulled back the edge. It was all packed tight in there, the engines and filters, lungs and heart, the dark liver, the fancy gloss of the intestines, the sheathed penis or buried female parts. Brud slit the membranes, made the separations, left it all for the ravens, carried home the hollow shape, might even leave behind the head with its antlers smooth and branched and sharp, or the head without antlers. Leota waited for them with the knives and the small bone saw. Gussie followed as Leota and Brud carried the deer through the yard, hooked it in the shed, sliced the flesh from the structure of bones. That hollow carcass with the ribs like the ribs of a ship, like the beams of a church, holding the possibility of movement, of flight. Brud twisted the bones, separated the joints. Leota made her quick cuts, cleaned her hands on her white apron. They smoked the meat, cured the fragments. Gussie thought she could probably reconstruct the creature, arrange the flesh on the hollow structure, a puzzle, dress it in skin. But proving a sex for it was another matter—whatever clues they'd cut away had been scattered already by the ravens.

◆ ◆ ◆

The afternoon was gone. Evening came down with the last pale rays of sunset. Stars in the cradle of the hills. No one passed on the road. She found a bank of dry leaves, a roof of acrid brush, and lay down. With each breath, she heard the leaves rustle and compress beneath her weight. She was slowly breathing her way down into the deep bed. She moved her legs, felt the juncture of thighs and hips, felt her pulse submerged. The creek was a cold sound moving on.

A hundred times or more, many more, she'd run off, tracked the countryside, found a place to sleep, watched the stars, tasted the breeze. She might taste dust stirred by the deer passing through the north woods. She might taste bark or pitch or dying fire or fallen feather or moss thick and moist. She stared up through the brush, watched the sparkling pinpoint map, watched the pattern of leaves, branches, held her hands against the map. A bed of fallen leaves. The supreme dryness of the air. Stars flowing, endless, like minerals dissolved in the creek. She wrapped Jack's shirt close around her chest.

Jack would be watching those same stars, counting the patterns as they swirled, smelling coal dust, kerosene. Jack with his duffle slung onto the rack overhead. Jack with his forehead pressed against the glass, the train's speed vibrating his bones. She had felt his forehead press against her own forehead, felt his pulse shake her body, with the stars swirling beyond the hotel window, with the scent of cotton, of brass. She had mapped Jack Fisher in her mind. His broad, frail shoulders were built to take muscle. His chin was rough with the gold glimmer of whiskers. She remembered the balance of Jack's hands on her ribs, the hollow of his navel wet with heat, the sheet catching between them until they fought again for skin. The miles opened out, now, between them.

The night grew chilly. The creek carried the chill along with its sound, drawing from some vague elevation lost in the darkness, moving on to some other vague decline, washing out toward the plains. The sound of water shaping the banks, pushing at the cold round stones, digging down through the fresh filaments of roots just barely holding to the surface, down through layers to the fossil beds beyond memory or understanding.

Another sound worked in with the flowing water, and eventually the sound separated into something mechanical. She rustled herself upright in the leaves and looked south along the road. The white specks of headlamps bounced along, approaching slowly, like fallen stars dancing through a secret passage. Soon the vehicle passed right above her there, the scent of exhaust and the thin rattle of metal, the following scent of dust. She held still. She saw the figure perched at the wheel in the glass-and-fabric box, the faint light on his profile, intent on the ruts and ditches. She didn't run up to the road, didn't cut into the beams of the headlamps, didn't cut in from the endless darkness and the stars. The man was on his way north, his own way, and she was on her own way. The vehicle moved on among the pines, lit the clouds of sharp needles, beautiful and shifting. He was on his way home, she thought.

She would have a home, somewhere north. In Wyoming? Walls carved from the woods—spruce, pine, cedar, whatever blanketed the valleys—the scent of the woods boxed into the square joints, the gleam of amber pitch like jewels caught in the hard light. She would have bowls of leaves and seeds, flowers hanging head-down from the beam, bleached bones gathered in that new country, insect wings with the pattern of dark open eyes, an uneasy shimmer. Where she would be or if she would be alone, she couldn't see, but she tried to scan through the image—she found the window, found the delicate curtains closed against the view, touched the curtains and found a softness there where they touched the hewn walls. The cloth had been carefully sized and cut, hemmed with a straight row of tiny, even stitches, and as she stared into the pure whiteness its pattern swam up from beneath the surface—they were Leota's violets like flecks of beauty spaced, Leota's work (Gussie startled at the idea, that Leota might know her years from now, that she might turn her skill toward decorating Gussie's home), and among the flowers, less frequent but carefully rendered, almost by way of apology, were tiny flecks of branch dark with dusk, and moss ranked on cedar trunks, and moonlight on rime, and a jet raven feather suspended where it fell on the splay of a fern. She parted the curtains to look out, to see where she would arrive, north, but the glass was black, too black even to throw her reflection.

She nestled deeper in the bed of leaves. The moon had risen. The air was still and cold, exposed in the flush of silver light. Beyond her bower, she thought she could hear the vastness of the world, the empty miles of the road, the weave of echo.

She dreamed.

She held a square of parchment, unfolded it, and there on the crisp yellow surface, secured with a black ribbon, she found the shock of her grandfather Einar's silver hair. This was all she had of him—he'd died before Brud found Leota. Gussie ran that soft silver across her cheeks, across her closed eyes, held it to her lips and inhaled.

Far north in the spruce forest, she came to Einar. He was walled in by heavy boughs and darkness, old cedar and cold. A flame burned in a cup of rock. Smoke obscured the light, but still she could see Brud in Einar's features, Brud as he might appear in forty years, old and alone and banished from the center of life and yet still full of anticipation and desire, full of his own maps of the world. Einar reached for her through the smoke, pulled her to sit beside him, his rough skin icy, and together they held their hands to the warmth.

"Where am I headed," she asked, "that I've looped all the long way back to you?" For she knew vaguely that she was far from where she was supposed to be, on the Laramie road, near Virginia Dale.

"I can't know where you're headed," Einar said. "This is all I can say for sure: If you know where you're headed, then turn left at the black spruce. If

you don't know where you're headed, then turn right. There's fast-running water in both directions, good for drinking. There are turns you might take, if you see something that catches your fancy.

"I remember finding what was left of an Ojibwa lodge, just the ribs with all the covering gone, huge, the wind whistling through the structure, and I stood inside and tried to hear the old voices. I remember coming in to the brink of a village, and hearing the sounds swirling with the evening smoke, and trying to separate the human voices from the voices of machinery and wind and animal, and I waited until night filled in among the trees, the night sky and stars falling and settling against the windows, and then there were no voices at all, and I entered the maze of the village—I didn't know where to start, and I didn't know where the village ended."

Gussie looked at Einar squarely, looked at the firelight giving out to the enormous cold starry sky. "Look at me," she said.

Einar took the girl's chin in a tight pinch, leaned to her, studied her, placed his lips quickly to her lips, and she felt the parchment of his skin.

"Here's what I know," he said to her, his grandchild he would never meet. "You awake on a cold morning in late fall to find your breath has beaded moisture on the fallen leaves, drops of water tainted with your blood, your heat, from deep inside you. You're constantly leaving your traces. You move on. You follow raven calls. You listen to the skeleton trees rattle their bones. And once in a great while you see yourself in a sheet of morning ice, alone, and you're startled, you're sure you're a stranger, sure you aren't human, just a creature, breathing, unlike any other."

"What am I?" she asked. "What creature?"

"Dark. Smart. Like your grandmother."

"Who was she? Who was my grandmother? I don't know her name. I don't know her face."

He looked at her a long while, then he grabbed a pile of fuel and dropped it on the fire. A cloud of sparks rose among the boughs, the red challenging the stars, cooling into the void. And she was alone.

She thought that the forest had fallen away, thought she walked across open fields, but then the moon swung up and the surface of the forest far below her feet shone silver and dark, and she saw the trees as nothing but a mat branching and holding low in the sway of gravity, earthbound. Across the country the creeks and waterways gleamed with the cold pure moonlight, as if the globe shone from within with its own light, mapping its valleys and declines. She closed her eyes and saw that map imprinted at the back of her eyes, and she opened her eyes and the sun had risen hot and stark. She was up against the heat looking far down to the long curving shore of Superior and the forests marching north into their own green haze, broken by the beautiful dark pools and the reflected sky that made the pools appear immensely deep and thin-surfaced. She drifted on north and still she found the map of that country sharp at the back of her eyes. And then she saw rising from the forest a swirling cloud of smoke, but the smoke fragmented and grew darker until she saw that it was a large flock of ravens, nearly a hundred riding an updraft from their roosts in the canopy, from their grips on the cold hard wood, free now in the day's warm currents. On they came until she heard their voices, their rolling calls.

The ravens swept up around her and past her and she was caught in their momentum, effortless, rising another thousand feet. She heard the males call to the females and the females reply with the joy of altitude and heat, and she knew, although she didn't know how, which were the females and which were the males, they all were black and large and strong but to her they were distinct. The females looked to the males to start the dive, the females turned their black eyes from the stark sun, the females thought of how when they landed they would beg for a scrap of food and squawk with their bills wide, but for now they were strong with the males. The males spoke of speed and cached meat, the males turned their black eyes to the females, the males thought of how they would strut the ground and fluff their feathers and flash the white membranes of their eyes, later, but for now they swirled with the females in the high places where the clouds floated.

They drifted. They paired and split. They fell, and Gussie fell with them. They tipped a wing and rolled to their backs. They tipped the other wing and rolled upright. The wind of their descent fingered through their feathers and tightened their skin. They rolled and rolled again. They called and called, in *harsh and beautiful codas, and Gussie heard the notes and understood. They sang of the long fall down the rays of sun, of the tall air free now of cloud and eagle, of the sleek speed of their weight, of days and nights and the scattering of the horizons and the cliffs cold with rain and the lonely groves where thousands roost. She felt the air and the songs around her, she felt each black feather anchored in the glorious strange stretch of her skin, she felt the whistle of her nostrils and the sharp danger of her bill, she felt the grip and flex of her talons, she felt the whole weight of the earth drawn up at her with incredible speed, and she wondered at her power to attract the earth so violently and wondered at her fearless snap of wings and tail as the ravens caught the merest layer of air above the treetops and broke off each to his own direction. She chose north.*

She flew on, and the sun angled cooler by degree, by the miles. She tried to understand the patterns of the world, the carvings of the water, the shifting textures of leaf and stone, the clouds painting fast shadows, and then she felt the compass swing in her mind, she felt the map align, and she flew on toward a valley she knew would open, a break in the dark forest where a slow marsh ringed a pond and early spring broke through the papery buds. And there it was, aglow with fresh green. And there a man walked through the grass, left silvery tracks, looked up at her as she wheeled, as she circled down into that breach of the black spruces.

Einar held out his arm, and she alighted, held on with the wiry thin strength of her claws, and he walked on, took her with him. Ahead, above a black trunk that rose bare for thirty feet, up into the clouds of soft needles and the architecture of crooks and elbows, secure in the branches, was a pile of sticks and soft scraps shaped into a massive nest, and on the edge of the nest stood a large black raven preening the feathers of her long wings. She paused, looked down at their approach, hopped and took to the air and glided to meet them. Einar held out his other arm, and she alighted. Einar said, "The air is clear this morning." The raven gurgled deep in her throat. Einar said, "I've found nothing yet today. I took the ridge at first light, took the trails where the deer pass, looked along the water where the frogs sometimes bask, but it's all still quiet, and I wanted to see you, to hear of the high calm chill of the morning air and the miles you've already circled, to see your black feathers hold you in the air. How is he?" He looked up at the nest. The raven gurgled again. "Go on, Gussie," Einar said. "Go on and take a look."

Gussie left them there, Einar and his raven, and pulled herself up through the air and landed on the lip of the nest. In the dimness beneath the boughs, in from the bright morning, she took a moment to see what she thought she saw. Here in the halo of woven sticks, in the padding of deer fur and soft petals, lay a child, its pink skin stretched about its drawn-up angles, its eyes closed and roving beneath the waxy lids, its small sharp mouth gapped and dark inside, and a fuzz of black hair. She looked at the shape of the bones, his skull a soft ball, his hand a delicate instrument, his knees shapeless, white in the creases. It was Brud.

◆　◆　◆

Gussie wandered toward Wyoming with empty pockets, empty stomach. Her new boots muted the stony road.

Here was a crossroads, Virginia Dale. A dog twisted back on itself, chewing its hindquarters. There was a tavern with a long front, different facings, windows high and low, a mess of old stage station and postal office and porch falling off one end and screens streaked with rust and a sign swinging from noisy chains: VIRGINIA DALE—LODGING—MEALS—POST—STOP PLEASE. She came in from the road, onto the porch, stood at the open door. This was a place to stop if a storm had drifted the road, but not on a clear day. The afternoon light spread in long squares across the battered floorboards. The bar was scuffed at the base, the bottle racks nearly empty. Electric cords strung like vines from the low ceiling, the bulbs all cracked or missing. And behind the bar, lit only by reflected light, stood a man, a mass of gray sprouting from around his hat. His beard was grizzled black. He muttered, tapped his fingers on the bar. "Saturday will be busy. Unlikely. Check the stock. Don't bother. Crowds and crowds. North and south. Too much for me alone, don't you think? No." He whistled, a falling note.

For Gussie, this man was another start—every man was another start, and would be for miles and years to come. She would greet him, judge what he thought when he looked up and greeted her. She stepped in through the open doorway. "Hello, hello," she said, striding. "Sir? Are you open?"

The man startled to attention. "Afternoon, young man." He doffed his hat, replaced it, met her out from behind the bar.

She extended her hand, squeezed his hand, looked up at him. "I'm hungry."

"I ain't serving."

"I can't pay."

"Fair enough." He smiled, moved on across the room with her in tow. "Sit. Sit. Here at the window. In the sun. This place is chilly." He took hold of her shoulders, pressed her down into a chair, and she landed hard, winced for his benefit, but he had moved on, fast across the room. "A bit of meat and potatoes, yes? Some gravy? A sweet drink? You ain't old enough for a beer—of course not, a boy like you. But a boy needs a beer these days . . ." He busted out of the room through the swinging kitchen door. The crash of pans. For all she knew, he hadn't hardly seen her.

She looked at her bright face in the windowpane, removed her hat and fluffed her hair—not much to fluff. She had thought that maybe her scent had changed, now that she was a woman. "Must be Jack's shirt." Her voice wouldn't help—she heard the roughness of it, as if she'd just awoken, as if she'd barely spoken in her life (not far from true, short of bird calls and quick exchanges with teacher, student, father, mother—Leota, soft voice . . .). She smelled her sleeves—starch, sweat, nothing specifically masculine, unless soil was masculine. She dug the grime from beneath her fingernails, laid her hands out flat on the table. Her hands were tanned, rough at the knuckles, strong. She saw where she'd bruised herself against the boy—purple swirls pressing up from beneath.

In the windowpane, there was nothing but her face. She was not a particularly handsome boy. If she'd seen herself sitting there, a boy alone, she would've watched for a while, waited to see what he'd do, this boy, this quaint creature. The boy didn't move, not for a long while, just thinking, his thoughts most probably off on a wander through the oily tubes of machinery, and greased bullets, and thighs, and how to secure a good hard drink that would burn his throat, and then the image of a chair, and then a blade, then a breast, a shiny dime. Something like that. She supposed that his thoughts must filter somehow through his veins in a manner perfectly opposite from her own thoughts. His blood pooled in his muscles, heated at the thought of power, of anger. He slid his fingers along the tabletop, pulled them in against his palms, tested his fists—they were solid enough if he put better thought behind them. He banged his fists on the table, judged the weight of the thump. He could be hard. But he startled at a movement caught in the corner of his eye, felt his heart jump, looked at the window, held himself calm again. It was nothing—just a strange girl looking back at him, her features bunched in a questioning smirk.

The man returned from the kitchen, and Gussie squared herself to him, pulled her hat back on over her curls. "Thank you," she said, testing a smoother tone.

He banged the plate on the table, pulled knife and fork from his pocket and laid them at the edge of the plate, sat across from her.

Thin strips of meat afloat in a brown pool, swirls of iridescent oil, rising steam. A healthy dollop of potatoes flecked with peel and pepper. She took up the fork, ran the tines through the gravy, stabbed a strip of meat, chewed it, smiled at the man. Plain food, hot, on a plain plate. The man smiled too, moved his lips a second as if he too were chewing, with pleasure.

"It's been a long time since I went a day without food," she said. "Didn't know it could hurt so bad."

"Oh, sure, that hollow tummy. Like fire. Like a wound. I've had my share, son. You walk past it, though. You move on. Where you headed?"

"North."

"You got a reason to be in Wyoming?"

"I don't have a reason to be anywhere."

"That's handy."

"I'll figure a reason when the time's right."

"You're young. It'll all come down on you shortly enough. If the war don't get you . . ." He reached across, took Gussie's hand, whistled a long low breath. Just sat there, looked out the window, looked again at Gussie, reached and ran his thumb across Gussie's cheek, beneath her wincing eye. "Don't you go volunteering. They want you, they can find you. Wyoming's a big place. Could lose your name up there."

"I'll need to find myself some work."

"You get yourself off the roads, far into the back country. What kind of skill you got?"

"Don't know. What do you know about jobs?"

"I ain't got a job for you, if that's what you're asking. Sorry. All I got is I could use a laundry girl, so I don't keep bleaching my poor hands, but that's just luxury for me, and it ain't for someone like you. I don't think so. You'd be insulted by girls' work. Not for you, is it?"

"I don't know. I don't have anything particular in mind. You look at me and tell me what I should do."

"Well, all right." He pointed at her, pointed at the floor, twirled his finger. "Let's see what you got going."

She stoop up, shook the miles from her legs. Her trousers settled low on her hips. She locked her thumbs in her pockets, gave the man a squint. "This is all I got. What do you see?"

The man looked hard at her, from her boots to her shoulders, down to her hands. She thought he might be trying to count her fingers, so she freed her thumbs and held her hands palm-up to him. His eyes flicked from one hand to the other. She felt the damp heat on her skin. She moved her hands lightly at the wrist, thinking of Leota, of the smooth, pale movement, as if she played some delicate instrument, fingers pulsing, a music the man would hear, notes he'd see, see Leota on her, see everything that was Leota and nothing that was Gussie, see a beautiful girl.

"You're sturdy," he said. "You'll do what you want. Take a good breath. Feel your lungs. You're strong, son. I'm sure of it. Strong and steady."

Laramie Plain

She kept walking north. For a few miles, the pines were taller, and then a narrow meadow, and then shelves of stone, and the WYOMING sign ahead, and she passed the sign, and the sky opened. The Laramie Plain stretched between the Red Buttes to the east and Jelm Mountain to the west. She traced the line of the road as it took the folds of the plain, and far ahead she saw a stirring of dust. As she continued she saw the machinery, the horses, heard the engines of the road crew. Behind the crew, the road was pale and straight; ahead of the crew, the road was gouged with shadow. For all the miles she could see, the crew was the only activity. The Laramie Mountains, gray and distant, dipped beneath the northern horizon.

She came close enough to count the number of men on the crew, to see how they went about their work. The horses weren't calm—they fought their commands, pranced before the Fresno scraper, tangled the lines. Gussie had walked among the legs of horses when she was small, in Ravenglass, she'd fed them from her palms, slipped onto their backs as they slumbered. She watched the man work the reins, follow the scraper, and she took the same stance, held her hands out and gripped the air, tried his moves and thought she could do better. And she saw the men with shovels and picks—work without the need of language, hardly even the need of a brain. The man in the truck pumped the pedals, the gears screeching through clouds of blue smoke. The foreman checked his measurements, drove stakes into the ground. The crew unloaded a culvert.

A good job, she thought. *A man's job.* If not this crew then another crew, farther into Wyoming. If not road work, then man's work, mindless. She dropped her hat, drew her knife, cut her hair close to her scalp, watched the hair separate and take flight in the wind. How long before the strands were taken up and woven into a nest, carried into a burrow, for warmth, for comfort?

She pushed her trousers low on her narrow hips. Slowly she started her approach, trying to add a rougher edge to her stride. Her toes caught against rocks, jolted her bones. A man might walk like that, not care what he dislodged. She growled a bit, tested the low notes.

She came up to the crew. The foreman was at work beyond the truck, saw her standing there, waiting, motioned her over. Gussie met the man, took his extended hand, felt his wiry grip, and she gripped back, hard as she could. He released her hand, rubbed his fingers, scratched at his trim blond beard. "Where are you headed?" he said. "Are you lost?"

"Do I look lost?"

"Just thought you might need some help."

"I'm fine by myself. Could use a job, though, if you need a man to beef up your sorry little crew here."

"So you're a traveling comedian, eh?" He looked her over, poked at her shoulder as if testing for resilience or density. "No, I don't have any need of a comedian. I got enough problems slowing me down."

"I can do whatever you need."

"What makes you think that? You're a pup."

"I'm not stupid. I'm not lazy. What more do you want?"

"You have enough sense to work hard and pay attention?"

"I have enough sense to do what I'm told, sir." She shoved her hands into her trouser pockets and tried to spit. "I've built roads all over the place. Did gravel roads in Minnesota. Did oil roads in Colorado. Uh-huh. I'm your man."

He nodded gravely, crossed his thin arms. "You're a liar, son. But I'm short five men, and I'll never catch up if I don't hire on. So you'll work for me. My name's Mr. Dunn."

"My name's Gus, sir," she said, feeling she already needed to be working, pushed by the man's attention. "My name's Gus Locke."

"Good deal, Gus. Don't you lie anymore. No need. Just work. That's all I ask."

✦ ✦ ✦

The crew camp sat at the near horizon, at the end of a long incline, the cluster of tents like a small army encampment. The spot was indefensible, exposed. Wind moved through the grassland in long sweeps of silver and green. The white canvas tents took every breath of wind, caught seeds from the grass. A few scrubby willows rooted along a slip of creek, the creek going dry already with approaching summer.

Mr. Dunn introduced Gus Locke around—she got no more than a quick hello or joke from Ben and Ernest and the rest, these filthy men—and then he showed her to her quarters, a small tent set off from the others. It was stacked with crates of necessities—canned milk and fruit and vegetables, machine parts, oil, inner tubes, tins of flour. And in the corner, a cot with a folded woolen blanket and flat pillow. "You'll be better off in here," he said. "Those other fellas are a rough bunch. I'll keep them off you, if I can. We'll see how it works out."

"I can handle myself. Always have."

"You're in with something bigger now, I'd guess." He snapped open the blanket, dropped it neatly along the length of the cot. "The last fella to use this cot took off and left us. He didn't have an answer for these men or this work." He sat on the cot, smoothed the blanket, his gaze on the trampled grass floor, the boxes, the dusty ceiling.

Gussie looked at his hands—they were bony, smooth. "Thank you," she said. "Don't worry."

He nodded, turned to square the pillow. "I'll worry enough to keep the project going. Got a tight schedule."

Such a nice neck, she thought. *Such a small ear.* He was a well-made man, perhaps thirty years old, his shirt as clean and white as salt or plain paper. And then Mr. Dunn was past her, out of the tent, and he climbed into the truck, the engine sputtered, he drove away.

She looked out into the camp. The crewmen were kicking about in the twilight, letting the day's work ease from their muscles. They all seemed burly and aimless. They were dark from the sun, baked by uneasy years. Gussie was a small girl, an even smaller boy. She lay down, waited, for what she wasn't sure, listened to the men's voices.

"I was wounded," she heard Ernest say. "I got a wild horse and a rope round my wrist, and the rope snapped and tore my skin."

"That's bad," someone said.

"You know it. I seen the white bone all shiny, and the flesh all raw, and the tendon looked like something uncooked. And then the blood come up. Wouldn't stop. Could feel every inch of my body at once."

"Not such a great thing to feel, judging from the looks of you."

"Could feel my guts. Could feel my lungs. Could feel the bones in my feet. You ever feel like your eyes are round and hard and full of tears? Ever think your lips are paper? Then I heard the broke gate fall. Saw the horse flat out across the field."

The men all whistled or groaned. Gussie squeezed her eyes shut and tried to imagine their structure, but she couldn't feel them at all.

"I'll tell you guys something, cuz I known you all now a few weeks," Ben said, "tell you I lost my wife to another man, years ago."

"That's bullshit."

"You had a wife?"

"A blind girl?"

"A human girl?"

"Missing her is almost as fierce as loving her," he said. "Missing her keeps me busy. There's things I can't do cuz it gets me thinking of her. Can't work the feedlots anymore, cuz she used to bring me my lunch there."

"Thought you got fired from the feedlot for lovin' the cows."

"I can't get comfortable talkin' to a woman no more."

"Hard to talk to a woman when she's screaming and tryin' to get away."

Those voices went on, and Gussie listened, tried to get her own stories started. *Lost my gear in a stampede on the Sand Hills. Got my heart broke by a gal that made great biscuits. Once killed a deer with my bare hands and a rock. Stole a Ford, drove it till the axle broke on a goddamn lonely road. Bit the head off a rattler . . .* And then, before she'd gotten far, the truck pulled into camp and Mr. Dunn was back into her tent. He laid out for her some trousers and shirts and a jacket, travel kit with soap, toothbrush, powder, and a razor and lather brush.

"When you get scruffy," he said, "I'll show you how to use that razor."

He'd bought her some long johns and work socks, and he tore at the brown paper package, handed them to her. "You need the whole outfit," he said. "You don't have anything." He left her alone to sort through the goods he'd chosen.

She guessed at how he'd gone about shopping for her, the packages from the mercantile in Tie Siding, a few miles south. Mr. Dunn had sorted through the goods with the shape of her body in mind, running his fingers along seams, leafing through styles and fabrics. Boy's clothing. He had held up a shirt by the shoulders, let it drape, placed the thought of her inside it, her structure of muscle and bone, and he'd thought of how the panels would envelop her, brush her small nipples. Trousers to warm the bow of her short legs. Long johns to pad the chafe of the trousers. He hadn't asked for her sizes—he must have held her naked body in his mind and judged her. She placed the male Gus on the mirror of her naked body, and she saw how his muscles clove the skin with sharper shadows, how his shoulders bulked, abdomen toughened, and she chose for him a sensible penis, pale in its shroud, and a nice pair of testicles, evenly round in their pouch, small enough to tuck comfortably in the long johns, stay out of trouble. Nothing like Brud's proud dangle. She blushed at the thought, held the stacked clothing tight and inhaled its newness.

Outside, she caught herself in the reflection of the truck door. She was a jaunty boy, cared for, neat. Mr. Dunn had dressed her well. Would Leota recognize this boy? Maybe not. But she'd admire the crispness of the outfit, the ruddy sun on the boy's cheeks. And Leota would imagine that she knew nothing of the boy's thoughts, his life, and the way he moved through the world. And maybe Gussie knew nothing, either. She took a few dancing hops, breathed deep and two-stepped around the edge of the camp, trying to enter Jack Fisher's moves.

Mr. Dunn was coming in off the fields. Gussie kept stepping. She saw clearly the pearl buttons of his shirt, the flash of his buckle, his loose gait slightly knock-kneed, hands looking for a place to rest. He was the age maybe of Brud the last time she'd seen him—he was old enough to have a home, to have a woman to love. He was almost at her. She turned, tried a dip and a twirl. She heard his steps as he passed. She thought of his feet in those black boots, and she wondered if his feet were the same as Jack's, the bones and tendons pressing up through the white skin. She thought of his chest inside that shirt, and she wondered if he had a few hairs at the sternum, like Jack.

She stepped lightly in his wake, reached and touched him on the shoulder, and the shock of her boldness stopped her, and she wished he would keep walking. But he turned around, faced her, and she looked up at him, at his dark eyes in the evening shadow of his hat. She looked past him, caught the last blush of sunset above Jelm Mountain.

"What?" he said.

"Just this," she said, and she forced herself calm, turned slowly for him, her arms out. "This is what you did to me. What do you think?"

"Did to you?"

"The clothes. You knew me perfect."

"Yes, well . . . I was a boy once. I remember."

"And now I got a song in my head. I'm happy. Thank you. I'm gonna dance a bit." She took a few sliding steps around him.

He shook his head, waved her off. "Act the man, boy."

"Which man is that?"

"The man you're going to be. You're almost a man, aren't you? Are you fifteen? Sixteen?"

"Something like that."

"Good enough, then."

Mr. Dunn left her, walked toward the center of the camp, toward the fire. She saw how his shoulders cut flat against the night, square and straight. He sat with the others, remained square. The firelight licked the line of his jaw, washed thin and flat across his pale face. He was somehow different from the men on the crew. The silent men watched him as he held his hand out toward the flame, the long shadows of his fingers obscuring the curve of his lips, the dark set of his eyes. The men couldn't see clearly who he watched in return. They heard his steady voice—he said something about the look of the clouds approaching or the span of the next morning's gully. Whatever he said, they were attentive—they would all be expected to remember his words, or so they believed, given his serious tone. But it was a ragtag crew, and they didn't all have the faculty for remembering detail, so they leaned forward around the fire, or they stood and shifted their positions closer, trying to catch Mr. Dunn's expression or inflection or glance, trying to commit some vague moment to memory. He was the boss. He stood up from the group, left the fire circle, and disappeared beyond the tents.

She would never be a man like Mr. Dunn, she was sure. But the men on the crew—they were well within reach. She circled through the darkness, let the firelight catch each man. A lineup of weak chins and squashed noses. A heap of bad posture. Someone spit, and the fire popped. She came on into the circle, into the smoke. She squeezed between two men on the edge of a crate. Coyotes yipped along the Red Buttes, pups testing their lungs.

"Hey, Gus," Ernest said, pinching her side. "You're going to have to work hard. No slacking. No special favors for yearlings."

"You guys ain't worth your salt," she tried in return. They laughed, looked at each other but not at her.

"Hey, fellas," Ben said, "this boy is gonna hold us back."

"You guys ain't nothing but a bunch of steers getting punched," she said. "You got no sense but to do what you're told."

They didn't laugh. They looked at her. She saw their small eyes, tried to squint the same hard expression, twisted her mouth into a tight button, raised an eyebrow, knew she was a pathetic sight. They smiled a bit, went back to their conversation.

◆ ◆ ◆

She started with a shovel. As the culverts were laid, she came in behind and scooped dirt around the curved edges. The wooden handle creaked in its joint with the metal blade, and she used that sound to judge the weight of each scoop. The music of her work stayed with her long after she'd dropped the shovel at the end of the day. On into sleep, she dreamed of the shovel against the weight of soil and stone, her palms torn by the constant rub of the handle. But when she awoke, she found her palms tough and calloused, and then Mr. Dunn was at her tent—it was dawn—and he said, "Let's go, son," and she heard the men at the fire, and she was ready again for the rhythm of the shovel and the heat of the sun unbroken on the plain and the sputter of the truck coming and going and the horses hauling the Fresno scraper, opening a new surface north.

Through the long day, there was no pressing need to speak—the men moved along behind the plan that had been laid, each man taking his turn, adding his bit of muscle to the design—but still the men chattered on, endless, by the hour. "Lift that." "Move that." As if the world wouldn't rotate without their attention, without proof that they could see action and name it. And each time someone said, "Gus, now, shovel the dirt, here, here," she said, "Thank you for pointing that out."

Ernest followed her closely. He grabbed her biceps and squeezed. "You're not much," he said.

"I'm enough," she said.

"You're barely enough to keep us going."

"We're going fine." And she worked harder, until she felt the sweat draw the strength from her muscles and leave a salty pain. Still she kept at it, even as the men sat along the gully and watched the clouds. They yammered a steady stream, until their voices wove with the hot pulse at her temples. *Ten miles to go . . . A ton of lumber . . . You're the bastard won't give . . . Dumb as a dead mule . . .* She moved the earth, watched herself plant the blade, lift, expel. Yes, she knew the job required no thought—the job was just an animal rhythm, no more than breathing, a natural motion without choices, and the dusty air filtered into the deep pockets of her lungs, she tasted it, she thought maybe the plain was slowly rising up inside her, until she couldn't breathe. She was buried inside the hot expanse of the plain. Her movements were locked. Shovel buried. Arms buried. Her body had stopped.

"You gonna do any work worth noticing?"

She was sitting cross-legged, the shovel dropped to the side. She looked up. Ernest stood against the sun.

"You gonna do anything?" he said.

She grabbed at the shovel, climbed to her feet, brushed past him. "Just thinking of the next step," she said. And she focused her vision and walked as straight as she could, and she passed by the truck and took a long drink of that metallic water in the steel drum, and she kept walking far to where the next set of stakes laid out the work, and she planted the shovel and forced it deeper with the kick of her boot, and her head cleared, and she saw that far behind her the crew still messed with the finished culvert, and Ernest looked her way and shook his head, and she heard his small voice—"Don't do nothing till I get there"—but he made no move to catch up. So she looked back to her shovel, and she cleared away the roots the Fresno had left, and then she dropped the shovel and started moving the lumber from the stack that had been deposited. She smiled. It was nothing, this man's life.

When they returned to camp, she took her supper to her tent and lay down, stared at the potatoes, the congealing butter, the strips of meat stewed to gray fiber. She wasn't ready to eat. Her chest hurt, ached, her lower back was almost hot to the touch, her stomach had an emptiness that food might not cure. But she'd heard all the men complain—no way to escape the constant strain, the tender joints. And she was getting stronger. She took a spoonful of potatoes, worked the gritty paste across her teeth, swallowed, and her stomach fluttered.

Mr. Dunn came into the tent. "Here, Gus," he said. He handed her her pay. "A few extra dollars in there for a good week."

"Sir?" She took the cash, ran it through her fingers, thought that the touch of that soft paper was sweet, rich. She slid it into her pocket, felt the padding against her tender skin.

"I saw you out there today," Mr. Dunn said. "You're moving along."

"I'm not going anywhere."

"No—you're moving *ahead*. You've got a step on this whole crew. I don't want you leaving. War has taken all the good men, one way or the other. But I've got you. I need you. Just lost the Fresno driver."

So Mr. Dunn put her on the Fresno scraper, that sharp-edged

bucket, the blade that tipped to cut the plain. The first morning, he led her through the harnessing of the four tall horses, and she echoed his movements. "You remind me of someone I knew," Mr. Dunn said. "A boy like you. But maybe he didn't have your potential. I'll never know."

He walked with her behind the Fresno, laced his fingers together with the reins and her fingers. She felt his long muscles as he pushed her thighs with his thighs, as he made her step forward at his pace. She felt his heat magnifying the day against her, felt her hands caught in the guidance of his hands.

"Like this?" she said, but she couldn't have moved an inch outside his plan for her.

"Like this, young man," he said, with a gentle tug that brought the horses around. "You're in command. Your slightest move—they're waiting for you—they don't know anything else."

Then he sent her off on her own. She still felt the pressure of his thighs, the steady progress. She made his gait her own, down to the square of his shoulders and the steady set of his hips. If the machine slipped sidewise, if the horses shied, she took more strongly to the memory of his stride and drew it all back.

She threaded the reins through her fingers, set the handle on the scraper, followed the heavy steel and the music of its runners. She peeled the surface of the old road, then moved on to cut fresh ground. The grass dragged to ruin beneath the blade. The top layer of the earth held the roots, the prairie dog holes. Then she made another pass, exposed the layer of moist soil that dried quickly in the wind.

◆ ◆ ◆

Gussie dunked a washrag in a pan of water. If she went slowly down her legs, along her arms, if she dropped the washrag back into the water and ran her fingers over her chilled limbs, there in the darkness with the moon glowing through the canvas and the pillar of stars at the gap of the tent door, she felt how her skin contracted around her muscles, how her muscles bulked around her bones, how her bones held a new body, Gus's body. She had hardened. Her cycle, that iron flow, was a memory—more than a month she waited for the ache that pulled her elbows and knees to center, and then she stopped waiting, knowing she had vanquished it through long hours, painful work. Her thin wrists were marked with veins that rose from her darkening skin like a lazy, mannish script—she pushed at the veins, but they wouldn't recede.

She reached for her clothes in the darkness. She touched the buttons, metal and mother-of-pearl, heavy seams with raised stitches, pockets, worn cuffs with trailing threads. She guessed blindly which were Jack's, which had come from Mr. Dunn. It didn't matter. Jack was gone, and she remembered only parts of him, as if he'd been refracted through a panel of cut glass, beams of light rainbowed around the edges. She saw his shoulder with its barely concealed structure of bone, and she felt her own shoulder, the tightness of her clean skin. She saw his chest with its small, pale nipples, and she felt her own nipples, shrank from their new tenderness. But her arms were as wiry as his, her legs as muscled. She felt her sex, the small of her back, the soft pooch of her buttocks. Did she miss anything about being a girl? Would a man stand like this and study the smoothness of his mother-of-pearl buttons, as she did? Maybe. Mr. Dunn had taken the time to select clothes for Gus, to dress the boy in sturdy colors.

Even in the summer heat, she shivered. She pulled on her long johns, her socks and trousers and shirt, buttoned away her wrists and neck and waist. She could breathe easily again, concealed.

She took her blanket, walked out into the warm night, out from the too-close stacks of gear and food. The tents were mostly dark, the men asleep and dreaming—she tried to imagine the dreams they dug themselves through, the blank sky and the rank scents and the frail creatures always fleeing ahead, out of reach.

A lantern lit one of the tents, and the shapes of two men stretched up across the canvas. They worked at something—

cards—and then a golden shadow flashed and danced from hand to hand, raised and passed again—the clank of the bottle against the edge of the cot. Then the lantern moved, and a man ducked out from the tent. The light swung at the joints of the man's knees, and the shadows flashed out from his gait—unsteady, the toes of his boots gouging up red clouds of dust. Gussie looked to move beyond the reach of his light, but he had seen her.

"Gus," he said. It was Ben. "Why you out lurking? Can't sleep? Miss your mama?"

Gussie stopped, stood her ground, readied herself, the endless male chatter looping in her ears. "You couldn't touch my mama," she said.

"I'd bring you into our tent for a good hard drink and a game, relieve you of your pay, but it's hands off the child."

"If it's hand off me, it's by my own say-so."

"Sure. Right. And I'm the goddamn foreman."

"You the foreman? Not for a road. Maybe for digging a latrine."

"You ain't the foreman, either."

"That's right, Ben."

"Not gonna be."

"Don't want to be. Just want to do my job."

"That's good," he said, scratching his head, moving on. "Stay to your job . . ."

"I can handle my job."

"Stay out of my way . . ."

"Wouldn't touch you, Benny."

"Don't touch me, boy . . ."

"Wouldn't touch you unless it became necessary."

Ben was gone. The light moved among the tents, disappeared beyond the truck. She was left in the dark to think of her mother— Ben had put Leota's face in her head. She did miss Leota, she was sure. She did miss Leota's thin waist and the touch of her fingers, the way she spread her fingers and combed Gussie's hair, the way she ran a fingernail through the channels of Gussie's ears and flicked the dirt away, the way she squared Gussie's collar, the way she waited on the porch for the girl to return.

Gussie walked away toward the willows, tried to force her mother's gait down through her own strides. She floated for a few steps, fell back into her usual shuffle. She tried tilting her head to the side, glancing from the corners of her eyes—Leota could catch whomever she desired with that look, a glance to stop a man like Ben, a man without grace or a moment's real thought.

Good evening, Ben.

Evening, ma'am.

Walk with me awhile?

A pleasure, ma'am.

Gussie felt her square hips inside her trousers. She felt the calluses on the balls of her feet. She felt the bristle of her hair about her scalp. No glance of her own, no matter how well calculated, would stop a man for anything more than a question or a fight. For now, maybe forever, that was alright. She was never the image of Leota, never even the shadow of Leota. She had walked a thousand times beside Leota, and each time she might not have been walking at all. For as long as she could remember, Leota had always been ahead or above, alone. And only at a time before memory was Gussie *within* that beauty—she'd been a small yellow lump floating in an alabaster vessel.

She went on to the edge of the camp, spread her blanket beneath the arching willow bushes, lay down. Above her, the stars wrapped around the arms of the willows. The stick fingers dragged across the constellations, the gods and creatures lost their tails or arms or weapons before the turn of the earth made them whole again. The Laramie Plain seemed to be suspended in the night, tagged to the elevations east and west, as if even a faint late-night breeze might riffle the plain, snap and luff, send Gussie and the crew bouncing, flying high into the cold gap between earth and stars, and then they would plummet, she thought, voiceless, black as ravens, clawing for each other, as if taking hold of each other would somehow break their fall.

She saw one of the crew walking among the tents. No lantern. Maybe Ben, maybe someone else, Ernest or Mr. Dunn or one of the others. As if testing the air, judging the earth, the man wandered the corners of the camp, and then he came toward the willows, stepped lightly, stopped and held still for a long while. The minutes passed to an hour or more. The stars slid around the man's tall, steady shape, and a star nestled against his neck and entered from sight, and a star lodged in the gap between his arm and side. And then the moon leapt up small and white. All the distances were laid out flat. At some point, the man might move again, approach.

Gussie rose, slunk away through the willows, headed far out. There was something beneath the surface of the plain, she was sure, out here in the open. Each day she felt the taut thinness of the earth as she drove the Fresno, felt the resonance of the horses' hooves tapping at the dusty drum. She felt the plain as a thin drapery between the Red Buttes and Jelm Mountain. She thought that if she found the right seam, if she located the bubbling spring or cutting creek, she might be able to see down through the water, down to the underworld. What that underworld held, she couldn't know. She imagined blackness, warmth, scents like memory, cedar brushing softly, and finally a vague view as skewed and strangely lit as the reflection in a raven's eye.

She listened to her boots grind the dry soil. No one followed. Bats zigged across the sky with the soft patter of their skin. She made a long, slow decline, felt the lay of the land give way, and finally she saw a creek, no more than a thread of water in a buffer of dense vegetation. She held her hands to the scrub willows and wildflowers, felt the day's lost heat caught in the darkness of the branches. She looked down into the water. She saw a boy looking up at her. The sky above, the sky below, was muted with moon and galaxy.

◆ ◆ ◆

On into summer, they worked the road north from the border. Mr. Dunn was a good foreman. He walked north until he was no more than a flicker of shadow in the afternoon. He guided the survey, planted the stakes, felt the density of air settled in the hollows, guessed where the season would turn and the snow would drift and bury the highway.

And from the placement of the stakes, from the way Mr. Dunn swept his arm north, using the angle of his palm to describe the lay of the road, from his words—"We come off the hill softly, Gus, so we hit the next bridge square"—from all this Gussie had to plan her passes, marshal the strength of those four huge horses, lay her thought of the finished grade upon the old road and the plain, and then flick the reins, take a step, hold it all together. How it must have looked to the crew—this slight boy, eyes hidden beneath the brim of his oversize hat, no more than a doll bouncing at the end of the reins but somehow controlling the weight and the power. She moved the long handle until the blade struck, and then the bucket filled and overfilled, and she kept the overfill contained as she moved on to a lower spot and again adjusted the lever, let the soil discharge to a good depth.

And there was Ernest again, always after her, or getting the others after her, egging Ben, trying to make her out to be young and slow, but she could hold her own against any of this lot. Mr. Dunn had driven off to Laramie that morning, left them to follow his last orders. She moved north with the horses, passed the men all sitting on a stack of lumber, sitting unmoved during her last five passes, and she said, "There are some edges up there you might want to smooth before I gotta do it myself." They didn't respond. They passed a canteen, drank, shook the last drops onto the ground. She swung around, came back at them. "Any time would be fine," she said. "I don't really care." They all climbed down off the lumber as she passed, and then they were behind her, and she nodded and tried not to smile.

The horses skittered. She pulled her focus back, tightened the reins, looked past the rusted bulk of the Fresno to the smooth dusty flanks of the horses. And then she saw the pebbles fly in from behind, strike the flanks, and she glanced back, the men all in a line, lobbing rocks, smiling. She turned back to the horses, couldn't speak, not words, just uttered a string of soothing sounds, worked the reins to let them know she was there, she was strong, she would hold them together. They pranced forward, huge hooves clipping the road. Then a volley of larger stones arced in from behind, struck, and that was it, the horses were off. She ran, felt the reins stretch and tear her skin, and she released. A great clatter moved south. She followed. Didn't look back, even when she heard the men's whooping shouts. Wiped her bleeding hands against her trousers.

The Fresno skipped and threw sparks and broke free from the harness, and then the horses accelerated, loosely held by the strips of leather, but the leather flew and the hooves pounded and left the road, and the plain rippled beneath that frenzy, a beautiful flight, four horses yoked together by more than harness, yoked by inarticulate fear and a view of the horizon. Gussie ran in their wake, caught the ground behind them even as the torn sod still rolled, and she whistled, high and quick, and she left the work behind and for a mile she ran free toward the Red Buttes and their strange elevations, ancient erosions. But she caught the team, still on the flats, and she rubbed their necks with her painful hands, and she turned them back, led them slowly. She saw the crew bent at their work— no one had followed. She saw the Fresno, a speck on the road. She thought only of righting the Fresno, repairing the harness, moving again past the crew without a word, making her precise cuts of the plain.

As she came down the long slope toward the road, she saw that Mr. Dunn was pulling up to the crew, the truck's dust still settling along the plain to the north. He climbed down from the cab, talked a moment to the men, shaded his eyes and focused in her direction. She looked down, followed the progress of her own steady steps, and finally heard Mr. Dunn's voice carried on the wind. A warm and soft and even wind.

". . . can't have it. The boy could've gotten killed . . ."

He yelled at the men. Gussie looked up. He pointed north along the path of their work, pointed south along the work they'd completed, pointed out to Gussie and the horses.

"You won't get paid for today. Don't deserve it . . ."

And then there were too many voices. And then the men turned and walked away in a mass, slow across the plain.

Mr. Dunn climbed back into the truck and drove to the Fresno, waited. "I'm sorry for this," he said when she finally approached. He took the reins, held her hands a moment and examined the slashes and blood. "This isn't going to help this operation."

"They're not going to bother me, Mr. Dunn."

"They've already bothered you. They sure as hell bothered *me.*" He led her to the back of the truck, tied up the horses, washed her hands carefully, made her drink. "You've done all you're going to do." He climbed up onto the bed of the truck, helped her up, and they sat there against the boards, in the shade.

"I couldn't hold them," she said.

"I know. Don't worry. They told me what they did. A joke. It's all gone bad. Don't worry. We'll just rest here a while, till you get your wind back."

"I'm fine."

He placed his hand on her knee, jostled her. "Let me tell you something. Something bad that happened. A long time ago. Okay?"

"Okay."

"Just listen." He removed his hand from her knee. He leaned his head back against the boards, closed his eyes. "There was a boy who stayed with my family when I was maybe your age. He'd lost his own family. He was a good kid. I took him everywhere with me. He shared my bed. Shivered all winter. Drove me crazy.

"He didn't follow close enough, never close enough. My fault, I'm sure. Never had a chance to teach him proper. Out on the Nebraska plain, the storms come from the west, storms like we've got out here. Big mountains of cloud. You know.

"The boy and I walked miles cross-country. We passed through windbreaks. From the edge of the break we looked far across the field to the next break, and then we kept going through the wheat. A storm came up when we were out in the middle. I hadn't seen it coming. At first it was just a breeze that pushed us along, but then we felt the cold and looked back. The sky was dark green, and the far windbreak trees were all wild in the wind. And then the full force hit us and it was hard to breathe.

"We ran. The boy kept pace when he could, or I slowed for him. We were afraid, the wind stung, it didn't seem we could reach the next trees before the storm got us. The boy was laughing and trying to keep his breath and keep his legs moving. Then the rain caught us. I looked back and the boy was behind, not far but too far to reach him with my hand. The whole storm came down on us. The sun was gone. There was a thrill on the boy's face. But then we were struck apart. I didn't know what I saw. A light flashed on his body. The light lifted him and took him away. The light was so close that it was like it came from inside my own eyes. The boy was gone. I couldn't see him. My soles burned.

"I found the boy laid out in a furrow. Hail was falling. Everything was going white. The boy was small. There was no warmth at his nostrils. His shirt was torn open, his shoes were gone, his forehead was burned. I scooped hail and held it to his forehead. The skin was ruined.

"On his trunk and arms and shoulders I found some markings. I tried to wash his skin with hail that melted in my fists, but the markings stayed. They were like leaves branching from his veins and nerves. I thought it was the shape of plants from far west, maybe from the mountains where the storms rose up. I left Nebraska. Years ago. I came west. Never forgot it."

He sat quiet for a while. The wind was picking up. She looked at his hands where they gripped around his legs, the fingers woven tight and white. "I'm sorry," she said. "You couldn't help him." She laid a hand on the knot of his hands.

He made to get up, rose above her. "No. I couldn't help him." He jumped from the bed of the truck, helped her down. "And now I've got work to do. I'll take the Fresno from here."

"I can do it. I'm fine. Just help me get it going."

"No. Your hands. You rest. Go lie down." He pointed to a line of willows that transected the road. "You've been hurt. Lie down. I'll take over."

He untied the horses. She walked off through the grass, found shade where the willow leaves hinged stiffly in the afternoon, where the air seemed colored by the moisture veining through the green, drawing from a thread of creek. She watched Mr. Dunn work. He righted the Fresno, brought the horses around, attached the harness. His hands on the reins and the Fresno handle—the strong action of his pull, the stirred dust, the protest of metal. He made a pass, testing, stopped, rested the reins on the handle, looked toward the boy, Gus Locke, just looked, no smile, a steady glance before he looked up at the sky, shaded his eyes against the brilliant edges of the clouds, the quick rays.

Gussie felt her own heat, her pulse. She saw Mr. Dunn take up the work again, saw a brother—maybe Mr. Dunn was her brother now, maybe he'd watch out for her—she felt the way a brother would feel when he thought of Mr. Dunn, the easy looseness across his belly, without fear, the way Mr. Dunn's shape almost didn't register in the brain, the shape replaced by the memory of other afternoons, evenings, childhood, meals around the table, voice from across a field, footsteps in the boxy dimness of a barn. Yes, if Gussie had had a brother, it would be an easy wait in the shade for his approach.

But Gussie had never had a brother. She waited in the willows. Mr. Dunn's brow was slick with sweat. He bent to his work. If he was not her brother, then what did she feel when she saw him? His steady progress, his gradual approach, the slight dust kicked by his boots, the puff of his shirt around the wire of his torso, the grind of his jaw as he squinted in her direction. There—she felt the tightening of her skin as if he had touched her, and the touch moved on in her mind, followed the lines of her nerves, and she caught at her throat as if the gesture would somehow calm her, and the touch of her fingers to her warm pulse could have been Mr. Dunn's touch, and her skin heated, and she closed her eyes, and Mr. Dunn was there against her, pressing, insistent.

+ + +

That evening, a storm came in. The rain sent the crew to their tents directly after supper. Gussie lay on her cot, watched the canvas gray and go black through the roar and spatter of the storm, lay awake for hours, listening, beneath the musty comfort of the wool blanket. She heard the rain pummel and soak the ground, and where the ground was logged the water began to flow, so that in with the rush of the clouds and the angle of the drops she heard the passage of rivulets into streams, the plain alive with water and gravity.

With a slowly passing gap in the storm, she heard something moving out there beyond the heavy canvas. There were steps that pressed slowly against the ground, and she tried to guess the weight of the creature, guess the form it took, sleek and keen-eyed, or low and sharp and hunting, or tall and chilled, approaching. And what the creature could judge of her by scent or sound, she couldn't know. She was a weak force in the vast night, her heart a cringing little fist, unsteady, her breath whistling across her dry membranes. She was defensible by nothing but her intellect, and even that seemed incapable of moving her from beneath the blanket, taking her to the gap of the door, showing her the night and the danger and the need for flight. But she wasn't going anywhere. Her fear passed, or it became just part of what made that small tent and its supplies and the warmth of the blanket her home, for now, where she listened and tried to give shape to the world beyond. She heard the steps again. She felt a chill of fear, felt the night leak in around the edge of the blanket. She pulled the blanket tighter, looked toward the door.

The canvas gapped. It was Mr. Dunn. His dark shape moved quickly against the darker clouds and distance, and then the canvas closed and he was inside. She heard him breathing. She heard him find a place to sit among the supplies. He was close enough to touch her, but she couldn't see if he reached, if his hand hovered at her shoulder or neck or hip. She waited. The rain started again, swallowing all sound. She felt something brush her lips, realized it was her own breath from against the blanket. The rain shook the tent. A mist of pulverized storm fell from the canvas, swirled in slow currents through the enclosed space, coated her cheeks, the channels of her ears, her open eyes.

"Mr. Dunn," she said, or she'd only thought his name, she couldn't be sure, couldn't hear herself. "Mr. Dunn," she tried again. Nothing.

She couldn't be sure now if he'd even entered the tent. The darkness was complete. The air was wet and heavy in her lungs. *Alone,* she thought. *Alone.* She played again his shape at the dark doorway—surely he was close to her.

All she knew for sure was the cradling cot beneath her and the blanket. All else was the sound of water. She had shaped Mr. Dunn and placed him out there in the darkness, in the unshaped space, but for all she knew in that dark night he could have been inside her, inside her thoughts and dreams, floating in the storm. *Inside,* she thought. She felt a flutter low in her gut—it seemed to float, to swim. She felt the movements of another body inside her, the waxen limbs nearly luminescent in the darkness, the pulse a steady contraction that animated the limbs. She tried to see that other body inside her. Maybe it was the image of Mr. Dunn. No. Maybe it was her self, her *other* self, Gus. No. It was something else. She placed her hand low on her belly—there was something there, something that was small, beautiful, frail as thread, soft as petals.

"Mr. Dunn," she said suddenly, again. She wanted him to feel that strange flutter. "Mr. Dunn," she said.

"I'm here," he said.

But the feeling was gone, though she could still see its shape on the insides of her eyelids—lines of light like veins, gathering into nets and branches. She thought of a fern, deep in Minnesota winter, those perfect miniature symmetrical fingers, sheened with an immaculate skin of frost.

"I'm here," he said. He sat on the edge of the cot. He rubbed her shoulder, patted her head. "Just checking on you. I need to take you somewhere in the morning. You sleep."

He got up, moved away. In the darkness, she couldn't tell where he'd gone. She watched the darkness. For hours. Listened. Maybe she slept. Finally, she rolled from the cot, felt her way along the stacks of supplies. Cold heavy cans. Dusty boxes. No Mr. Dunn. She found the door, opened the canvas.

For a long cold minute she looked out into the rain. Slowly the earth turned or her eyes grew accustomed, and she saw the streaks of rain, each drop carrying the faintest echo of faraway light. Curtain after curtain of gray. And then the camp slowly rose into focus, deep behind the water. The clouds rushed overhead, almost within reach. Then she saw Mr. Dunn in the cab of the truck, sitting at the wheel, looking away. Maybe he was asleep. He wasn't moving. He wasn't looking toward her, wasn't coming for her.

Shaken with cold, she climbed back onto her cot, lay there as the dawn fought through the end of the storm. She listened for the truck's engine to cough into life. Nothing. Then the truck door slammed.

Mr. Dunn was at the tent, holding open the canvas. "Get your things, Gus," he said.

◆　◆　◆

They drove north along their own road, taking the curves they'd calculated and graded, crossing the hollow echoes of the new culverts and spans. And then they left their work behind, and the road was all ruts and muddy drainage. The sun came up over the Red Buttes and started to work on the mist that hung to the plain. The mist failed, the sun shifted from pink to white, and the plain blazed with light reflected from the endless drops heavy on the grass. They shaded their eyes against the glare. For miles, they saw only a lone antelope far off, a line of fence that had lost its wire, an axle swallowed in a sandy ditch. Snow on Jelm Mountain seemed far too high in the pure blue.

Gussie watched Mr. Dunn's hands go white on the wheel and his face go red and then pale again, intent on the road. They weren't talking, didn't seem that they would talk. He nearly closed his eyes against the glare.

Windmills. Fences. The Laramie Mountains were clear now. And they drove on into Laramie, the streets quiet, the truck a bulky reflection in the shop windows, and then they sped on out from the last pickets and telephone poles and followed the northward curves of the Laramie River. Layers of the earth peeling away in the strong rush of the storm flood. Left the river behind. On through Bosler. Through Rock River. Across the Medicine Bow River bridge and through the town, past the great concrete-block edifice of the Virginian Hotel, all the curtains drawn against the sun, horses tied to a rail. Heading due west now, with the railroad to one side and the pure flatness of the world to the other. Locomotives steaming. The tracing of far ranges.

And when it seemed to Gussie that they wouldn't stop, that they would travel until the road ended and then keep on traveling into the desert, Mr. Dunn pulled north off the road onto twin tracks through sagebrush, and he rumbled on at too great a speed, and they skirted the edge of a ravine, and he slammed the brakes and cut the engine and the truck skidded and stopped. The view west. Nothing but open country. Nothing but the wind picking at the seams of the cab, the engine cooling through small metallic groans.

And there they sat. Mr. Dunn leaned forward over the steering wheel, squinted against the miles. And Gussie watched him. He released the wheel, sat back straight. That was all. Afternoon was coming up. They both watched the sky. They both stared straight ahead. And then, as if they'd thought the weather into being, the horizon darkened, the clouds approached. Great high thunderheads. A huge sheet of storm dipped down and caught the sun in a brilliant orange unearthly mass before going utterly black.

Lightning flashed shadows through the cab. Then hail slammed the roof, deafening. The view outside fell to white, the white as smooth as ice until lightning shattered it again into motion, then smooth white again and the rolling sound of distance. They sank together from the force of the storm, shoulder to shoulder. Gussie couldn't separate her own breathing, her own heart, from the great shaking, the spring-loaded rocking of the truck.

"This is going to wash us away," Gussie said, unsure if he'd heard over the roar. "This is terrible," she said, louder.

"I just need to rest for a while." He looked sad, exhausted.

She didn't know what to say. "I could drive, if you're tired."

"You can't drive. You've never driven. You're too young."

"Then what is it?" She couldn't think. They were far from the crew. They were alone. She placed her hand on his knee, and he flinched. She placed her hand on his shoulder, shook him like a brother, as he'd shaken her the night before. "Where are we going? Are we going together?"

He looked at her. "I can't keep you on the crew, Gus." And then he was crying. Tears slow on his pale face. Too old to be crying. He rubbed at his face with his sleeve, shook his head to send the tears flying. "The men are going to walk off. I need them. They're almost worthless, but they've got numbers on their side. I got you a room with my cousin in Rawlins. I'll take you there. I don't want you to be sad. You'll be fine. She'll watch you. Let you grow. Let you work for her, if you want. She's a good woman."

She looked at him a long while, watched him catch his breath, calm himself. The storm leaked into the cab. She shivered. And then she heard what he'd said. He didn't know who she was. If he knew, he wouldn't send her away. "Here," she said, and she pulled at her shirt, yanked it from her trousers, buried her face against his neck, worked to open her buttons, and she dragged his hand, cupped it to her belly. In the lightning, they looked down at her breasts, her rounded belly, a soft extension. She was carrying Jack Fisher's child.

THREE

Rawlins

Gussie lay in darkness, in a room high in the eaves of the Brunswick Hotel, drifted near the end of a long, deep sleep. From far inside the wind she heard a train whistle. She knew it was the two A.M. Union Pacific, a freight train drawing from a great distance. The tracks swooped along the curve of Sugar Creek.

Off Buffalo Street, men's voices echoed through the alley. *Johnny lost his hat . . . He's lost without his hat . . . This way . . .* And then the voices faded, and the wind rattled the roofs, whipped branches against the dark sides of the Brunswick Hotel.

Wind shaped this town—Rawlins, Wyoming—this low place on the verge of the Red Desert. Wind fingered the mortar of the brick facades, the sandstone arches and foundations, sandstone quarried north of town, the blocks of stone as cold as night, as old as history, as faded red as the hillsides in their decline. Wind caught at the meanest scraps of this place, scoured the gullies, dusted the gardens, swirled back on itself. A small town bare to the winter sky.

Gussie lost the sound of the wind, opened her eyes. She saw the icy, unsteady stars in the tall window, but she couldn't see enough of the sky to puzzle out the constellations. She closed her eyes, slept, dreamed.

The baffles of the aurora borealis pulse across the northern sky. A bruised cosmos, lime and violet. Small inside the aurora, only the brightest stars shine. Gussie looks at those stars a long while, tries to discover their constellations, but she can't find a way through the colors.

Against the aurora, the pines are clearly cut. She follows the bearing of the branches, gauges the lay of the land, and soon she is deep again on the trails she knows, with the aurora a hazy wash in the strata of conifers.

She makes her way for long hours, the night cleaving to the trail, the aurora fading into past or future, fading as completely as the sounds of Ravenglass. She knows that these are the northern woods, Minnesota. Beneath her steps the fallen scraps of forest give up their sounds—flakes of bark, the black spruce, eggshell, snakeskin, lichen as dry as an old man's beard. She counts the miles by the steady pulverizing of her steps, the dust of forest and memory in her wake.

A faint light comes in among the trees. Then the trees are gone. A constant gray as if rain will soon fall, as if the season is waiting to move on. She keeps walking. A train whistles, without location or echo. The mild ripples of the earth—winter in the roots of the brown grass. Snow slants in from the west. She tastes the bleak wind in her lungs.

She is following a single line of tracks, heading west. Where the snow is thin the animal has opened the color of the soil, an ancient red. A long series of marks scribed on the snow in undulating ribbons. Beside the ribbons are tiny prints, two to the left, a space, two to the right, like hands. A salamander? She looks for its bright stripes, its flat head, the beautiful large eyes, but it's lost in the distance.

The ribboned marks diminish until the last vestiges are nothing but an occasional flick, then gone completely. Only the tracks remain, left, right. Farther along, the tracks have grown, and she stops, places a finger into an impression, sees now the claws, sharp.

Ahead, something moves. She hurries forward. The gray light is failing— it must be evening, or the earth has turned farther toward winter. Hills rise into the underside of the sky, with darkness flowing into the gaps where hill shoulders against hill. She runs, in pursuit, but whatever runs ahead is too fast, is uncertain to her, remains uncertain.

She sees the animal's hopping stride, the limbs fancy in the air. She sees colors like quick reflections in black feathers—bark and ice, bloom, willow.

That creature digs at the crest of the hill, baring the red desert, the veins of mica and bone, and as she rushes up the hill she sees that it's a raven digging at the horizon, and the bird lifts, black into black, and she runs up beneath and looks into the blank night, and the raven is lost though she hears its wings, and then she sees its course, sees it against the light that it releases from the clutch of its talons, mica chips scattered like stars, and the raven's wings set the stars to flowing, settling in her wake, settling into dragons and gods, maidens and bears, and a great white river flowing high and away.

◆ ◆ ◆

Gussie awoke to darkness. She remembered, as she had remembered each time she awoke during these last five days, Dr. Bradley's voice—"In time, Augusta will come out of it. I almost lost her, but she's as tough as any I've seen."

She held her hand to her soft belly. She was a mother now, but she wouldn't be a mother again. She had lost blood, faltered, survived, here in this room in the Brunswick Hotel. She reached for the light beside the bed, turned the switch, closed her eyes against the pain of the sudden brightness. She thought she had been in this room too long. She thought she hadn't been out in the town for months. Pain drifted deep. The mattress held her shape. She laid her hands on the pressure of her breasts, felt the hard pockets, pushed until the pain subsided, the milk heating the cotton of her gown.

Her child. Anne, it was called. A girl. She had held the child—she remembered its slick blue skin, at first, its wrinkles clogged with white, the pinched scream of its face, the way it batted at her breast and tried to gain purchase on the nipple, a sharp discomfort.

She opened her eyes. The empty room. The ceiling and the bare bulb at the end of its wire. She draped the covers aside so that she could feel the chill, cool her pains. Nothing was as it had been. She felt the looseness of her viscera, the misshapen marrow of her body.

Pulling at her nightgown, she exposed herself, her belly, to the light. There were shadows on her skin, low against her sex, swirls of violet fading toward green.

She wanted to fold herself back toward sleep, lose sight of herself, and shut down the pressure of the milk. She switched off the light. She wanted to dream, to wander back to other days. Tears stung her eyes—not sorrow, she thought, just a reaction to the cold and the splintered pain. But she couldn't sleep, wouldn't sleep again that night. She was exhausted from too much sleep.

She slid from the bed. The weakness of her battered center, her legs as if the muscles had lost their grip on her bones. At the window, she held herself steady, chilled by the air, by the view.

Buildings blocked a fraction of the sky, and, above, the stars rose, the patterns nearly overwhelmed by fainter patterns overlapping, the planets lost in their slow wanders. Down the hill, past Front Street, a train charged into the wind—the sudden flash of the engine, the clatter and steam, the pulsing of the cars, one after another, the caboose's red beacon, and gone.

Gussie traced the patterns of the rooftops—the North Star Lodge across Third, the chimneys of Blake House behind the bare trees. A light shone from far inside the frosted window at the back door of the railroad employee club. She knew the boardwalks, the rutted streets, the saloons, and if someone passed, she might know him by the shape of his stride, the speed and direction.

Gussie heard a cry—somewhere outside in the streets, a cat or a bird, or somewhere inside the hotel, a baby's cry, her baby. Someone had taken the child away—it had been Mrs. Shayd. Gussie remembered the woman's large hands on Anne's chicken torso. Mrs. Shayd had removed the girl, hid her away—to let Gussie sleep, to let her heal, "You need time alone. I'll take Anne"—hid Anne somewhere down the hall, somewhere in the closets, in the gables, in the shelves of neat linen, the mops and lye and ashcans. Mrs. Shayd had secreted the girl away—Gussie was sure of it. Those guests in the hotel who heard the girl's cry, who wondered at the lonely sound,

Mrs. Shayd must have put off with a distracted wave, saying, "That's nothing, that sound, don't think about it, it's nothing . . . ," sending the guests down the hall, down the stairs, until the baby's cry became part of a memory, the guests often passing through Rawlins as quickly as the trains from east or west, embarking, disembarking, spirited away toward the shores of a thundering sea, speeding on to the sameness of the plain, away from Rawlins, or the guests went north on the trails, by horse or wagon or automobile, past the Rattlesnake Hills, through the gaps and into the broken and open country, where the thought of a baby's cry would serve no one. And why shouldn't Mrs. Shayd secrete the girl away? What was the girl, anyway? A mistake. Couldn't be a beauty. But Gussie couldn't picture the girl, though she'd held her, nursed her through the groggy numbness and pain, through the five long days and nights.

Gussie heard a cry again, and she remembered the touch on her skin of Anne's tiny fingers. Gussie's nightgown was wet with milk. She made her way through the dark room, pulled off the gown, rolled it into the bottom drawer of the bureau. To suppress the pain, she found a scarf in a drawer, Katherine's long soft scarf, and she bound her breasts tight, pinned the scarf taut. The pain subsided enough for her to think clearly. She sat on the edge of the bed, wrapped herself in a blanket, watched the stars, waited for dawn.

Beyond the foot of her small bed, two other beds were empty. Even in the darkness she saw their white metal frames. The girls had slept elsewhere, waiting for her to heal, Katherine and Elizabeth with their gold hair and hazel eyes. They were sisters, tall and supple, the same long stride with the slightest spring to the step, as if their feet couldn't quite bring themselves to fall square on the ground. Through the past months they had lain in their beds, waiting for her to undress and extinguish the light. How runty her limbs must have seemed to them, how sad her belly with its cargo. But the girls hadn't looked at her—they stared at the ceiling, spoke straight up into the space where the bulb hung from its wire, where the storms had leaked through in brown blossoms, petals of loose plaster.

"Those boys in 22 came in from a Bell Springs ranch," Katherine had said. "You saw those sod-roof boys?"

"I saw them," Elizabeth said. "Don't know a thing about Bell Springs except it sounds pretty. Sod-roof cabins aren't so bad if you have a husband in there. That's my guess."

"You been to Bell Springs, Gussie?"

"I'm not in any shape to go sight-seeing, ladies," Gussie had said, bracing on the edge of the bed. Laid out, she had pulled the blanket over her shifting belly.

On one occasion, shortly after Gussie had arrived at this hotel, this job, with Mr. Dunn having turned back so quickly for his return to the Laramie Plain that he'd only had time to give a pained look and say, "This boy . . . this girl . . . care for her . . . ," the innkeeper Mrs. Shayd had come into the darkened room, said to the girls, "Good night, sweethearts—Elizabeth, Katherine, Augusta," and all three girls had answered, "Good night, missus," and the door shut, and Gussie thought that was a marvelous feeling, far from the Laramie Plain, this cozy bed, the tight walls, the lovely girls fading toward dreams, and Mrs. Shayd with her large form, rich voice, serious manner with love just beneath the surface. She thought that Mrs. Shayd had left them, but then something moved her bed in the darkness, someone laid a hand on her neck, cheek, patted her hair—it was Mrs. Shayd. "Did my cousin Dunn do this to you?" Mrs. Shayd said, not a whisper at all, a full-voiced question, so that Gussie thought that the other girls must have sat up to listen, but she heard nothing from them. "Did he get you with child? I wouldn't claim him as family if he did."

"You don't have to break your family on account of anything that happened to me," Gussie said, her voice low to draw Mrs. Shayd's voice lower. There were lies Gussie could have told Mrs. Shayd by way of answer, making Dunn or some other man the villain. She could tell of a man's hands at her waist, at the seams of a beautiful dress. She could describe the calloused pads of a man's palms. Could tell how one man transformed with time and circumstance to another man and another man, each more handsome, persistent. But she'd known only Jack Fisher, and he wasn't dangerous, hardly handsome, and it wasn't a story she would tell. "It wasn't your cousin Dunn," she said. "It was another man."

"Do you want to tell me, Augusta? You can tell me."

"He was someone . . ."

"A good man?"

"Yes."

"And you lost him? You can tell me. You're safe, sweetheart. Tell me. You lost him?"

"Yes. I lost him. I don't know where he is."

Mrs. Shayd had left the room then, her silhouette quick at the swing of the door, the door shut and the hall light extinguished, the room dark before the lights of Rawlins began to bleed across the ceiling. No sound from Katherine and Elizabeth. In their silence, Gussie thought, the girls were guiding their dreams back to the night of Gussie's fall, the girls were imagining a pursuit, the pressure of a storm, the constant irritation of the wind, their lovely whiteness marred by fear and heat. But it was not them in peril. The girls lifted themselves back from the shameful bed and watched. They saw Gussie beneath the weight and labors of a man they could not know or recognize, and as Gussie's small hands were lost to sight in the linens and shadows, as her ankles and toes withdrew, as her square brow slipped behind the man's shoulder, the girls saw the man's skin as nearly as they could imagine—the pores that stretched and pooled, the fine hairs that might darken with age, the maps of freckle, lines of scar. Beyond the skin, beneath the surface, what could they dream? These girls could not dream the weight of a man upon them, the way their breathing would struggle inside the crush of their ribs, the staccato of their nerves as pleasure roamed, and finally the release of the man's weight, the chill of skin suddenly exposed. And these girls could not imagine the quick forgetting, the way the man fragmented until they remembered only the warmth of his earlobes in the pinch of their fingers, the point of his nose pressed at their closed lids, the pox-scar crater tiny on his brow. These girls could not guess at how that brief moment with Jack had taken hold in Gussie, how her stomach had cramped, the first flutter of movement, and then the weight of it and the ache of her back, and that night in this room in the Brunswick Hotel when all the lights were turned high, when the night was blocked by heavy curtains, when Dr. Bradley stood over her with his hand on her belly, pressing at the child hidden there, until Gussie lost the room and the doctor and Mrs. Shayd and herself, ranged in fever, dreaming of the child that had left her body.

◆ ◆ ◆

The room was gray with dawn. Gussie rose from the bed, stood at the closed door and listened. She heard a cry from somewhere down the hall. The sound was too high and pure for a raven, though it made her think of young ravens out of sight in the trees. She tried the sound herself, fit it to her lungs and throat, forced the air, startled at the sound of her own voice, a reed, delicate, remote. She couldn't remember ever making such a sound. She heard the cry again, and she was sure of it now—it was Anne's cry. Mrs. Shayd would bring the child to nurse. Soon. Gussie backed away from the door, wrapped herself tighter in the blanket, watched the knob, the strip of hall light at the bottom of the door.

Gussie thought of her mother fat with child, Gussie weighing Leota's narrow frame, wondered how Leota's slim hips and flat belly had expanded to accommodate a girl as square as Gussie. But maybe Gussie had been a frail little creature. Leota held her child, her Gussie, rocked her, carried her down the stoop and through the tall grass, to the gate and the edge of the forest. At dawn, the first light sharpened the pines, the million-fingered branches. Maybe Gussie had fed at Leota's breast—she must have—that delicate white breast. Maybe Leota had cupped the back of Gussie's head with her small hand, held Gussie's lips to the tender nipple, told Gussie to drink, to dream, to hear the day rise.

And now Leota, on her porch at dawn, two hundred miles to the south, watched the end of night, the mist across the snowy fields, the road. From which direction would Gussie return? Gussie was long gone. Lost. And maybe Leota's pain was lost too, if there had been much pain at the disappearance of a girl who'd started leaving as soon as she could first walk.

"You mustn't just wander off," Leota had always said, as if Gussie's treks had been accidental. But Gussie had always had something in mind. "I needed to see if the snow has left the pond," Gussie would say, or "I heard the next town has a chimney a mile high, and I wanted to climb it, but it wasn't there," or "Denver has trains on its streets, and the bell clangs to send you out of the way." And Leota's gaze would dart away, a quick squint, and she'd return to whatever task Gussie had interrupted and say, "Don't do it again, Augusta. I worry."

Yes, Leota worried. But worry isn't serious, doesn't entail wailing, tearing of the hair, a deathly pallor, the blood gone cold. Leota would set her needles to clacking, the yarn to knitting, and another row of something delicate would emerge. Steady progress, year after year. Leota's hands were always calm, skilled, pulling at the stems of the lupine and snipping with the shears, smoothing the linens on the large bed, tipping black tea leaves into a jade-green pot, dusting sugar across an apricot galette.

Gussie looked at her own hands. They were dry from the Wyoming air, the skin cracked around the nails. Her old roadwork calluses had mostly peeled away. This hotel was a soft place, with its carpet runners down the halls, the settees in the parlor, the plash of warm water from the boiler. Not the place Gussie had imagined as she'd rushed away from the Laramie Plain, although she wasn't sure what she *had* imagined. She had spent her days here doing whatever a pregnant girl could do, following the uniformed girls with a feather duster, wiping spots from the crystal, sorting mail behind the desk. Mostly she had stayed out of sight, a closed door between her and the guests. "You're not uniformed," Mrs. Shayd had said. "I'll have your uniform ready when you're ready. Till then, you do what you can do, keep out of the flow of the guests." And now her new uniform hung on the back of the door.

She looked closer at her hands, at the fine lines of her prints, the ridges taking delicate turns, ending in a block of scar or scrape. Leota had never injured her own hands, not that Gussie could remember. Leota had opened a jar, spread citrus beeswax ointment on her fingers, her palms, slowly smoothing the gloss into her skin. Leota had pulled on white canvas gloves. Leota had held a towel to grip the black handle of the cast-iron pan. Leota had reached for her daughter, Gussie, a small girl in the sweet grass and sun, and Leota had touched a strand of hair errant on the girl's brow, moved it aside, almost absently, but it made the girl's thoughts flutter, *how beautiful, gentle,* and Gussie's hands couldn't touch anything like that.

At the washstand, she plunged her hands into the white bowl, beneath the cold water, watched her fingers turn whiter, never as white as the bowl. She soaked her hair and buffed it dry, shaped the curls. From the hook on the door, she took her uniform, new and pressed and waiting for her, waiting for her small figure, small enough but never boy-hipped again. Now she would finally match the other girls, Katherine and Elizabeth, the lovely sisters. She buttoned the white blouse, felt the starch in the cotton, the slick buttons. And the skirt, its tight waist, the bib and suspenders. She tipped the washstand mirror, checked her profile, wouldn't have known herself passing on the street, not with the serious stiff fabric of the uniform, not unless she looked close.

She leaned in at the glass. Her skin was ashen, her eyes set in dark hollows. She wasn't different, no new luster—she was only weaker. She tried to remember Leota when she'd first seen her, a memory from deep childhood, to imagine if Leota's face had been anything more than eyes and mouth and shape of the jaw, anything more than a basic familiarity. She saw Leota hover above her, soft as a moon on a misty night. Gussie opened the drawers of the wash-stand, found the scraps of Elizabeth's cosmetics, the leftovers with a drift of color. Slowly she disguised the contours of her face, touched red to her lips. Now there was a pale flatness to her face, as if she'd lost her features, but the lips were thin and rich.

◆ ◆ ◆

Gussie made the bed, tucked the corners tight, and sat on the edge of the mattress, carefully crossed her ankles and smoothed her skirt. She faced the door. She held her arms various ways, as if cradling a weight. She tried to make a pigeon sound, a calming flutter, but her throat was rough. So she sat, frozen, silent, hands gripping her knees.

Minutes passed. Daylight sharpened the corners of the room. And finally she heard the creaking of floor joists, footsteps approaching, and she laid her hands in her lap, exhaled. With the swing of the door, in from the hall came Mrs. Shayd, the sudden soft bulk of her, the starched uniform, as crisp as fabric could be in its drape of her ripe figure.

"You've roused yourself. Good. Five days is enough. There was talk we might lose you. I told the girls that today was the day you'd rise from the dead. They didn't believe me. 'She's too sick,' they said. But a mother won't let go when a child is waiting. Isn't that right?" Mrs. Shayd swept past, tipped the window open an inch, smoothed the bed linens behind Gussie, came back around, landed her rump on the mattress, arm around Gussie's shoulders. "And you've made yourself ready. I knew this uniform would fit you. It's a little tight, but that will change. No more toss-offs. No more smocks." She shook Gussie, leaned into her with her full weight, her breath warm against Gussie's ear. "You're dressed. Are you ready?"

"I don't know, ma'am. Was I ever ready?"

"Ready enough, I guess, for things beyond your control." Softly, she said, "Light work for you until you're strong. Don't want you bedridden again, not with your girl waiting. She's a mild thing, you know, your Anne, no trouble at all. I love the girl. You love her too, I'm certain. Don't you? Don't you love her? Come."

Mrs. Shayd was up and to the door, looking back, her face a charming oval framed in flyaway gray. *Love the girl.* Gussie didn't know. Couldn't be sure. She should feel something more than ruined inside, should feel more than the painful pressure of her breasts. She should feel something like Mrs. Shayd felt, there at the door, smiling in anticipation of leading Gussie to the girl, Gussie's daughter, a stranger, tiny, barely born. "Come, Gussie," Mrs. Shayd said. "Come along. You can't wait."

Gussie moved slow in Mrs. Shayd's wake. Into the hall. Past the closed doors and the cave of the back stairs. Into a small gabled room, all window and sky. And the crib. Mrs. Shayd reached in, cradled the child, turned, backlit, large against the window and that pure blue dawn. Gussie wasn't ready, wanted to sleep again, to dream, to take herself far away. She wouldn't look at Mrs. Shayd, looked only at the sky, tried to draw from the empty blue a horizon or a cloud. Nothing. She was here in the room. Her legs shuddered with her heartbeat, and she backed against a chair, sat down.

Mrs. Shayd approached, holding the bundle with care and strength, looking down at what she held. Must be precious, Gussie thought. Gussie saw how the woman's arms folded at the elbows, saw the span of the forearms, the white blanket, white skin. Gussie's arms were icy. But she sat forward—this was her girl—and she shaped a nook with her thin arms, and she smiled.

"Good," Mrs. Shayd said. "Good for you. Here she is. Your Anne."

And the bulk of the woman stooped, and the child was wide-eyed and squirming, hands caught in the blanket. Gussie took the weight of the girl—no weight at all, as light as the memory of the girl at her breast. She felt the tight mask of her own smile, and she tried to blink, but her eyes were dry. She wished for tears, thought

tears would be beautiful, thought the pools in her eyes would glis-
ten, distract the child, amuse her, fall on the child's face, glitter with
the clean light from the window. But no tears. No words. Nothing
but the girl's small face. A face without a single shadow. Lashes like
wisps of spun glass. Hair like a fuzz of silk. And the features—
Gussie tipped the girl, brought her own eyes in line with the girl's
blue, a blue as free of obstruction as the Wyoming sky, the pupils
locked on Gussie's eyes and working at focus, pupils as small and
unfathomed as the first far hint of dark that swallowed Wyoming
from the east, the dark that left Gussie alone, nightly. This girl.
Translucent skin. Nothing of Gussie. Nothing of Jack Fisher. She
looked closer, searched for Jack, searched for herself in this creature, leaned until her nose nearly grazed the flat early form of the
girl's nose, sure to grow from sprite to beauty, soon enough.

"Anne," Gussie said. The girl opened her mouth—the wet pink
gums. "Little girl." And the girl stiffened, arched her back, shut
tight those blue eyes, screamed.

Gussie leapt to her feet, held Anne away, held the sound out toward Mrs. Shayd, and the woman took Anne and cradled her, saying, "There-there, peanut, there-there, sweet pea, you're an angel,
you're a dove, you're my girl . . ." And Anne was quiet again. And
Gussie came close and looked at the girl, saw how the girl's eyes
watched Mrs. Shayd's lips, and Gussie too watched the lips, the
shapes of the soft words, the red of the puckered skin. On and on
Mrs. Shayd talked, her lips a soft dance, and Gussie moved her own
lips in imitation, shaped the words, soundless, wanting to learn
how to love the girl.

Red Desert

The final spring storm came down into the streets of Rawlins. The air went gray and blue, a dense swirling of shadow. Gussie sat on the cot beside the crib, in the small gabled room she shared now with Anne. The heavy crib, painted glossy white, was Mrs. Shayd's gift. "Your girl needs nice things, Augusta, if she's going to learn to appreciate the world." Pale yellow flowers on the white. Green stems and quick leaves. The linens a faint robin's egg. And down in the nest of color, Anne slept. Light on the girl's face, the fluid light of drifting snow.

Inside the weight of the storm, sound was buried. Gussie heard nothing but the slide of snow from the hotel roof. At the rail of the crib, Gussie leaned in to hear Anne's breath, touched Anne's brow, felt the small heat, touched Anne's neck, felt the soft tendons and pulse. She leaned closer, smelled the exhalation of milk, her own milk, a rich scent. She tasted that smell, tasted the product of her own veins, her blood and marrow, strange that she could nourish the girl, wanted always to nourish the girl.

"I'm sorry," Gussie said, her voice no more than the breath of the storm. "I'm all you have."

She straightened the blanket, wouldn't disturb the girl further, though she wanted to peel back the layers, lay her hand flat on that hand-size rib cage. The daylight was gone. In the streetlights, luminous currents sheared against the buildings, seeped in around the windows.

Then Mrs. Shayd was there, a hand on Gussie's shoulder. "You need to let her sleep," Mrs. Shayd said.

Gussie shrugged from beneath Mrs. Shayd's hand, reached again into the crib, almost touched the satin hem of the blanket, made a move as if smoothing the girl's hair. That static blond silk rose toward Gussie's fingers, settled again. "I'm not bothering her. She likes to know I'm here."

"She needs to learn that you won't jump at the first whimper."

"She's barely two months old. Why would she need to learn that?"

"You'll spoil her. I know these things." She took Gussie's arm, pulled her away, too strong for Gussie to stay there in the tight little room.

Out into the hall, in through the next door, into Mrs. Shayd's bedroom. The smell of sleep trapped in the paper roses, gauzy curtains. Mrs. Shayd knelt at the row of moth-stained cartons beyond the bed. "The departed Mr. Shayd's effects," she said, "and whatever I haven't use for." From a carton she pulled out socks; an olive bandana ironed into a small square; a pristine black ledger, embossed with gold—*Jean-Louis Shayd*; and she laid it all on the bed. Then she found something deep in the carton, drew out a small wooden box, a tuft of cotton pinched by the lid. She came back around the bed, sat on the edge, motioned to Gussie. "Sit with me, child."

Gussie sat, and the mattress sagged, forced her shoulder-to-shoulder against the woman. "What do you have, Mrs. Shayd?"

"This is for you, to help you. It didn't always help me, it hurt me finally, but it will do you fine, keep you safe." She dug her nail under the lid, pried it open. In the whorl of cotton, a gold wedding band. She held the ring toward Gussie.

Gussie accepted it. Tested its cool metal weight on her fingertip.

"It was mine," Mrs. Shayd said. "It was from my husband. Look here." She held out her left hand against the bedside light. Her ring finger was indented in a smooth band of skin, low against the palm. "I haven't worn the ring for ten years, but the mark's still there." She rubbed at the finger. Then she took Gussie's left hand, worked the wedding band onto the ring finger. It hung loose. "We'll wrap some thread on the underside to make it fit."

"Why should I have this? It's yours, Mrs. Shayd." She slid the ring up to her knuckle, settled it again.

"You have no husband. Am I right, Augusta?"

"Yes."

"Never had a husband?"

"Never."

"There are things you don't know. There will be men passing through Rawlins. They pass through daily on their way to somewhere else, or on their way home, north or south. They'll see you working here, see your child. They'll want you to work for them, to marry them, to help them stake another claim. They can't fill all the acres themselves, not without help. You can cook and . . ."

"I can't cook."

"Anyone can cook. And you can give a man children."

"I can't. Doctor said . . ."

"They won't know that. They'll just see you and know you can do their work for them. That's all. Way out in the desert, in Shirley or Difficulty or the Ferris Mountains. You'll end up alone with your precious girl and a man who seemed good enough at the time."

"That sounds okay. I don't need much."

"Maybe, but Anne needs a real home. So you wear that ring. You say, 'I lost my husband. I'm waiting for him to return.' And I'll care for you and Anne."

"Maybe I *could* find someone good enough, ma'am, if I looked."

"No easy task for a girl like you." Mrs. Shayd reached for the bedside table, picked up a framed photograph, passed it to Gussie.

"This is my son, Robert. Dear boy. He's more like me than like his departed father."

Gussie tipped the photograph toward the light. Robert was an empty shape, the sun behind him, the rolling cut of Wyoming hills, a bare horizon. This young man could be any young man, his face in shadow. Gussie looked to see Jack Fisher in the boy. Perhaps the curve of the neck—a slender form, waiting to mature into a broad column of muscle and bone. She looked at the hips, only a shadow, and she almost felt the keen-edged ridges of Jack's pelvis, the weight of his body. Jack could be stronger now, taller, a man.

"Robert has gone to the war. He'd defy the angels to come home to me, if I needed him. Do you have a photograph of the man you lost, Augusta, the father of your child?"

"No, ma'am." She tried to sharpen her memory, to form an exact image, but Jack faded into the silhouette in the photograph.

"Robert is a handsome boy," Mrs. Shayd said. She took the photograph, replaced it on the bedside table.

"Anne's father was handsome. He was good enough."

"That's a sweet thought, Augusta. Hold on to that thought." She circled Gussie's shoulders in her sturdy arms, gave her a shake. "You may look at this photograph any time you'd like, dear. It will help set your goals for the future."

Through the thin wall, the sound of Anne rousing. Mrs. Shayd released Gussie, and both women were out into the hall, the stark shadows of the bare bulbs, but Mrs. Shayd had the advantage, laid her hand on the knob, blocked the way, urged Gussie on down the hall with a few blunt fingers on Gussie's back. "I'll look in on her. You have your chores. If she needs you, I'll find you." Mrs. Shayd was in through the door, and the door latched.

Mrs. Shayd would still be sitting there in Gussie's room in an hour or two, whenever Gussie returned. Or if Anne truly needed Gussie, Mrs. Shayd would carry the girl through the hotel, find the mother, the teat, and say, "She's ready for you, Augusta. There's nothing I can do about this girl's appetite."

Gussie descended the stairs, felt with each step the slack, weedy bands of her muscles. She was not yet fully herself again, and she thought now that she might never grow to the tough, able woman she had always expected to be.

At the parlor window, she rubbed a handprint from the glass. Out in the storm, the passersby hurried uphill or down, looking for shelter, bundled beyond recognition. The snow kept falling, leveling the ruts, softening the roofs. Gussie looked to see Jack in any young man who passed through Rawlins, that night and the months that followed. There were hundreds of young men these days. She looked to see any part of Jack in the faces, limbs, strides. But Jack Fisher was gone. Lost to her. Lost to Anne.

◆ ◆ ◆

From the crest of Monument Hill, Gussie looked away from Rawlins, looked west toward the Continental Divide. She had never made it to that dotted line on the map, though she'd been in Rawlins for almost a year, never hiked to the final hilltop to gaze into the Great Divide Basin. The basin was surrounded by a circular split in the divide, cut off from the West's cold rivers. There was no easy escape from that basin—water leached into the soil, evaporated into the ceaseless wind. The near corner of the basin held the Red Desert—she'd seen the words on the map, heard men talk of it. The Red Desert, the haunt of wild horses, herds of sheep on the sere grass, the herders' wagons, blood rivers, Honeycomb Buttes, pools of amber.

If she walked west, four miles to the divide, she could look into the Red Desert and judge the place for herself. And she could carry Anne that far, no problem. Down from the rim of the desert, on across the wild, she would look for pools of water before they evaporated, pools in the shade of wasted trees, the ground paved with broken stones. She would find the tracks of the sheep wagons, find the sinks where grass drew life from beneath the red surface. And in those brief acres of green, she would sit on the ground, feel the day's heat rise through her bones and scatter. And in Anne's face she would see the color of the falling sun, the gold, the violet, the coming night. Then the stars and the spectered darkness, Anne's breath against the endless desert.

Gussie turned back, shaded her eyes in the afternoon sun, crossed the hilltop, the fossil shells and prickly-pear blooms, toward Mrs. Shayd on the picnic blanket. And there was Anne, belly down, arms and legs slowly swimming. Mrs. Shayd stroked the girl's back, moved her lips as if singing. The wind carried the sound away, but Gussie knew the song, a melancholy lullaby full of shadow and distance. Anne laid her head on the blanket. Mrs. Shayd placed her hand on Anne's head, cupped the curve of the skull with her heavy fingers, looked up and saw Gussie approaching. And then Mrs. Shayd lifted Anne, rolled her up into her arms, bundled her, kissed her forehead.

"That's a good girl," Mrs. Shayd said, nodding toward Gussie. "Come join us. Be social." And as Gussie sat on the blanket, Mrs. Shayd tipped Anne up a bit so Gussie could see her face, then held her down again, rocked her. "I'm a little dizzy from the richness of it all," Mrs. Shayd said.

A summer feast. More money in this luncheon than Gussie's weekly pay—Mrs. Shayd had shown her the bill. Gussie still felt the oily residue of the oysters on her lips, the sugar on her fingertips, orange from the candied peels, yellow from the lemon cake. Asparagus. Olives. Slices of white cheese. She felt the precarious weight of those delicacies in her stomach. Maybe the food would taint her milk, turn it spicy or too sweet. "Do you think Anne will like my milk? All this fancy food might've spoiled it."

"Don't you worry about that, Augusta. Enjoy yourself. It's a beautiful day. I've given this to you as a special treat. Accept it."

"I accept it, ma'am, of course. Thank you. It's just that this food's mostly all new to me."

"That's what makes it special." She rose to her feet, rocked the child, looked out over Rawlins.

Gussie too looked out over the town. Rawlins was low down beneath the sky. The grid of the wide dirt streets ran straight in all directions, petering out into the color of the plain. Wood houses with dark roofs, sheds and ruined barns, pale paths in weedy lots, scattered trees. And at the center of all the blocks rose the churches like brick mesas, the abrupt steeples, and the commerce blocks, the long facades, the Brunswick Hotel, smoke and steam from a locomotive paused at the rail station. The dark rail line stretched east and west, lost finally in the clutter of erosion and rising heat, the curve of the globe. But even as the world all around faded beyond sight, Gussie thought of the room in the eaves of the hotel, the strength of the rafters against the weight of a storm, the late-night sound of Mrs. Shayd rustling in her covers, pouring a glass of water, pacing, just beyond the wall, Mrs. Shayd always thinking of Anne, offering a gift, making a plan.

"There'll be guests from the train." Mrs. Shayd started away, left Gussie to pack up the picnic. "We have things to do."

By the time Gussie had gathered the leavings and folded the blanket, Mrs. Shayd had already carried Anne halfway down Monument Hill. Gussie hurried along the trail, down toward the walls, the sounds of the automobiles, the scents of horses, wood fires, potentilla. The trail angled along the state penitentiary, where behind the iron barriers the men worked at the gardens, moved in the shade of the young trees, watched in silence the passage of the woman with the child, the passage of the girl following, burdened.

Then onto the streets, toward the school, where girls in white circled in a celebration, and a crowd attended, and a white awning fluttered above the school steps. Mrs. Shayd stopped at the school gate, and Gussie caught up and stood with her. "These girls are lovely, aren't they, Augusta?"

"Yes, ma'am."

"Too young to know they're lovely."

But they weren't young. Some of them were Gussie's age. Arm in arm, in pairs, they circled, celebrating something, maybe celebrating their graduation or their beauty or the purity of their white dresses in spite of the dust in the wind. The younger girls smiled, blushed.

"On we go," Mrs. Shayd said, and Gussie fell into step. "I guess you must have gone to school yourself, Augusta."

"Of course." She paced Mrs. Shayd, tried to move her legs in the same stride as the girls, couldn't, tried to move with the same steady stride as Mrs. Shayd, impossible. Maybe it was the weight of the picnic goods. Maybe it was her shoes, made for work. The shoes had been Mrs. Shayd's choice. "I've learned enough to make my way," Gussie said, "wherever I choose to go."

"But there aren't many places for a girl in your situation, Augusta. Not many who would give you a home."

"My parents would give me a home."

"Well, yes, but then you'd be there now, wouldn't you?"

"I could go there."

"If you could go home, sweetheart, you'd be there now."

Surely, Gussie could go home. Leota would come out from the house, watch Gussie's approach. Leota's smile, her hands reaching. *Let me see what you have here, sweetheart. Ah, such a surprise, such a wonder. I've dreamed of a child like this. It's as if she were my own child.*

They came down to the tracks, turned east toward the station. A train passed, a huge commotion, moved on west. "The mail will be in," Mrs. Shayd said. "I'm looking for a letter from my boy. Always looking. Do you correspond, Augusta?"

"I don't write letters," Gussie said, "and I don't get letters."

"Well, no, of course you don't. How could you? To whom would you write? What news could you possibly report?" From the pocket of her skirt, Mrs. Shayd pulled a small square of folded paper. "I've read this letter over and over," she said, struggling to open the paper, balancing Anne. The paper fluttered in the wind. "Listen to this, Augusta," she said. "It's from my boy. *Dear Mother. I meant this to reach you by Easter, but perhaps I have waited too long. I am sorry. You will forgive me as long as my heart was right? I am safe and sound. Nothing has harmed me, unless you count the bedbugs. They are awful, and I shan't ever accept them, but I'll leave them behind soon enough, and anyway they keep me alert."*

The wind took the letter, sent it down the street. Gussie ran, nearly lost the picnic gear, caught the letter from the air. She held it, the creases nearly worn through, looked at the crabbed script, the paper stained by bad weather or time. Walking back, Gussie couldn't find the words Mrs. Shayd had read, the words lost in the ruin of the paper. The only clear words she found: *I love you, dear Mother, I think of you each hour.*

"Thank you, Augusta," Mrs. Shayd said, and Gussie handed over the letter. They continued along the street. Mrs. Shayd tucked the paper back into her pocket, blew a puff of air into Anne's face, kissed the girl on the forehead. "I remember Robert at this age. He was perfect."

Gussie shifted closer, looked at Anne, the girl four months old. Fingernails like flecks of white ash. Her eyes closed, her skull fuzzed with nearly colorless hair, too blond. Gussie had stood at a mirror and examined her own hair, found strands at her temples that were almost a match to Anne's. Hard to fathom that something from her own body could match the girl. "Do you think Anne is perfect?"

"She's like my boy, yes. But you can't know the way I miss Robert. Missing him makes him more beautiful than you can imagine."

"More beautiful than Anne?"

"You've never lost a child."

"You haven't lost your son. He'll be back when the war is ended."

"I can't know he's safe."

"You have his letters."

"Paper is nothing like skin."

◆ ◆ ◆

In the hotel laundry, Gussie pushed towels and aprons down into the steaming water. The coals were hot in the stove, high summer light in the windows. Anne was asleep, curled in a sheet, in a basket, beside the stove, left there for an hour while Mrs. Shayd took a list to the mercantile.

The Brunswick Hotel was full of boys—a final night before the train swept another batch of Wyoming volunteers toward war. There was one last shirt for ironing, for the boy in Room 7. The boy would be gone on the morning train. His shirt was nearly worn to thread. The iron's heat was a soft breath. She worked her way carefully around the pattern, then set the iron aside, folded the shirt, held her palms on the warm cloth. The shirt would cool, to be warmed again by the boy's skin.

She tried to remember the boy in Room 7, to remember if he'd said where he'd lived, how he'd traveled, how his family had bid him farewell. He could be an orphan. He could be a sweetheart. The sole child of a lonesome man. The twin of a missing twin. Which boy was it? She couldn't conjure his eyes, his neck, arms. She thought maybe he was the short boy with the scarred lip. How would that lip feel against her lips? The scar was a tough ashen line—the shape of it drifted around her nerves, unsettled.

Gussie closed her eyes and listened to the sounds of the laundry, the swirling bubbles and steam. She could have been listening to rain. She wanted to tell Anne a story, but the girl was asleep, and it would be years before she understood. In the story, Jack Fisher is sheltered beneath a tarpaulin. The rain pools on the tarp and drains away. He's dry. He has a stub of candle. He's warm enough. He's writing a letter. *The rain is very soft. It makes me forget where I am. I could be near my home. Maybe I'm just camping. No war. Maybe when I'm ready I can find my way back through the woods to my stoop and the door and my mother's voice. Or back to you, Gussie. Back to you, Anne. I'd dearly love to see you, little girl. I think of you both more often than you can guess, and I am yours,—Jack, and "Daddy"* A light enters the trees. It's the moon. The clouds are going thin. The rain is gray and straight. In the moonlight Jack can see the ropes strung tree to tree, the miserable tarpaulins pegged and drooping.

Katherine and Elizabeth came into the laundry, each carrying a brimming hamper. Anne's eyes opened. The girls approached the stove, dropped the hampers, gathered over Anne, and the girls and Gussie watched Anne, and Anne watched them back. They all three reached down and tickled the girl, and Anne grinned, jabbed at their hands, tried to sit up. Gussie pushed the girls away and lifted the child, held her. "You've brought more work for me," Gussie said.

"These boys come into town without any sense," Katherine said. "They're traveling with everything soiled or half wrecked. We can't send them off like that. They think laundry happens by magic."

"I guess I'm a magician," Gussie said. "I like that title better than washerwoman."

"Better than *sporting* woman," Elizabeth said.

"Elizabeth!" Katherine said.

"I don't mean anything except boys think they can follow a girl all day and say nothing and the girl will turn around and love them."

"The boys want to love you?" Gussie wasn't surprised— Elizabeth was a beauty, same as Katherine.

"They don't want her," Katherine laughed, "not as much as she'd like them to. She reads love in every 'howdy.' But in truth, the boys were just now asking about *you*, Gussie."

"Which boys?"

"Does it matter?" Katherine rubbed Gussie's shoulder, patted her back.

"Sure it matters."

Katherine leaned in closer to Gussie, ran a finger across Anne's forehead. "I told them you're married, of course."

"You know I'm not married."

"Come now. What's so bad about being married? It's an honor. You've got that beautiful ring. And Mrs. Shayd told us to say you're married if anyone asked."

Elizabeth nudged Katherine aside, came in and held her hand to the side of Anne's face, brushed at the white skin. "Don't listen to her, Gussie. They weren't asking about you, not directly, but they'd seen Anne. They wanted to know who she was. That's close to asking after you, isn't it? They think she's precious."

"The boys are all sweet and lovely to look at." Katherine reached into a hamper, picked up a pair of drawers, shook them and held them out toward Gussie. "But they're threadbare. And not very clean."

"I don't care about that."

"You'll care soon enough, if it's his body that made this dirt." She shook the drawers again, dropped them into the hamper. "A lady should at least pretend to look for a decent man."

"I'm not a lady."

"You seem like one sometimes," Elizabeth said.

"When you get a chance to hold your child," Katherine said, "you can seem almost like a grown lady."

"A married lady," Elizabeth said.

Katherine and Elizabeth stared at each other hard for a moment, then laughed. Linking arms, they moved on to the door and out of the laundry. Their voices faded into the hotel, turned a corner, out toward evening.

Gussie sat on the stool beside the stove. Anne seemed content with the steaming sounds, the steady bubbling. Gussie turned her so that they sat alike, mother and daughter, facing the brick walls and the bare bulb, the starchy fog, the pinned clothing in limp ranks. She pulled the ring from her finger and dropped it into the water, and it sank. She pulled the chain, and the tub began to empty.

◆ ◆ ◆

"You're not wearing my ring, Augusta," Mrs. Shayd said. "Where have you left it?"

"It was loose," Gussie said. "It made my skin itch." She thought her way quickly through the hotel, back through the recent days. "I left it in your room, on your bed, where you couldn't miss it."

"When?"

"Monday."

"Monday . . . Monday . . . The day I had Mr. Chin air out the blankets."

"Yes. Mr. Chin. That's right."

"And you didn't tell me?"

"I was working. I forgot."

That night, Gussie heard Mrs. Shayd pacing beyond the wall, opening and closing the doors of the chifforobe, clattering the bureau drawers, looking for the ring. The sound of the bed being dragged aside. Something fell, burst. The movement went on.

Mrs. Shayd wouldn't find the ring, but she would find everything that had come to her as a result of the ring. Photographs of her son in his father's arms. Presents from past holidays. And the small scuffed shoes wrapped in brown paper. And the silk scarf from Daniels & Fisher in Denver. The room was stockpiled with her married life.

In Gussie's small room, a hunt would take less than a minute— the floor under the cot and crib, the five drawers in the bureau. Nothing but her uniform, the clothes she'd taken from Jack, the clothes and duffle that Mr. Dunn have given her. And Anne's things, all chosen by Mrs. Shayd. Gussie's baptism dress was gone. Her bloomers were gone. And she had none of what she'd carried from Ravenglass—she'd lost the pebbles, the feathers, the eggshells.

She remembered Brud's wedding ring. It was not nicely cast and smooth like Mrs. Shayd's. Brud's ring was not graceful. When Gussie had weighed it on her palm, she'd thought it was made of something other than metal—nothing could be so cold and heavy, like a lump of something foreign. When she held it close to her eye, out in the dawn toward the red pines, she saw how scarred the ring had become through the years, through the miles north, along the rocky steeps. A whole map of scratches and scrapes like creeks and ponds, tracks and clearings. But as dawn grew, she saw the world in shadow and light on the gold, and slowly the gold was gone and the shapes were colored. Blue sky cut by the wandering birds. Nervous pines waiting for heat and wind. A blaze of daybreak. She understood that everything Brud loved could be seen in the surface of that ring, if he carried it far enough. And then she returned the ring to the top of the bureau, and when Brud awoke he slid it onto his finger and moved out into the rising light.

And Leota's first wedding ring, passed from her grandmother, from Sweden. The ring was narrow, flaring where it held the stones. The two pale green gems might have been ice chipped from a slow pond, holding the notion of snowlight or low skimming sun. That ring on Leota's finger, and the way she twirled it, so that sometimes the stones were open to the light, sometimes closed to her palm. And the occasion when she would remove the ring, hand it to Gussie, and Gussie would feel its small heat, waiting, looking close at the prongs that held the stones, looking at what had caught there between gold and gem—a fragment of hair, a splinter of wood from the fence or forest. Leota was mixing clear liquids in a jar, and then she summoned Gussie, and Gussie turned her palm and let the ring slip into the jar, and there in the fragrant liquid the residue of the world around Ravenglass dissolved.

Mrs. Shayd stood at the door, the light from the hall bulb making a bright ghost of her loose hair, a scrim of her nightgown. "You're sure, Augusta?"

"Sure of what, ma'am?" Gussie squinted against the light, the dark shape of Mrs. Shayd's curves inside the light.

"Sure you left the ring on the bed?"

"Yes. Monday."

"Mr. Chin didn't see it. I'd hate to think it was gone." She came into the room, sat on the edge of the cot. "It's something I don't want to lose."

"But you gave it to me."

"That wasn't losing it."

"But it was mine?"

"It was always close, if I wanted to look at it."

"It was a gift, wasn't it? I could have left with it, if I'd wanted."

"I suppose. I hadn't thought. You might have given it back if you were going to leave."

"I did give it back."

Mrs. Shayd turned her legs tighter against the edge of the cot, looked down at Gussie in the plain light. "Are you going somewhere?"

"No. The ring bothered me."

"Irritated your finger, you said."

"Yes."

"But you thought it was nice to have a ring, to be married?"

"I'm not married. I might want to be, might not want to be."

"You have your eye on someone to marry?"

"No."

"Good. We'll watch out for each other, us two."

"I'm not sure if I know how to watch out for you."

"Don't you worry about that." She took Gussie's hand, massaged her fingers, worked at the place where the ring had rested. "Just let me care for you."

◆ ◆ ◆

Mr. Chin was let go. In the morning, he wasn't in the kitchen, and Mrs. Shayd said, "He's back to his family in Green River City. You blame him? These are trying days."

For a few minutes, Gussie stood at the alley door and watched the sky slowly go gray with dawn. It was chill and quiet. The last train had passed west an hour ago. Already Mr. Chin would be nearing Green River City, looking ahead for the shroud of woodsmoke, the bridge across the river. He would walk to his uncles' livery, past the horses agitated with hunger and pent energy, out into the narrow yard where the house stood. Inside the house, one of his old uncles sat at the table, hunched over a small porcelain cup of tea. The uncle looked up, said, "You're home, boy. That's good. Sit here with me." And Gussie thought Mr. Chin would sit, inhale the smell of the place and want to hold the air in his lungs, listen to the sparks in the stove and want to hear that song continue.

Gussie took over Mr. Chin's duties. Mrs. Shayd stood behind her at the kitchen sink, Gussie's arms red from heat and abrasive. "This is work to support a person through hard times," Mrs. Shayd said. "Do you mind?"

"This isn't much. I know real work." Gussie pried dark yellow egg from the plates.

Mornings, before dawn, Gussie rose, passed through the halls. She boiled water, sliced bread, stacked napkins. The cook bundled in through the back door, hooked her musty loden coat on a chair. She was a plumpish woman, a refugee from the rail, Slavic without much English, eager for her apron, eager to drop balls of dough into scalding oil.

With platters, with scoops, Gussie followed the cook. "Yah," the cook said. "Dats my girl." Then silence in the brightness of the bulbs, the whiteness of walls and counters, the steam in evaporating puffs, silence in the rhythm of flame and crockery, a routine, the cook's brow beaded with reflection. And through those hours at the cusp of dawn, Gussie counted the turns and stairways that separated the kitchen from the attic room. She knew the noises the building made, the way the rousing guests set the kitchen ceiling to groaning. She could hear nothing of Anne—too many floors, too many layers—but she knew that Anne needed to sleep, needed the long silence beneath the window and the dark sky. "The kitchen is no place for a child," Mrs. Shayd had said. "Too many dangers."

Daybreak flashed pink a dozen times over in the windows across the alley. The guests' chatter suddenly filled the parlor. Into the kitchen, Mrs. Shayd carried Anne—Anne in a long white gown, lace at the collar, the billowing cloth tied below her feet. Mrs. Shayd came straight to Gussie's side. "She just woke," Mrs. Shayd said. "I heard her the instant she cried, and I changed her and dressed her. This new gown is a gift from me. You like it?"

Gussie dried her hands on her apron, touched the glossy white fabric, touched Anne's cheek. And when Gussie nursed the child, fresh from Mrs. Shayd's arms, Mrs. Shayd said, "You should wean her. Then you won't be tied to her." Gussie pulled Anne from beneath the nursing blanket, handed her over, turned back to work.

And late into evening, from the kitchen, Gussie listened to the guests who gathered in the parlor, shut off from the night. They were excited. She took a rag and wiped the counters. Light gleamed on the tiles. Drying her hands, she emerged into the bright parlor.

The room was hot with the bodies crowded there. Cradling Anne, Mrs. Shayd stood at the center, beneath the chandelier, with the snarl of electric light above the unruly cloud of her hair. The flash of the crystals, the blue of the girl's eyes, the men crowded around, smiling at the girl's laugh. "She's my angel," Mrs. Shayd said, and she turned, opened the view of Anne's face. The young and old men, the graybeards, the smooth chins, all closed ranks, following the woman's turn. She held the child up to her cheek, that freckled ashen skin against the girl's pink, those long fingers cupped around the skull. The child let out a sound—no more than a sigh, so faint that Gussie barely felt it in her nerves—and the woman lowered her again, and the men closed again, their voices a steady murmur. *Apple flesh . . . Columbine . . . Evening star . . . Watercress . . .*

"My sweet girl," Mrs. Shayd said, and she kissed the girl, and those who were close enough leaned in to kiss the air near the girl, near to Mrs. Shayd's lips.

A small sound from Anne, and Gussie felt the girl's voice spark her limbs, weigh her breasts, and she stepped forward. The men and boys were a wall, the shoulders locked, but she pushed in, fingers on a boy's belt, elbow into a man's back, and they barely turned. She smelled the hotel soap on them, saw the barber-scraped shadow of their beards, the delicate ears with their curving channels, she whispered *Make room for me . . .* but they didn't hear, and then she reached Mrs. Shayd, looked up at the woman's face, the eyes narrowed, the lips still pulled into the shape of a kiss, and there in the woman's arms was Anne, the buzz of the electric light refracted just above the girl's skin. "Augusta," Mrs. Shayd said. "I brought her down. They wanted to see her. Isn't that right, boys?" They nodded in reply.

Gussie held out her arms, took Anne, looked down into the face. Gussie was a shadow in the girl's eyes, dark against the bright ceiling. Gussie turned away from Mrs. Shayd and the woman lingered close to her back, Mrs. Shayd's breath on Gussie's nape, her hands hovering beside Gussie's elbows, ready to catch her movement, correct it, and she whispered, "I'm here, Augusta, if you have work to do."

"No, ma'am, I'm free for a few minutes." Gussie stepped into the crowd, gained distance.

Here were the men and boys. Their heat and the smell of their nerves filled the air around her. Here was Gussie, venturing into the crowd, testing Anne's charm. She looked up from her daughter. These faces, the faint sweat that gave a shine to their ruddy skin, even the youngest of them had been challenged by the Wyoming air, the wind without break, the cold without pity. She moved among them, saw how they shaped themselves to her path, how they backed against a pillar, leaned around the corner of a table, as if this were the entertainment and they each wanted full value, circling closer where the room allowed. She held Anne up, lowered her face to the girl's, so that their skin was close. The men and boys were against her now—she allowed them—and their fingers touched Anne's hair, her brow, her ears, near to her small creased lips, and the fingers were thick, dry, the nails split or black, but such timid movements. And the men touched Gussie, too, a graze, a mistake, a finger drawn along her cheek, taking the narrow space between mother and daughter.

◆ ◆ ◆

From the attic windows of the Brunswick Hotel, the whole of Rawlins was laid out, the rooftops jutting into the sky or dark against the hills. As daylight arced from east to west, the layers of rooftops shifted, a constant deepening or flattening of perspective. At noon, the town seemed fragmented and widespread, but at dusk the buildings merged into a band of constant gray without depth, untold windows alight against the budding stars.

One evening view in particular, from the north attic window, stopped Gussie a moment as she passed. Uphill, the ranks of windows stairstepped, the prison rose with its banks of slim openings, and farther to the west a single window curved its bright light high above the other lights. There was something inviting about that window, the way it hung there at the limit of electricity, on the brink of the wilds, and she thought sometimes that it was a window not of the town but of the night, where the dwellers of the Red Desert could blow in on the wind and take a gander at the construction of this place, listen to its sounds. Why would a man need a window so high? She dragged her fingertip across the windowpane, left a faint greasy mark to help her locate that high window in the daylight, although for a week or more she was reluctant to look when the sun was up, preferring to watch that window float in darkness, ungrounded.

But finally in daylight she found herself at the north attic window, a stack of sheets in her hands, and she positioned herself and looked through her own smeared fingerprint and found the window, found the building, a tall Queen Anne Victorian, with a round turret at the front corner, a metal spike at the tip of the cone of tiled roof. Behind the turret, the rest of the house was large and sweeping, rust-red brick with wood trim and filigree in bright colors. And she could make out the black iron fence that surrounded the property. And the trees still young. And bursts of flowers beside the walk. On another day she watched a lightning storm move in from across the divide, and the town darkened, and the hills were lost, and a blue bolt struck the spike at the top of the turret, and sparks rained with the rain. When the sky cleared, the house looked untouched, at least from that distance, except for a slight darkening from the water.

On a warm August evening, Gussie wandered toward that house, that window. Anne perched on her hip, watched the way ahead, held to Gussie's collar in a vise grip, looked back when she could in the direction of the hotel. They came up from a row of whitewashed shotgun cabins, and then the wide street opened left and right, and she turned left and saw the house. The high window was dark. She came up to the fence. From the light post beside the walkway, a small sign hung, FOSTER in gold on black. She knew the name—banker, miner, speculator, heir to a man who had extracted his fortune from the acres of this dry country. "Foster," Gussie said. "Mr. Foster." And Anne made a sound, reached for the glow of the lamp and the gilt name. "Yes, dear," Gussie said. "Edward Foster. I've heard that he's a single man. And a rich man. I've known a rich man, sweetheart. Sometimes they'll give you things."

She remembered the feel of Frank Locke's banknotes against her skin, the weight of the paper, and the clothes she was supposed to have purchased. She had almost become used to the starched lines of the hotel uniform, but she might never have grown accustomed to the costumes Frank Locke desired for her. He had wanted her to shroud her lines. She looked at her shadow on the street. No legs—just the blocky outline of the skirt beneath the waist—no way to move without floating, it seemed, no way to climb or flee or do real work. She remembered the miles that Frank Locke's banknotes had taken her. She thought of the desert miles beyond Edward Foster's high window.

Turning from the iron fence and its spikes, she started back toward the center of town. She felt the weight of her uniform against the movement of her legs.

On another night, she saw Mr. Foster at the high window. He was a young man, perhaps thirty, a restless man. She took care to note his graceful style, the sleek cut of his hair, his slender height. Then she watched for him in town. She saw him enter the automobile garage, and she came forward to the open doors. In the dim recesses, he stood beside a stout black automobile, talked to an attendant, climbed into the automobile, sat for a while, hands on the steering wheel, climbed out. "Store it for me," he said to the attendant. "Keep it tuned. If I ever want to escape from town, I don't want any delay." Gussie appreciated the sentiment. He came toward the doors. She stepped aside. He squinted out toward the afternoon, brushed past her, whispered "Pardon" as he continued. The dust he stirred seemed nothing in the wake of his steady gait, his haste.

She saw him other days, nights. He entered the bank, and she was beside the door an hour later when he emerged. He stepped around her. "Excuse me, please," he said. She waited in the shade along Sugar Creek, Anne in her arms, the sun and heat filtered to leafy green, and he passed in the company of other men, and she stepped out into the heat, followed. Anne made a sound. Mr. Foster glanced back, focused on Gussie a long moment, his eyes pale and fine and pleasant, then returned to his conversation. She heard him say, "I believe I'm being shadowed . . ."

And on still another night, she saw him on his porch, pacing at the rail, as a group of others sat and talked, laughed, drank. He paused, looked out over the town, beyond the town, glanced down just long enough to catch Gussie and Anne there at the gate, and he cocked his head to the side, shrugged, gave a little wave, and went back to pacing. Long strides. If he had a mind to, it seemed, he could stride right through the railing and keep going.

Gussie made her way down from Walnut Street, with Anne looking back over her shoulder toward the remarkable house, sounds at her small lips, supple sounds like laughter in the balmy evening. Gussie turned down Third, saw Katherine and Elizabeth ahead, almost didn't recognize them outside the hotel—she thought at first that they were ladies drifting, ghosts, something else, so smooth was their gait. "Girls," Gussie shouted. "Wait for me." And Anne turned and looked ahead, reached a hand toward the girls.

Katherine and Elizabeth glanced back, slowed their strides. "Where have you been walking?" Elizabeth asked.

"Just taking air." Gussie shook her head back toward the hills. "There are some lovely mansions on Walnut Street."

"Oh, yes," Elizabeth said. "I bet you've never been in a home like some of those places. That would be a nice life, to move up the hill. I'd like to give it a try."

"You don't know any of those people, Elizabeth," Katherine said.

"*I* know one of them," Gussie said. "Edward Foster."

The girls laughed. "You don't know Edward Foster," they said.

"I know him to look at. I'll know him better soon enough."

"Well," Katherine said, "if you're going to try the impossible, you might as well try the most impossible."

Gussie smiled. "Tonight's a perfect night. Do you two have your sights set on anyone particular?"

"Sure we do," Elizabeth said, "but his name keeps changing. I hope he doesn't leave town before I meet him."

"You get on home, Gussie," Katherine said. "This is not your milieu."

"*Milieu?*" Elizabeth said.

"French. It means 'place where you're comfortable.' "

At the corner of Cedar Street, Gussie stopped. The sisters straightened themselves and walked away down the street. The girls' skirts, long and pale blue. The girls' arms, linked at the elbow. The girls' hair, arranged in riffles, ribbons. They moved in step, the shadows and light from the establishments meeting their advance. They passed beneath the strung cables, the drooping banners still hanging from Independence Day, tattered red-white-blue, no one brave enough yet to tear down the patriotism, and now the girls were the only parade. And then they paused where the light glowed most faintly, and they waited, facing dead ahead, as if they expected the world itself to carry them on of its own accord. The music leaked from the saloons to each side and met the girls at the center of the street.

They looked left and right, from saloon to saloon, and the men drifted out to greet them. The men wouldn't get too close to the girls, not at first. Katherine and Elizabeth unlinked their arms, turned slowly from side to side. They reached subtly toward the men as they greeted them, then linked again, waited. The men came closer, jostling each other, almost dancing a step, circling in behind the girls, and the girls started to move again, keeping just ahead, and the men followed, a ramble.

Gussie didn't move until Katherine and Elizabeth were out of sight, and then she proceeded along Cedar, down the center, in their wake. Summer air blew easy and parched. "Soon enough you'll walk with me," Gussie said against Anne's ear, and Anne leaned away, looked up. They passed beneath the frayed banners, the hiss and flutter against the stars. They passed the bank, the automobile garage, telephone office, stopped in the oblong of light in front of the Red Ore Saloon. The place was full of noise, full of men. In the low angle of the light, the dust of the street was cratered with footprints, and Gussie thought she saw the girls' small, keen prints moving on. She waited there, listened to the music glide from the open door, the laughter. No one emerged.

Gussie turned, continued along the sidewalk. The storefronts were mostly dark. Then, ahead, coming down from a side street, Mr. Foster emerged. He turned in her direction, came along fast. His black suit was dull. He was tall, lean, with the uncomplicated grin of a man who'd taken his father's success and strengthened it. She stepped out into the street. "Mr. Foster," she said, directly in his line. He stopped. "You've left your guests behind."

"Pardon me." He tried to step past her, but she took his arm, hindered him.

"You don't care for their company?"

He levered his arm free. "Why are you stopping me?" He tried to pass.

Again she blocked him. She held Anne up for view. "You've seen my child?"

"Excuse me, miss." He seemed unable to back away, unable to fathom how such a small person could block such a wide street. He looked over her head toward the saloons, the voices and music, then his shoulders slackened a bit, he looked squarely down at her. "You were just passing my house, not twenty minutes ago. I know Rawlins is a small town, but I see you often. Too often. What do you want?"

"I'm Mrs. Locke."

"And?"

"This is Anne."

"No, I mean . . ." But he stopped, leaned closer to view the girl.

"She's mine," Gussie said. She smelled the dark spice of Mr. Foster's pomade, saw the furrows in his slick black hair.

"Goodness. Where'd you find her?" He ran a finger along Anne's jaw, and the girl didn't flinch. He traced her ear, smiled, tilted his head, retracted his finger and touched it absently to his lips.

"We live in the Brunswick Hotel," Gussie said, and she turned half away, taking Mr. Foster's attention with her. She started walking, and he walked with her. "I work for Mrs. Shayd. Some would say it's hard work, but it's no problem for me."

"What do you do with Anne?"

"She's looked after."

"Your husband . . ."

"Lost."

"I see." He followed Gussie up onto the sidewalk. They paused against the front panes of the seamstress shop. There was light behind the glass, shadows on the floorboards. A young clerk was working at the table in back, laying out bolts of cloth. "Again, Mrs. Locke," he said, "what do you want?"

She leaned her forehead against the glass, peered into the dimness. "Mrs. Shayd provides for us. A place to sleep. Meals. This uniform. Anne's clothes."

"No, Mrs. Locke. What do you want from *me*? I think you've been following me. That's not proper for a young mother on her own."

"Maybe. You must need a lot of help with that house of yours, sir. You have room for all your friends just on your porch. But you left them. Left your friends behind."

"Yes. So you said already." He cupped his eyes against the window, looked inside.

"Is it proper for a gentleman like you to leave his guests and go wandering?"

"That's not your concern."

"Fair enough."

He glanced at her, smiled vaguely. "Point made, Mrs. Locke. So, my guess is that you're looking for a new position. Is that what you want? I already have a housekeeper."

"I'm not cut out for housework."

"What position do you desire?"

"I would like to get out of Rawlins. I can work horses. I could work a mine."

"This is not a good time in the world to be asking for something. But maybe it's not the worst time for a girl to ask for a man's job. You have more important concerns, though."

"I do?"

"Your girl. You have to keep her warm and safe. Is there something you need? Something for Anne?"

Gussie looked up at Mr. Foster. There was a softness in him. He glanced at her, a slight wink, a sad smile. "Yes, sir. Thank you," she said. "I saw a white gown in there. It would be beautiful."

"Alright." He rapped his knuckles on the glass. "I can do that for you."

The clerk peered in his direction, nodded, came and unlocked the door. "Good evening, Mr. Foster," she said, looking up at him. They shook hands. "Always nice to see you."

"Good evening, Miss Baggott," he said, nodding to her, nodding to Gussie. "Mrs. Locke here has seen something on your shelves."

"Would you like to come in?" She stood aside, holding the door wide.

"Yes, dear," he said, and he walked inside. Gussie and Anne followed.

They looked through the small nightgowns, and Anne's hand reached as much as Gussie's, touching the smooth white fabric. Gussie pinched a hem, felt the fine, even stitches. "This is nice work," she said. "I don't know anything about work like this."

"That's okay," Mr. Foster said. He pulled a gown from its hanger, held it against Anne. The girl leaned back from Gussie, looked down at the gown, hugged it with her small arms, dipped her chin and rubbed against the collar. "Anne likes it."

"That's a good choice," Miss Baggott said. "What do you think, Mrs. Locke?"

"It's beyond my means."

Miss Baggott smiled. "It's not beyond *Anne's* means."

Mr. Foster patted Anne's head, left his fingers on her pale hair. Anne reached up and took hold of a finger, drew his hand down and looked at it, smiled.

Miss Baggott wrapped the purchase in brown paper and walked them to the door. Mr. Foster paused a moment before following Gussie into the night, and she heard him say, "If Mrs. Locke comes in again, you may telephone me before you bill her."

"Yes, sir." The door closed.

Anne hugged the package. Gussie stepped down into the street. "Thank you, Mr. Foster. Nice of you, sir."

"Nothing, actually. Now that I know you're not haunting me, I'm relieved. And a gift for a child in these times lightens a man's heart."

"You must need to get back to your guests."

"You must need to get back to the Brunswick."

"I'm afraid it will be too hot in my room."

"Well, I don't need to get back to my guests. They're talking about battles and business."

"What would you rather talk about?"

"Nothing. Not tonight. The air is perfect. Or maybe I'd talk about the wild horses in the desert, or the sheep I've run north toward the Ferris Mountains. Something quiet."

"I understand." She looked up at him, and he smiled at her. "I'm not a city girl. This isn't really my milieu."

He laughed. "I wouldn't guess it was." He turned them toward the Brunswick. "We should get you home. It's late. You can tell me about your milieu some other time."

As they came to the corner of Fourth and turned downhill, Katherine and Elizabeth came uphill with their posse of young gentlemen. The girls smiled at Gussie as they passed, nodded a greeting, the whole group stumbling as they turned onto Cedar. Quiet laughter.

◆ ◆ ◆

In her room that night, Gussie laid Anne down in her crib, felt the heat of the fresh air still on Anne's skin. "Edward," Gussie whispered. "Foster." Anne smiled, reached up to Gussie's close face and pushed her away.

On the cot, Gussie folded back the brown paper, smoothed the white gown. She opened a bureau drawer, pressed down on the small stacks of Anne's clothes. Mrs. Shayd had bought some quality garments, all pastel or white, all too nice. Mr. Foster's gift slipped in perfectly among the rest of Anne's things. And now he knew Gussie, and he would talk to her later about his ventures in the Red Desert.

She undressed, turned off the light, pulled on her nightgown, slid between the sheets. The window was open, the air slowly cooling, seeping into the room. A train clattered through Rawlins, carrying with it the echoes of the streets, the bare hills. The sound reverberated, shook the window in its frame, shuddered the cot's springs. Gussie felt the momentum of all that weight moving past this gathering of buildings along Sugar Creek, this series of artesian springs and wells, this nest of electric wires, telephone wires, this state penitentiary town, this downwind vessel for the ghosts of the Red Desert.

She still knew little of this town, knew mainly that it held for a night or two the sleep of men and boys, their dreams of further roads, strange destinations, knew that it held the dregs of Wyoming behind the prison's white stone blocks, and that those men and boys also continued, daily, nightly, to travel the roads back to their crimes, to travel forward toward some other place, some muddle of hope and desire, a remembered shade tree, a caress, a house. Gussie saw her own muddle out there, heard it too in the silence as the train moved beyond hearing. She saw pine and distance, and she heard the footsteps of a toddler Anne entering in through a back door, and she saw the full run of the sky, a trail to the horizon, and she heard Anne beside her, no one else.

Anne was asleep. For a long stretch of minutes Gussie listened to Anne's breath, the shallow quick pulses, watched the stars in the high window, the sparks wandering off the point. Then there were voices in the hall, the girls returned from their roundabout, and Mrs. Shayd caught them before they could shut themselves away, the frank pitch of Mrs. Shayd's voice, a mother's voice. "It's too late," Mrs. Shayd said. "Girls, it's much too late. You cannot be out like this."

"We know," Katherine said. "We're sorry."

"The boys are scared," Elizabeth said. "We had to listen to their stories. Didn't we?"

"Which boys? Come . . ." And the voices moved from the hall, into Mrs. Shayd's room, and then the voices were muffled, caught in the lath and plaster, no longer clear who was speaking. Gussie listened, took whatever she could hear. *From the north . . . no, no, gone, all of them . . . seen in the streets . . . at this hour . . . Gussie . . . Foster . . .* She remembered nights at home when she would listen through walls and windows, learn of herself.

Then Mrs. Shayd was in Gussie's room. Gussie saw the woman hold still a moment in the moonlight. Mrs. Shayd lifted Anne from the crib and held her. Anne struggled a bit, made a small sound. Mrs. Shayd rocked the girl.

Gussie lay there, dazed, watched the lustrous sleepy scene, thought of home, thought that Mrs. Shayd's shadow could be Leota, with the moonlight at the window and the baby Gussie in her arms, the smell of the northern air passing through the windows thrown wide, the green roof scattered with fallen red-pine needles, the silence of the rooms, the old bachelor cabin swallowed into grander design. For Leota, the Ravenglass forest scent was the scent of the earth, not the scents of the plains beyond Greeley, where the altitude blistered the air and the cottonwood cotton flew like snow.

But Frank Locke's house, with all its height and dark windows, might be the home Leota had dreamed of once her first dream ended, once she left Ravenglass. Leota at midnight, on Frank Locke's porch, watching the stars fall toward the mountains, the moon swim the clouds, the moonlight fill the undulations of the fields. Leota is satisfied. She thinks that view is enough of the world, that there is enough of the flow of the seasons and the fall of rain, snow, hail, the rare passage of an automobile or wagon, enough birdsong, tractor roar, to last a hundred lifetimes, to last eternity. And then Leota turns from the night and enters the house, up the stairs, to the bedroom she shares with Frank Locke, Frank's sleeping breath humid on the pillow. She drops her gown and slides in quietly beside Frank. She hears the house shift a bit against the night breeze, the tall wooden construction flexible, strong, forgiving. She is home.

"Poor dear," Mrs. Shayd whispered. "Quiet now. No one's taking you anywhere. You're safe with me. You're home. This is your home."

Gussie roused, sat up on the cot. The waxing moon was vast in the open window, its crescent horns hooked toward the west. The moon in the mare's nest of Mrs. Shayd's hair, in the hollow of her throat, and as she parted her lips, her teeth flashed against the white but caught nothing.

Gussie touched Mrs. Shayd's hip. "This isn't Anne's home," Gussie said.

Mrs. Shayd drew back. "This is her home."

"She should be sleeping," Gussie said, pushing again at the doughy flesh in the nightgown. "It's late. I want her to sleep."

"Augusta," Mrs. Shayd said sharply, and she took Anne from the room, pulled the door closed behind her.

Gussie waited in that empty room, felt her lungs likewise empty—the jittery void—felt that emptiness, that new dread, push at her. She heard footfalls on the back stairs, climbed from the cot, followed out into the hall. Nothing in the dimness. She stepped into the dark pit of the stairwell, started down, paused at the second floor. There was no one in the long hall. All the doors were shut, all the guests asleep in the numbered rooms. She descended to the first floor. Another empty hall. She came to the end of the hall, looked out into the parlor, BRUNSWICK HOTEL etched in reverse in the moonlight, the streetlight. No one on the settees. No one among the potted palms.

Gussie heard the clink of glass, turned from the parlor, down the side hall to the kitchen. Mrs. Shayd in a cone of light at the table. A glass in her hand. The child cradled.

"I'll take her," Gussie said. She needed to feel Anne's weight, couldn't quite remember the feel of that body, the fit of that small shape, afraid now, seeing the girl content, quiet.

"Sit," Mrs. Shayd said, not looking up. She held out the glass, indicated a chair across the table.

Gussie came forward, didn't like the woman's voice, the depth of her lungs, the size of the hand gripping the glass. She waited for the glass to crack, but it just hung there above the table, the light in an amber disk on the tabletop. Gussie sat, looked at the tabletop, the scars on the wood, the black scorches, didn't look up. Mrs. Shayd leaned across, touched her with the glass. Gussie looked down into the glass, smelled the sweet sherry, saw the white grip of the hand.

"Drink," Mrs. Shayd said.

Gussie didn't move, just looked at the liquor.

"Take it, Augusta. You've tasted spirits before, no doubt."

"I'll take my Anne back to my room, thank you."

"Your Anne . . . this girl . . . your room . . ." Mrs. Shayd withdrew the glass, downed the liquid herself, clanked the glass on the table, reached across and took Gussie's chin in a pinch, made Gussie look at her. "Cousin Dunn was well rid of the trouble you could cause him. Am I right? I take you in when you're nothing but a castoff. Of *course* this is Anne's home."

Gussie shook free of Mrs. Shayd. "Anne is my daughter," Gussie said. "Where she came from is my own business."

"It's my business, too, little girl. I have an establishment here, a reputation."

"Nobody would care."

"You might be surprised. People don't go around accepting . . . I've tried with you . . . This is a town. A prison town. A growing town."

"Do you want me to leave?"

"You couldn't care for Anne on your own."

"I could."

"No one to care for her while you worked."

"That's for me."

"No man is going to hire you on. No man is going to understand the needs of your child. No man is going to give you a room, love your child as you love her. This is her home. You're not going anywhere. No man is going to love you, not after what you've done."

Mrs. Shayd pulled a paper from the yoke of her nightgown, palmed it flat on the tabletop. "This is a letter from my Robert. He's sick with a fever, laid up in a hospital tent. That's all he's got—canvas walls—do you understand that? I gave Robert this hotel as a home when he was three. He knows good walls, and a roof from the rain, and heat, and nice things. He knows all the people who pass through on their way to somewhere, and he knows that he has to be kind, because they're sleeping under his roof. He knows the attic room you're in with Anne, because that was his room from when he was a child right through to when he was a man, and now he's gone and I give the room to you, and when he returns we'll see what we'll do about it. He's a good boy, good as the earth around here. I wouldn't want him to know you, not right now. So you take your child back to my son's room, and you tuck her in, and you leave me here to gather my nerves back into my head, and I'll be along shortly, and we'll forget what you said."

Lincoln Highway

This is not Anne's home.

Late into night, on toward morning, Gussie sat on the cot beside the crib, held her child. The room was tight, warm. Anne was small, a feather. Gussie tried to concentrate on holding the baby, on the sensation, the force of her muscles. At the brink of sleep, Gussie startled awake, held Anne tighter. She thought of Anne alone, or herself alone. The moon had passed far beyond the window. The moonlight was a faint wash in the stars. And the desert where the moon now traveled was an infinite vessel for that pale light. A girl alone, looking out at the desert in moonlight, would see a perplexing distance unmarked by wire or post. A girl alone, looking down at her body in moonlight, would see only her legs folded on the ground, or her hands limp and palm-up to the sky, or her shoulder with its subtle knobs and freckles, no reference, no way to judge her beauty or lack.

I just want you with me, Anne.

Gussie was alone. In truth, no one knew her in Rawlins. No one knew of Jack Fisher and his thin shoulders and his sleeping breath on the pillow. No one knew that Gussie could work a team of horses within an inch of a survey, or that she remembered the north woods clearly and the paths through the cedar brakes, or that she dreamed sometimes that her daughter was beyond her reach. No one knew that she'd left her mother in a house every bit as tall as Mr. Foster's house, that if she'd chosen she could have looked down on the world from the frame of a high window.

But here she'd met Mr. Foster, dreamed a gateway to the Red Desert. Here she'd seen the banknotes slipped from his wallet, heard the gurgle he made when he looked at Anne. Gussie didn't know him yet, not well, but maybe she knew enough about him already to trust that he would help her, given time. But how much time? And how would he help her? She thought of his house, of the curved brick turret. He might glance out the turret window at Rawlins and think of the men and women he knew, had known all his life, and think of how they must know him, the man in the grand house in the square of lawn. They might think of him as the man who had hired and fired the dreams and desires of a good many rawboned local souls. The men and women of Rawlins counted their coins, watched for winter. Did Mr. Foster understand that Gussie was alone, that she found herself confined, afraid, unsure if she could take Anne away?

On the nights that followed, Gussie heard Mrs. Shayd come upstairs later than her custom, enter her room next door, sounds sharpened by the dead silence. Gussie traced the sounds. Mrs. Shayd placed something hollow on the bedside table, sat on the edge of her bed. The bedsprings strained and released. She hung something in the chifforobe. Then water in the basin, a splash, stillness. Only the building settling in the night, it seemed, but there was a rhythm—it was Mrs. Shayd moving slowly back and forth in her room, her weight bearing down on the boards and beams.

Then a conversation started, and it built through the weeks, into fall. At first, Gussie tried to place the voices, sure they must rise through the floor, through a vent, funneled from some other part of the hotel, from guests too agitated to sleep. But as guests moved on, as rooms below sometimes remained empty, still the conversation continued, intensified, and finally Gussie leaned at the wall, pressed her ear to the plaster, listened through the layers to Mrs. Shayd's voice modulating female to male, in conversation with herself.

"It's cold. Close the window. Come here. Beside me." The higher voice.

"The window's a crack open for the night air." The deeper voice.

"I'm cold. Come here."

"I'm here, sweetheart."

"Settle in, husband. Here. That's good. Everything's fine. The hotel is full tonight. Full again."

"That's good for you. That's good."

"Good. Maybe. I'm waiting for the roof to blow off. After all these years. Waiting for the walls to come down."

"Let them come down. What loss would that be? I have a thousand places to go."

"You've gone already, husband."

"I know."

"The wind always comes from the west. I can hear the shingles. How long before the wind tears the roof away?"

"Maybe this year. Maybe in twenty years. What then?"

"My hair, my skin, will blow away. Gone to wherever."

"Gone to wherever I am, sweetheart."

"I don't know where you are."

A nightly conversation, Mrs. Shayd one half, and the other half someone lost to her, must be Mr. Shayd. Mrs. Shayd's ceaseless pacing. The sound of the bedsprings. The clank of the glass on the table. The light switch. Two voices in the bed, talking toward sleep.

Gussie left the wall, rubbed life back into her ear, fell silently beneath her blanket. Was there room on her cot for a man to sleep with her? She felt the blanket warm with her warmth. She felt the pillow cup her face. She knew the heat of a man's nostrils. She'd touched a man's belly and felt the muscles, the banded fibers. That was more than a year ago, and her memories had weakened, become confused with all these men and boys passing through Rawlins, all these necks and bellies, these eyes dry in the dry air, these whiskers starting out from the reddened skin. She hadn't touched these men and boys, but she had cared for them. She had sliced their bread, boiled their coffee. She had taken their laundry, washed away the miles they'd traveled, flushed out the soil of their homes, the sweat of their fears. All that cloth, all those empty shapes, the buttons sewed by mothers, the patches cut from fathers' toss-offs.

Gussie tried to imagine a husband pressed against her through the seasons, his voice repeating his thoughts until she could speak his thoughts for him. If she made herself small against the wall, Jack Fisher might lie beside her, face-to-face, shin to toe, his scent rife with the places he'd been. In Rawlins, he worked freight, she thought, unloaded the goods from east and west, rolled them through town—crates of peaches, apples, barrels of nails, lengths of pipe, silk, sugar. And he entered numbers in the ledgers, knew each merchant's name and need. He booked the outgoing freight, the stone, coal, and wool all drawn somehow from the claims and holdings of a few men. Jack Fisher knew each man who gathered riches from the encircling territory, called the men by name, shared a drink or meal on the odd day when the men were feeling large-hearted.

And then home to the attic room in the Brunswick Hotel, where Gussie lay on the cot, where Anne slept in the crib, where the stars blazed in the foursquare panes. Gussie watched him undress in the dark room—his stoop and careful balance, his sweet attempt at silence—and then he was down with her. He smelled of pipe smoke, coal oil. She touched her lips to each scent, judged his day in a slow progression from brow to jaw, shoulder to rib. In that small bed, there was hardly space between them. She found him behind her, on top of her, his hand on her hand on her belly pressed against his belly.

She worked to separate them, to draw a clear picture of each, even as they locked on the wavering cot, the sham of a marriage bed. She could feel her own hips, the low creases where the baby had stretched her skin, the cool uneasiness of her navel, the toughness of her legs. She saw the window, the stars, the way the wind tore at the light and sent it drifting. The sky was too wide, the wind too constant. If Jack had found this place, if he had accepted Gussie and child, if they had listened together to the winter squall, then she might have heard his voice fill the late hours, understood his thoughts. Even if he had stayed with her only a few days, a week, she might have come to know him well enough to understand how it should feel to have lost him, never to hear again the sound of his voice.

◆ ◆ ◆

In from the gate, up across the porch, Gussie approached Mr. Foster's door. Holding Anne on her hip, she turned the brass crank, and the bell clanged. A long minute passed. She heard nothing from inside the house, heard only the sounds of Rawlins and the sky. She could have retreated, continued to circle the streets and breathe the windborne dust, but, however pitiful she might appear, she had resolved to make this social call. She needed to tell him something, ask him something.

Then Mr. Foster stood at the narrow crack of the door. "Mrs. Locke," he said. "Anne." He touched a finger to Anne's arm, and Anne touched him back. "What can I do for you ladies?"

"We were out walking, Mr. Foster. We thought we'd stop."

"That was kind." He smiled, looked back into the house, paused as if listening, looked out toward the street. "I can't ask you in— nobody else is home. Shall we sit on the porch? I'll get us something warm to drink, a sweet for the child."

"She doesn't need anything."

"You know best." He stepped away, into the dimness, left her.

Gussie waited, turned to look out over the porch railing. The town was melancholy in its haze of bare trees. She paced the length of the porch, stopped at the far curve of the rail, found herself posed with a casual angle to her hips, her head tilted, as if the house had made her settled and assured. She wished that someone would see her there.

Gussie held Anne tighter, kissed her ear, backed against the wall, turned and looked in at a window. Nothing distinct beyond the near table, the brass lamp, crystals hanging in delicate ranks. She didn't need these heavy casements to block the draft. She didn't need these curtains to shut out the daylight or the stars.

She remembered climbing a cedar toward the northern lights, the pitch gathering on her palms, gathering bark and needles, high into the night, above the surface of the forest. The world stretched in soft undulations without break. The stars skimmed the icy currents. The voices of Ravenglass were lost in the sheer volume of open. No one to see her there. She held to the cedar, inhaled the wilderness. She wondered if she would always track the byways, conjure a better horizon, look away from home, away from whatever soul it was who waited for her, called her name, called her to come inside and sleep.

Gussie turned again, faced the town. Down Sixth Street, Mrs. Shayd approached, walked steadily, glanced squarely at Gussie and Anne, no sign of recognition, and then snapped her face away, looked at the sky. Mrs. Shayd flashed beyond the black iron bars of Mr. Foster's fence. At the street corner she paused as if she were unable to decide which way to proceed, unable to keep walking, but she didn't look back. In the wind, her skirt sucked around her legs, left her lopsided. Finally she hurried out of sight, down into town. Mrs. Shayd, beyond her usual paths, away from her duties. The woman was as restless as the weather.

Mr. Foster came out from the house, blankets and steaming drinks in hand. Gussie settled into a rocker, spread the gray wool over her legs, took the cocoa, held it away from Anne's reaching hand. Mr. Foster sat in the next rocker, laid a blanket over his knees. Leaves blew along the street, gathered in drifts against fences.

"I'd almost forgotten how brown it was last winter," Gussie said. "I didn't get out much. I was laid up."

"You had a difficult time with the birth?"

"I'm not delicate."

"But you're young."

"I almost died."

"I'm sorry." He sipped from his drink, looked at her over the rim of the cup, an unsteady moment, eyes half-closed and weary, then looked away. "I didn't know, of course. But you had Mrs. Shayd to look after you. She's a good woman."

"I've been thinking that I won't work for her anymore. She loves Anne."

"And I could love her . . . could love a child like her."

"Mrs. Shayd takes her away from me."

"Is she trying to help you?"

"I don't need help."

"What do you need?"

"I don't know." She dipped a finger into the cooling cocoa and let Anne taste. The girl wriggled with excitement, held tighter to Gussie, laid her head on Gussie's shoulder, watched Mr. Foster. "I need to move, to keep going."

"Do you want to go home?"

"No."

"Is Rawlins your home now?"

"I don't know." She found a sudden tightness in her voice, couldn't look at Mr. Foster. "How am I supposed to know?"

"You have friends here."

"I'm alone."

"You have your daughter. You're with Anne."

Gussie couldn't answer. She tried to sip from her cocoa, but her heart was pounding, her lips wouldn't obey. She found tears in her eyes, at her nostrils. She looked out at the street, tried to focus through the refracting light, thought she saw movement at the corner, past a light pole, along a fence, but each blink erased the form and sent the movement elsewhere. Mrs. Shayd wasn't there. "Mrs. Shayd will take her."

"So you said. She helps you."

"No. She'll take her."

"No. No." He reached to pat her shoulder, but retracted his hand, thought a moment. "She's a good woman. She has a child of her own."

"I don't know . . ."

They sat in silence. Gussie controlled her breath. The chill wind kicked up. They tucked the blankets more tightly about their legs. She caught his cautious glance, and they smiled, relaxed.

He nodded, started again. "What do you need, Mrs. Locke?"

"A wool blanket would be nice." She laughed. "There—I finally have an answer."

"You need to be with your child, always, Mrs. Locke, so that you don't worry. If she were my child . . . If she were me . . ."

Mr. Foster told Gussie of his dead father. His father loved him, he thought. They slept under the stars in the desert, in wool blankets. He remembered a morning with frost on the sage, ice in the water pail. He awoke to the crackle of flame. His father was low over the fire, steam from the pan, sizzle of meat. He remembered clearly, would never forget, the way his hip settled in a divot of rock and sand, the way the blanket held heat to his legs and bare feet. And he remembered a night, his father close to him, when he heard something pass through the Red Desert, didn't move to rouse his father, heard hoof falls, the jangle of metal, the mutter of a strange language. He listened for hours, long after the sounds were lost to distance. "No," his father said at dawn, "no one passes these miles but us." That day they found a hammered fragment of bronze, a scrap of worked flint. The desert was full of possibility. In time, his father took him to the quarry where the earth was cut and raised from darkness. And those blocks built the town, built towns in other territories along the rails. His father took him south to the mines, where black buckets rose from the tunnels.

He told Gussie of his dead mother. She had taken him east. The miles slipped past, the sky went green with rain and leaf. She took him to a boarding school, past the old New England battlefields. "There's nothing for you to learn in Rawlins," she said. "There's my father," he said. "There's more to the world," she said. He sat at the window, high in the face of the white brick building, and watched her walk out the drive to the road. She stood there at the gate, her pale skin and yellow dress, the dappling of late summer. The carriage stopped, and she boarded. He would stand sometimes at the gate and look down the road, the macadam in the dim tunnel of elms, or the road buried in snow, crazed with the shadows of the bare trees.

"You can't leave your child for even a day," Mr. Foster said.

"I don't want to leave her."

"What can you do?"

"I can take Anne and leave."

"No. What work can you do? I need to think. Don't despair. You're safe, I'm sure. Anne's safe. Give me time."

◆ ◆ ◆

In the last hours of darkness, when Anne was deepest in sleep, when Gussie had already traveled her dreams and found herself alone again in Rawlins, Mrs. Shayd entered Gussie's room. Slowly, hushed, Mrs. Shayd pulled the chair against the crib, sat close to Anne, reached her hand through the rail and smoothed the blanket.

Gussie didn't move. She listened to Mrs. Shayd's slow, steady inhalations of the dry air, the whistling exhalations, smelled the dense accumulation of sleepless nights. Gussie wondered if Mrs. Shayd knew where she was, if she was awake in a dream, if she paced her breathing to Anne's breathing. Mrs. Shayd leaned more heavily, seemed to bend the starlight down into her focus on Anne, to extinguish the world beyond. And she whispered in the dark room, too softly for Gussie to gather words or thoughts.

With dawn approaching, with Mrs. Shayd looming close, Gussie tried to drowse a few minutes before she would have to descend to the kitchen. When Gussie again opened her eyes, Mrs. Shayd remained, unmoving. The incandescent white and heat waited, the pots and griddles, serrated knives, but Gussie didn't dare break Mrs. Shayd's vigil, unsure of what would happen. Slowly she rolled beneath the blanket, the dry wool sparking blue against her nightgown.

Mrs. Shayd turned full square to the cot—she was dark, without feature but for her large shape. "Tell me what you plan," Mrs. Shayd said. Her hand fell on Gussie's shoulder, pinned her to the cot. "Tell me your intentions."

Gussie tried to sink away from Mrs. Shayd's hand, but the cot wouldn't give. "Mrs. Shayd," Gussie said, "I need to get to work."

"You don't, Augusta."

She looked up into the blank of Mrs. Shayd's face. "You're firing me?"

"No." She released Gussie's shoulder, leaned closer. "Tell me what you plan to do. I know you walk up the hill to Edward Foster's house. I know you take Anne."

"Yes, ma'am." Gussie wouldn't deny it. What use? *Give me time,* Mr. Foster had said. And so she needed time. "I live in this town, Mrs. Shayd. I come and go and meet people. That's all."

"And you take Anne."

"Yes. I take her."

"There is too much you don't know yet or won't ever know or would rather ignore. You are the mother of a child, but you don't know what it is to love a child or to lose a child."

"I haven't lost my child."

"You are a lost child yourself." She backed off a little, smoothed the blanket across Gussie's throat, continued more softly. "You like Mr. Foster's house because it's tall and beautiful, but that house isn't a cake or a painting. You don't know anything about Edward Foster."

"He's my friend."

"But you're not his friend. He pities you. He looks at you and sees a lost girl with a beautiful child. He thinks he can help you. He'll give you whatever you ask of him. He's a rich man. Richer than I will ever be. I don't have half of what he has."

"But you have this hotel, you have your son."

"I don't have anything, Augusta." She pushed her chair back, stood and turned, held to the crib rail. Her broad shoulders blocked the sky and the hint of dawn. "How could a man like Mr. Foster know the value of anything? All he ever wanted was laid out for him to take. He's dug up every acre that showed promise. He's taken people's money with the pledge of return. No regard. None. He has all he needs, but that doesn't stop him from wanting."

"He's alone."

"He can buy someone."

"He's my friend. He hasn't bought me."

"Listen, Augusta. Up in Chugwater, when I was a young lady, I met Mr. Shayd. He courted me, and he asked permission of my father, and we were married. He knew the order of things. We made a plan and moved to Rawlins—we didn't just drop into town out of the sky. And no one took us in. We didn't depend on charity. We found our own place and did our own work."

"You want me to leave, to find my own place, do my own work."

"No. Listen. We built our lives here, and no one in this town would say that we couldn't be trusted, not unless they were cheats or cowards. No one would say that our word wasn't true. I could balance the accounts. Mr. Shayd could expand our holdings through pure goodwill and fine service. Robert could charm a convict out of a lie—the boy knew our lives depended on trust and honesty and grace. So, after all the years, I've still got this hotel. No one is going to take it away from me unless I decide to let it go. But I won't let it slip away. I know what's worth keeping, and I keep it."

◆ ◆ ◆

November 11. *Armistice.* Gussie dropped her work, came out from the kitchen to the parlor window. She saw a sliver of the parade on Cedar Street. Wind snapped the flags, carried off the smoke of the stuffed Kaiser in flames. An army truck, a white star on the door, churned out a fog of exhaust. Leaning against the glass, she felt the vibrations, the shocks of the afternoon. *Armistice.* She kept repeating the word. She hadn't realized how much she had wanted the war to end, not until now. All day she had imagined a stream of the healthy and the wounded flowing west from each port, the men all finding their way up turnpikes and tributaries.

And all day, in shifting layers of detail, she had imagined the door to the Ravenglass house, although she wasn't sure why she'd placed herself in that house, that memory. She thought Jack might find his way there, that she would startle at the sound of a knock, open the door to the night, take him in. He would stand with his back against the door, and she would stand near to him.

"Gussie," he would say.

"Jack Fisher," she would say.

And he removed his battered hat and dropped it to the floor. His head was nearly shaved. He sat at the table, cupped his hands around an earthenware bowl, tipped the bowl to look inside, raised it to his lips and drank the last warm swallows of broth, lowered the bowl to the table. Then he rested his chin on his palms, seemed unlikely to move again. Gussie stood behind the chair, looked down at his skull.

If he found her, how would she know where he had traveled, what he had seen? She imagined the bristling swirl at the crown of his head. The light slid along a strange line—a scar. And then she saw the pattern of damage that streaked toward his left ear. The skin had been rent and sewn, the needle scars pacing the hardened lines. She thought that if she studied the pattern, she might somehow decipher the miles that took him away, the sounds of the engines that pulled across rail and sea, the touch of rain on fallow fields, branches heavy with storm and cold. Somewhere inside the pattern was the instrument of the injury, the force of the projectile, the tone of the torn air, the arc through night or bright sun, the print of the man who aimed the weapon.

She couldn't bring the image clear enough to know where he'd been, who he was. "Come with me," she said. He followed. The house in the red pines was warm with wood fire, tight with lamp-light. Into the room with the iron bed, the window closed to the winter, she might sit him on the edge of the bed, hold her palms to his cold face. His bones were clear beneath his skin. "Here," she said. Slowly she loosened his buttons, pushed his shirt back off his shoulders, shifted his weight as she pulled off his trousers and drawers, kicked his boots aside, bundled his clothes with the tattered socks. She lowered him onto the bed, arranged the pillows, not ready to look at him yet, not ready to know the rest of his wounds. She left him there.

As the water heated in the copper, she laid out his clothes on the kitchen table, inspected the fabric. Here Gussie might find the mysteries of Jack's time away. It all smelled of smoke, cold, salt. When the water was steaming, she filled the laundry pail, pushed the clothes down in, sprinkled the soap, and began to work the travel from the cloth, wring away the fear, the nights, the miles, the hours, the sounds of fire, foes. At the surface of the water, darkness accumulated among the dying suds. She might scoop a palmful, hold it to the light. Suspended above the creases of her skin, pale and black flecks circulated. Could be ash. Blood. Iron shavings. Gunpowder. Lost skin. Blight. Rust. Taint. She rinsed it all in a rush of cold water, pinned the clothes to the strings above the stove, listened to the falling drops sizzle on the stovetop. Slowly the refilled copper heated, and the water started to roil.

In the bedroom, Jack Fisher lay where Gussie had left him, one arm cocked up behind his head, exposing the dry hollow of his underarm—that space seemed to tremble with his pulse. His legs were pulled up, one leg slightly farther than the other, leaving a shadowed crux where his sex settled, the whimsical fleshy cluster that she could never remember clearly. Strange to think that that soft extension could have brought anything more than laughter and pleasure. But it had brought her Anne, although Jack knew nothing of that.

She touched his leg, the soft skin, the streaked dirt, and said, "I have water for a bath, if you'd like." He opened his eyes, and she helped him up from the bed. Taking his hand, she walked ahead, and he followed, waited as she mixed hot and cold in the tub, and he stepped into the water. She looked at him fully now, walked around him to reach the lantern, raise the flame. His skin was too grimy for her to separate surface from scar. His bones held his muscles too loosely. She helped him down into the tub. The water hissed and gurgled. He was held in warmth. She watched for the water to color with the ache of his travels, to leave only the indelible marks of his skin for her to decipher. But in that water he was unsettled, wavering—each breath moved the water, altered his contours, until there was nothing constant or knowable. She couldn't remember Jack Fisher. She couldn't imagine that he would ever find her.

Armistice. Gussie had work to do, but who could work on such a day? She turned from the parlor window, went to look for Anne. The street noise followed her up through the Brunswick. A train whistle blew, died into echo, swamped by the celebration. In the attic room, Anne sat in a corner of the crib, watching the door. Lifting Anne from the crib, Gussie opened her blouse and held the girl to nurse. Anne was nearly weaned. One more feeding, maybe, and that was it. Good timing, if they were to travel soon, leave this place.

"You're free after tonight," Gussie said.

Gussie lay Anne flat on the cot, stripped away her little gown, unsure if it had come from Mrs. Shayd or Mr. Foster, the gifts equally fine, unpinned the diaper and put it aside, and saw that small form, the smooth kicking of the legs, the clutching of the fingers, the freshness of the skin. Gussie leaned down, smelled the girl's warm tummy, felt that scent flutter in her chest, swirl in her head. She kissed Anne hard on the soft pooch of her belly, her slack muscles, her cheek. Anne laughed, kicked her legs as if she ran.

"Soon enough you'll run. A family trait."

Gussie remembered Brud's white skin in the low humid slant of the Minnesota sun, his speed into the farther openings of branch and turf, the run of shadow, leaf-light, the Ravenglass smoke caught in the tangents of paper birch. Brud ran into the black spruce, on into the boundary lands where the sun cooled and the mist drew winter from the air. Brud was caught in a cycle of winters, asleep in the lost bowers that his father Einar had built, asleep in the soft skins that Einar had tanned, hearing through his sleep the current of storm, the skeletal cedars, the lanky moon shadows. Brud awoke to human voices, unsure if he was awake, but the voices haunted that night and the seasons that followed, voices that puzzled through the branches, that settled on the leaves above his head, just out of reach, that skimmed the lakes with the black wings of loons. No sense to any of it, but slowly the voices pooled in the hollow throb of his chest, he understood without understanding that the voices were Leota, a fair song of bird or breeze, the voices were Augusta, a tinge of animal or insect.

Gussie held her naked child against her shoulder, felt the spring of the girl's limbs. "Maybe I was like you, when I was young," Gussie said. "Maybe you are like me. My father would love you. Sometimes I think that he might go back to the Ravenglass house and look for me. Wouldn't he be surprised to find me there, and you there with me? If there's even much left to that house. The yard must be grown over. The walls must be soggy. I could show you the porch where I slept. I think you'd enjoy the fresh air out there and all the things I collected, and maybe you'd be smart enough to tell me why I chose what I chose to keep. There was dry bloom and bark and bone and feather. There was my father's hair in single strands. You're a part of me, so maybe you could understand and you could tell me what it means and why it's gone."

Gussie pinned Anne into a new diaper, found a nightgown with small stitches, buttery yellow trim, sat the girl up and dressed her. She held her above the crib, turned her in the light from the window. Twilight. There was firelight now, bonfires along Cedar. Gussie wrapped her in a blanket.

"I swear you could almost take care of yourself, little girl, by the looks of you," Gussie said. "You could attract all you could ever need, but I'm going to care for you as long as I can. You will stay with me. We won't be apart."

Gussie carried Anne into the hall, to the sliver of light outside Mrs. Shayd's door. From that spot, the celebration was filtered through the brick and plaster of the old hotel. Still she could hear bells and sirens in the cold air. Rifles aimed at the clouds. And the sound of Mrs. Shayd in her room, the heavy bedsprings.

Gussie stood at the door, said softly, "Mrs. Shayd? I need to get outside. I'm going. I want Anne to see this, even if she won't remember."

Mrs. Shayd stepped out from the door, blocked the light, stood close. "You'd better leave Anne here."

"The whole town is on the streets. Haven't you seen?"

"I've seen. I don't care for it." She loomed closer, clasped her hands to Anne's shoulders, as if she'd wrest the girl away, but then she slackened a bit, only reached to smooth the blanket around Anne's head, shield the child's ears. "All that racket. What does it mean, to celebrate war?"

"Celebrate the *end* of war."

"Nothing changes."

"Your boy will return home." Gussie placed her hand on Mrs. Shayd's shoulder. The woman was chilly to the touch, her face ashen. "You'll be alright."

Mrs. Shayd winced. "Yes, Augusta, I'm alright."

And for a second Gussie thought she understood the sadness of the moment, all the voids that couldn't be filled by moving forward, by celebrating, by shouting against the wind. And Mrs. Shayd would sit in her room, alone, and talk her way back into better days, lost loves. "Why don't you come outside with us, Mrs. Shayd? We won't stay long. Just a chance to knock out the cobwebs and see the crowd."

Mrs. Shayd shook her head. "You go on, if you have to. But it's too cold outside for a child." She pulled Anne from Gussie's arms, and Gussie allowed it. "Don't stay long. There's work to do." She backed into her room.

Just inside the doorway, letters lay scattered on the floor. Mrs. Shayd stepped across the letters as Gussie stooped to gather them up, saw the dates and salutations. Mrs. Shayd retreated and sat on the bed. There were more letters laid out on the white expanse of the bedspread. "Bring those here, Augusta," Mrs. Shayd said. "I'm looking for something."

Gussie stepped on into the room, saw the grim look on Mrs. Shayd's face, thought she should shut the door in case anyone might pass by. She latched the door closed, came forward. "What are you looking for?"

Mrs. Shayd lifted one page after another, let them fall. "I've mislaid a letter."

Gussie stood beside the bed. The letters drifted. *Dearest Mother . . . 1914 . . . 1916 . . .* "What is it?" Gussie said. "What are you missing?"

Mrs. Shayd reached, took Gussie's hand, made her sit beside her. She hoisted Anne tighter against her shoulder. They all three sat among the letters, the open papers, the black script. "I have something to tell you, Augusta. On armistice, of all days. I did not tell you the full truth. My boy left Rawlins years ago. My husband isn't dead, not that I know—he left me, and all I had were the letters he wrote. 'Prospects are improving,' he would say, or 'Expect money in the next communication.' He was on the St. Lawrence Seaway. He was in the Caribbean. He was in Texas. All those years, fifteen years, he told me he'd return. He was cruel. But I kept those letters, so I'd know he was alive. And then my boy found the letters. He read them and took them all away."

Gussie picked up one letter and another. "Then what are all these?"

"These are all from my son. Robert sent new letters, to replace his father's letters. He followed his father. He didn't know the man. He used his daddy's letters as a map. He never promised to return."

Gussie smoothed a few letters flat, touched Mrs. Shayd's arm. "Mrs. Shayd . . ."

"He was always a loving son. He thought of me every day." She rose, carried Anne to the window. Streetlights and bonfires glimmered on her face. "All the boys will be returning." Mrs. Shayd leaned on the sill, her forehead to the glass, Anne's face to the evening. A long series of gunshots. Anne tapped her hand at the pane, and Mrs. Shayd caught the small hand and held it.

"Was Robert actually in the war?" Gussie said.

"He was in the war."

Mrs. Shayd remained at the window, and she trembled slightly each time the revelry boomed. She kept smoothing the blanket around Anne's head. Then she started to speak, and her voice steamed the panes, dimmed the reflections from the street.

"He rode the train east from Rawlins. Robert was a young man when he left, too young, but he was already as tall as a man. He never knew Mr. Shayd, only knew the letters. He worked first as a teamster, those long strings of horses, the overloaded wagon—I didn't want to think of the danger.

"Then he trawled the Caribbean. He cut sugarcane on the islands, ate crawfish. He wrote to me about the Gulf heat, and the insects on the beaches, the barren pines, border towns, and the bells in the church towers."

"You knew that he missed you?" Gussie said. "You knew that he loved you?"

"I got a letter every day sometimes. Other times he was silent for a month or more. Then I had to wonder if he was running cattle somewhere, or if he had been bitten by a dog or taken up by a young lady."

Gussie looked again at the photograph beside the bed. Robert Shayd could probably find a girl who would love him, no problem. But she couldn't think of him as anything but alone. She thought of her night in the open, below Virginia Dale. She thought of her tent on the Laramie Plain and the silence that seemed vast and constant, soon to evaporate with the dawn. Robert Shayd would switch off the light, undress, lie flat on the bed. Gussie knew that time of night—at first his senses are drowned by his pulse, the heat of his muscles, but slowly his body settles, his fingers stiffen. He would retreat into his day's work, the rhythm would infiltrate his pulse, push him toward sleep. Then he would be moving again as he had moved all day, whatever the work, wherever—his dreams put him through it again. "I've been away, too," Gussie said. "He must dream of you. He must find you each night, even if you don't know you've been found."

"My son wrote to me about the wind in Rawlins and the spring leaves along Sugar Creek. He remembered the red dust at sunset. And he said that he remembered the sound of my steps in this hotel, and he missed the morning hours in his room—your room now, Gussie—when the doorknob rattled and the door swung open, and I came into the room and sat on the edge of the bed, and I said, 'It's morning, Robert. You come downstairs when you're ready. For now you can sleep.' Maybe I said that. I can't remember."

"I'm sure you said it, Mrs. Shayd." But Gussie couldn't be sure. She thought of Leota's slender neck and her icy eyes. One afternoon, Gussie had seen Leota pass, far below, Leota in a slow wander through ferns, through sunny veins of grass, pausing once to glance back as if she'd heard someone following, but she was alone, and she continued, moved from sunlit clarity to a momentary flash to no more than a fragment in the weave of branch and needle, shadow and leaf, until all Gussie saw was a shoulder, an ankle, an ear, part of a jaw line, and finally Leota was gone, vanished into the rise and fall past Ravenglass. And then, from far in the afternoon, Gussie heard her own name called, her mother's voice, and the sound worked into her memory, lingered, intensified through the years, until that voice, that afternoon, that warm sun and crystal air, that glimmer of ethereal skin, became for Gussie the essence of love, and that's what she remembered, and that's what she controlled. Leota, in her house beyond Greeley, still moved as she'd always moved, still paused to look into Gussie's room, the early light from the window in a flat grid on the bed. Leota would always say, *Come downstairs and I'll fix you something to eat.* "Robert knows what you said, Mrs. Shayd. I'm sure he wouldn't forget."

The sky had gone dark. The noise of the street continued, blew around the western wind. "It will storm tonight," Mrs. Shayd said finally.

"Why have you told me all this about Robert, Mrs. Shayd?"

"Because maybe you're like him."

"I'm not." She could deny it.

"There are many ways in which you're not like Robert, yes. But maybe he has left a son or daughter behind in some town along the way. That child is my flesh and blood, my grandchild. Maybe you'll keep traveling until it's too late. You should stop."

"Too late?"

"Too late to turn for home. I have a home here, for you and your child." She turned from the window, came back to the bed, sat beside Gussie, among the letters. "I've shown you some of his letters from the war. Now the war is over. There's a particular letter I've misplaced. At the end, he could no longer write—a nurse wrote the letter for him. I've read it often enough that I don't need to see it, but I like to touch the paper, and it smells of the hospital and Robert and the others there. It was strange to see his words in someone else's hand.

"He said the nights were colder and the noise of the battle had moved east. All he could hear was the other men around him and his own breathing. He liked the nurse. She was a French girl. She told him about her town in the south, and he thought of Rawlins when she said the sun sank right down into the hills. I haven't received another letter. I think he might have taken up with that girl. I think she might have taken him home. He would have been too sick to fight again. She would set him in a room. He will write when his head clears. Unless he's dead, of course."

"Ma'am," Gussie said, and she took Mrs. Shayd's hand, tried to hold her still, to feel her warmth, her own hands small, the woman's skin parched and yielding. "I'm sure Robert isn't dead."

Mrs. Shayd removed her hand from Gussie's grip, took Gussie's hand and turned it over, looked at the palm, turned it and looked at the fingers, the small nails. "You're a rough girl," Mrs. Shayd said. "You couldn't know. Your child is not the same creature as you. She could almost be Robert's child. She could be my own blood."

Gussie tried to pull away, but Mrs. Shayd held her. Gussie looked at the woman's wrist, the tendons high, tight. The sleeves of the woman's blouse a light cloth, white as cloud, and the buttons like drops of rain. The way the collar lay broad and flat, its scalloped edges stitched with subtle thread. The way the blouse veiled the woman's shape. This was her Sunday blouse, her church blouse, for the prayers and the hymns and the passing of the plate and the tasting of the blood and body. An exquisite creation. And then Mrs. Shayd's neck, the deep hollow at the base, the cluster of jagged freckles at her jaw. The tight lips creased with pain. The eyes as stark as blue granite, a hint of moist red at the ducts.

Gussie saw Leota's eyes, the fragile ice and buried color, and Anne turned, her face small in the shadow of Mrs. Shayd's face, Anne's eyes an equal to any, cloudless, boundless. "You're nothing like Anne," Gussie said. "I'm sorry, Mrs. Shayd. I'm sorry for your son. But Anne is nothing like you."

"You don't know. You can't know. Not until you've lost your child."

"I don't intend to lose my girl."

"Intentions are useless."

Extracting herself from Mrs. Shayd's grip, Gussie was to the door, the squeal of the hinges, and the dim hall. "I *am* sorry for your boy," Gussie said, "and for you."

"No pity."

"But how could I not pity you, if you think you've lost your child? I don't hate you. Do you think I hate you?"

"I've been nothing but good to you."

"Of course. Thank you for all you've done." She wouldn't argue.

"And for all I've done for your girl."

"Yes. For everything. I can never thank you enough."

"Are you saying good-bye?"

"No." Not yet.

"There's no life for you out there, not for a girl like you."

"A girl like me . . . You've said that before." Gussie held to the cold doorknob, nearly swung the door shut, nearly made her way down the hall, but Mrs. Shayd seemed locked there on the bed, Anne too watching Gussie. And Gussie couldn't bring herself to be harsh, seeing her child held in the woman's arms. "I'll be fine, Mrs. Shayd, whatever I choose."

"You'll be alone. Anne will be alone."

"I'm going out, just for a while. That's all."

"You'll be alone. What do you know? What do you know of a girl like Anne?"

"You can sit here with Anne, Mrs. Shayd. I would thank you for it. You know best. If you think it's too cold outside, then she should stay with you. I'm going out to the celebration."

"There's nothing out there."

"I need to go."

"You'll get caught up. You'll get carried off."

"I'm not going anywhere." But she thought of the air, of the bonfires, of the distances, of Mr. Foster and the expeditions that always took him beyond the bounds. "I fed Anne, but if she fusses, you can feed her a bit of milk."

"I know."

"Or give her some porridge."

"I know how to care for a child."

"I appreciate it."

"You don't appreciate it."

"I'm going outside, just for a short while."

"Go, then."

◆ ◆ ◆

From the hotel stoop, Gussie looked up toward Cedar. The crowd swarmed the intersection. The evening was packed with voices. The noise wouldn't stop. Gussie tried to separate out the voices, but she heard only the chaotic roar, the pitch of engines, shouts without shape. The stuffy box of Mrs. Shayd's room, the woman's voice— *You'll be alone*—followed her, turned her away from the crowd, looking for a stretch of land where she could hear her thoughts.

Gussie started downhill toward the rail, the station lights a warm nimbus. Across the tracks, she cut south onto the old curving streets, among the ruined buildings, the warehouses on their gravel flats, to the banks of Sugar Creek. Feeling her legs and the depth of her lungs, she walked beside the creek. More than a year had passed since she'd found herself abandoned in this town, and in that time she hadn't walked straight toward anything without circling back before dark. Now she walked west toward night. On through the scrub and cottonwoods, the trees bare against the sky and silver clouds.

At the narrowing of Sugar Creek, she came finally to Rawlins Spring, the green seep on the edge of winter. There was watercress here. The spring brimmed, sheened the sand toward the creek. At the edge, she crouched, cupped the cold water, drank the sweetness, shook the drops from her fingertips. The last gleam of the fallen sun brushed the hilltops, bled into the clouds. She looked back toward town.

For a moment, the clouds shredded with the wind, and the stars washed suddenly over Rawlins in astounding numbers, dazzling the earth. There was moisture on the air. A train inched in from the west, the snake of lit windows alive with passengers hanging out into the chill. They all yowled at the clouds, at the looming night, at the black machinery of the train, the steam and coal dust, the rails hot from the pressure of all that rolling weight, yowled at the open directions, east and west, north and south. The beacon was a solid white beam in the thick air. Gussie, too, yowled, a lone sound beyond the edge of town, a sound that caught her by surprise. She cut her voice short, listened to the sound die in the loose ends of dusk.

She came back into Rawlins along Sugar Creek, crossed the rail where the train idled. The passengers shouted from the windows.

"Let's hear a song!"

"Throw me a bottle of something."

She waved, smiled, moved on. They could all find their own diversions. There were thousands of miles to go. Up onto Cedar, she stopped in front of the Foote icehouse, took the long view down the street. The crowds roared. Horses shied at the flare of horns. Folks danced out into the wide street, jumped the ruts. Great bonfires spit and sparked. Men challenged the flames, caught women and dragged them toward danger, freed them at the brink. Gussie stared the whole throng down, but no one stared back. She scanned for Katherine and Elizabeth among the waves of sparks, the smoke in black screens, but the girls were nowhere.

Gussie looked back up at the facade of the icehouse. The lettering had mostly faded, flickering now with red, the same flicker that lit her own arms, her skirts. In the end, everything in Rawlins yielded under the blast of the sun, under the wind laden with bits of desert, and the sudden storms that rose from the west. In the vast shallow platter of Wyoming, the town was defenseless.

She left the icehouse, moved along Cedar, wove among the bonfires, the heat tightening her skin. Boys flooded around her, past her, into the seethe of burning wood, the fume of paint and varnish. Long-spun currents of joy stirred the dry street. And then the young men caught Gussie—no escape—merged her into the flow around the largest fire, all the young women drawn into the circle. They danced, hands linked, ran sideways, heads thrown back as much from the pressure of the heat as from the thrill of the night. And then the line broke into groups and they all ran along Cedar, past the men and the saloons, crowded the steps of the post office, and the boys kissed the girls. Gussie felt the bodies all around her, the heat of their limbs from the fire, from their desire, and she saw the firelight on their lips—and then they all jumped the edge of the marble steps, the boys first, the girls in pursuit, pulling each other, hand to hand, retreating. Gussie watched them go, still felt the fire's heat on her neck, on her hands.

Mr. Foster came out of a saloon, headed east, passed Gussie, slowed and tipped his hat. "Good evening, Mrs. Locke. These boys want a bit of tomcatting, don't they?"

"Yes, sir."

"Given the right fuel, people go off their heads, don't act themselves. You should keep yourself out of harm's way. Walk with me, won't you?"

She took up his pace, followed along. Mr. Foster cut north a block, walked straight west down Buffalo, toward the edge of town, where the small trees ended. They passed the last of the bonfires, the last of the businesses. Buffalo Street lost its curbs, lost its straight line, headed down a long hill toward endless ranks of hills farther on, blackness without bound. The buzz of electric wires was lost. She felt the road beneath her feet, heard Mr. Foster's steps in the pattern of her own steps. He slowed, stopped. He was a black shape. He turned, and she turned. They looked back into Rawlins. The bonfires were far, intermittent, a fallen constellation.

"That's a small place, Mrs. Locke," Mr. Foster said. "It has everything you could want, if that's what you want. Light, and people, and the rail." He peered at her in the dark. "Mrs. Locke?"

"Yes?"

"You ought not to be off by yourself. It's dangerous. You know that, don't you?"

"But you asked me to walk with you."

"Yes. That's not my point. The world is dangerous."

"What could happen?"

"Nothing. Something. I don't know. Coyotes. Lunatics."

"I can handle myself."

"I don't doubt it."

"And I'm not alone."

"Of course. I'll watch out for you."

"I can't stay in Rawlins. I can't stay with Mrs. Shayd any longer."

"Has something happened?"

"It's a long string of things happening. I'm just at the end of it now. I can't stay with her. Anne and I can't stay."

"She seems a good woman, but I'll take your word."

"I can work for you?"

"Yes. That's what I've been trying to figure."

"I can tend sheep. I can repair a road. Anything. I can work beside a man. As long as I'm not alone."

"Mrs. Locke, you'll have Anne. Always will." He laughed, started them back along Buffalo, placed his hand on Gussie's elbow to guide her. "Things will go crazy now, with the war over. But I'll find something for you. We'll have to think about your daughter. We can't have a girl like that in rough circumstances."

♦ ♦ ♦

Gussie and Mr. Foster entered into the brightness of the hotel parlor. Mr. Foster stopped. Gussie walked a few steps, turned.

"Thank you," she said. "I appreciate what you've done."

"I haven't done anything, Mrs. Locke," he said.

"You saved me from lunatics and coyotes."

"Well, yes, certainly." He smiled, tightened his jacket, readied to leave. "I'll come by tomorrow to talk with Mrs. Shayd."

Katherine and Elizabeth came into the parlor from beyond the desk. "You can't talk with Mrs. Shayd tomorrow," Katherine said. "She's gone, sir."

"Why are you still here, Gussie?" Elizabeth said.

"What do you mean?"

"Mrs. Shayd told us you were leaving, Gussie, that you'd already left," Elizabeth said. "She was going out to meet you, to take you where you're going, to help you with the girl."

"The girl?" Gussie said.

"To help her?" Mr. Foster said.

"She got Anne all packed up, like you wanted," Elizabeth said.

"I wanted?" She looked at the girls, the tall slender girls, shoulder to shoulder, watching her. Their hair was smooth against their skulls. They nodded, the clusters of electric lights in their dry eyes. "What did I want?"

"To take Anne," they said.

"She took Anne?"

"Yes," they said. "To meet you."

"When?"

"Two hours ago," Katherine said. "Maybe three hours ago."

Mrs. Shayd was gone. Anne was gone. Gussie stood there in the parlor, on the Persian carpet with its intricate whorls and blood-red shadows, with the potted palms a vision of a far-off climate, with the light hot and close and sparkling, and she thought she didn't know the place, she had the time wrong, it was morning not evening, it was last year or next year, or she'd forgotten something, a plan that had started without her, carried her child away. Those lovely girls approached, reached for her, their heads tilted in concern, the light stringing through their hair, light shaping the whiteness of their skin. She didn't want to touch them, almost feared that they'd pass right through her, pass right on and leave her in the empty hotel. She turned, found herself against Mr. Foster, his tall form in black. The weight of his hands on her shoulders. "Where did they go?" he said.

"I don't know," Gussie said. "I can't think."

"No," he said. "Girls, where did Mrs. Shayd take Anne?"

"To find Gussie," Elizabeth said.

"We thought it was Gussie's idea," Katherine said. "We thought Gussie was leaving us without saying good-bye."

Mr. Foster held Gussie tighter, pushed out through the door into the cold dark and wind. "We'll find them," he said, and they stood on the stoop a moment, looked up toward Cedar at the bonfires dying away. "Don't worry, Mrs. Locke. Just a bit of confusion—I'm sure that's all it is."

She saw the flames and embers in the distance, felt the touch of Mr. Foster, warm and firm, inhaled the scent of him, pipe smoke and road dust. He took her out through the town. There was no sign of Mrs. Shayd and Anne at the rail station, and the clerk said that Mrs. Shayd hadn't bought a ticket, hadn't boarded a train. Up and down the streets, no one had seen them, and then Judith Lucero said, "They gone to the livery."

And at the livery, Joseph said, "She took a buggy. Just for a drive, to go visiting. Told her to wait till morning, but she had a buzz in her hat. I seen her go west on the Lincoln Highway. My guess is she'll stop in Creston Station. That's about twenty-eight miles, ain't it? You got your automobile, Mr. Foster. Ain't too fast a horse I gave her that you can't catch her up if need be. Ain't much choice of a road once you get out of town. But she ain't a thief. She'll be back, sure as rain."

"She won't be back," Gussie said. "And it hardly ever rains around here." But she imagined a cold rain streaked with scraps of hail, Mrs. Shayd flying flat out across a landscape, the horse roiling the highway with its hooves, the hood of the buggy scooping too much cold air, Anne bound in a blanket, her breath icing the wool, her eyes open to the storm. Too great a distance already?

Mr. Foster was pulling her back to the center of town, and she went with him. "You grab something warm, Mrs. Locke," he said, "and I'll swing around to pick you up." He left her, ran toward the garage.

She made her way back to the gabled room, and there she sat on the cot, the only light a faint slice from the hall. If there was anyone else in the hotel, she couldn't hear a single movement, already couldn't remember if she'd seen anyone in the parlor, in the long halls, steep stairwells. She heard only the wind trying to work its way in around the shingles, the sashes, whistling the chimneys and vents. If she sat there long enough, she might learn the meaning of that wind, hear the shape of the land it crossed, understand its patterns, but for now the sound seemed to be pure pressure, growing colder, sealing the box of the hotel. If she had ever lived in that room, she now wasn't sure. If she'd ever awoken to the soft cry of her child, she now couldn't bring that sound to mind. All of Anne's clothes were gone. The mattress from the crib was gone. And the blanket. And the soft rabbit with the black eyes.

Gussie saw the duffle that Mr. Dunn had given her. She knew suddenly that she was late—late for meeting Mr. Foster. She knew she would not be returning to the Brunswick. She quickly opened the duffle, pulled the drawers from the bureau and placed them on the bed. Here were the clothes she'd arrived in, that Mr. Dunn had bought, and she remembered the Laramie Plain and the sun huge as it cut up from the Red Buttes and the long early shadows of the four horses tethered to her small hands and the power of the turn of her wrist. She felt her palms, couldn't find the old calluses, the ridges, the tough work, work she'd done with ease. And here were the clothes she'd taken from Jack Fisher. Gussie quickly opened the buttons of her uniform and stripped it off, left it underfoot. Then she pulled on long johns and Jack's trousers and gray shirt, remembered his stride as he led her through the snowy Estes Park streets, he wasn't going to let go of her, wouldn't let her totter in her ridiculous baptismal boots, kept her walking straight without a moment to look back, to see if anyone followed. They were together. They were safe. And she would lead Anne too, wouldn't let go, would hold her straight.

Gussie's old walking boots felt tight on her feet, high on her ankles. The rest of the clothes she stuffed into the duffle. She didn't have a proper winter coat to wear with trousers, only a dark blue cloth coat that matched the coats Mrs. Shayd had given to Katherine and Elizabeth. Gussie swung into Mrs. Shayd's room, switched on the light, and searched quickly through the boxes on the floor, some marked MR. SHAYD, one marked ROBERT. Dust and cobwebs. In the Robert box she found a heavy wool coat, dark brown, too small for a grown man but a good fit for a small woman. She pulled it on, fastened the elk-horn buttons, took up her duffle, and dove down the stairs, through the parlor.

Katherine and Elizabeth rose from a settee, tried to stop her, their slim arms outstretched. "Look at you," Katherine said. "You're not you."

"What have you done?" Elizabeth said.

"I'm gone, ladies," Gussie said. "I have a different job." She shouldered out the door, jumped the curb.

With the clatter of a cold engine, an automobile pulled down Fourth and stopped. Mr. Foster peered from the dim cowl of the cab. "Is that you, Mrs. Locke?"

"It's me, sir. Finally me."

"Right on time, young lady. Get in."

She maneuvered the running board, climbed into the automobile, her duffle in her lap. Mr. Foster swung around in the wide street, the headlights throwing weak yellow. The air, the remnants of smoke, the dust of Rawlins, flowed in over the half windscreen, in through the open sides, riffled the cloth top. No great speed, but Rawlins was soon gone.

◆ ◆ ◆

Mr. Foster drove as fast as the ruts would allow. Where stars had swarmed, there were now the mounting peaks of cloud. The long white Lincoln Highway fences stretched beyond the reach of the headlights, drawing the automobile west down an endless chute that seemed to create itself from the night. At each gap in the fences, north or south, they paused and looked into the darkness, but there was nothing to be seen. A train shunted past on the rails to the south, the sounds swallowed in distance and wind. Slowly the clouds devoured the stars. Soon there was nothing to the night but the long white fences and the road they contained.

And then snow started to sweep in from the west, long lines drawing through the headlights' beams. Mr. Foster stopped, closed

the top windscreen, took Gussie's duffle and placed it in the back
seat, pulled out wool blankets. They wrapped themselves against
the cold. The snow drifted in, settled in the ridges and valleys of the
blankets. And now all was white—the fences, the road, the air.

The automobile slipped between the fences, continued. Mr. Foster leaned forward, stopped on occasion to clear the snow from the
windscreen. "Don't worry," he said. "Your girl will be fine. Mrs.
Shayd is confused. That's all."

"She's not confused."

"She won't hurt the girl."

"I know."

"We'll find them."

"I know."

"Something happened. What happened?"

"She lost her son."

"Yes. Years ago. He left. Took to the rails. A good boy."

"He's dead."

"Goddamn . . . I'm sorry. You know that for sure?"

"He's dead, unless some miracle brings him back. But he's not
coming back, one way or the other, so he might as well be dead."

"No, you're wrong. Even if you never see a person again, you
want to know he's alive."

"What difference?"

He looked over at her. She looked back at him. They turned to
the road again, to the snow and the white. Miles passed.

The raw air filled the automobile, blasted and swirled, drew
Gussie's skin tight. Cold tears welled in her eyes. She wiped at the
tears with the blanket, huddled down in the seat. From stars to
snow, from Rawlins to nowhere, always without warning, Wyoming
changed abruptly, washed from sight in dodgy weather. They could
have been driving inside a cloud for all she could see—no way to
know if they were still on the highway that stretched from east
coast to west coast. No traffic, no passers, just the headlights' gradually diminishing reach, the fences nearly lost in white against

white, and a sudden ghostly passenger train, the string of lit windows pushed east by the wind, ungrounded and quick.

Even sunk into the blanket, Gussie still felt the wind. She held herself from shivering, held herself still against the jolts of the road. Immovable as she could make herself, she listened to the grind of the engine, the sputter and surge, the rattle of the sheets of metal, the hush of the snow. Gussie felt the cold in her belly. She struggled to wrap the blanket tighter, to ward off the cold. And in that engine sound, in the dampening snow, in Mr. Foster's cold cough and tap at the windscreen, Gussie heard Leota's voice muted on the drive from Frank Locke's house to the baptismal river. "Gussie," Leota said. "You're a sweet girl." And Leota turned back from her seat beside Frank Locke, reached for her girl, touched Gussie's skin, caressed her beside the eyes, beside the ears, brushed at her lips. Gussie sat still, unable to shift into her mother's touch, watched her mother's hand, the gentle working of the joints, the fragile bones and pallid skin. In all that wide-open storm, Leota was there with her, traveling, still with her, always. And if Gussie could speak to her mother, she would say, "I know. I understand what I've done. I did it for you."

Mr. Foster reached over, rubbed her back. "You okay, Mrs. Locke?"

"I've left my mother," Gussie said. "Left her in Colorado. She doesn't know where I am. I just left."

He rubbed her shoulders, his large hand soothing her locked muscles. "And what's the story of your husband?"

"I don't have a husband. Never did. Just a boy who entertained me for a day and a night. He went off to war."

"I think I guessed that already. But I'm not going to judge you, Mrs. Locke. There's enough trouble in this world already. Will this boy be returning to you and Anne?"

"He'll never find me."

"You don't want him to find you?"

"How could anyone find me out here?"

"Does the boy know your mother?"

"She doesn't know where I am."

"Alright." He brushed the snow from her hair, turned his focus back to driving. "Don't worry."

"I'm not worried. I can handle myself."

From Leota, the miles were stretching. Ahead, no telling how the road to Anne would twist. And the thought of Anne brought a heaviness to Gussie's chest—her milk still lingered. Anne was not fully weaned, not yet. Gussie felt the girl's grip on her, the vacant space in the automobile, the tenuous speed over the icy highway, the flecks of illuminated snow diving into the darkness of the automobile, the prickling assault.

Miles west, the snow thinned and fluttered and stopped altogether. The clouds split, long streaks of stars in the widening gaps. Gussie leaned out over the automobile door, looked up. The constellations emerged. The desert was white. The stars sparkled on the snow. The automobile wheels spun, pursued by a waxing moon. The moon's cold-captured sunlight brought a strange distance to the Red Desert and its vast eroded spaces, the lips and promontories, the road's careful plan, the rail line cutting away from the road and curving near. The clouds would close again, open again, teasing out the years to come, but for now the sky was clearing.

Mr. Foster slowed, stopped. "Look," he said. Down the center of the Lincoln Highway, tracks stretched beyond the light, the long even lines of wheels flanking a line of hoofprints. "That's Mrs. Shayd's hired buggy. What else could it be?" He pressed the accelerator, moved forward. "Your child is out here."

Maybe the tracks were nothing but a trick of the snow and the road. Gussie wanted to climb from the automobile and run ahead. Or she wanted to climb into the back seat and cover herself in the blanket and hide from the empty white. Or she wanted to run back along the Lincoln Highway and leave the task of finding or not finding to Mr. Foster. But she sat forward, focused long.

The tracks swerved right, passed through a gap in the fence. Mr.

Foster slowed again, turned at the gap. The headlights shone north into the Red Desert. He started slowly, off the highway, the engine hot and running a low murmur. Gussie watched the moonlight on the land. There was a hint of road, not much more than a trail, and for a long way it ran straight. The buggy wheels had compressed the snow into brighter reflection. The hooves had picked up the snow, moved it, left dark holes through the snow to the desert soil beneath.

The approach of dawn on the Red Desert, the moon still white in its ascent. A pale rose suffused this world, the snow washed with faint color, as if the desert glowed red from beneath the snow. On the steeper slopes, where the snow hadn't stuck or had slid away, dark slashes waited to claim their true colors—rusty stripes, charcoal layers.

The tracks continued. The automobile kept its momentum, Mr. Foster clutching the wheel. They hadn't spoken for miles, not since Mr. Foster said, "I don't know where she's headed out here. There's nothing. No road, even." The rabbitbrush scraped along beneath the chassis. The automobile lurched over buried stones, but it was a good machine, and it kept going.

Gussie watched the blades of grass tremble in the snow, the moon shadows multiplying the desert grass—a ghost prairie's worth of feed. The Red Desert rose and fell in ruined hills. She tried to guess where the tracks would turn, where they headed, but the only true guide was the reach of the headlights. The tracks took sharp turns, long curves. Mrs. Shayd would drive Anne north until the sun rose and the snow melted and the trail was lost. Maybe they would never find her. Maybe they weren't on the right plain.

"Are you sure she's out here?" Gussie said, and she felt a burn in her chest. She coughed, couldn't stop coughing until Mr. Foster slapped her on the back. She slumped in the seat.

"The tracks are clear," Mr. Foster said. "Look there."

She opened her eyes. She saw only the sky from her low vantage. The stars were gone. The moon hung in space, the horns pointing west. "A pink moon," she said. A delicate curve alone in a sky gone gray.

"There," he said. The automobile stopped. He pointed ahead.

She sat up, felt the crisp air at her lips, her nostrils. The whole Red Desert was there, all the miles opening to the sun ready to rise. No stars, but a small light shone on the near slope, a lantern hung from the hood of a black buggy. The lantern sputtered out or was lost to the brightening day. A horse stood near, head low, steam from his straight back.

Gussie dropped the blanket from her shoulders, climbed from the automobile, and ran ahead. Her steps plowed the dry snow. She moved fast. The automobile followed, Mr. Foster blowing the horn, the blast moving across the plain. Gussie passed the horse, saw the white salty streaks on its black coat—he had been driven too hard. And then the buggy loomed, a cracked wheel, the whole contraption leaning, not broken enough to tip, but it seemed to have stopped just as it had started to drive beneath the surface of the desert. Then she was at the buggy, looked in beneath the hood. Nothing.

The sun slivered up from the horizon, a brightness that burned away the dawn, bleached the moon, snapped long shadows behind the hills, gave a sharp depth to the footprints leading on up the slope. Gussie ran. The slope leveled, then fell away, and she gained speed. Now she saw the woman ahead, walking north, her shadow like a gray banner across the white. And in there, in the sound of the wind in cold swirls, in the full round of the sun risen and the tongues of its heat, in the miles toward distant mountains like hints of a farther world, a cold world, in there was the sound of Anne's voice, and Gussie accelerated, and the automobile crested the rise behind, and the automobile horn blew and blew, coming on.

Mrs. Shayd stopped, turned back. Gussie fought the air, seemed to run finally without breathing. Mrs. Shayd's head wrapped in a red scarf. Her body in a long dark coat. Anne on her hip. The girl in her blanket, her hand small and white on the dark of Mrs. Shayd's coat. And Anne watched Gussie. Anne moved her hand from the dark coat, let her small fingers stretch in the cold and the light. And there was Gussie. She stopped. Mrs. Shayd above her. The woman's large shoulders, the grip of her arm cradling the girl on her hip, the width of her hand red from the cold, scarred from the reins. Gussie looked into the woman's eyes. There was only the brightness of the unending white in there. Gussie looked at Anne. Anne looked back, made a small sound, not much more than a catch in her breath, that said she was hungry, that she needed to be taken from this woman. Gussie held out her hands. Mrs. Shayd handed Anne to her, and Gussie took that small weight, learned the feel of it again, almost as if she'd never known it at all. She wouldn't let go. She wouldn't forget that warm breath against her neck.

"You lost her, at least for a while," Mrs. Shayd said. "Now you know how it feels. I hope it hurts forever."

FOUR

Eden

Driving a rig with four horses, carrying gear, tools, supplies to Mr. Foster's operations, Gussie traveled the Great Divide Basin with Anne. The desert was immense, mostly untracked. Mr. Foster had sold his cattle, kept the sheep. He'd tapped out the copper at Encampment. He was digging around for something new. He was looking for oil. Didn't find much. Looking for gold. If he were looking for sand, he could have found enough for the entire world.

Mr. Foster said, "It takes a fortune to keep a fortune," and Gussie thought, *I won't ever be rich,* and Mr. Foster said, "This whole land here is a lid on a pot of whatever the country needs," and Gussie thought, *I'm just glad you're looking, because it gives me a job, and that's all I need.*

Buffered by pillows strapped to the wagon bench, Anne rode beside Gussie. Anne was three years old, a quiet child, always watching, listening. The light changed through the seasons. Spring light fresh in Anne's eyes, light on the dune grass and the blooming brush. Summer light red on Anne's cheeks, the flush of her white skin. Winter light immaculate and enveloping.

To keep Anne safe from serpents, cold, coyotes, from whatever slunk through the draws, and to calm Gussie's fears, Mr. Foster built a sleeping box for the child. The box was squared of mahogany, padded with silk, ceilinged with pressed zinc, ventilated through rows of curtained holes. Anne was safe in there, her cheeks pink with warmth and the perfume of her small body. In the wavering shadows of the campfire, Gussie cradled her daughter down into the soft chamber, arranged the blankets, slowly closed the lid against danger. Anne made no sound, no struggle, showed no fright at the darkness, the confines—Anne knew the soft fabric, the smell of the wood, the leak of desert air through the hidden vents, and maybe she knew the sounds Gussie made, the ritual of closing the camp for sleep. Gussie had thought to lock the box, but if she were to lose the key she'd have to break the box open—the hinges were inside—and she wouldn't risk the blows of a hammer, the splintered wood.

It was a moonless night. Gussie knocked the fire to coals, shook her blankets out and laid them beside the sleeping box, pulled the blankets around her settle on the cold ground. Starlight fell like gauze across the plain. The hills stood black in the night, the gullies channeling deeper shadow. The horses shuffled beneath the feeble trees. The branches reached into the mix of star and void. The leaves sheltered the small birds that flew boldly all day—the birds huddled now that the sun had set, the distance had disappeared, now that noises moved without focus or meaning, and fear shaped the darkness.

Gussie closed her eyes. She saw her daughter as she'd laid her in her sleeping box, the fall of her hair across her profile. But already Gussie couldn't reshape the girl's exact beauty, as if she had shut the lid before she'd gotten a clear view. Were the fingers laid flat on the pillow, or did they curl? Were the lips, those small petals, parted to breathe? Gussie couldn't remember the heat of the girl's skin. Couldn't remember the curve of her ears. The line of her chin. The planes of cheek and brow. Gussie touched her own face in the darkness, but she found no clues. She opened her eyes.

Starlight. The shape of the fire circle, the stacked pots. The shovel planted upright beside a barrel. The crate with the food. The wagon with its walls, small window, canvas, a solid square against the sky. In the cold months they would sleep inside those walls, Anne's box nested in the larger box of the wagon, suspended above the ground, rattled by the wind. But tonight the sleeping box was down in the roots, its brasses glinting, and Gussie beside it, her back pressed against the wood. Someone passing by would see no more than a crate of fine construction, and he might guess that it held instruments for triangulating the heights, hammers for breaking stone, vials for collecting specimens, potions for drawing out the secrets of the dust. And the passing soul would see Gussie lying there, rifle at the ready. No one would guess that a mother slept beside her sheltered girl.

Gussie lay close to Anne's dreams, but she didn't hold the girl, couldn't judge the small twitches of the limbs, couldn't catch the sleeping sounds at the girl's lips. She held her ear to the curtained air holes. Although the box was not magic, although the box could not make the girl disappear, still Gussie couldn't hear her daughter in the soft space, and for the length of a heartbeat each night Gussie thought that Anne was gone. Gussie laid her hand on the lid of the box. It might be her own pulse she felt in the grain of the mahogany, the smallest grain of perception. Anne's dreams might be smaller still, more faint, infinitesimal in their peaceful rambles. What those dreams could be, Gussie could only imagine. She saw her girl traveling over the desert, mute, nothing but the creak of the wagon and the dry steady wind to tell the passage of the miles. Anne might dream of sage plains as soft as a blanket, sunsets as red as a cherry phosphate, and skyfall stars like sparks. Anne was a bright girl. She might dream of long faint roads through the desert, roads that turned back and crossed themselves, that never issued out from the badlands and alkali sinks.

When Gussie reached to open the box each morning, she always paused a moment, ran her hand gently across the lid, some sort of superstition that she never quite deciphered. Then she worked the latch and raised the lid. Anne, eyes wide open, looked up at her, made a sound, stretched her arms.

◆ ◆ ◆

Mr. Foster came along on the wagon, once each season—spring, summer, fall. He wanted to see the samples his crews laid out for inspection, run a fingertip through the soil and flecks of stone. Gussie sat straighter, wouldn't let him take the reins. "I can't have you doing my job," she said. "Least I can do is ferry you where you need to go."

Mr. Foster was probably the closest friend Gussie had had in her life—the hours on the wagon, the time in Rawlins huddled over maps, the long cold nights with the sky slowly whirling, the way he knocked the dust from his hat, his squint at noon. He asked her about her life, and she tried to answer.

"What was your father's occupation?" he said.

"My daddy was a trader, a laborer, nothing constant, but he'd take on any job that came along. I saw him chop wood for five hours straight without stopping. He was strong."

"He was like you. What about your mother?"

"Leota is slender and pale. Her eyes are blue as ice."

"Like Anne."

"She's good with beautiful things, like books and sewing. She's smart, I think, smart enough to care for me when it was just her and me alone. If she had to work, she worked—probably didn't give it a thought. Thin crust, rhubarb—I always remember her pies, ain't ever tasted anything as good."

"Did you want to be like her, to learn to sew or bake?"

"I got my own interests, and she helped me with those when she could."

"No pressure to follow her. That's good."

He could have asked her anything—about the pain of childbirth, the headaches that came with her menstrual cycle, the space Jack Fisher took in her memory—and she would have worked up an answer of some sort, even if it had embarrassed her. Given the chance or the nerve, what would she have asked him in return? *Have you ever loved anyone? Have you ever taken a girl to bed? Have you forgotten the girl, and has she forgotten you?* Maybe these were the things a friend could ask a friend. But, of course, he was upstanding, and he would not have behaved as she had behaved, forgoing innocence. And even if he had strayed he wouldn't tell her, make it public.

She was nervous with him near. He was as unlike her as a person could be. He was smooth, educated. She saw his long fingers, and she wondered if his grip was strong. If he were to lace his fingers with hers, would she be able to extract herself? He never reached for her. He watched the miles pass beneath the wheels. He whistled long notes without shape. Sometimes he would not utter a word for half a day, and then he would start talking a steady stream until they reached camp for the night. He described his acquisitions—a telescope that laid out the dance of Saturn's moons; a bronze statue of a bighorn sheep.

Winters in Rawlins, together in Mr. Foster's guesthouse, Gussie and Anne stoked the fire, listened to the wind and the trains, watched the sky. When the weather cleared, they drove the wagon west to Rock Springs or Green River City, east to Cheyenne, not always on an errand for Mr. Foster, sometimes just to be out of reach of the night sounds on Walnut Street. "I'd rather have strange sounds in strange places than the sounds that I remember, that take me back to my time in the Brunswick Hotel," Gussie said, and Anne said, "I like to travel. I like a room in a hotel. I like to come back to Rawlins."

Mr. Foster took Anne and Gussie to the picture shows. He had his cook lay out meals for them at the kitchen table. He taught Anne checkers and gin rummy, and as they played Gussie would return to the guesthouse, sort the gear for the next departure. The hours passed, she moved in the dimness of sunset, folded warm clothes, wrote a list of staples for a week or a month in the desert. When she lit a few lights and turned the covers on Anne's bed, the girl returned. Mr. Foster watched from the kitchen door as Gussie took her safely in.

"He let me win the games," Anne said. "I don't want him to let me."

"He's being nice."

"He don't play as good as he can."

"He wants it to be easy for you."

Gussie didn't know what Anne and Mr. Foster talked about when they were alone. She could hardly imagine them sitting across from each other at a table in the front parlor or the library, a bright light casting shadows. If Anne was asleep, if night had taken the view and the lights burned a steady low wattage, Gussie might sit across from Mr. Foster, though it hadn't happened yet. She always put Anne to bed, extinguished the lights, climbed into her own bed—it seemed a luxury to sleep when her child slept.

Mr. Foster was not the right man for her, or she was the wrong woman for him. Gussie had seen how his eyes caught only her edges, though sometimes she thought he was just being a gentleman. Maybe he looked at her when she looked away. She couldn't imagine his hands reaching to touch her arm, shoulder, to rub the back of her neck—she knew she would laugh, duck from beneath his touch. She knew him too well, no mystery when she saw him, no surprise. She remembered Jack Fisher riding his wobbly bicycle in the Sunday morning light, and he seemed to want to jolt her, knock her down, and then the altitude and the sun against the rocks, his shirt gone, the shock of skin, the closeness. She'd seen Mr. Foster secrete himself behind a big sagebrush to make his morning ablutions, while she would stand right beside the wagon and wash her arms and face. And she knew of his closet of handsome clothes, the felt hats, waistcoats, the trousers that never lost their crease or shine—she couldn't dress well enough to grace his parlors.

Across the desert, Mr. Foster held Anne in his lap, and Anne leaned back into his narrow chest, her gaze half-lidded, languorous.

The girl wore whatever Mr. Foster had bought for her. Depending on the season, Anne would be in white skirts or wool overcoat, a hat to channel away the rain, or just a ribbon to fly with her hair. Gussie had seen Anne finger the hem of a new dress, inspect the lace, worry over the damage—sagebrush caught the fabric, red dirt shaded the white.

Anne held Mr. Foster's hand, sat tight beside him at supper. Gussie sat across the fire from them, watched Anne watch Mr. Foster, knew Anne's look from her own young rambles with Brud north of Ravenglass, knew that Anne waited for Mr. Foster to talk about the next miles they'd traverse or the danger of poisonous snakes or the ritual dances of coyotes and wolves. Of course Anne listened to whatever Mr. Foster said—he was as close to a father as she had, might be the only father she'd know—no way to predict where they would travel, mother and daughter, where they would find themselves in years to come, who they would love or lose. Sometimes Gussie wanted to take Anne back from Mr. Foster's side, hold the girl in her own lap, but she knew that pleasure and company were scarce in the Red Desert and that soon she and Anne would be alone again, only the smoke and the distance, the open miles, and Anne would lean against Gussie's side, take Gussie's hand, tuck the beautiful dresses away in the wagon, and put on clothes that could take the wear of the desert. And then Anne would be vigilant again, counting the spikes of the blue gramma grass, scanning for raptors, warning Gussie of sand or boulders ahead.

At night, when the weather allowed, Gussie and Mr. Foster laid out a tarpaulin on the ground, their bedrolls padding their bones, the sleeping box as windbreak. Anne had outgrown the box, and now she carefully laid out her own blankets, tugging at the corners to square and smooth the fabric. Beneath the stars, they all lay side by side, Anne in the middle. The stars filled the entire basin, no forests to catch the constellations, only the famished cottonwoods. Gussie looked directly up into the night. The earth turned. The stars surrendered their positions.

Gussie separated the sound of the night air from the breath of the two beside her. There was damp warmth to the air they expelled. Anne was already asleep, her nostrils whistling. Mr. Foster hadn't yet fallen into his usual deep rumble, the indecipherable words that emerged from his dreams. Anne was small in the space between them. Anne was safe—the bones and smarts and muscles of these two people to protect her. Gussie couldn't remember ever sleeping between Brud and Leota. She thought it might have become a habit hard to break. The iron bed, the springs, would have conducted each pulse, set up opposing rhythms. Gussie would have slept to those rhythms, to the gradual shifting of weight. With each inhalation, she would have tasted her parents' musk, the mix of their work and soap and sweat. She might awake and find them entwined against her, might feel the force of their bodies, their sleeping minds placing them alone together. No, she'd never slept in the bed with her parents. And she never slept on the tarpaulin with Mr. Foster without Anne lying between them. But if Anne took sick, slept in the shelter of the wagon, if Mr. Foster and Gussie were alone, would their sleep and dreams roll them together, would they startle awake, find themselves entangled?

Gussie sat up, looked toward Mr. Foster in the darkness. He was no more than a shape, darkness against darkness. He could have been looking directly at her, but she wouldn't have known. He would see her small form, her wild hair, in the lower stars. He could have been looking at Anne, thinking—what?—that the girl needed a home? Needed a father?

Gussie lay back down, looked up at the constellations, named each shape she could remember, named them again, finally closed her eyes, said, "Mr. Foster. What is your plan for us?"

She heard him roll away, the movement of his blankets over his body. "Tomorrow we go up to Freighter Gap," Mr. Foster said, a whisper, nearly as faint as the starlight. "I got a new map. A treasure map." He laughed. "I can find something else for you to do," he said. "Two years out here is enough."

"Enough for what?"

"For your daughter. The desert is empty."

"She has me."

"She doesn't know any different."

"I'm not enough?"

"It's dangerous out here."

"I know how to take care of myself."

"There are other jobs I could give you that would be easier on the girl."

"What could be easier?"

"A house job. A town job."

"I've tried that."

"You could try again. I'll watch out for you. You'll have a clean job."

"I don't care about clean."

She thought of Mr. Foster's cook, and the white kitchen, and the cook's fresh uniform. And beyond the kitchen, the carpets that dulled the steps in the halls, the draperies that killed the winter drafts. It was possible to shut down every window, to close off the sunlight even at the height of a summer day, to live in electric light. Gussie would have her own uniform, the black skirt, the pockets for keys and rags, and the schedule—service at dawn, attention at noon, the sheets ironed. At some point, she thought, she would descend the stairs, and below, in the foyer, an oblong of sunlight would flash across the floor, a moving form at the center of the brightness, and then the light would cut with the shutting of the door, and as Gussie waited on the stairs, halfway up, Anne passed, the crispness of her schoolgirl uniform, the ribbon in her hair, no glance to the side as she proceeded straight out of sight, toward the parlor, and then Anne's voice was swallowed into the mixture of other voices. Gussie heard Mr. Foster. She heard a young lady or two or three. And other men. Gussie continued down the stairs, alighted in the foyer where the sun had just passed, and she turned, found a corridor, continued into darkness where light bled from beneath each closed door. She opened a door, crossed the room to the window, leaned to the glass, forehead to the pane, and looked out on Rawlins. For a while no one passed. She saw only the spruce and cottonwood branches growing higher into the wind, and smoke shearing from a chimney, and clouds toying with the horizon of barren hills. Then a woman approached from the lower streets. Gussie judged the gait—it wasn't Mrs. Shayd. The woman turned east, quickly out of sight. Then a man passed. Then two women. A wagon. A truck. She watched a long while. Later, when she returned to the corridor, she would hear Anne's voice, but already it would be lost in the maze, and Mr. Foster's voice would be in there somewhere too—*Come here, Anne, little girl. Tell me your plans. What do you need?*

"I won't work in Rawlins, sir," Gussie said. "Do you understand? Because of Mrs. Shayd, of course. Please don't ask me again."

"I won't. But God will damn me if any harm comes to you or this girl. I'll damn *myself*. Let me do what I can. Please. I'll buy you a thicker blanket, a longer rifle, a pistol."

◆ ◆ ◆

At a spring below Chalk Butte, Gussie filled the water barrels. Anne peeled off her shoes and socks and tested the spring with her toes, then lay flat on the rocks, lowered her face to touch her reflection, waited for the image to settle again. How could she hold herself that still, still as marble? Maybe she looked down through the spring to the underside of the desert, or she looked at the clouds moving in the captured sky, wondering which clouds were real, which sky held the real blue. She might ask a question of that pretty girl in the spring, but even a whisper would wreck the image.

"Come away, Anne," Gussie said. "Come away from the water."

Anne didn't move. She hovered at her reflection.

"We have to go," Gussie said. "North."

"I want to stay." But slowly Anne rose, pulled on her socks and shoes. She came toward Gussie, watching the ground. When her shadow touched Gussie's feet, Anne stopped, looked up, stared at her mother, seemed to study Gussie's shoulders, neck, face. And she reached to Gussie's upper arm, pulled Gussie forward and down, so that they looked at each other eye to eye. Anne's fingers combed up through Gussie's hair, worked to shape the tangles. With a sigh, Anne abandoned the hair and took a moment to dig the sleep from the corners of Gussie's eyes. Then she pushed Gussie away, stood back and stared again.

"Am I okay?" Gussie said.

"Look in the water," Anne said. "You will look different in the water."

"No. I always look the same." She turned from that small, waiting face, climbed onto the wagon and took hold of the reins. Anne sat beside her. As the wagon started to move, Anne patted her mother's hand. The girl's touch was cold, and Gussie moved her hand away.

◆ ◆ ◆

In late May, they descended the plain from the distant teeth of the Wind River Range. Gussie followed a long, straight road south across the flats. They neared the Big Sandy River, and a marsh came in beside the road—a confusion of birds, cottonwoods, willow scrub. Gussie stopped the wagon, watered the horses and let them loose in deep fodder, took Anne to the cool grass where the buck-bean bloomed. Anne picked the stalks of clustered yellow flowers, laced them around her wrists, ankles.

The sun climbed, and the blaze flattened the reddish hills. In the morning heat, Gussie heard the air moving through the brush, the catch of birds' wings, the slow bubbling water, the shuffle of the horses. And she heard Anne's small sounds, always there, the sighs as she bent to her work, the snap of the buckbean stems. Gussie patted the girl's pale hair. Focused on a garland, struggling to split the stems and attach each to the next, a multiplying of yellow, Anne tipped away from Gussie's touch. The joints of the garland were beaded with white sap.

"Will you give me a necklace?" Gussie said.

"These are mine."

"Will you make one for me?"

Anne didn't look up. "Pick me some more buckbean."

Gussie reached for the buckbeans in the sunlight, came back with a burst of yellow. She placed the stems at the cross of Anne's legs, and Anne began to weave. She made what she could out of what Gussie had provided, her small fingers working swiftly, and then she rose to her feet, looped the garland over her forearm, and stood there facing her mother. Anne took Gussie by the ears, tilted her mother's head, trying to level it, focused close on Gussie's forehead, on her hair, touched her mother on the brow as Gussie would touch her child. "There you go, sweetheart," Anne said, and she took the garland from her forearm and placed it on her mother's head. "You are pretty, my dear," Anne said. "You are my sweetheart. Do you know that?"

"I know."

"You are the only one I love."

"Of course I am."

"I'll never leave you, little girl," Anne said, and she kissed her mother beside each eye.

Gussie felt the quaver of the girl's lashes, saw the focus of the blue eyes. "We'll go now," Gussie said, and she stood, scanned for the horses.

"We'll go now," Anne said, taking Gussie's hand.

◆ ◆ ◆

Down the cloudless miles they traveled through the Eden Valley, across the Big Sandy River and Little Sandy Creek. Here, west of the Great Divide Basin, the land was fertile, plowed in dark curves, budding with alfalfa, timothy. Fences strung wire beside the road, sectioning the land. Far to the left and right, groupings of ranch buildings anchored windbreaks of young trees, black Herefords in the shade. The Eden Canal fed the ditches, drew water from the cold-rushing sources, flooded the fields.

They passed on south through Farson. And then the dark squares of Eden, the flash of a windmill, gleam of windows. To shake loose the lazy heat, Gussie urged the horses into a trot, and Anne sat up straighter, shaded her eyes against the afternoon. Soon a broken corral drew past, then a shed, and a house with a deep porch, clapboard losing its white. The horses' steps echoed clean and close. Rapidly the far end of town approached, and Gussie didn't want to speed into the empty view. Not yet. She reined the team slower.

Children came out to the fences, onto stoops, to watch the rig pass, small children, brown from the sun. Anne leaned hard against her mother's side, watched as the children ran along, threw sticks at the rig's wheels, circled, shouted—

"How far north you been?"

"You stopping?"

"Seen anything?"

"Hello?"

"She's a girl."

"What's her name?"

When they got no response, the children dropped behind. Gussie parked the rig beside the Eden store. Anne held to Gussie's side as they rounded the building, came up onto the boardwalk. Already the children were far toward the north end of town, their voices lost in the dust and shimmer.

"Where are they going?" Anne said.

"To get ready," Gussie said, "in case another wagon enters town."

"Is that fun?"

"They want to see new things."

"I'm lucky."

"How?"

"They want to see me."

In the store, Gussie searched the shelves for something to ease the miles—a pair of gloves, a tin of powdered chocolate. Anne touched everything Gussie touched. They turned a spool of ribbon, unfolded cotton towels, tried the weight of a can of kerosene, tested an apple—"Where can something like this grow?" Anne whispered.

The clerk emerged from beyond the shelves in back, came up behind them, tapped Anne on the shoulder. "How old are you, little lady?" he said.

Anne spun around behind Gussie, didn't answer. But when Gussie said, "Anne is four," Anne took a step forward and said, "Anne is four."

The clerk led Gussie through the Eden store, and Anne followed. "It's been a year since you've been through, ain't it?" he said, pulling a cone of sugar from a barrel. "One of these years you'll figure this is a good place to settle." He laughed, tore a length of brown paper from a huge roll, wrapped the sugar.

"One visit a year is about right for this town," Gussie said, and she laughed too.

"Have I been here before?" Anne said, following them toward the canned goods, the potted meat, fruit in syrup.

"Sure you have, little lady," he said. "I remember you. You come through town in May. But you leave too quick."

"Can we live here?" she said.

"I don't see why not," he said. "It's a nice place."

"There's nothing to stop the wind," Gussie said. "Those sad windbreaks won't do much."

"There's nothing in the whole of Wyoming that can stop the wind," he said. He took from Gussie the cans she'd chosen, returned to the counter, laid the cans beside the sugar. He wrote the items on a pad as he placed each in a box. He gave Gussie the total, and she paid. Then he leaned out over the counter, looked down at Anne. "You hungry, little lady? I could set you at a real table and give you a lunch of cold chicken and potatoes."

"Can we stay, Gussie?" Anne said.

Gussie looked at the clerk. He was a young man with a scarred, closed eye. The store was empty except for them.

"I won't charge you for the meal," he said. "If you see a soul only once a year, you should feed that soul."

"Is that in the Bible?" Gussie said.

"I wouldn't know. It's my own thought. Don't need a book to tell me how to be a good person."

"Okay. We accept. Wouldn't want to get in the way of someone being good."

He led them through a side door into the café. That room was also empty. Back among the tables, into the kitchen, he sat them at a table below a window. The view was open to the east, no ranches, no houses, just a fence and a fallow field, diminishing to nothing across the miles. He uncovered some dishes on the counter, made up two plates, set them on the table before Gussie and Anne, gave them napkins, clanked down some silverware, poured glasses of milk. He pulled out a chair, sat with them, helped Anne cut her chicken. "It's good?" he said. They nodded. He kept reaching, helping Anne with her meal, and the girl would stop and watch his hands, then sit forward again and take her fork in hand.

Anne finished her meal, raised her glass, drank the cold milk in big gulps. "We could live here," she said to Gussie.

"We could," Gussie said, "but why here more than any other place?"

"I want to see those children again."

"There are children in every town. They aren't special."

"They want to know my name."

"Even if you told them your name, you'd be gone before they could use it."

The clerk stood, cleared away the plates, poured more milk. "Drink," he said to Anne. "There's as much as you could want." He watched her drink, the glass unwieldy, the milk bubbling. Then to Gussie he said, "Where are you two headed?"

"East past the dunes, to the Red Desert, and back to Rawlins."

"There are easier roads if you go south and around."

"I know that."

"And it would be faster, I'm sure, going south. Might save you a day. So you could stop here." He looked square at Gussie with his one good eye—it was green, flecked with gold, damp around the edge from strain or rheum. "Give the girl a night in town. It must be a while since she's seen sheets and a mattress and maybe we could get a dance together—we got a hurdy-gurdy—and a game of marbles for the children." He kept looking at Gussie, slid his hand forward till his little finger grazed the side of her hand where it rested.

"I'm not a hurdy-gurdy girl," Gussie said, trying to smile at her joke.

"I didn't imply any such thing." He looked out the window, a square of daylight deep in his iris. "I was just talking music. Innocent music. A musical instrument."

"This town is too small for a hurdy-gurdy house anyway, I guess." She felt a moment of heat on her cheeks and neck.

He didn't look at her, just squinted slightly against the view. "I'm saying we could have a dance in the café. Move the tables."

"And marbles?" Anne said.

He looked at Anne, smiled. "If you don't know marbles, there are other games."

"I want to learn marbles."

"Someone will teach you."

"One of the girls or boys?"

"We have to keep going," Gussie said, and she slid her hand a fraction away from his, but he didn't look back at her. She knew how small the town was, how few the inhabitants. From the north edge of town, the Wind River Range could be seen thin on the horizon. From the south edge of town, the road ran on straight through the short grass, and if an automobile approached, its cloud of dust could be seen for twenty miles. At night, this town would float on the plain, a small glimmer south of Farson's slight glow, and in the

Big Sandy River and the net of irrigation ditches the stars would ripple, fight the current. "We can't stay here."

He turned to her. "I know," he said. "I just thought you might enjoy it."

She saw his bad eye, the stretched-smooth skin of the scar, the way only the bottom sliver of the iris showed beneath the fallen lid. She wondered if he wanted her to touch that eye, to lift the lid and allow him to see both sides of her at once. She was sure there would be no gathering that evening if she didn't stay. And even if she did stay, would the townspeople gather for just another teamster bound to disappear?

In the window light, she saw now that his scar skipped below his eye and caught his jaw with a thin white line. No way to know what had struck him, left him marked. The people in town might notice only his thick black hair, his small straight nose. And a dance, with food carried in, with the tables dragged to the walls, would get everyone moving too fast to notice much more than male or female, rhythm or lack, all too starved for company to care. At some point, Gussie would turn in this young man's hold, away from his scent of soap and flour, away from his neck and his white shirt, turn to see Anne, to let Anne know that she was seen, and there Anne would be with the other children, and a woman handing out sweets, cups of punch, reaching to turn Anne away from the dance, to lead her off to some other amusement.

Gussie stood and walked back to the store, with Anne and the clerk trailing behind. Then outside, the clerk followed with the box of goods, loaded it into the back of the wagon.

"Thank you for the meal," Gussie said. "I'll see you next year."

"I'll be waiting," he said. "Maybe you'll have a truck by then and more time to spare."

Anne held to Gussie's pant leg, looked up at the clerk, said, "I want to see those children again."

"I'll get them for you, little lady. You go ahead and climb up and get the rig turned around, and you'll see them." He walked toward the front of the store, waved his hand high without looking back, said, "Safe journey, ladies."

As Gussie pulled around, onto the road, they heard a bell ringing, and then voices from the north, and the children rushed into the street, stopped and watched. Anne waved, and the children waved back. Then the wagon turned fully south, and Anne settled again at Gussie's side. The last house was gone. They continued a mile into the open, then left the road.

◆ ◆ ◆

They drove east, away from the Eden Valley and the falling sun, and that night they camped in the Killpecker Dunes. Gussie stood beside the fire, looked straight down into the flames, the white tips of the windblown heat. She looked down at her own stark shape— trousers reddened by the dusty miles, creases flattened in the bright light, boots splitting from wear. Looking away into the desert, she held a smoky breath deep in her lungs, thought she heard the wolves on Steamboat Rim, guessed at the passage of elk, heard the rumble of wild horses in their flight from the ghosts of conquistadors. Each sound was a picture she'd been sketching mile after mile, year after year, until she almost didn't need sunlight to guide her.

No hint of the day remained on the western horizon. She could follow the path of the stars, beyond the dunes, toward the band of thicker air above the Eden Valley. Barefoot, she would feel the tracks her wagon and horses had made, feel each dig of a hoof, each long trace of a wheel's progress, until the hills sloughed away north and south and the lights of Eden wavered, ungrounded on the plain. Then the walls of Eden, the faintest buzz of electric wires, the turn of windmill blades, a dog huffing at something it had cornered, and music buried somewhere. She might face the Eden store and the attached café, the large windows full of music, full of men and women, some sort of waltz. This was no hurdy-gurdy house, no dance hall—that had been an unfortunate joke, and it had made the clerk uncomfortable. These dancers were upright, straight-backed, intent, but they let loose with a laugh or a whoop when the momentum whipped them off course for a step or two. Certainly, if the clerk had wanted to dance, he could have found enough souls. That's all he wanted, surely—to feel a beat take him beyond thinking, with someone guided safely within his grasp. She wondered why she had joked with him, refused his offer.

Gussie stepped away from the campfire, followed the path of her shadow, until her shape spread out on a thin layer of dark water. She sat down on the sand, removed her boots and socks, rolled up her trousers, extended her feet into the water. It was tepid, refreshing. From beneath the Killpecker Dunes the water had seeped, a pool of old drifted snow drifted again by sand, melted in the warming desert, a shallow pool that tasted of frost. The stars came down into that water.

Across the pool, firelight washed the wall of a dune, the sand steep and golden. Anne danced at the foot of that dune, on the narrow beach beyond the water. Her shadow extended far up the wall, shifted through poses, limbs stretching over the sand. Anne raised a hand, leapt to the side. And she was making sounds, rhythmic. Gussie waited for a pattern to surface. It might have been the desert cold driving the girl. Might have been the day's heat radiating from the sand. Or the clerk's offer of a dance. Or the glide of reptiles, insects, airborne seeds. But Gussie saw none of that in Anne's moves.

Had Anne ever seen a couple dance? Not that Gussie could remember. Had Anne ever heard music? Gussie thought back through the seasons. Birdsong, always, fast toward the next break or the sky. Songs through a church window, not for dancing. And in Rawlins there had been Mr. Foster's Victrola, set out on the porch above the town, and Mr. Foster and Gussie sat in the chairs, Anne in one lap or the other, listened to an orchestra glide through a symphony, with the pop of the needle across the black grooves, those pops the same sound as a sagebrush fire, so that Gussie's thoughts wandered more to the far miles and the starry sky than to Rawlins laid out below or to the crowded hall where the orchestra had recorded. People would wander up from the Rawlins streets, toward the sound, stand at the limit of the porch light. No matter the music, the people didn't dance—they remained still. So these steps, the way Anne ran across the base of the dune, trailing her shadow, jumping ahead, these steps could come from the girl's dreams, from her blood, from the surge of a desert spring, from the passage of clouds, the wind that sometimes tasted as if an ocean waited beyond the ridge, an ocean as broad and dark and unsure as the desert, the beach dry and blowing with the husks of dead things.

Gussie stood, rolled her trousers up her calves, stepped out into the water. It was little more than a large puddle, soft water in a depression. Reaching down, she trailed her fingers, raised her hand and tasted the drops that hung from her fingertips. The water tasted of sunlight and minerals, salt, ceaseless evaporation.

Now she was closer to Anne, closer to the wall of the dune that caught the firelight, seemed to gather and multiply the brightness. Anne drew her movements through the brightness, shaped her shadow tall or squat, long steps or short. Gussie heard the girl's voice, a whisper. "You stopping? Seen anything? She's a girl! What's her name?" The voice, the girl, the light against the dune. Gussie knew the words, the children of Eden not fifteen miles behind.

"Come here, little girl," Gussie said.

Anne stopped, turned, full on toward the light. "What do you want, Gussie?" she said. And she slipped down the sand into the water, and even to such a small girl the water was shallow. "Where does this pond come from?" she said, stepping slowly. "There's no creek here." Anne touched Gussie's hand, took hold.

Gussie bent to the girl, kissed the top of her head. "The water finds its own trails. There are lots of ways in and out."

"A creek's the easy way."

"Yes." She swung Anne's arm, turned the girl in a pirouette, and then they were both turning, sloshing through the water. "Do you know how to dance?" Gussie said.

"Do you?"

"I've danced before." She lifted Anne, held her on her hip. "I'll show you." Anne light as air, her arms linked around Gussie's neck, her cheek against Gussie's shoulder. Gussie turned, thought of what moves to make. She stomped her feet, and she added higher notes to the beat—a song she could remember just well enough to hum, to take them one-two-three through the dark and the firelight, destroying the mirror of the water's surface.

◆ ◆ ◆

In the wagon, in the dark, they laid out their blankets, and then they were together in the warm wool. The night sky was high in the small window, the distance muffled by the thin walls. In the morning, Gussie would cut southeast, cross the divide, find her way along Table Wash, follow Black Rock Creek toward Emmons Mesa and the Leucite Hills. There were few roads along those miles, roads so barely scratched into the surface that a shift in the angle of the sun would erase them altogether.

Gussie thought of the months, the miles, the sameness of the distances, the first sight of a crew camp when Anne would say, "There, I see the smoke, I see the tents, there." And then Anne would go quiet as they drove within earshot, and she'd climb down with Gussie and stay a half step behind as Gussie greeted the men, gave a list of the supplies she'd hauled. Always, at supper, Anne first sat against Gussie's side, but as the sky darkened, as the fire rose into fresh fuel, Anne would wander the circle, shyly standing near one man or another, watching him speak, watching him laugh, until the man reached for her, patted her shoulder or back, and then she'd move to the next, until finally, late, when sleep had almost taken her, she would be sitting beside a man, leaning her weight into him, and he would momentarily look down at her, smile and keep talking, and she would look up at him, watch his words.

The wind died completely. The horses shifted in the cold. Gussie laid her hand on the side of Anne's face, on the girl's shoulder, rubbed her back.

"Teach me another dance tomorrow," Anne said.

"I don't know but one dance," Gussie said. She remembered Jack Fisher's loud boots on the dance floor, the clock face that seemed to be deep behind ice. For a moment she thought she felt the pressure of his slender hand on the small of her back, thought she felt the queasy heat of wine in her gut. But the memories were gone with one big breath, and she laid her hand on her tummy. She was hungry. The lunch at the Eden café had been filling, so she'd made only biscuits for supper. She could reach out in the dark to find something to eat, but she held still, traced the faint pains and bubbles in her gut.

"Who taught you that dance?" Anne said, laying her hand on Gussie's back, rubbing slowly.

"Your daddy was the boy I danced with."

"My daddy. Do you know him?"

"I knew him." Gussie stopped a long moment, didn't breathe. And then she caught her breath. She rolled away from Anne, lay on her back, looked up at the window. The stars were swimming, unfocused. She cleared her throat, cleared her thoughts, spoke gingerly, carefully, teaching her child. "He's called Jack Fisher. I knew him before he left for the Great War."

"Is he dead from the war?"

"I don't know."

Gussie told her daughter what she could remember of Jack Fisher. She told her how in the morning light Jack had ridden a bicycle, coming at her as if he would run her down.

"He was teasing you, Gussie."

She told her daughter how Jack hefted his duffle onto his shoulder, how he carried it lightly balanced. He was careful setting it down—it held all his belongings.

"What did he have?"

"He had some shirts and sweaters and oilskins. And some trousers. And other things that boys carry. He gave me a shirt when I was cold."

"Would he give me a shirt?"

"I think he would."

"Would he give me a dress?"

"If you asked for one."

"Can I ask him?"

"I don't know where he is."

Five Finger Butte

Gussie traveled the desert, read the maps, set the shapes of the land in her head, picked her way along roads that were hardly roads at all, roads destroyed by their own poor design, no design but a man's desire for the quickest line. The wheels dragged their own tracks behind them, crushed the meager green. Gussie tired of the ruts, tired of the gumbo that trapped her wheels, and so she moved off the roads, remembered Mr. Dunn's hand held out against the distance, the way his hand swooped across the lay of the land, judged the driest way, the firmest ground, the snow shadows.

The desert light at dawn, ice on the water in the pail, frost on the red soil, and Anne asleep in the wagon, a five-year-old girl now. Anne with her chin pulled down toward the warmth of the wool, with her head on the pillow, beside the hollow where Gussie's head had just rested.

The desert light at noon, when the sun was tiny and far, when the shadows hid and the contours of the land were secret, and Gussie pulled the brim of Anne's hat tighter on her brow.

The desert light at dusk, when the miles lost dimension, and sound carried farther on the gray empty air, rarely any sound but the air itself as it pushed against the stones, the dry-scoured riverbeds, the sage and shrubby cinquefoil, rabbitbrush and sego lily.

Too many horizons between here and there, too few roads, and none of them marked, too many days of cloudless wind, too few nights when the day's heat lingered after the last white hint of sunset. They could travel for weeks without crossing paths with another traveling soul—no human figure to give scale to the buttes, rims, plains, erosions. But still, Gussie watched the distance, learned to differentiate wagon dust from the trails of migrating elk, a wild horse from a working horse, all at the full limit of the view.

They drove the rig up to the lip of a ridge, paused to spy the easiest way down, to note the gullies on the plain below that might send them off their line. This day the cloud shadows rode fast and small, and what green there was sparkled silver in the breeze. Anne pointed to where Gussie had already focused—the glint of sunlight on burnished metal, moving from the west toward the east, miles away. Gussie urged the horses, and the wagon started slowly toward the plain, the wheels fighting the brakes. When they reached the flats, they continued north, a notch in the far hills drawing them straight. Still the glint progressed from the west, and Gussie could now see the dust that the soul stirred. In an hour or two, their paths would cross.

Gussie kept to a direct line. Brush crackled beneath the wheels. She handed the reins to Anne—the horses kept pulling straight north. Gussie took out the new pistol from behind the seat, checked the chambers, returned the pistol to its spot among the boxes. She unlatched the door that concealed the rifle, took out the Winchester, found it loaded, placed it within reach, in plain sight. Then she took the reins back from Anne. They passed a scattering of white bones—no skull to identify, but it had been a lithe creature, probably a doe antelope. A rattlesnake slept on a flat white rock. The northern hills rose higher. The glint converging from the west was now clearly a person on a horse leading another horse or a black mule—two dots moving in tandem.

"Get on in the back," Gussie said. Anne climbed among the boxes, pulled a blanket around herself, her eyes deep in the shroud, looking forward past Gussie. This was the routine.

Through the years, they had encountered a man hunting wild horses, a man tracking elk, a man lost on a parched shortcut, a man too lonely to stop talking even when he'd ridden on into the morning, his voice drifting back in broken conversation, more than one sheepherder trailing sheep from the last green hollow to the next.

Earlier that summer, a man had taken an odd angle in their direction, pulled up behind them and followed their dust, slowly closed the gap as he scanned the empty land, and he had kept pace when Gussie urged her team faster. He'd drawn his rifle from his scabbard, fired ahead into the ground to each side of the rig, and Gussie had thought for a moment how fast she might make the miles, but toward what she didn't know, twenty miles at least to Mr. Foster's closest crew, so she said, "Anne, get on up here." Anne climbed from her shroud and settled on the bench and took the offered reins from Gussie, who said, "Pull the team up short, set the brake, hold the reins tight, get under the bench, as fast as you can, sweetheart, now." Anne did as she was told. The rig slid to a quick stop, and as Anne rolled down under the bench Gussie landed square on the ground beside the rig, raised the rifle to sight, took the best aim she could manage, took the recoil of two shots against her shoulder, and saw the man's hat fall away as he turned and fled.

"Okay," Gussie said.

Anne emerged, tied the reins to the brake pole, climbed down, stood beside her mother and looked back. "His horse is fast," Anne said. "Can I have his hat?"

The hat, white and broad, sat neatly on top of a sagebrush. Gussie and Anne walked back, and by the time they reached the hat and inspected the hole in its crown, the man had neared the far ridge, soon to disappear. Mother and daughter walked back toward the rig, and along the way Anne collected leaves in the upturned hat, and stones, and a length of shed snakeskin, a feather.

"This is a nice hat," Anne said. "Thank you for getting it for me."

"Lucky shot," Gussie said. "But luck or not, I had no choice in the matter." She glanced back at the ridge—he was gone—looked ahead to the trail she had plotted, judged the camp she would make at dusk, the small fire lit only long enough to heat water, the darkness full of sound, her pulse rushing in her ears, unlikely ever to slow, her breath unlikely ever to come easy again. As she lifted Anne up onto the rig, her arms lost their strength, the sky went white. She found herself prone, awaking, her face cool. She opened her eyes.

The sky was cloudless, so deep blue that it seemed stars would shine through. The edge of the rig loomed, and she could see how the westering sun angled, striking the ground beyond reach, the rabbitbrush blazing gold. Anne leaned in over her, poured water from a tin cup, and the water ran over Gussie's brow, channeled across her temples, circled her ears in cold lines.

"You fell asleep," Anne said.

Gussie sat up, cleared the water from her eyes, found that the hair at the back of her head was heavy, muddy. She thought a moment. She was in the Great Divide Basin. It was July. She was to supply the crew at the camp below Five Finger Butte. She would reach the butte tomorrow, if she kept a steady pace.

Anne stooped beside her, held the tin cup to her lips, and Gussie drank that spring water dense with the layers of dark, buried worlds. Anne removed a broad, white hat from her head and fanned Gussie with slow strokes. Gussie looked at the hat, took it from the girl, saw the bullet hole. And then Gussie was on her feet, out into the sun, looking north and south, turning to take in the red miles, the sand dunes ahead. No movement. No dust rising. No animal.

Gussie turned back to Anne, knelt before the girl. "You took care of me, sweetheart," Gussie said.

"Yes, I did. Are you sick?"

"I was scared. Were you scared, little girl?"

"I wasn't scared, Gussie. I thought you were sick. So I did for you to make you better."

"How did you know what to do?"

"When I'm sick, you cool my forehead. Don't you?"

"Yes. Always."

"And you talk to me."

"Did you talk to me?"

"Yes, ma'am."

"What did you say?"

"I patted your head and your shoulder. I said, 'There, there, Gussie. I love you, sweetheart. What do you need? Do you want some food? Do you want a blanket? You're on fire.' You didn't say nothing."

"How long?"

"I don't know."

"An hour? A minute?"

"I don't know time."

They climbed up onto the rig and continued north. Gussie handed the reins to Anne, and Anne took them without question, adjusted the leather so that it laced comfortably between her fingers. The girl leaned forward, squinted, made small sounds to the horses, turned the team around a brushy depression. Gussie watched the angles of her daughter's wrists, her forearms, listened to her calls, saw the trail still centered beneath the team's hooves. Anne was as much a shadow of Gussie as could be made from such a different quality of blood and breath, such a finer shape. Gussie touched Anne's knee lightly, and Anne jerked the knee away as if her concentration couldn't be disturbed.

"What if I hadn't woken up?" Gussie said.

"If you was dead?" Anne said, her eyes hard on her work

"Yes. What would you do if I was dead?"

"You're too heavy to lift into the rig by myself. But I don't want you tore up by a coyote. So I put stones on you?"

"That would work."

"Then I have to keep going, 'cause I can't reach the harness and the team has to get free to graze, so I find a man tall enough to reach."

"And where do you look?"

"For the man?"

"Yes. Where are you driving us now?"

Anne glanced sidelong at Gussie, raised an eyebrow, said, "We're going to Five Finger Butte, to Mr. Foster's crew."

"That's right. And how would you find it?"

"I just go to it. I make the horses pull me where I tell them."

"But where? Do you know where you're going?"

"Five Finger Butte," Anne said, and she handed the reins back to Gussie, stood up on the bench, shaded her eyes against the distance. "I go the easy way, if the horses don't get no rest or no grazing. I can give the horses water in a bucket. I can give them oats. I go 'round the sand dunes 'cause I can't get the rig out of sand—I'm too small. Then I go to Red Creek—it is dry now, so it is flat like a road. I look for mud and go around. Where the sand is in the creek I go up on the side. If I see it rain somewhere, where it falls around Red Creek, I drive out of the creek so a flood don't catch me. Then I see the butte. Yes?"

Gussie hadn't known what her daughter had learned. Anne knew the way. "And if you went from Rawlins to South Pass?" Gussie asked.

Anne explained the route.

"And from Honeycomb Buttes to Jep Canyon?"

Anne gave the quickest route and then the route with the most water.

"Killpecker to Flattop?"

Anne talked about the way the sun came around the hills. She balanced high on the bench and let her palm soar out flat across the land. She knew where the water gathered, where the creeks swelled to impassable, where the gumbo stopped a wheel dead. She told of the pollen green in the breeze. The walls of the badlands raining down scraps of red sand. The scent of dawn, when the stillness is icy with dew and the sagebrush dark and heavy. The way the Great Divide Basin spun beneath the stars.

"Well, then," Gussie said, and she laughed, brought her girl back down onto the bench with her, held her tight against her side. "There's nothing I can tell you. You're fine on your own."

"I'm not. I told you—I'm too small."

"That's changing fast, sweetheart. I'll lose you."

"Don't lose me, Gussie. I don't want to leave you."

"You'll leave me, sure as time. But don't worry. We have a thousand places to go. Here"—she handed Anne the reins—"take us to Five Finger Butte."

That was two months ago, and still Gussie felt her pulse race if a stranger drew close. And increasingly, this summer especially, the desert was tracked by men searching for clues, trying to dig up answers and riches. Now, the glint of the horse and mule had come near—Gussie had been right, it was clear now, a tall man on a fat horse, his mule pulling on the lead, the sun flaring off the fancy bridle, the decorated saddle, buckles, the man's spectacles. He was traveling about as secret as a meteor. He looked toward Gussie, raised his hand, touched the brim of his hat. Gussie raised her hand in reply. The man's rifle remained in its scabbard. Gussie glanced back at Anne in her shroud, the girl's eyes tiny and focused out toward the man.

"He's okay," Anne whispered, and she emerged from the shroud, came forward to her spot on the bench. "He's too silly to hurt us."

"You might be right," Gussie said against Anne's ear.

"He wouldn't know a gun from a stick."

"A wolf from an elk. Yes? An elk would eat him for the salt. Wouldn't it?"

Anne laughed, leaned against Gussie's side, Gussie laughed too, they both shook and snorted until they pulled right up to the man, reined the team to a halt, and the man worked to control his horse, the pack mule prancing in an arc.

"Howdy, boy," the man said to the smiling Gussie, and "Howdy, darling," to the smiling Anne.

They laughed again, and the man laughed too, though he seemed unsure why, and his horse jumped, the lead tightened, the mule swung around, the man hooted and swayed, and he and his animals went floundering off through the brush. "Lead on," he shouted back over his shoulder, "and I'll follow and share my sup with you." Gussie continued on her route as he slowly gained control and fell into step behind the wagon.

That evening they set their camp on a long open plain, nothing but sagebrush and short grass and the distant rounded hills like sleeping beasts. Each time the man called Gussie "boy," Gussie and Anne glanced at each other and laughed, and the man would smile or whistle, scratch his whiskers, tug at the bandana that circled his neck, bend again to raising his tent or tending the meal. He fed them bacon and beans, and they ate heartily, Gussie answering the man's questions about her travels in the basin, her memory of the color of the soil, the layers exposed.

Clouds started up from the horizon, swamped the sunset, and it was cold, seemed it might sleet or snow. Anne wandered off beyond the light, returned with more broken lengths of brush. The flames sparked taller. Anne sat on the crates, between Gussie and the traveler, Mr. Borman, his eyes blocked by the glare off his spectacles.

"I found these," he said, and he unrolled a length of canvas, exposed a collection of stone shells and bones. "What do you think?" He tapped a finger on Anne's knee.

"Those are everywhere," Anne said.

"Maybe," he said, "but I know what they are. I can fit them into the puzzle I'm solving."

"But I know what they are, too" Anne said, and she tapped his knee right back.

"Be nice," Gussie said. "He's a guest in our home." Gussie smiled at him.

Again, he touched the brim of his hat. "That's alright," he said.

"She can say whatever she wants. I don't mind. Glad of the conversation. And this desert isn't anyone's home in particular, so we're all fair game."

"It's mine," Anne said, and she pinched his knee, looked up at him. "My home. So these stones are mine too, but you can have them. Tell me what you think they are."

"Okay," he said. He arranged the fossils on the canvas, ordering them by age, and named each. He told them the story of ancient oceans, the rippled sand beneath the tide, the face of the moon on the waves. "There was no one to see it," he said, and they all looked beyond the firelight.

No coyotes yipped that night. The wind tasted of salt, imminent storm. They leaned closer to the heat. Maybe his words had gathered an ocean around their camp.

He told them of the world beneath the ocean sky, the ancient stars as nascent as the phosphor of cells, the swirl of heaven, the life sleeping there, feeding, a quick spark before the tide moved on. And along the shore, the creatures wandered, leaving angled tracks, swishes of the tail. The water and the wind, the dunes. "Here," he said, and he held a tiny fossil bone on his palm. "This is the creature's hind leg." He told of the slow wander from the push of high tide, the sliding steps up the face of cascading sand, the pause at the crest where the view expanded, where the eons of Wyoming painted themselves in greening marsh, pink granite, crystals of feldspar, quartz. What could a creature like that see or understand, its brain no larger than a few grains of sand? To it, the world might be flat and close, no focus beyond the nearest obstacle, no sense of night beyond the need to seek warmth, to sleep. And the water recedes. And the ranges rise and are buried and are exposed again. And into this desert wander men, and they find the stones where God has written the story, and they begin the slow translation, line and verse, rock and bone. "God has walked here," he said. "God has curled to sleep in the bowl of the basin. You can see it in the veins of the creeks. You can read it in the salt that sloughed from his skin.

You can hear it, if you stand still long enough." Mr. Borman sat back on the crates, looked up into the rising smoke. He inhaled deeply, set his shoulders, hummed his exhalation, nodded to himself.

Anne looked up at him, seemed to study him, touched the back of his hand where it rested on his knee. He startled, his gaze came down on her, and she snatched her hand back, leaned away. "There now, child," he said, laughing. He patted her on the head, gave her shoulder a tweak. "Didn't want to scare you. It isn't ghost stories I'm telling. Just the truth. But you're a sweet thing. None of this means anything to you. Maybe it won't ever mean anything."

Anne smiled weakly, slid from under his touch, slipped off the back of the crate, ran a finger along Gussie's neck, circled the fire, and moved on. Gussie watched the girl take the firelight with her on her small form, her even steps, farther than the flames could light the brush, until Anne was just a glimmer, a memory of warmth, and gone.

"You want me to keep an eye on her?" Mr. Borman said.

"She's fine." Gussie watched the dark space that had taken Anne's shape. She would have followed, would at least have stood at the reach of the firelight, but she faced Mr. Borman. "She knows her way around."

"I don't doubt it. But there are traps for a girl alone, even in the empty desert. You'd be safer without her—any traveling man is safer without a woman. Especially a woman of such beauty, even if the woman is only a child. Beauty is a trap. Beauty is a millstone. She'd be best off in a home or school where she wouldn't be such a lure."

Gussie removed her hat, ran her fingers through her short matted hair, fluffed it as best she could. "I'm not a traveling man," she said.

He squinted, fanned the air before his eyes, as if he'd been caught by the smoke. "I'm sorry, miss." He shrugged, gave a half smile. "I've been out here a long time."

"I've been here longer. And so has she. Anne. My daughter."

"Your daughter . . . But you are too young." He looked back into the flames. "This desert is a perplexity, and I've not figured it all out yet."

"You've tried."

"Yes, miss, I've tried."

"There's your mistake."

"Never a mistake to work a problem. But I think sometimes that I can't convey what I've learned. It makes me a touch melancholy."

"You've told us a nice story. Don't let us wandering girls make you doubt your game."

"Don't you worry, miss, I'm dedicated. No doubts. And there are a lot more things I could tell you that might be of interest, if you care to listen. Even your daughter might remember the tales I've told. Consider it the start of her education. It's as good a start as anyone could hope to find in this wasteland. I'm a doctor of philosophy, authority in geology, paleontology. Educated at the University of Chicago, ma'am."

"Well," Gussie said, "I'm sure that's very fine, and I thank you for your stories."

"It's a duty, don't you agree, in a place where encounters are rare? If a man sees a want, he tries to satisfy that want, nothing expected in return. It's the liberal way of an educated society."

"You find us wanting?"

"It's your daughter who's the object of my concern. Don't get me wrong; I find her lovely. But you indicated that you travel together always. Begging your pardon, but you're a teamster, by all appearances. What knowledge can you give her?"

"Of course, she'll need more than I can give her. But she's five."

"Can she read?"

"She knows her letters." The cold wind kicked up, and they both ducked from the shifting smoke. "She knows her colors and her numbers and how to tie a knot and she knows her way through the Great Divide Basin."

He came up out of the smoke coughing and laughing, slapping at the sparks on his trousers. "Yes, of course she does. She knows her way. But she can't read. What map? I can barely decipher a map myself. What map does she read?"

Gussie stood up. She looked off beyond the fire, out into the circle of scrub and light, up into the stars raked with thickening cloud. Mr. Borman's laugh died away, and he hunched, hugging himself toward the flames. She looked at him, at the ivory pipe he drew from his pocket, the bear's face carved on the bowl, the inset black eyes, the tiny metal tool he used to tamp the weed, his scraped and bruised fingers, the shadow of the stiff brim of his hat, the fumble with his matchbox, fingers thick with cold, and the struck match, cupped hand, inhaling the smoke through clenched teeth, the cherry smoke flowing in twin streams from his nostrils. He sat up straight, seemed to chew another dose of smoke, and held the pipe down, looked at the smoldering weed. What could she say? In the way he folded that tiny tool and slipped it back into his pocket, she thought that she could see how, given the right milieu, he might command attention, might lead his students to the edge of a ravine, to the sweep of a prairie fire, to the curve of a river where the current pulls too swiftly for escape from the looming rocks. "So," Gussie said, "you can't hardly read a map. And my girl doesn't even need a map."

He stood, looked down across the fire at her, took a puff on his pipe. "Miss," he said, "don't reject advice just because it makes you feel small."

They faced each other. The fire hissed and popped. Rain was blowing into camp in long streaks, thickening into sleet, snow, hissing to steam in the fire. Gussie felt strong—her arms were warm with the flow of blood, her legs were tightly sprung. She barely felt the nettling ice. How would she appear to this man as she leapt above the flames, descended on him through smoke and storm? She smiled, a hard line, and he scowled at her, fiddled with his pipe, shrugged, looked away, said, "I was going to suggest that alarum might be warranted, but here comes the winsome sprite now."

Anne entered quickly from the dark. She was barely herself—only her legs showed below a huge bundle of brush. She dropped the fuel beside the fire circle, looked from Gussie to Mr. Borman and back, shook her head. "Didn't you see the snow?" she said. Her hair was heavy with white, her arms and shoulders crusted. She began feeding sticks into the flames, and the fire rose, bellowed by the wind, hot enough to burn its way through the storm. "We need a big fire to stay warm. You would freeze if I didn't bring wood soon. Sit down." They sat on the crates, watched as the heat turned from red to white. Anne stepped to the wagon, returned with a tarpaulin, sat between Gussie and Mr. Borman, and with their help she draped the stiff sheet around them all, a waterproof shell open to the warmth. "That's nice," she said. "When you smell the snow coming, you got to get a bigger fire if you don't want to sleep yet. You got to get the flames big enough that the snow won't douse them."

Gussie and Mr. Borman were quiet. Gussie watched her girl, felt her own chill burn away, saw the white on Anne's jacket turn to clinging drops of water and evaporate. Gussie wanted to smooth Anne's hair, hook it behind her ears, but even for her closeness Anne seemed out of reach. Gussie wanted to tug at Anne's jacket, square the buttons, flatten the collar, wanted to tell her girl that it was late and she really should be ready for sleep. But she waited to see what Anne would do now, waited to see if Anne understood strangers and their whims and doubts.

Gussie looked across Anne to Mr. Borman. Sheltered in the tarpaulin, melt dripping from his hat, he drew on his pipe, his lips wet and working around the stem, a constant mindless agitation. He might speak again. Or he might have receded into his facts, laid out in his mind like text, like bones in a glass case. The facts were beautiful—long blocks of words washing slowly through the white pages, dark veins of leaf pressed in a stone cracked open like a book. Gussie saw how small Anne was, her fingers like twigs. What could the girl have learned beyond the surface, the elements of the desert—heat, moon, north, bluff, east, thunder, dune. What could Gussie teach her, finally.

Gussie hadn't read a book since she left Frank Locke's house beyond Greeley. She heard Leota's voice, the rhythm of words in the dim light of the parlor, the night plains hidden behind the reflection in the window. The dark green binding flexed in her hands, the whisper of page against page. *Devouring Time, blunt thou the lion's paws, and make the earth devour her own sweet brood . . .* Gussie remembered the tenderness of her mother's voice. And here was Anne warming in the heat from the raging fire. What would Anne remember?

Anne roused herself in the shelter of the tarpaulin, reached into her jacket pockets and began to draw out the objects gifted to her by Mr. Foster's crews, the objects found in camps and towns and the soft south-facing soil of winter cutbanks, the objects found this night or other nights in the light of star or storm, moon or final streak of sunset, first far gray of sunrise. She laid everything carefully on the sand before their feet, nestled it all into the hollows of footprints, planted it all in the lee of the blackening stones of the fire circle.

"Here, Mr. Borman," Anne said, and he looked at her, looked down where she pointed, at the pattern of treasures. "This is what this all is," she said. "This is seeds for my garden."

"What garden is that, sweetheart?" Mr. Borman said.

"Listen to me, sir." She picked up a green knuckle of jade. "This is a seed for mountains." She dropped the jade, picked up a fossil shell. "This is a seed for my house. You see the rooms. No one else has a house like this." Dropped the shell, picked up a piece of blue bottle glass. "This is the sky. Look through it—you can see the fire."

"And where will you plant these seeds, little lady?" Mr. Borman said. He tapped the stem of his pipe against his chin, smiled at her.

"There is a whole desert, Mr. Borman," she said.

Gussie looked beyond the fire, out into the snow, the laden brush, the clouds that seemed to skim beneath some higher light—

the moon, the stars, the constant heaven in the dark. Mr. Borman puffed on his pipe, and the sweet smoke lingered. They folded the tarpaulin tighter, hunched closer to the heat, reached for the pile of fuel Anne had brought, built the flames. Anne finally gathered her treasures back into her pockets, and she didn't flinch when Gussie circled her with her arm, held her against her side. The snow had already gone to huge flakes that lazed on the falling wind. The fire, full of the slow-gathered oils of the dry land, was fierce and pungent. And down in the fire were the chambers of red coal, the braces and arches of the blackening branches, the distances that kept crumbling to ash.

For years now, nights beside a fire, the silence of the dark, the snap of the wood. Gussie and Anne were slowly devouring the desert life, stomping on the branches to break them from the root, carrying bundles to camp like nomads on an ancient plain. And the occasional night in camp with Mr. Foster's rock crew or oil crew or shepherds, warming themselves again at a sagebrush fire. In the Leucite Hills, the men had been eager for their supplies, eager for an audience. They displayed their findings to mother and child— vials of gray sand, pumice, false gold. Anne accepted from the crew the milky green jade they offered, and she held it tight in her fists. Then the songs beneath the stars, the stories, Anne passed from one lap to another, bounced up into the smoke and sparks. Gussie wondered sometimes if she'd ever pass again through a crowded town and not shy from the everyday, the slide of a window in its frame, a woman shouting at a dog, the engines, the voices of the boys, the rough chins of the men.

And now, with the snow moving on, with the fire still hot, with the tarpaulin soft with heat, with Anne dozing against her side, Gussie looked across at Mr. Borman and thought that this was something she'd wished for—mother and child with a man of some sort of intelligence or means or vigor—but the man was never quite ideal. Mr. Borman had smoked down through his tamped weed, and now he turned the bowl over and, with his small metal tool, scraped the remains into the fire. Then he carefully, thoughtfully, patted his various pockets and found a home for pipe and tool.

"The morning will take me east," he said, stretching his legs. "I have collected enough to keep me occupied for many years. I hope to get tenure out of this expedition."

"Do you have company?"

"Company?"

"Is there someone waiting for you?"

"Ah." He kicked at the damp earth, glanced away at his pup tent sagging and tattered at the edge of the light. "I have an office, ma'am. Steam heat. A view of the quad. There's a bronze statue of a patriot—the university's namesake—and it seems he's looking directly at me, waiting for me to say something, but I'm not certain what he'd like me to say. I work very hard. I eat a late supper at the faculty club. I enjoy spirited discussions. I smoke too much. I have rooms in a lovely home not five blocks from the edge of campus. From my bed—pardon my indiscretion—I can hear the other residents conversing quietly or running water in the sink or descending the stairs, and I can see the weather passing high—the window above my bed is enormous. Then I choose my wardrobe according to the weather, and I join the other residents in the dining room, where the air is always warm and damp and full of the scent of coffee and bacon. One of my favorite moments of the day—standing there at the sideboard, deciding among the choices. Will it be toasted bread and jam? Will it be poached eggs and tomatoes? I love it. The food is wonderful. The morning light is filtered through the sheer white draperies. And the residents talk of nothing at all, and they repeat the same nothing every day, and I find it soothing. I hate to leave that morning meal, but everyone goes about their days, so there is no use lingering."

He sat still for a long minute, then leaned forward, let the tarpaulin slide off his shoulders, held his hands to the fire. The final lengths of brush were taking to the flame, and the silver-gray leaves curled and fell. The storm clouds had moved on, the stars were struggling against the moonlight, and the night was bound to get much colder. Mr. Borman's breath rose with the smoke, and the heat and moisture drew a river across the constellations.

"You are alone," Gussie said.

"You are correct," he said. He stood, worked the muscles of his neck, looked again toward his tent but didn't start in that direction. Leaning down to Gussie and Anne, he arranged the tarpaulin tighter around them, placed his hand briefly on Anne's sleeping head. "You'll want to stay here until the fire is spent, I suppose, as long as she's sleeping."

"Yes. I don't want to waste the wood."

"You're a good person."

"I hope so."

"Let me tell you something. This girl of yours needs a home. Whatever brought you out here with her, you'll just have to forget it. If you are her mother, then you need someplace permanent for her, where she can sleep in a bed and get some schooling. Will you take this advice from me? The only thing the girl has is a shell and some jade."

"She has me."

"You're a good woman, no doubt."

"I know you're right," she said.

"Good," he said, and he sat again on the crate. "I'll wait here with you until the fire cools."

Lost Soldier

Through a window of Mr. Foster's guest quarters, Gussie watched the late afternoon rain, the green light that filled the yard toward the house, the honeysuckle battered under the quickly passing storm. She opened the window, smelled the dampened dust—even here in Rawlins the desert loomed, ready to take hold. Anne ran on the lawn, catching the drops in her outstretched hands.

There were things Gussie would miss about these quarters. The softness of the mattress. The endless supply of heat, light, and water. The heavy curtains that dulled the lash of the wind. Small things—white marble on the dresser, leaded glass at the tops of the parlor windows, the dense red patterns of the rugs, the depth of the bathtub. The cook would often add something extra to the food—figs with the pork, wine in the sauce.

And there were moments here that she hoped to forget. Anne halfway out the gate, onto the street, and the automobile that came too close, the wild cloud of dust and exhaust. Katherine and Elizabeth strolling past Mr. Foster's corner, a calm wave toward Gussie, the sway of their skirts, their long hair pinned in swirls above their necks—they seemed taller, more womanly, more bold in their stride down the center of the street, and Gussie wondered that she had ever been clad in the same uniform, embarrassed to think how gawky she must have looked. And the day Mr. Foster's cousins came to Rawlins on their way from Illinois to Sacramento, and Gussie and Anne moved into the loft above the storage shed, a perfectly tight space, and they lay awake in the nighttime, in the comfort of the beds they'd laid out, and listened to the cousins sing and stumble from the house to the guest quarters.

When the rain moved east, when Anne stopped running on the lawn, Gussie came out from the guest quarters, toward the house. Anne followed her up the steps to the side door. Gussie knocked, and the cook let them in. They sat at the kitchen table, ate the food the cook laid out—beef in broth, sliced potatoes roasted in milk. The cook went back to preparing Mr. Foster's supper, paying no more attention to Gussie and Anne. When they finished eating, Gussie said, "Is Mr. Foster home? I need to talk to him."

The cook glanced at her but kept at her chores. After she slid the roaster into the oven, she smoothed her apron down her legs and left the kitchen.

Gussie leaned in toward Anne. "You need a home."

"You told me that already."

"I need to say it again so I'm brave enough to tell Mr. Foster."

"Don't be scared, Gussie. He always does what we ask."

Mr. Foster followed the cook into the kitchen. He squinted in the brightness of the room, smiled at Gussie and Anne. "How're my girls?"

Anne slid down from her chair and took his hand. "We're leaving, Mr. Foster," she said.

"Not for a few days, sweetheart," he said. "The equipment hasn't arrived."

"Good," Anne said. "I want to see a picture show."

"Whatever you want to see, I'll make sure you see it."

Gussie took Anne from Mr. Foster's grip, hoisted her onto her chair again. "You wait here," she said. "I have to talk to Mr. Foster."

And then Gussie said to the cook, "Watch her for me. Don't let her go outside."

"Of course, dear," the cook said. "I won't let her get away."

Gussie led Mr. Foster out into the hall, with the afternoon radiance far at the windows. She said, "I can't work the desert anymore."

"I've been waiting for you to say that. Now you can work for me here in town."

"No, sir. Thank you. We're leaving. Anne needs a home."

"I've said that a hundred times."

"We're leaving Rawlins. Going north."

"I have a home for Anne here."

"She's my daughter."

"But I have a stake in her too. Have you forgotten?"

"Forgotten?"

"All I've done for her."

"I haven't." She feared her voice might crack, and she moved past him into the sunlight in the foyer. She looked back at him—still a young man, still slender and dark, a bit handsome. He approached, into the brightness. His face was pale, the sun-color suddenly gone, and his eyes deeper, unsteady. "I need to do this by myself," she said.

He took hold of her arm, squeezed too hard, but she didn't flinch, just looked up at him, the flutter of his heart at his temples. He seemed to be holding his breath, locked in thought, indecision, and then something broke and he turned Gussie to the stairs, led her up. "Let me show you," he said. And they hurried down the second-floor hallway—Gussie for the first time—where the walls were plainer, the space narrow and tall. Doors opened left and right onto lovely soft rooms with white beds, windows filled with sky. And then, halfway to the end, he turned, and they entered a room. "This," he said, and he released her arm. "When I was young, this was mine. Now it's for Anne." He stood aside, allowed her to see the room.

She stepped forward. At first, she saw only the glass doors open to the wrought-iron balcony, and the white curtains settled around the view, the tops of the trees gold and alive, and the sky grounded by a faraway southern horizon of peaks, the town of Rawlins invisible. Gussie had seen that balcony's incision into the face of the structure, the black iron against the brick, filigree of vine and leaf, a place from which to look down on the yard, the spiked fence, from which to view the street through the obscuring branches of the trees. Then she saw the walls in the room—smooth plaster, as pale green as new leaves. The room a cloud of light, placed up in the weather. She shaded her eyes against the glare from the honey-wood floor. Inside the light on the floor, she saw the curtains' pattern, the waffling shapes of faintly stitched blooms. Everything seemed newborn. The crisp squares of the quilt on the bed. The dark leather books behind glass in the shelves. The fine black lines on pure white paper—etchings of a steel-beam bridge across a blank river, a platter of mushrooms, a bottle of wine beside two glasses, a bowl of pears. The thin gilt frames were high, widely spaced. And Gussie was centered in a full-length mirror set in an oak-wood stand, claw feet, pinecone carvings, chamber pot on the shelf beneath the glass. She was lit with sunlight, her hair a winged mess, her trousers frayed at the cuffs, her white shirt shadowed with indelible red stains from desert mud. Behind her, Mr. Foster crossed the room. She turned away from the mirror.

He sat on a wooden chair near the balcony doors, pointed to the second chair, waited for her. She sat beside him. They looked through the light to the bed, the books, the electric fixtures, brass and frosted glass.

Mr. Foster placed his hand on Gussie's knee. No pressure. His hand almost floated there. "Miss Locke," he said, "I used to lie in that bed and see the town lights on the ceiling. You don't have to worry. This house can protect a soul from anything. The locks are heavy. The staff is alert. I would lie there and know every sound I heard. It's good to become familiar with a place, as you know, to let the patterns replay enough times that little will startle you. It's better that the sounds lull you, not frighten you. This room is for Anne. She should live here. She's from Rawlins. She could be my daughter."

"She's not."

"But I could make her my daughter. Adopt her. Give her a name."

"You want us both?"

"Both?"

"She's your daughter and I'm your wife?" She looked at his hand on her knee, his bony fingers and small nails, but he pulled it away, and although the sudden absence gave her skin a chill, she was glad it was gone. "If I'm not your wife, she isn't your daughter. I don't want to marry you, Mr. Foster."

"No." He rose, walked away, sat on the edge of the bed. "I'm not asking you to marry me." He leaned forward, looked at his feet.

"So you want to take my daughter?"

"No. Not take."

"You want her to have your name."

"Isn't that why you brought her to me? So she could have the things I have?" He stood again, the bed rocked from the sudden shift, he took the three steps across the room. She pulled her feet back under the chair, afraid he wouldn't stop, but he stopped directly and looked down at her. He jutted his jaw. "And now you'll be gone. She'll be gone. I don't like it. It's false. Somehow false." He left the room.

She waited until she heard his footsteps on the stairs, and then she stood. At the bed, she pressed her hand into the depression he'd left. There was warmth, but only a degree or two more than the air. No, she didn't want to marry him. But she loved him. She thought of him lying in that bed, trying to decipher the lights on the ceiling, trying to unravel his parents' moods, trying to will a child into one of the empty bedrooms, a brother or sister. He might have stood on the balcony in the night's stillness, his feet cold, the air filling the loose space of his nightshirt, and looked down through summer branches, pieced together the life out there, imagined the place he might arrive when the time came, the girl he might embrace beyond the glow of the streetlamp, the marriage, the voices in the hall. He couldn't have known. The things he thought he wanted. The years.

Gussie lowered herself flat onto the quilt, pulled her legs up, her head on the pillow. She looked at the ceiling, at the reflections of sunlight, mix of leaf shadow. This was Anne's bed. Anne's room. Nicer than Gussie's own room in Frank Locke's house, the first night when Gussie slipped between the linens, waited for sleep to take her, waited for her eyes to see the stars through the high window, the view wide and empty, no light from beneath the door, the house settling, waited for the sounds that would wander, find a way around the corners, through the halls, Leota's voice as Gussie remembered it from the moonlit window of the Ravenglass house.

Anne, her first night in this room, in this bed, would test the tightness of the sheets against her legs, try to see into the dark corners of the room, wonder at the lights of town playing on the walls. She would listen to the faint sounds of Rawlins, trace the trains as they followed the creek, paused at the station, moved beyond hearing. She knew the smell of the wind, the patterns of echo, church bells, clank of the prison gate, streetlights high and pale, the faces, the slow changes in the faces, stone facades, bright signs. But in this room, the view would be fresh for Anne, the sounds new. Someone would pass in the hall, and she'd gauge the stride—it was Mr. Foster turning in for the night. Mr. Foster alone. At some point, a woman's steps would follow him, and his bedroom door would seal shut with a click. Anne alone. Anne judging how this room caught and amplified sound.

Gussie couldn't place herself. She lay where Anne would lie. There was only this narrow bed, straight and solid. Would Gussie have a room in the house, hear Anne through the walls? Or would she have a basement room beside the cook's room, or a room in town, or nights in the Red Desert? If Gussie and Mr. Foster stood at Anne's door, wished her sweet dreams, if they closed the door and backed away, if they waited there a moment before turning, both slow to move, as if they expected Anne to call out, but Anne never called out, if they went their own way and paused at the reach of the hall, looked back, caught a quick good-night flicker of smile, then gone, what would Gussie's life be, what would Mr. Foster be to her? This would never be her home.

Gussie left the room. She would tell him that he would learn to forget, though she wasn't sure how. He was resourceful, he could find anything he wanted in this country if he set himself to the task. He hadn't found gold. Hadn't found oil. Yet. Even with all the expense. But there were things out there that could be found without any expense at all. He'd have to decide.

She descended the stairs, looked in the front parlor, in the solarium, ventured into the side hall, found Mr. Foster in the library. It was dark—splinters of light angled from the black shutters. He stood at a wall of shelves, held a book open before him, though he couldn't have seen more than shapes without meaning.

"I'm sorry, Mr. Foster," she said.

He turned toward her, snapped the book shut, held it to his chest. "There's nothing to be done about it." He motioned for her to enter the room, and she followed him to the davenport, settled onto the cold leather. He laid his hand on her knee again, but this time with teasing roughness, and he released her, placed the book on a side table, settled back. "If you've made up your mind. I don't own you. Maybe I can explain." He sat square, looking forward, took a few deep breaths. Then he began slowly, shaping his words.

"When I first met you on the street," he said, "I thought you were probably looking to turn a crooked deal, but I found you amusing, and I can afford a small crooked deal without lasting harm. And you had Anne, which softened me. So I purchased a few items for the girl, and that kept you engaged. I looked forward to your visits and to seeing you in town. I don't know that I ever would have found a position for you—you didn't seem suitable for housework, and I had only your word that you were otherwise capable."

"You didn't believe me?"

"I had no way to know."

"Do you believe me now?"

"Believe that you're leaving?"

"Believe that I can do the work I say I can do."

"Yes. But I've worried every day that I shouldn't have put you at risk in the desert."

"I wanted the work. I would have left if I had no job."

"So I only postponed your departure. And now I pay a deeper price."

"Mr. Foster. You'll find a wife. You'll have a child of your own."

He laughed, threw his weight forward, and Gussie shrank away as he rose to his full height, looked down at her. He was slashed head to toe by fine bright lines, hot white sun. She saw his knuckles, his throat, his pupils struggling to focus, his brow rippling, the skin whiter than the light. "You have no idea," he said, "you who made this child out of air and light and water and your own base appetite."

"What do you mean?" she said, but she knew. He thought that Anne was beyond her. "You have no idea how frightened I am every day."

"I do know," he said. He backed away, turned, stood at the window, touched his forehead to the blinds, peered into the afternoon. "The night we went looking for Anne, I thought we wouldn't find her. Then I knew I loved her. And I thought that the trail would go cold, and Mrs. Shayd would live in a town someplace and watch the child grow. We'd never know. The child still had milk on her breath."

Gussie joined him at the window, leaned her forehead too, saw a line of sky, a white hole where the sun burned. "I'm not stealing her. I'm going to find a home for her. So that I won't be frightened, maybe. So that I won't lose her. I can't live in Rawlins. Anne needs a school. But I can't sleep here, even in your beautiful guesthouse. And the winter work is rough. And . . ."

"I know all that. Of course, I know."

"I've learned the country north and west. I'll find a place. I'll find something to do."

"I want to hear from you."

"I don't know where I'm going."

◆ ◆ ◆

Gussie and Anne drove north in a sturdy little wagon pulled by a gray horse, both gifts from Mr. Foster. They followed the Rawlins–Fort Washakie Stage Road, which skimmed along Separation Flats, passed Cow Spring, Chicken Spring, Buck Spring, the rare soddy ranch in the hills. No stagecoaches passed—not anymore. These days the traffic was over on the Rocky Mountain Highway. Still, some horses and wagons traveled this way, and a few automobiles rattled across the ruts.

That first morning, they overtook a freighter, four coupled wagons tethered to twelve horses on a jerk line. Gussie pulled up alongside the driver.

"Where you headed?" she said.

"To my death, probably," he said.

She thought that maybe he was dead already, a ghost of the long road. When she continued ahead, when she looked back before cutting into a draw, the freighter was nowhere to be seen. No dust rising.

At Bell Springs, they stopped for the night at the old stage station, ate a meal of mutton and biscuits, sat on the steps outside as night fell. The stars pressed the bluffs low. Sounds from the barn. Sound of the wind.

"This is a good place," Anne said. "Let's live here."

"You think so?"

"The supper is at the supper table. I don't smell like smoke."

"I think we can raise our standards a little bit higher than that."

In the morning, they dismissed Bell Springs astern, took their time along Coyote Rim, came down toward Bull Springs. For a long mile they watched the small buildings draw near. There was not much there, just a station house and some outbuildings, a maze of fences, corrals, some greenery along the creek. Always the same huge sky. Here the lady of the station came out to greet them.

"Are you stopping?" the lady said.

"Depends," Gussie said. "Do you need us?"

"Need you?"

"Can you give me work?"

"Not likely."

On toward Lost Soldier station, which they found as the Milky Way came up like a cloud across the stars. Here a boy came out to take their horse to the stable. Meal of antelope and onions beneath the oil lamp. Coyotes yipping in the hills.

Some men came in from an oil crew. They couldn't wash the black from their hands, not that they gave it much of an effort. "Cold water," they said. And "no" they said when Gussie asked for work. "You're too small. It takes a big man to roughneck. You'd lose your fingers or an arm." Some of the men were big. Some weren't.

That night, Gussie and Anne slept together on a bunk, curtained off from the station parlor by a suspended sheet. Cold seeped down across them from the window, and the moonlight played strange shadows. They huddled closer, tucked the blanket under their shoulders.

When the men had had their fill of food and drink and left, when the others in the station had finally fallen quiet, when the last lantern had been extinguished, Anne whispered, "We can't stay here."

"Why is that, little girl?"

"Because of the men."

"They've gone back to their wells."

"No. The men in the story."

At supper, Mrs. Kirk had told them of the lost soldiers. Forty years ago, a company of riders from Fort Steele came up that way. Three of the men heard of a whiskey still in the hills east toward Big Camp Creek. They took their ponies out after supper and rode that direction. Then the snow came up from the west, and they got waylaid. One survived. The other two were lost, presumed dead. The survivor was found by the rest of his company.

"Where are those two lost soldiers?" Anne said.

"Dead, like the story says."

"They're not dead. I think those men are in the desert."

"They would be old men by now."

"They're not old; they're lost."

The coyotes yipped again. Anne and Gussie sank deeper into the lumpy bunk.

"I heard them," Anne said.

"The coyotes?"

"No. I heard those soldiers in the snow, when we was in Mr. Costa's sheep wagon." Anne told the story. Gussie remembered.

There had been flocks of Mr. Foster's sheep toward the Honeycomb Buttes, and Gussie had found them, found Mr. Costa's sheep wagon, the smoke from the black pipe in a thin layer among the hollow hills. Gussie and Anne unloaded the supplies, helped Mr. Costa stack them in the cupboards under his built-in bed. And then they shared supper in the herder's wagon. Anne sat up on the bed, watched Mr. Costa heat the canned beans, brew the coffee, break bits of biscuit from the wax paper packaging. Gussie and Anne slept that night in their own wagon, beside Mr. Costa's, and when they woke in the morning a low-slung September storm had come into the desert, snow gusting horizontal in the wind. The hills were lost in white. Gussie and Anne hurried from their cold beds to the heat of the sheepherder's wagon. Mr. Costa was gone, but he'd left the stove stoked, the lantern lit. They watched the storm through the wagon's small window. They saw the drifts slowly rise to the hubs of their own wagon. Ice accumulated on the panes until they could see nothing more than swirls of blue and gray light.

Mr. Costa came into that small space, the snow blustered around the door, and then he shut out the storm. He told them he'd found all the sheep he could find, that he'd left them with the dogs, against a wall of the buttes. They would sleep there, safe in their wool, and the dogs would keep the wolves off. He told them that he'd found their horses dragging their pickets downwind, and he'd brought them back, tied them to Gussie's wagon, out of the wind, and they might survive if they all stood together. How long could this snow last?

Through that day and into evening, the three of them sat in the sheep wagon, Anne on the bed, Gussie and Mr. Costa on the bench at the pull-out table. They drank coffee. They ate canned apple pie. Mr. Costa kept the fire as hot as the little stove would allow, and yet small currents of cold drifted, chilled them all on occasion. They wrapped themselves in blankets and sheepskins, played cards, told stories.

That night, Gussie and Anne slept together on Mr. Costa's bed, and Mr. Costa slept on the bench. Anne awoke late, unsure of where she was. The small windows were silver. She touched the nearest pane, and the cold was wet and frightening. Anne remembered hearing Mr. Costa's breathing, and the groan of the stove, and the whistle of the wind across the stovepipe, and the shake of the storm. She remembered the strange smell of the bed, the same smell as Mr. Costa, the musty sheepskins, the smoky grit in the sheets, the valleys in the mattress that must have held the contours of the man's legs, hips, shoulders. She awoke again, later. This time she heard nothing for a long while. She thought she was alone, but then she heard Gussie and Mr. Costa, their breathing smooth and even now. And then she realized that the silence was the end of the storm and the deep snow muting the distance. The wind was gone. She looked at the windows, and in the icy glass the stars skewed. The wagon was alone and stranded. The horses could be dead. The sheep could be suffocated. The dogs could be lost. She listened, tried to hear.

Then she heard footsteps. Someone moving through the desert. In the cold, the snow creaked faintly under the weight of the steps. The steps came closer, and separated, and she knew it was two people. They were circling. They were stopping to inspect the wagons, to test the strength of the horses, to judge if all this had been abandoned, to smell the woodsmoke and wish to be inside, in the warmth. Anne heard a rattle. Could have been the door handle. Could have been the latch on the window.

"I woke you up," Anne said.

"Yes," Gussie said. "I remember."

"I said, 'Who is it?'"

"And I couldn't say."

"I said, 'Are we safe?'"

"You were scared."

"You didn't hear them."

"I didn't hear anything, sweetheart."

"I didn't know who it was. They wanted the warm wagon. It was cold outside."

"Mr. Costa took good care of us."

"Mr. Costa would have hurt the men if they came in to get us."

"What men?"

"The men outside. The lost soldiers. It was them."

Anne was quiet, tangling deeper into the blankets, heavy against Gussie. The coyotes had moved on. Somewhere out on the road a wagon passed, didn't pause for water or warmth, kept going north. The creak of the wheels and the thump of the hooves retreated into silence. Gussie looked up at the window. There were shapes in the stars. Could have been clouds. Could have been a tree. If someone had been looking in at that window, would he have seen mother and child lying there?

Rongis

They left Lost Soldier at dawn, continued north toward the wall of Green Mountain, Crooks Mountain, and Crooks Gap between. Sweetwater country lay beyond, the great strange knobs of the Granite Mountains, but before Gussie and Anne could pass into that land they stopped at Rongis. Abandoned a few years earlier, the station looked like a week's labor might get it ready to open its doors, to issue smoke and music. A dead rose vine on a fallen fence. The post office sign down on one nail, sandblasted. And there were sounds from somewhere among the buildings, could be intermittent hammering, the groan of metal, as if the town was trying to keep itself in repair for the return of its kin.

"I don't see no one here," Anne said. "Does that make this place better?"

"That's not the exact idea, little girl, but I guess I've never shown you any different. You'll need people and a school."

"You think children live here?"

"If anyone at all lives here, we should've brought them paint and window glass. But maybe they'd need more help than we could offer. There's that noise, though. Let's see if it's anything human. Could be the wind."

They pulled the wagon up beside the post office, took their lunch and headed out, past the station, among the outbuildings and empty houses, following the sound. Echoes turned them left and right. Broken bottles in the grass. Bedsprings. They lost the sound, kept going past the last building, turned back at the sound of voices. Two men—one tall, one short—beside a half-dismantled shed, sorted their booty into piles of lumber, tin, nails. Gussie thought of her weapons left in the wagon.

Anne reached up and took her hand. "Who are they?" Anne said, barely a whisper.

"Scavengers."

"What's that?"

"They will take what they can find."

"Will they take from us?"

"I can't tell yet." They backed away a few steps, lowered themselves onto folded legs, into the shadow of a big sagebrush. "Let's see."

The men inspected their progress, discussed the best way to bring down the next wall without hurting themselves, and then they returned to hammering the shed loose at the joints. Anne glanced up at Gussie, pointed to the lunch pail, and Gussie nodded—the men wouldn't hear anything across fifty yards.

So Gussie and Anne ate their lunch—apples, bread, soft white cheese—shared water from the canteen. Slowly the shed disintegrated. The last wall fell, and the view opened back across Rongis, Gussie's wagon and dozing gray horse plainly framed. Now the men would know they weren't alone in this ghost town—nothing to be done about it. The parts of the shed separated—boards and beams. The shorter man dropped nails into a bucket with the battering sound of hail. The taller man yelped, dropped a sheet of tin, sucked at a cut on the heel of his palm. The shorter man looked up at him, smiled, said, "The shed don't like us, Charlie."

"And why should it?" Charlie said. "We razed it."

"Raised it? More like we skinned it. Nothing left but the space where it used to be."

"You're a man of strange intelligence, Arthur." Then Charlie looked directly across the fifty yards to Gussie and Anne and said, "You, there. Ladies. Do you have any water to spare? This cut stings like heck, and I'd like to wash it clean."

Arthur looked at them too and said, "An apple, if you got extra, a green one, would make me happy. I love apples."

"Scavengers," Anne whispered. "They'll take from us."

"Only what you can spare," Charlie said. "Or nothing, if you're strapped."

Gussie felt her face flush with heat, and she jumped up, advanced with the canteen. Anne came behind with the lunch pail. "I'm sorry," Gussie said. "We didn't want to bother you." She handed Charlie the canteen, and Anne dug in the pail, came up with apples and cheese.

"We got lots," Anne said. "Can I give it to them, Gussie?"

"Of course, you can. We find people in the desert, and they want food, so we feed them."

"Salt of the earth," Charlie said. "We thank you. Where are you two headed?"

"We don't know," Gussie said.

"North," Anne said. "We're going home."

"Where's home?" Arthur said.

"Someplace I can learn things and have a bed."

When they finished eating and making introductions and discussing the terrible condition of the road toward the Sweetwater and judging how soon winter would come, Gussie pulled her wagon around, backed it directly to their work, told Charlie and Arthur to load it up, and they did. She drove the wagon on into Crooks Gap, where the creek was low and the boulders were jade. The men led the way on their bony horses, turned onto a track that curved up Crooks Mountain. And then they all arrived at a squat log house, and a water pump, and a walkway edged with stone, brambly hedge of wild rose. The men unloaded their plunder, stacked it beside the house. Gussie and Anne released their tired gray from the harness, led him into the corral. Arthur pitched hay over the fence.

"Alfalfa," Arthur said. "Oats in the morning. You two going to stay?"

"It's late," Gussie said. "We'll stay."

Dusk came early to that eastern hollow, but far out in the distance, the sun still angled brightly. East across Crooks Gap, the face of Green Mountain caught the full red setting of the sun. Gussie looked at the basin to the south, could see the day's trail disappear into haze and stacked horizons. To the north, the promise of the emigrant trails, the green of a river bottom, the shadowless plains, were blunted by an abrupt rampart of spent granite. She had strayed from whatever route she had planned or expected, and already the next morning's departure seemed too distant to be considered.

Inside the house, Gussie and Anne sat at the table as the men lit the lanterns and set to cooking supper. The house was small but neat, with bunks in an alcove, open-face cabinets stacked with canned goods, curtains at the windows, rafters hung with drying flowers and herbs. They laid out a meal of salty ham and biscuits. "Not fancy," Charlie said. "We've been too busy to gather up anything fresh."

It was clear by the place that they had indeed been busy. They'd staked their claim on the land only a year earlier, and already they'd worked through a whole list of improvements, run their wire down onto the flats, where the bulk of their 640 acres lay, bought ten head of cattle. They wouldn't get rich, but they didn't seem to care.

"I don't expect to get rich, either," Gussie said. "I've had my chances to live with money, but the chances weren't perfect."

Arthur cleared away the plates. Charlie took Gussie and Anne to the chairs beside the woodstove, told Anne of the sights to be seen on Crooks Mountain. "Child, you can see elk pass right outside the window."

"I seen elk a thousand times."

"You can see eagles."

"I seen eagles dead and alive."

He looked at Gussie. "Will nothing surprise her?"

"Anne knows the wilds better than is maybe good or natural. There are other things to know about the world."

Arthur finished with the dishes and joined them. "Charlie's the opposite," he said. "He don't look up often enough to see where he's placing his step. Rattlers and holes and barbwire. He learned everything from books."

"Are you brothers?" Anne said.

"They're not," Gussie said. "Look at them." But she didn't know, and they just smiled. Charlie was tall and very thin, maybe mid-twenties, his clothes slightly too crisp. He had the clean blond look that she remembered from the boys in Minnesota, a shadowless blue to his eyes. And Arthur was a good half-foot shorter, stocky, with a big set of whiskers carefully shaped. He was not crisp—his overalls seemed too ripped and breezy for the Wyoming seasons. He'd been tested by the dry wind, could have been Charlie's age or ten years older—he never said.

One of the lanterns sputtered and went out. The room shrank into long shadows. No sound beyond the breath of the fire, the breath of the four gathered there. It seemed to Gussie that they could all have sat there, unmoving, for years. No sound of wind. Stars deep in the pine branches outside the windows. Arthur and Charlie both leaned forward in their chairs, squinted toward the heat of the stove.

Finally Charlie said, "You'll stay here for as long as you need." He stood and pulled from a cabinet a bottle and three glasses. He returned, sat, poured a few fingers of reddish liquid in each glass, passed it around. Gussie sniffed at the glass, let Anne sniff too. Then Gussie took a drink. The sweetness burned and fizzed on her tongue. They all glanced at each other, downed the rest of the liquor, set the glasses aside.

"Come on outside," Charlie said. "I think you'll like this." They all rose and emerged into the dark, sat on a bench against the house wall, the logs still warm from the day's sun. It was crowded on the bench, not enough room, the pressure of thighs and shoulders. The air was still, the distance empty. The stars seemed somehow less cold, Gussie thought, with the box of the house holding her upright, and the drift of stovepipe smoke. "This is what I wanted," Charlie said.

He talked slowly, quietly, told of his stoop in New York, the walls of the buildings all around, the stars swallowed in electric light, the sky cut in strips. Always the sound of voices or machines, always the coal soot or the vented fumes. He would sit on that stoop for hours, in heat, in rain beneath the awning, waiting for something, waiting for a voice that would move him, make him drop his cigarette, stand from the stoop, follow the sound. But nothing drew him out—nothing broke through his thoughts. In his room, he slept beneath a window, but he kept the shutters closed. The lightbulbs in his room were high and weak.

In the summer he would travel far north to the Maine coast, and there his grandmother would greet him. They fixed their tea, stirred mayonnaise into clumps of lobster meat, sat on the cottage porch. Wind spun the hanging pots of geraniums. Wind hissed in the pines. Through the heath, birds raced, fought, chattered. But always the view was farther out. A finger of bay crossed from left to right, drawing in from the distant sound of breakers. The tide cycled. For a few hours, the tiny white triangles of the boats skimmed the blue, skirmished with each other, carved their wakes. But then they sped to shore, the tide turned, and slowly that luminous surface pulled back, and the mudflats emerged. It was like geology played out in a wink. Gone was the brimming. Risen were the dark ridges and ripples, the murky lakes. Out onto that momentary plain wandered the searchers, poking at the mud, looking for something buried and rich. Before they could extract enough to satisfy, they had to turn for shore, they had to find their way among the flooding channels, and then suddenly the contours of that underworld were lost, and again the sails raced above. Charlie counted the inrush and outrush. When the land was hidden beneath the water, he tried to remember the muddy contours. When the land was exposed, he tried to imagine how deep the water had been.

After university, Charlie went to the war. He was in France. Winter came down through the windrow. He remembered the dusk, the way the last hint of sun whitened the clouds at the horizon, and he thought he saw smoke rising, and hills crowned with flame, and the jumble of a village trying to hide in its own darkness. He tried to sleep. He remembered the damp cold, the tree roots that twisted his back, the branches above that flashed with distant light, sometimes red, sometimes white, the throb of his injured shoulder, the jolts of the ground, the jump of his pulse, the slow freeze along his collar, the dread that he would dream himself into ice.

Charlie stood up from the bench, walked away into the gap in the pines where the lowest stars shone. Gussie thought of the scent of the woods beyond Ravenglass—this place was different, as if the air were too thin to carry more than one scent, just a hint of lodgepole dampened further by the cold. Gussie thought of the open ways beyond Ravenglass, the stars filling in from the branches of the black spruce, the dry cedar, paper birch, stars right down to the ground, and then a shape passed there, no more than an absence of stars making its way through the radiance. Gussie thought of the old bachelor cabin in the red pines beyond Ravenglass, thought of Leota sitting on the back stoop, waiting, newlywed, new to this place, unsure of the sounds, unsure of the shapes that broke the arcs of the stars, unsure if she had been left in this clearing, alone, with only the bachelor walls to hold back the wilderness, until she heard the steps approaching, heard the rustle of the fallen needles, the crush of desiccated leaves, and she backed up the stoop, waited with the kitchen light at her shoulders, her shadow centered in a square on the overgrown yard, and Brud stepped into the square, complicated her shadow, pushed her in through the door, and the warmth and closeness of the cabin was all around her. Gussie thought she could rise from that bench, turn and step into the house, and she would know something of what Leota felt in that bachelor cabin beyond Ravenglass. And here Anne was beside her on the bench, and Arthur also, and Charlie was downhill in the stars, soon to return, a man with a certain pale virility, and she listened for him. He would not be as quiet as Brud, and he would not take such long circuits. He was settled—she'd heard it in the steady focus of his voice. He had been places, but they were all on the way to this place. She understood.

Anne slid down from the bench, and Gussie reached for her, but the girl was already out of reach. Anne headed off into the dark, following Charlie's path, her steps small in the gravelly dirt. Gussie felt a jolt of fear, but it subsided as soon as she inhaled, blinked. Her girl was wandering alone, invisible, but Charlie was out there, this was his land, he was gentle, and Anne would be alright.

She leaned deeper back against the logs. Arthur was still beside her, but there was space now. She looked at him. In the lantern glow from the window, he seemed small, frozen, waiting for something to pass, something to rise from the darkness.

"How did you boys come to this place?" Gussie said.

"Come to this place," he said, slowly, as if he were unsure of the words. He faced the night. "I was never much good," he started. "I been going around, here and there. Got myself into Wyoming, though I couldn't prove one way or the other how it happened. Caught on with a geology crew, did the ferrying and cooking sometime."

"I did that too. No cooking, though."

"Cooking ain't bad. People appreciate almost anything." He laughed, a high, rapid sound, silly. "Had to go up to Casper to pick up the latest tenderfoot rockhound from the rail. Got to drive the company truck—that's a great thing, that engine, so loud. I get to the station and there's Charlie St. George. He got a cardboard suitcase. He got a dark suit on. He looked like he was waiting for a train to get him out of there quick as possible. But I called out his name and he picked up the suitcase and stepped lively right over to the truck, so I guess I got the right man. 'You gonna need something rougher than that suit,' I say to him, and he agrees, so we go on over to Smith's and dress him up. Then he looks passable, though you wouldn't've mistook him for a person who knew where he was or where he was going. It took a while for his new clothes to get worn in.

"We drive on down along the North Platte, all through the rocky areas, and he's hanging out the window the whole time, looking at the sky, looking at the hills and ranges, and when we stop for a break he runs down to the river to soak his feet like he's just hiked a thousand miles. 'Am I the first person to sit just here?' he says. 'I ain't got the foggiest,' I say, and he says, 'Close enough, I guess.' 'Close enough for what?' I ask him. He says, 'Close enough for me. For someone who's by himself in a new place.'"

"Did he leave a sweetheart behind?"

"I wouldn't know about that. He never said. He wasn't a hang-dog sad sack, if that's what you're meaning. He wasn't a heartbroken paramour, not that you'd know. He just thought he'd found himself a place to start. 'Just look,' he said to me. 'You can see right down to the genesis of nothing, of everything. You can see all the elements laid out, right from the past to the future.' He worked the survey for a season . . ."

"I should have seen you in the basin."

"We weren't obvious, not our outfit. We stayed out of sight. Don't want no one knowing what we find. We looked like a hunting party, mostly, or lost adventurers. We had a leader telling us where to turn, but I could tell that Charlie St. George knew more than all of them . . ."

"Still, I should have seen you."

"There's a lot of miles down there. No way to know when you might cross someone, or if you might never. Charlie, at the end of the season, says he ain't keen on leaving Wyoming, so I help him think it out, and he got this acreage up here, and I help him get more land—each person gets his own lot. I'm fine with it—I'm a good worker. I'll stick with Charlie St. George, because he's already got me more than I would've ever thought I could have."

"This place."

"Yes."

"This home."

"Yes, ma'am."

"And where's the nearest town?"

"Nothing of size or value until Lander. Sixty miles."

"Is that okay?"

"It's a fine little town."

"Is that okay with you, being so far out here?"

"Well, ma'am, if you been working the desert like you say you have, you know that heading into town, any town, gets your nerves on edge. Yes?"

"Yes."

"You dip into town for what you need, and then you head right back where you belong."

"How does it feel?"

"The dipping into?"

"No, the getting home."

"Well," he said. He thought a minute. "I don't know. Maybe I ain't been here all that long, just a year. But I come up the mountain and I see the rocks set in the sky, and maybe the sun going west, and the trees getting dark, and I smell the smoke and see the light, and I always stop, every time."

"You stop." She nodded.

"I stand a minute on foot, or I rein my pony. I don't know. I like the light. I like the door. I like that I'm almost there."

"And going inside?" She touched his shoulder.

"Why do you ask?"

"Tell me, please."

"You forgot how it feels to go home?"

"Yes." She remembered, for herself, but she wanted to hear this man tell her. "Coming home to this far place. Going inside when it's dark outside."

"It's nice," he said. "It smells right."

That's all he said. Gussie tried to see his face, judge his eyes, but he was dark. She patted him on the arm, stood from the bench and passed in through the door, closed it behind her. From the middle of the room, she looked around. There was the remnant scent of the ham, the underlying scent of dust that filled all log structures, and the woodsmoke and kerosene. No hint of decay that she could discover, no ghostly trace of sweat. Still, it was a man's home.

Leota would have stepped for the first time into Brud's bachelor cabin, stood at the center, judged the place. Would it be her home? The light came in through the red pines, and Leota stood at the window, saw the world through the skew of the old panes, saw how the trees hemmed the view, how the sun separated the pines into bursts of spiked shadow. And the floorboards, paced through the years by her new husband, the knots standing up from the plain. And the stove with its dented pipe. And the bed—Leota sat on the edge, must have heard the springs and wondered how long it would take for that sound to become familiar enough to disappear. She sat there as the day lengthened, as the western windows brightened and then went gray, and she listened for Brud, for the beams to creak as they cooled, for the skitter of night things, the flutter against the windows. But she would need to light a lantern to draw anything to the windows. She sat as the walls disappeared, and slowly the cabin took fresh shape in her mind. She would leave this single room as a corner of a new structure, as a reminder. She saw the walls multiply out into the clearing, the rooflines complicate, the walls flocked, the windows shrouded. Her home.

Gussie walked through Charlie and Arthur's house. There was heat contained there, soft against her skin. In this one space of all the many spaces she could possibly occupy, she touched the table-top, the jars, the surface of the mirror, took the one small step down into the sleeping alcove, touched the cold metal frames of first one bed, then the other, smoothed the brown wool blankets, laid her hand flat on a pillow. She sat on the edge of a mattress, no way to know if it was Arthur's or Charlie's, both beds identically clothed and tucked. They would sleep there, hear the weather push at the home they'd built, hear the wind draw smoke from the stove, hear the darkness fill the miles and set the mountain farther from the world. Gussie listened. She waited. No telling if anyone would arrive, or when. No telling who she waited for. Could she shape the face or stride of the man? She might already have forgotten this stranger—two, there were two strangers—might have made a mistake. If he passed through the door, whoever, if his appearance was unpleasant, if she felt a deepening fear with each second his bulk blocked the door, would she be able to face him calmly, to talk to him with ease, joke with him, as she made her plans to move on? She tried to sit as Leota might sit, hands in her lap, eyes on the door. Leota must have known the shape of the darkness beyond the lamp-lit form of her husband. She must have known the pace of his footfalls. Must have known the change he'd bring to that space, the change in the flow of the air, a baffling of the acoustics.

Gussie faced the door. She heard steps approaching. She heard voices, or maybe just one voice, couldn't make out the words. Sitting up straighter, she manipulated her features into a smile, held it there on her lips and in her eyes. The latch rattled and the door swung in—a block of darkness centered on the far wall. Then a figure developed, rising into the lamplight, a man all paper-thin height and legs. He teetered there on the step, seemed to search for balance, his hands clasped in fists at his chest. His face—yes, she knew the Nordic beauty of his face, and now the joy that seemed to thaw his edges. He came another step forward, and his knees buckled slightly, and she thought he might fall forward, but she saw that he was only dipping to make it through the doorway, though the doorway was plenty tall, but down he went, and there in the light was Anne, winging high on his shoulders, and his fists on his chest held the girl's ankles. Then Gussie felt Leota's strange blood in her veins, the pulse that got her to her feet in a single fluid stroke, that moved her to greet a beautiful man, and here the man held her beautiful daughter aloft. The cold night air came straight through the cabin—Gussie felt it tighten her skin, squint her eyes—as Charlie St. George advanced, laughing, and reached up, took Anne by the arms and swung her to the ground, tiny shape at his knee.

"That's my little hauntress," he said, patting her hair, pushing her forward, though she was reluctant, her feet scraping on the floor, her face turned toward the side, back toward Charlie. "This sweet belle tracked me in the dark," he said to Gussie. "You were right—she knows the wilds. She can see in the dark. She can move like a catamount, though she's prettier still. She could have taken me. No effort given. Just her musical voice nearly stopped my heart."

Up from the alcove, Gussie converged with the others, taking Anne's hand, and Anne reached back for Charlie's hand, and he stooped and took hold and Gussie looked from the man's blue eyes to Anne's blue eyes, and she thought she knew something of home and Leota and what Leota had lost. "Yes," Gussie said, "she's a beautiful girl, my child."

"She is, ma'am."

Gussie took a quick loop in her thoughts, back into Ravenglass, west into desert, back to Crooks Mountain, and the words shifted from mouth to mouth, the order now somehow correct, and she wanted to hold on.

"Let me tell her a story," Arthur said, and suddenly he had closed the door, moved into and past the group, breaking their bonds, and he knelt at the stove, opened the grate, inspected the coals, Anne at his shoulder, waiting. "All girls like a good story."

FIVE

Crooks Mountain

On the eastern slope of Crooks Mountain, a thousand feet above Crooks Gap, Gussie found a broad stone, and in the cold quiet she sat, bundled tight in her coat, and waited for dawn. Over the past months, since winter, she had barely slept. She'd come to know too well the progress of the late-night sky.

In September, in Wyoming, the season can swing from heat to snow and back in the turn of a day. The air, dense and heavy against the mountain, waited for the stir of heat. Gussie could hear everything for miles around—she could have heard a voice from across the distance, if there was anyone out there, wandering, shouting for help, lost. No ghost lights flickered from the ruined buildings at Rongis, far below. No automobile followed the Rocky Mountain Highway, five miles to the north, kept speed across the ruts and gumbo, gravel and bridges. She knew the miles of that highway, northwest to Lander, had graded the way over Beaver Rim, over the bones of old wagons.

A raven's call echoed from down toward Crooks Creek. And Gussie thought she could hear the Sweetwater River funnel through the far rift of Devil's Gate. And she imagined she could hear the travelers on the emigrant trail, the sounds of hooves and wheels caught for sixty years in the seams of the Granite Mountains. She could do better than those pioneers, had already done better—she lived in this place that they had passed in haste and fear, lived without craving a gentler horizon.

She slipped her hand into her coat, drew out a small bottle, the glass hard and warm. She pulled the cork, took a few long swallows, held the mouth of the bottle a moment in her lips, tasted the bite of the captured air. A burn spread behind her ribs. She released the bottle, sealed it, slid it back into her coat. She waited for what she thought must happen, but the liquor didn't make her drowsy—it awoke her to everything she didn't want to know. She drew the bottle out again, finished it, secured it in its pocket.

More and more, even awake, she found the same dream replaying, but if she was awake it couldn't be a dream, must be a memory. Dream into memory. Always, she saw the same place, a ranch, a summer day.

At the top of a windmill—four-sided wooden box tapering toward the sky—she stands beneath the slow-circling blades cocked powerless from the wind. Far to the west, the sky is black, but here the sky is its usual searing blue. She isn't sure if she knows the ranch—the bright acres, the hills. She has come to adjust the pump mechanism.

She lowers herself into the metal tank, and now she is held aloft inside the wooden structure. She thinks it would be better if the windmill was an airy construction of boards and fittings, if it pumped its water into a trough on the ground, instead of secreting the water away. She squats, pokes the seal where it grips the rod. Touching her wet fingers to her nose, she smells steel, cold, phantom sagebrush and bison.

Then the whole structure shudders, a rumbling that seems to be outside the windmill. Is she surrounded? She finds the rope, drags herself up into the day, stands there and looks out. The whole ranch is awash—the outbuildings, the main house, the fences and pastures, the gradual incline to the hills that channel the flood—the immense surface colored by the sky. The flood rushes in from the west, from the distant storm, kicks up mud at the corner of each building, swirls in the wake of trees.

She remembers—Anne must have come with her to this ranch, and maybe Anne has caught onto something, holds herself against the current, sees Gussie far up in the Wyoming sky, Gussie holding steady to the timbers, immovable.

Gussie looks toward the line of the creek, but the whole plain of the creek is submerged. Then she sees Anne on the roof of a shed, flying above the water, but Gussie is higher. Anne shouts to her. "It's beautiful . . . it's terrible . . . look . . ." And the shed gives way, rafts into the rush of the submerged creek. Anne holds on, sails past the next willows, around a bend in the valley.

Gussie tried to see the details she must have missed, tried different angles, thought herself to greater altitudes, looked far down on the flood, felt the sun hot on her back, yet the water never drained away, the land beyond the bend in the valley never rose into view. She thought that some parts of the story might already have happened, but she didn't know where. Over the years, she'd traveled across most of the country within a fifty-mile radius of Crooks Mountain. She'd dug through the stacks of maps that Charlie St. George had collected, laid out the hills and valleys. Still, she couldn't place that flooded ranch. The story—dream or memory— persisted, and she'd lie awake, finally rise and head out onto the late-night mountain.

She tightened her coat against the cold, scanned the darkness north, east, and south. The earth thrust against the stars. If a man wandered those miles, paused and gazed toward Crooks Mountain, toward Gussie, would he guess at the life hidden in the stands of lodgepole and aspen? Gussie and Anne, nine years now on Crooks Mountain, nine years with Charlie and Arthur.

Gussie was known for miles around, known as Gus, a road worker, a tough hand, good with a horse, drove Charlie's truck when there were supplies to be retrieved or product to be delivered. But would anyone know that she was Augusta Locke? That she had been Augusta Tornig? Would anyone say, Yes, she's the girl from Ravenglass, the girl who remembers the Minnesota ravens, who listens now to the trills and yells of the Wyoming ravens and wonders what orders they give, what memories they hold, how this country paints itself in their thoughts, if Wyoming is somehow painful without the vast green mat of the north woods of Minnesota. Augusta Tornig, the girl who thinks often of the cedars and paper birch, though she wouldn't admit it, thinks of the bare winter shadows like a stave on the snow, and the notes that drew her on—the brush of wing on windblown snow, the crack of a weakened limb. She knew the notes of her own movement, the memory of following, the tone of her steps as she crossed from drift to scoured ridge, the whip and scratch of dry branches.

In winter, in the whiteness of the land beyond Ravenglass, she found the raven nests. Some nests waited intact in a pine, on a rocky ledge, to be taken up again. Some had fallen. Gussie toed through the snow, through the sticks as thick as her fingers, sticks snapped from the branch with the twist of the black bill, woven into the bristling nest, the platform high out of reach, but here on the ground the structure was lost, and Gussie studied the marks on the dry wood, the few black feathers broken and dropped, the clean bones of a frog, shreds of moss, fur of moose or some other mammal, colorful bits. In the ruins she found a blue ribbon still tied into a bow, a pearl, a torn piece of photograph (the hem of a woman's white dress, her small shoes), a sliver of porcelain, a human tooth. All that industry, to collect the wood, to construct the safe cup for the eggs, to gather color and softness and ornament, all left behind for a season or lost forever.

Once Gussie thought she knew the scrap of cloth she pulled from a fallen nest. She remembered the sad umber, the texture, and the shirt it had been a part of, and how the shirt had held her small torso in fall and winter, the fabric finally worn at the seams, outgrown, gone to rags, just a remnant rinsed and hung on the line behind the house in the red pines. And Leota, at the kitchen window, might have seen a raven swoop into the clearing and carry off the scrap, the bird racing its shadow across the last snow toward spring.

Leota waited at the kitchen window through every season—at

dawn sometimes, when the grass was bent in the dew; at noon sometimes, when the sun angled starkly but couldn't warm the air; at dusk, when the grayness seemed permanent. Leota waited into darkness, waited into daylight again, her breath growing ice on the panes. Then out into the world, at least once, pushed finally by her pulse or the desire to touch her daughter's hair, Leota wrapped her throat tighter in her wool scarf, felt the weight of long johns and two pairs of socks, the animal-skin gloves and hat, the sweater with its impenetrable weave, the hulking dark coat reaching to the ground, the boots high-laced and flat-soled. Leota's shape was muffled, stifled. She almost couldn't hear her own steps—the hat and scarf held her breath tight against her ears—and she thought she would miss something she'd need to hear, so she kept her eyes wide and focused, wiped away the cold tears. There was no trail to follow, just the white openings, the sky avenues, the icy sun.

Leota walked north into the Norway pines, the bear-marked trunks. It could have been the shortest day of the year, so quickly the light waned. Another hour and she might be pushing through dusk as thick as evergreen brakes. Soon, Leota thought, I'll be lost, but my girl will keep on going, my girl won't find me, won't know I followed her. She entered into the last light, and there in a white space walled with spruce the ravens rose from a wolf-killed carcass, black rising into the first black.

Leota approached—she might have been brave enough. The sky shot over with red, the clouds splendid. In the glow of reflected light she saw the ribs of the deer, the skewed limbs, the skull rising through. She knelt close. The snow was written with tracks, mammal and bird. Maybe Gussie's tracks were there. Leota pulled off a glove and touched the icy indentations, the bloody bits of fur and skin, yellow fat gone crystalline. And then she touched the bones. The cold structure. Arc of rib. Battlement of teeth. And the frozen eye. She wiped her fingers on her coat, pulled the glove back onto her hand, stood.

Her presence had silenced the woods. She listened to the miles she hadn't covered. She hadn't taught Gussie any of this country. She wasn't sure that she'd taught Gussie anything at all. Her own daughter. She couldn't have traced, even in her mind, the structure of Gussie's form. She hadn't counted the girl's teeth. She hadn't followed Gussie's gaze often enough to guess where the girl would go.

Leota turned west, toward the end of sunset far beyond the trees. There was a clearing, as if the world opened without closeness or distance—a long frozen lake beneath unbroken snow. No tracks. Leota couldn't have known which way to turn next. Even a full moon might not give up her own tracks, much less lead her to her girl.

Gussie looked out from Crooks Mountain into the brightening east. Soon the first heat would reach her. Soon, if she climbed higher, she might see south all the way to Colorado, east to Nebraska, but only on a perfect day when the air was empty, air like a lens that made the view simple. She could draw a map of anywhere she needed to go within a hundred miles. Anne, too, could draw a map, but Gussie couldn't imagine how that map must differ from her own. If Anne left, how would Gussie follow?

◆ ◆ ◆

She rose and took the path down from the rocks, among the pines, cut onto a side trail, passed through the maze of granite and broken trees, faced a small window, small door and narrow wall, a dugout tucked into the mountainside. Smoke spread from a black stovepipe, dulled the early light. Charlie was at work. Gussie advanced through the haze, ducked in through the door. She inhaled the moisture, held it in her lungs, the whole dugout like a lung drawing in fresh air, processing it through heat and water, sugar and darkness, expelling sweetness and waste. Gussie thought it would be easier never to leave that space, easier to live off the air.

The steam hissed. Charlie touched a drop of distillate to his tongue. Gussie tapped him on the shoulder in greeting. He nodded.

"Whortleberry," he said, giving the thermometer a shake. "I had to fight a grouse for what fruit I could find. I'm on the heads now."

She knew the origin of each piece of the still—the copper collected at abandoned work sites, the kettles from Rongis, the firebox and stanchions fashioned by the blacksmith in Hailey. Charlie fed wood into the fire.

She scooted past him, deeper into the dugout. The shelves were stacked with empty glass, the barrels heavy with sugar beets, white yeast, fruit. From her coat she took her bottle, removed the cork, inserted a funnel into the bottle neck. The gallon jars on the bottom shelf held liquid in shades from amber to clear. She knelt, worked her bottle into the sandy floor until it balanced upright. She studied the jars, screwed open the most full. The raw smell, the underlayer of sugar and something drier, almost bitter. She thought of the small yellow flowers on the plain beyond the mountain, the way the yellow floated in the shrubby green, constellations of papery petals, and the pollen falling among the branches, down to the shaded ground, ruined leaves, roots.

Gussie took the dipper, drew liquid from the jar, funneled it into her bottle. She returned the lid to the jar, pushed the cork into her bottle, and the bottle went back into her coat pocket.

She stood at the shelves, not ready yet to turn around. She heard Charlie make the necessary adjustments toward the end of his run. On the top shelf, there was a loose heap of textbooks, dark leather bindings, gilt letters. She knew that the first page of each volume had been embossed—*Property of Charles St. George*—knew the weight of the paper, the shape of the equations, density of the text. She was no scholar, but Charlie was Princeton 1918.

She turned. He seemed to have finished—he sat on the low bench beside the door, his knees high, his small blue eyes shadowed, though clearly he was watching her. She patted her coat where the bottle rested. "Thank you, Charlie," she said, and she crossed the dugout, sat beside him. "No doubt it'll be good."

"No one cares about the quality."

"You care."

"I care about the chemistry." He raised the lantern globe, blew out the flame. The space went dark.

Daylight slowly leaked through the grimy panes. The copper tubes gleamed, and Gussie followed the lines down to the orbs of the kettles, the embers in their box.

"Did you sleep?" Charlie said.

"I've been up the mountain."

"If you drink enough *medicine,* you should sleep. This whortle-berry might do the trick. It'll be subtle. It'll be like late summer heat, I think. The kind of heat that makes a person dozy."

"I can't keep drinking your best product."

"I want you to sleep."

"I want things too. Sleep is just one thing I want."

"What else?"

"I want to know some answers."

"I can try to answer anything you need to know."

"You know more than a person like me could ever hope to know." She spoke with more heat than she'd intended. She looked hard into the dugout, counted the jars on the bottom shelf.

"Tell me. Ask me." He rubbed her knee, but she twisted away, leaned heavily against the wall. "I'd like to help you."

"I'm a grown woman. I don't need help."

"I know."

"If you need to help someone, help Anne. She's a child."

"I teach her, don't I?"

"Yes, you do." She relaxed into the wall, closed her eyes. There was a desperate hollowness to her thoughts.

Almost every day, Anne sat at the table in the boys' house, leafing through the books Charlie had laid out, writing her assignments on a pad of paper, her script square and precise. Sometimes the girl would read to Gussie what she had written. Anne with her eyes squinted just a fraction, holding the pad to the light, working to bring clarity to the rhythm of her sentences so that even without real understanding a listener might glean a bit of meaning. Anne's pause, her glance at Gussie, her moment to judge if Gussie was following along. Anne's small sigh, her lips going thin and pale, a shrug. If Gussie circled the table and stood behind Anne, if she leaned close enough that her daughter could sense her heat, if she tried to focus on the girl's prose or the equations that tangled on the surface of the page, Anne would slowly brush her palm across the paper, as if revealing a magic trick, and then pinch the corner of the page and delicately flip it over.

"Don't look, Gussie," she'd say.

"Why not, sweetheart?"

"Because it's mine. I'll share it when I want to. It would take too long to explain. The complexity is very great."

Very great. Gussie heard Charlie's accent in the girl's soft breath, and the girl's Wyoming accent sometimes in Charlie's voice when he was tired or off his guard, Charlie taking the rhythm or shape of the girl's voice onto his own dry lips. Each morning, over the years, Gussie would prepare to leave for whatever job she held that week or month or season, if there was a job to be had, and Arthur would lay out the breakfast, sometimes a rich meal, sometimes just enough to pad their hunger. And then, while Arthur cleared away the dishes, Charlie packed a satchel with Anne's schoolwork for the day.

"The mathematics," Charlie would say to Gussie. "Keep after her about her sums." Or, later, "Ovid for the whole month of May. There's water in all the creeks. Everything has gone from brown to green."

And Gussie and Anne would climb into their wagon and descend to Crooks Gap, head north or south toward the day's work. Anne read her books, solved her problems, sat beneath a tree or in the shade of the wagon as Gussie labored on an irrigation project, painted a house, crept across the flats with a road crew. Anne grew taller, watched the work when she could no longer focus on her studies, led the horse to pasture, met Gussie with the lunch pail at noon. There were ranch girls sometimes, station girls, schoolgirls, who found Anne alone at the wagon, sat with her awhile and talked. Gussie would see them, Anne and the girl, thought they might run together into the hot afternoon, find a creek, a pond, rocks to climb, but Anne wouldn't leave, never went any farther than the pasture to show the girl the gray horse. Gussie never heard what Anne and the girl said. Twice, she saw a girl try to lead Anne off toward a ranch house, maybe to sit with Anne, brush her hair, let her try on a dress. Anne's trousers were a rough sight, her shirts rolled up at the cuff. But Anne was as lovely as any of those girls. She waited at the wagon, opened her books and read aloud to the girl, until the girl finally disappeared.

On the drive home, Gussie would say, "You made a friend today?"

"She wanted to give me things, show me things, as if she knew what I had and what I didn't. I scared her off with Charles Darwin."

Wyoming was a tough state for many of those years—the coal mining and oil weren't steady, the ranching was boom or bust, though there wasn't ever much to the boom. Charlie and Arthur lost their cattle, ran sheep for a season, went back to cattle, gave up livestock altogether for a few years, looked for other income. Charlie signed on as a geologist one summer, but he didn't like to be away from home. Gussie kept at whatever she could find, usually road crew. Arthur ran the ranch—cut hay for the horses, hunted, put up preserves, searched out mushrooms and greens. None of it was enough. So Charlie St. George built his dugout. He learned the distilling process quick enough, and then he tinkered, tried different sugars, perfected it. There were dances in Hailey, ranches below Beaver Rim, far-flung operations where men were thirsty for something. Charlie rode down the mountain, sold the first batch, returned with a truck.

"I'll show you how to drive it," he told Gussie. "You'll be my distributor. If we want to make a go of this, we need volume."

"Just point us in the right direction."

"You'll go alone. I have to make the stuff. Can't spare Arthur, or we won't be eating, and I can't sleep if he isn't there snoring. And you'll need to go to some rough places, some places off the map, but you could find anything you wanted to find, and you're tough, Gussie, and I have no doubt that you can be professional and secret, what with the life you've led, but I can't let Anne go along on these deliveries. You understand the risk, the law. She's a child. Arthur will watch her. I'll keep her at the books. You won't ever be gone more than a few days at a stretch."

So Gussie drove down off Crooks Mountain alone, a strange silence even with the roar of the engine, the bottles clinking in the back. She looked at the distance ahead. Split Rock. Sweetwater River. Charlie was right—she could find her way to any corner of this territory, hardly had to think about it, could work from a name or a hint. *Clayton Danks in Miners Delight . . . Five men building a ranch north of Radium Springs . . . At the end of the Rattlesnake Hills . . . Leslie Engstrum on McGraw Flats . . .*

She laid out the miles, the turns she would take, wondered how her travels in this truck would compare to Brud's travels on the trails north of Ravenglass. He moved on foot, could rarely see the way ahead for the thickness of the forest, the carving of the creeks, and Gussie sped down the center of an unbroken prospect, the whole complex of erosion and uplift exposed to the sky. Brud left Gussie behind with Leota. Gussie left Anne behind with Charlie and Arthur. By this hour of the morning, Anne would have finished her reading, helped Arthur muck out the stalls. And now she might sit with Charlie in the dugout, recite her day's translations, answer his questions. Anne would be busy, challenged.

The truck lurched through the gears, strained to keep speed on the inclines—it was not an easy machine. At the passage of oncoming traffic, Gussie nearly drove into the ditch alongside the road. The steering was loose. Each rut and boulder whacked her backside, left her bouncing on the springs. And then, when the road headed down Beaver Rim without another vehicle in sight, Gussie released her pressure on the brake, shifted up, and let the truck fly at the limit of the engine. This was movement. She struggled to keep the truck centered, to return to her line after a skid across gravel, but she might not have been paying attention to driving at all, so fresh was the air through the windows, so rapidly the distance approached, the distance budding into further landscapes, canyons opening and closing to each side, and then the irrigated acres, the ranches that grew out of scrub, the horses rolling in the dust, men on threshers, children running from rain, dogs bolting from the shadow of fences. She could have driven that truck forever. At that moment, she could have kept going. She laughed at the thought. She looked as far as sight would allow, up across the storms and blue gaps. But then she turned from the road, took the way toward her first delivery, and she kept on driving for years, helping Charlie, returning to Anne.

She would pull up to a roadhouse or ranch, and a man would come out to take a bottle, a case, and a woman might wait in a doorway or hover behind glass. Gussie was always surprised to see a woman in that country, though she reminded herself that she also lived in that country. The men joked with the women the same as they joked with each other, and the women joked too, their lovely thin lips pulled back from their teeth. If the drive had been long or slow, if dusk had started or passed, Gussie was always offered a bunk for the night. A woman—sometimes the only woman—took Gussie aside to ask if she actually wanted to stay, if she wouldn't rather risk the road at night, this ranch or roadhouse being a rough corner of the planet, the product that Gussie had delivered unlikely to soften anything or anyone. Gussie often stayed—she had other places to travel the next morning, and a roof, no matter how rough, was a nice change from a ceiling of stars, which was her usual sleeping arrangement on her rounds.

So the woman led her deeper into the building, showed her to a room where she could wash her face, comb her hair. And there they sat, the woman and Gussie, and they talked quietly of the season, the roads, the distance from the rail line. After a while, when they exhausted the obvious, they fell quiet, heard the men beyond the walls. The men sang, poorly, they stomped, they hooted. The woman looked at Gussie, smirked, winked, and Gussie laughed, and then they both fell to laughing until they could barely breathe. Then they were sitting hip to hip on a chair at the mirror, and they watched each other in the reflection as they talked. Gussie described Anne's face, her eyes, her hair, her voice, and the woman looked Gussie up and down and nodded, made soft sounds deep in her throat, somewhere between appreciation and question. The woman pulled some flat tins from a drawer, screwed open the lids, inspected the colors—white, pale sunset, glacier blue, dun—and she touched a fingertip to a color, touched her cheek, touched Gussie's cheek.

"Is your girl as pale as this?" the woman asked.

"You can't apply the color my girl is," Gussie said, " 'cause there ain't such a color in nature."

The woman thought a moment, said, "If it ain't a natural color, then wouldn't it *have* to come from a jar?"

Gussie tried to work through the idea, her face frozen, mouth open, then saw herself in the mirror, her look of bafflement, and she startled, and she and the woman fell to laughing again, torrents, until they were sitting on the floor, slapping the boards. The men came to the door, looked in.

Gussie remembered a roadhouse in an elbow of badlands. Looked as if the place would sink in mud during a rainstorm, but also looked as if it might not have rained for months or years. Gussie stood at the back door of that place, looked up at the mass of erosion fading into darkness. At her feet, rusted cans lay scattered on the dirt, sparkle of shattered glass, ancient paper turned to pulp. There were bits of life—low wildflowers, lichen, red ants, burrows. Someone called to her—*Our Lady of Heavenly Moonshine*—and she turned, smiled, came back into the room, took a drink of Charlie St. George's creation. Hours passed. The room heated, shrank. She'd known some of these men over the years, others were new, passing along the byways, unsure if they'd find a reason to stay.

She walked beyond the roadhouse with a man fresh from Ireland. She liked whatever he said, a bit of a lisp in his accent, a vision of green in the tale of his home. She told him of Anne, and he said that Anne must be a dear girl and lucky to have such a mum. He touched Gussie's shoulder, pressed a whiskered kiss to her neck, and she turned to catch his lips, to taste Charlie St. George's liquor on his tongue. From where they stood, looking back, the roadhouse was a small collection of light—silent, far. The man took Gussie's hand, and they walked on, feeling the earth meet their unsteady steps, until they could turn and turn and see nothing of the roadhouse or any other light.

The Irishman kissed her through his whiskers, opened his shirt so that she could feel his heat. She opened her shirt too—whatever he did she also did, hats knocked loose and falling.

"If it's okay, miss," he said.

"Who's to say it ain't okay?" she said.

Trousers lost to gravity, trousers hobbling them, and they were down together, somehow warmer on the cold ground, the warmth of their weight. He entered her, and she laughed, thinking of the huckleberries she'd picked for Charlie St. George, the water she'd hauled, the wood she'd cut, and look what all that work had brought her—a delicious taste on her tongue, a strange accent in her ear, a healthy rut on the ruined soil. She hugged his shoulders, his back, his hips, helped him find rhythm and angle, until for a starry minute she forgot about him, but there he was again, hard at work, and she held her hands to the sides of his head, drew him against her lips, swallowed his yelps, felt so tender toward this stranger that she rolled with him when he rolled away, wouldn't release him, traced his neck, felt his ribs, loved his scent, made him talk so that she wouldn't forget his marvelous voice.

She never told anyone of her Irishman or any of the others. Each man had seemed a good idea. Each kept her thinking tender thoughts for months, lying awake in her bed on Crooks Mountain, listening to Anne breathe, the girl sure to take lovers of her own when she was ready, soon enough, daylight lovers. Gussie lingered mostly on touch and scent, on the shape of a man's jaw beneath her palm, the apple in his throat, the heft of the chest that protected the heart. She would kick beneath her sheets, let in night air to turn her flesh cold, hold her hands above her head to turn them tingling, numb.

And now, in the brightening dugout, Gussie turned on the bench, looked up at Charlie. He looked straight back at her. His small eyes were almost as blue as Anne's, with the edge of ice. He was steady. He was strong. She closed her eyes, leaned into his shoulder, felt the long sinews of his arm as he circled her, held her tight. "Tell me what will happen," she said. "The future."

"You can't let your fears control your sleep."

"Tell me."

"Alright," he said. "Prohibition will be repealed. This ranch will fail. We will lose touch with each other. This batch of whortleberry will be my finest. War will sweep around the world a thousand more times, over a thousand years, before peace takes even its first step. You will find Anne's father, either in this life or the next. The sun will die. The stars will fail. We will have mutton for breakfast." He rose to his feet, helped her up. "Let's get some food in your stomach."

"Okay," she said, following him. She felt somehow rested, somehow clearer. "Thank you," she said. The light was coming on stronger with the dawn. They passed through the maze, passed the corral, and as Gussie stopped at the pump, Charlie continued to the house.

Gussie worked the pump handle a few times, let the water surge, cupped the water to her face and neck. She worked the handle again, placed her mouth under the flow, drank deeply. When she first arrived on Crooks Mountain, the taste of the water, with its minerals and mysteries, had meant something to her, had given her pause. What had lived on this land, died here? What had settled in the low spaces and left its salt? What trees had gone to stone? Eons of death calcified into desert ranges. Water fell from the clouds, sank through sand, and in the unknown strata it found its gravity, its buried shores—without light, without knowledge, it found its way. Charlie had explained it all to her, explained that whatever path this well water had taken had rendered it unsuitable for use in the still, so he would send her down the mountain to Crooks Gap, to fill the barrels in Crooks Creek.

◆ ◆ ◆

Gussie left the pump, passed the house. The smoke already smelled of mutton. She walked a narrow path among the aspens, stepped into the single room of her cabin—the reincarnation of the Rongis shed, raised by the boys on her second day on the mountain—and opened the curtains. The room was cold. Anne was a vague shape beneath her blankets. Gussie knelt at the small stove, fed twigs and kindling onto the remnant coals, got the fire going again. On the stovetop, she placed a bucket of water. And then she sat at the window and waited for steam to rise.

Anne rolled slowly, faced the room, her eyes closed. The girl lay quiet, still, and Gussie watched the quiver of eyelids, the muss of the hair. Deep sleep. Gussie tried to close her eyes, to feel sleep approach, but there was a dull pulse that kept her aware if not fully alert.

Here was Anne—even in sleep, she was graceful. She must dream of floating, drifting, swaying to music. Gussie had seen Anne dance—wouldn't ever forget—starting on a night when darkness took the mountain early and storm clouds wiped the stars from west straight across to east. Charlie and Arthur had cranked the Victrola they'd taken in trade for a dozen bottles. With the table shoved aside, there was room to dance. First, Arthur alone, his moves rising gradually through his shyness, until he lifted his soles from the floorboards and took some turns, some jumps and dips. On a chair to the side, Charlie swirled liquor in a glass and tasted it, held it on his tongue, allowed it to vaporize, as he would teach

Gussie, a mist to draw quick into the blood. And Anne watched from the darkness of the boys' sleeping alcove, seemed to find a phrase or rhythm in the tilt of her head, the shift of her fingers, and she closed her eyes halfway, as if she dreamed, and stepped into the light, came past the stove, her steps slow, one step per measure, on the downbeat, advancing. Anne with her hair pulled back into a low thin braid. Anne with her eyes closed now and arms rising in long arcs, smooth hinge of the wrists. Anne taller than Arthur and so light on the floor that she seemed to be a current of air he stirred. Anne whose brown wool trousers and green sweater bagged at the knees and elbows, whose shape curved and softened the fabric, whose boots for all their age and wear shone black, freshly polished.

She moved around Arthur, and he moved around her. He kept his distance, tried to mirror her rhythm, let his arms rise loosely, but on him it looked foolish. He watched his own arms rise and fall, watched the flutter of his hands, and then suddenly he pulled his arms stiff to his sides, hands into fists, stopped. Anne continued cycling through her blind dance until she came up against Arthur, stopped too, shoulder to shoulder with the man, looked down at him, he looked up at her, they smiled, didn't move, seemed stuck, remained there as the music ended and Charlie rose from his chair, changed the record.

The fiddle, banjo, guitar took a scratchy tempo, and Charlie stepped out onto the floor, saying, "You two don't know what it is to partner, to really dance as if you care for patterns and control," and as Anne rolled her eyes and Arthur frowned, Charlie came up from behind them, took hold of their shoulders, turned them to face each other, and for that song and other songs through that night and nights to follow he led them into the give-and-take of dance as Gussie watched. Charlie taller than them both, his long arms weaving between them, tipping hand to waist, palm to palm, a release and a promenade, Charlie on their heels, hovering close to their progress. Arthur was not on a level with Anne, not as quick, and he seemed only to half dare to guide her—it seemed more that he tried to pursue her, a shadow shuffling forward. The room confused the music with the heat, the lantern light with the bodies passing, the snow needling against the panes.

Gussie stayed at the edge even when Charlie said, "Come, Gussie, we need two couples if this is going to work the way it ought." She slid toward the dry sink, the shelves, took down a glass, filled it from the bottle, drank the clear liquor as Charlie passed again, saying, "Drink all you want, if it'll get you to dance with us," and she drank another glass, and she didn't dance. From deep in the cushions of the aspenwood armchair, from deep inside the muddle of sight and sound, Gussie had watched her daughter dance. It had been a dream, a lovely memory, as she drank Charlie's elixir and wove the melodies silently in her thoughts.

And now, in the old Rongis shed, Gussie's home, the water on the stove began to simmer, a busy sound, and she stood, stripped off her clothes, the cold air a welcome shock. She saw herself in the tall mirror Charlie had rescued from a ruined boudoir in Rongis. She might have been as tall as Leota, stronger, the bones obscured by muscle and hard work. Maybe Brud's shape had filled in around her shoulders and neck. From carrying Anne, her belly was scarred with pale purple lines. Her exposed skin a foolish white, vulnerable, no defense—given a chance, the sun would blister the whiteness. From her wrists to her battered fingernails, from the hollow of her neck to her brow, her skin was a dusty brown. On good days, long days, unrelenting days, the brown took on a fresh blush. She liked the line where dark skin cut to white. She liked that the line was hidden. Who would believe her strength if they glimpsed that useless white?

She washed herself with the warm water. Her skin quickly dried. She pulled fresh clothes from her chifforobe and dressed, buttoned away her neck, wrists, waist. The wool socks heated. The long johns dulled her skin's sensitivity. She pulled on her boots, still damp from the night's wear. Then she lowered herself onto the edge of Anne's bed.

"The day has started," Gussie said, and she pulled the blankets down off Anne's shoulder. "It's already light."

Anne sat up, holding the blankets against her side, and leaned away, back to the wall. She squinted past Gussie, toward the window, as if the gray dawn was noon. "I can still sleep," she said. "I'm still tired."

"You're lucky you can sleep," Gussie said. "I can't."

"I have nothing to do today but read what Charlie's given me. Won't you leave me alone for another hour?"

"You can't accomplish anything if you're asleep."

"I could finish my dream."

"And where will that get you?"

"I have to finish it to find out where it was going."

"Somehow this dream will make you stronger or smarter, or it will feed you breakfast?"

"No." She pulled the blankets up against her throat, lolled her head to the side, her cheek gentle on her shoulder, inhaled deeply, gazed toward the window, silver panes of light on the globes of her eyes. "I was walking alone," she said, "and it wasn't this mountain. I know it wasn't. The trees were different—some sort of tall deciduous with silver trunks. They didn't seem to belong, as if their roots wouldn't get enough water. Still, they were very beautiful. I looked them up in one of Charlie's books, but I couldn't find their proper name. I closed the book. I was sitting in the middle of a field circled by those trees like a fence. The green blocked most of the sky, and I couldn't see where the sun had gone or if there were mountains. Then I saw something, down low. Beyond the trunks there was a whole other land all around. I want to sleep again so I can finish. I want to get up and walk to where I can see beyond."

Gussie fought to clear the tangle in her head, tried to sharpen the image, Anne walking toward those trees. Gussie hadn't seen trees like that in the Wyoming ranges. It seemed a part of her own dream, another chapter, a later scene or earlier. The valley bent, and the water kept flowing. And here Anne looked directly at Gussie, didn't blink, waited. Gussie couldn't look away. This was her daughter. She should have taken the girl's face in her hands, brushed the sleep from her eyes, but Gussie was frozen there.

She remembered an afternoon beside the Sweetwater, when the river had spread shallow across the rocks, the banks broad and flat and baked with old tracks. Antelope. Deer. Coyote. The turf was thick and cool, and Gussie and Anne had found a hollow where they could lie. Anne dozed. Her hair fanned on the turf, spent flowers spiking through the golden strands. The sky filled, soft shingles of cloud. Gussie could have gotten Anne to shelter, but she didn't want to disturb her girl, didn't want to move. The sun lowered, seemed to glow from beneath the clouds and turn them copper. Then the storm thickened. The clouds lost their color and built higher, loomed, far lightning. The first rain misted, glazed Anne's skin, jeweled her lashes and pale lips. Gussie could've watched forever. The sky opened. Lightning descended. Anne came up sputtering in the rain, blinked water from her eyes, tried to duck from the storm, her face blotched with fear and cold, until she saw where she was, saw what had happened, saw the drench of her clothes, and then she focused on Gussie in her perch there, close, Gussie unable to say anything or get them to their feet, to rush them toward the road, and Anne gave her mother such a look of scornful pity, as if to say *You don't know anything of the world.*

Gussie stood up from the bed, crossed the room, toyed with the fire in the stove. "You need to get up, little girl," she said, peering into the flames that slid across the coals.

"I'd rather not."

"Rather would or rather wouldn't, makes no difference. It is past the hour, and we can't keep the boys waiting."

"They don't care."

"I care. And you should care." She shut the stove, stood at the window. High in the aspens, the sun had struck the mountainside—the promise of a clear, warm day, with raptors in the blue, ants on the float-boulders of jade, wild horses in a long gallop toward the

Sweetwater Rocks. As far as those horses ran, toward whatever imagined safe canyon or plain, from whatever pursuing wind, they always circled back into their range, centered on what they knew or what they'd come to know. The bitter scent of blooming sage. The bright outwash of agate on the dry streambeds. Thickspike wheat-grass. Saltbush. Milkvetch. Needle and thread. "When I was young, I was always awake early," Gussie said. "My mother wouldn't need to drag me out."

"Leota."

"Yes. My mother. I would be awake first. Or if she didn't sleep she'd still be awake from the night before."

"So, because I've just woken, and because you've been awake all night, you've gained some sort of puritanical triumph."

"That's not what I wanted to say."

"Then tell me."

Gussie looked up into the aspen branches. Some of the leaves had started to fade—the first softened green toward yellow, toward gold. Soon the view would open up, the snow would fall, the glare would make the looking painful. She turned back to the room, stood aside, out of the light, against the wall. Anne remained in her blankets—the light from the window sharpened her to icy gray. The girl waited. Slowly her chest rose and fell, her nostrils flared, lids swept her eyes.

"We lived in the red pines beyond Ravenglass," Gussie said.

"I know," Anne said. "Your father put your mother there, in the bachelor cabin."

"Leota made the place beautiful."

"She did what she could to make it habitable."

"My father brought her gifts."

"He didn't want her to leave."

"I was their delight."

"You were the child they had."

"I was the image of my parents."

"You took the name they gave you, but you even gave that up.

Where are they? Where are the Tornigs? Where, Mother? Why
don't you take me to them? Are they dead? Are they lost?"

"Brud used to come in from—"

"Used to."

"Leota was at the kitchen—"

"Was at. You've never even told me what she looked like."

"She looked like me."

Anne rose to her full height, two strides across the floor, took
Gussie by the elbow—sinewy strength in the girl's grip—and pulled
Gussie to the mirror. "Look," Anne said. "See. You and I don't look
anything alike. There's no strength in our family's blood. Tell me:
You aren't anything like Leota. And I'm nothing like you." She released her mother, stepped away, to the stove, tested the water in
the bucket, pulled off her nightgown.

Gussie shook the dull pain from her arm, crossed to Anne's bed,
squared the blankets, smoothed the pillow. Turning back, she sat on
the bed. In this tiny home, they could never get away from each
other. They could hear each other's every breath. Each roll on the
mattress in sleep or wakefulness. The scrape of the bucket across
the top of the iron stove. The heavy careful sound of the bucket
lowered, placed on the floor. The deep sound of hot water as Anne
dipped her hands in, inhaled at the bite of the heat, began to
smooth the water up her arms, down her legs, working as if there
were real soil on her skin, scrubbing white.

From Gussie's vantage, the Rongis mirror caught Anne's far side,
the curtained north window. Gussie had often wondered who had
first purchased that mirror with its brass fittings, oak carvings,
bevels. The mirror had framed someone else's mornings and evenings, some man or woman, young or old. And then the world had
moved on, the whole town of Rongis had been left to dust, and
Charlie had pulled the mirror from the ruin, brought it up the
mountain in the back of his wagon, intending it for Gussie and
Anne, even though Charlie and Arthur had no such looking glass in
their own house. But the boys had each other to keep them in line:

Charlie St. George, your pants is gone dusty red as the desert . . . Arthur Tooley, you need a lather and a blade, before spiders make a home in your whiskers . . . Charlie had presented the mirror wrapped in a blanket, unveiled it with a smile and a flourish. "No lady's happy if she can't see herself," he said. He set it where they made their ablutions, and he brought mother and daughter together, squared their reflections. In those days, Anne was still a child, and she stood in her mother's shadow, looking up and down from her own face to Gussie's, reaching back to hold to Gussie's leg as if she feared falling into that other world. But she knew mirrors, knew her own reflection, so it was most likely something else she feared.

Gussie knew little of her own body, and here was Anne bathing naked before the Rongis mirror. Anne cupped the hot water to her neck, to her shoulders, and the water ran her contours, brought color and quickly faded. There was daylight in the water, like silver threads and chips of quartz. Gussie wondered how that light and heat must feel on Anne's skin, wondered if Anne lived in a world somehow different, wondered if Anne bathed inside a net of sparking nerves. Did every touch feel like bright light? Did Gussie see her daughter's actual skin, or did she see only the dazzle? But, of course, inside the run of water, there was Anne.

Anne held her hair up, exposed the white length of her neck. She cupped palms of water to her breasts, the soft rose of the nipples. The shift from the rib cage to the hips. Arms up as she ran her wet fingers through her hair, straightened the sleep-pressed wings and curls—beneath her arms, the blond hair darker, nearly auburn, like a shadow of another time of day. Navel high and shallow, pooled against gravity. Her hands dipped from the bucket, touched her belly, moved down and converged at the narrow auburn tangle, and Anne seemed to freeze there a moment, or Gussie let the moment freeze in her thoughts.

Up from the bed, Gussie crossed the room, unhooked a towel from its place on the wall, held it up between herself and her daughter. "Try to cover yourself," she said.

"Who will see me?"

"The boys."

"They don't come over here." She took the towel, dropped it on the floor. "They don't come if we don't need them for something."

Gussie looked away, toward the window. "You always argue. Won't you just do what I ask?"

"Cover myself while I'm bathing?" Anne crouched at the bucket, legs splayed, and cupped water again and again to her face, letting the water fall again like rain into the container. Then she stood, tall, her eyes half closed against the soaking, took her brush off the shelf, lined herself up directly in front of the mirror. "Look at this," she said.

Gussie looked. Anne traced herself with the back of the brush. The pressure of the wood left faint blushing paths on her skin. "What are you doing?" Gussie said. "Are you taunting me?"

"Oh, Mother, I don't bother about your modesty. I know it has nothing to do with me." She gave her hair a few quick strokes with the brush, clearing her brow and ears. "Charlie has me studying forms. I've been rendering with charcoal. He says to break things down to their basic volumes—cone, cylinder, globe. Then find the texture and the shadows that camouflage and give character to what lies beneath. Do you understand?"

"Of course I understand. It's not Latin or French."

"Not yet." She dropped the brush on the towel, pulled her hair back and braided it loosely—a few twists. She crossed her arms, then held to her own shoulders, inclined her head forward, held the pose. "What do you think? Underneath." She released her shoulders, ran her hands down and rested them on her hips. "Or is it possible to guess at hidden volumes and forms beneath the surface of a living thing? Sometimes I think that the skin and movement and breathing are too much of a distraction. Have you ever considered that, Mother?"

"I haven't."

"Have you ever examined yourself?"

"Myself?"

"Tried to make sense of the shapes that make the whole?"

"No."

"Tried to figure if lumpish things somehow combine into something graceful?" She jutted her sharp hips forward, moved her hands onto the flat plane of her belly, a slick sheen of water still evaporating. "You see," Anne said, "there isn't much pleasant about the body. Every part is a lopsided globe, an incomplete curve. The mass of the calf gets sort of stringy toward the ankle. The expanse between the last ribs and the hipbones seems to be insufficiently supported, so that its shape is constantly in flux. You see." She turned to face Gussie fully, moved herself in slow, open curves. On her lips, the makings of an almost-smile, her eyes on Gussie's eyes, not straying. The tilt of the hips, the slight outward bend of the knees, the flutter of the fingers as if drawing something closer.

"Why do you hate me?" Gussie said, and she turned away, fearful that another tick toward a smile on the girl's lips would bring tears. She felt Anne's fingers touch her back as she stepped past the girl and knelt again at the stove, opened the door. The dry heat on her face eased the tightness of her nerves. She picked up the towel from the floor, held it, blindly, and Anne took it. The sound of cotton on skin. The sound of flame settling into ash. Gussie fed more fuel into the stove. Slowly the heat took the surface of each stick, and what had seemed solid began to waver.

Anne passed through the room, pulled on her clothes. The stomp of her boots as she settled them on her heels. "Won't you come with me, Gussie? Breakfast will be cold."

Gussie didn't stand, didn't look at her daughter. She broke a twig into scraps, flicked them into the firebox.

"I've lived where you wanted me to live," Anne said. The latch on the door worked against rust, the door creaked open, the flames in the stove jumped and settled. "I can't live here forever."

The door was left ajar, cold flooding in. Anne was gone. Gussie shut the stove, stepped quickly to the door. There was Anne, off into the white pillars of aspen, kicking lively down the trail. And her voice came back—notes without words, bright, sharp. The light quivered in the first morning breeze, the green filter of leaves, the splash of clear brightness. Anne was soon nothing but movement among the aspens and light—her hair, her shoulders, a hand.

Sweetwater

Charlie St. George had been right—Prohibition would soon be repealed. But not before Charlie's still had been destroyed by federal agents, he'd paid a fine of $1,000, and he'd been shipped off to a Kansas prison. The Crooks Mountain ranch did not improve in Charlie's absence. With a roll of cash Charlie had hidden away, with Charlie's plans in hand, Arthur bought twenty head of cattle, gave real ranching a try again. The thirsty herd kept busting through the wires, trailing after the wild horses, down into the green swales of the Sweetwater Valley. Arthur rode the lines, poked at the leaning fenceposts, but most often he sat his horse on the ridge and looked east to where Kansas lay, out there somewhere. Each morning at breakfast, he laid out a new plan to spring Charlie from the pokey. *Decoys. Dynamite. Letters to the governor.*

"The days are ticking off," Gussie said. "Put your effort into something useful, or there won't be a ranch left for Charlie to call home. You wouldn't want it to fall to pieces."

"I wouldn't know what I wanted if it kicked me in the head," he said.

Arthur was distracted. He stopped shaving. He slept with

Charlie's books. Some nights he forgot to go to bed. Some days he forgot to wake up.

"What's wrong with you, Arthur?" Anne said.

"I'm sad."

"You'd do well to sleep with Charlie's thesaurus. Then you could be melancholy or bereft or lachrymose. Myself, I'm feeling the passage of precious time and the loss of my mentor."

"You're sad," he said.

"You could say so." She gave a sharp laugh.

"Damn hell. What am I supposed to do?" Gussie said. "Don't know any lullabies that'll work for two such gigantic whelps."

"Good idea," Anne said. "Sing us a song."

"Give it a try," Arthur said.

"Wish I could catch my breath long enough to sing," she said, "but I got to work. If I don't work, we don't eat."

◆ ◆ ◆

Months passed. Gussie walked through a chilly summer night. The aspen leaves blocked the stars. She almost wasn't sure if her eyes were open or closed. She heard her steps, the grind of gravel, the roots. She knew which trail she followed, how each step would fall. Years on Crooks Mountain.

She found the boys' house, felt its tight door, worked the latch, stepped from night to stillness. She held her breath, heard the last exhalation of the coals in the stove. No heat left in the metal. She knew the pattern of the house, passed through the spaces, came to the alcove, held her hand out in the air, couldn't feel a hint of Arthur's sleeping breath, the warmth drawn from deep in his blood. She reached far down to the mattress, found the bed empty, felt only the dents he'd pressed into the batting, the shape of hip, elbow, knee, shoulder, all his sharpest parts. There was no pillow she could hold to her face, smell his hair, taste his dreams. He'd crawled off to sleep somewhere else. She couldn't hold her fingers to his neck and wrist, judge his heart, calm him.

She turned quickly away. She wouldn't look for him—no way to find him on the mountain except by accident. Easier for her if he disappeared. She knew the dreams that tightened his limbs, thumped his ribs, jerked him upright, until she soothed him asleep again. He was weak. But she wanted to feel the shake of his nerves, the big violent moves, the sparks as his legs kicked beneath the wool. Easier for her if he never found his way back. But his gloom at losing Charlie seemed to be something she should study. The particulars of his nights scared her, thrilled her.

She ran a trail, out to the edge where the world dropped away. Darkness. Another step and she would fall. Here on the mountain, she had two charges now, Anne and Arthur. There had been a few simple years, times when the money was easier, when she did only her own share and most of Anne's. But Anne had grown. Arthur was a man. She turned, took another trail, skidded across needles and sandy gravel, stopped where the sky opened. The stars settled against the horizon, swirled up in clouds, rivers of light, milky pools.

North of Ravenglass, she had run in the wake of ravens, tried to leap onto their trails. She had dreamed of ravens so high against the blue that the earth lost its towns, roads, fences, people. A map of the world—patches of green, flat stretches of sky-colored water. From above Crooks Mountain, she would see the slopes without steepness, without obstacle, the mottle of aspen and evergreen, the chimney with its smoke, the rusty tin roof. Then she'd catch a thermal, rise beyond focus or understanding—just the ease of air, the wondrous tension of skin and feather, the distance covered with the tip of a wing, horizons rolling into horizons, the circling of the sun.

Gussie turned away from the stars, back down the trail. Trees closed in around her, opened again. She came in along the fence, slid a finger on the wire, skipped the barbs. Then the corrals. She ducked through the boards, crossed the dry enclosures, passed the sleeping horses—they took no notice of her, didn't startle. Passed the loafing shed, granary, swaybacked barn—a whole village of structures for the animals, the spaces empty tonight. Passed the house again—still empty, she knew—no smoke on the air. Through the aspen. To the black square of her shed. Stopped short. Could almost feel the weight of those walls. Could almost judge the volume of air the shed held separate from the night. Surely Anne was there, asleep in the old bed, beneath Mr. Foster's wool blankets.

Gussie passed in through the door, stood over Anne's bed, waited in the blackness for sound or scent. Gussie tried to imagine Anne's absence, the moment of discovery, the empty bed. She waited for something to happen, a response—could be a jolt, a shiver, a flash of light behind her eyes that would send her deep into dreamless sleep. What a strange place that would be—sleep without thought, sudden sleep, sleep not to be broken until the mind finished with its business of repair or forgetting. And then the slow waking. The water cupped from the basin, held to the eyes, throat. The stretch of the arms high, crack of the joints, and the settle into thought again. If she awoke after a long sleep, if she found herself alone on Crooks Mountain, if she had no place to be, no meal to fix, no ranch, no road crew waiting for her, no child to lose—if her child was already lost—she might sleep again, she might awake, take to the thermals, drift.

Gussie reached down—Anne was there—touched the girl's shoulder, stroked the soft fall of her hair, didn't want to wake her, didn't want to hear her voice that moment, that morning, easier to start forgetting before she was gone, bound to be gone. But Gussie said, "Up," waited long enough to hear Anne's usual "I'm awake." Then Gussie grabbed what she needed for the day, headed out. A cold light among the thin white trunks. Anne would follow.

In the house, Arthur sat at the table, his breath calming. Gussie lit a lantern, loaded the stove with kindling and lengths of wood, dropped in a match. Soon the room was bright and warm, full of the steam of boiling water, the smoke of heated fat. When she laid the plates on the table, Arthur rubbed his eyes, stretched the corners of his mouth, took a fork in his fist and stabbed lamely at the sausage, took a bite. "Morning," he said, didn't look up.

"Yes," she said. "Again."

Anne bundled herself in from the cold, sat directly at the table, drank down her coffee, started on the sausage. Gussie laid out the bread and butter. Anne's fingers touched Gussie's when they both reached for the knife.

"I'm sorry," Gussie said, releasing the handle.

"Of course you are," Anne said. She scraped a thick layer of butter across her bread. "You'll never be a cook, not like Arthur, but we don't mind."

Gussie flinched, pushed herself up from the table, dropped her plate on the counter. "Let's go, Anne. I'll be late." She took up her jacket, waited at the door. "And, Arthur," she said, "if you would ride the lines and actually fix the breaks, we might be able to hold our stock once we track it all down."

"I don't blame them heifers," he said.

"Fine," Gussie said. "Good."

He waved her off, laid his head on the table, a chemistry text as a prop.

"Don't drool on that book," Anne said. "I plan to get through the next chapter tonight."

"You haven't done any studying for weeks," Gussie said, and she opened the door.

"That doesn't mean I don't plan to."

"Don't bother me with your ambitions. Do it or don't."

The dawn was muted. Dew on the grass and blooms. Gussie carried her lunch pail, quick through the cold air, climbed up into the truck, started the engine. Anne joined her in the cab, arranged herself with blanket and pillow, settled in for the morning ride. Before the sun was a full diameter above the horizon, before wind began to strafe the plain, Gussie had taken her place with the road crew, and Anne was fully stretched out in the cab, back into sleep.

◆ ◆ ◆

Late morning, a mile past Sweetwater Station. A rocky draw cut down from the hills, crossed the line of the highway, the creek channeling nothing but dust. The crew followed the same plan for each bridge of more than a five-foot span—concrete, a bit of decoration, a date pressed into the wet pour. This puny draw hardly seemed worth the effort. Automobiles approached from east or west, touring, and they all easily detoured directly through the draw itself, leaving puffs of exhaust.

When the foreman called lunch, the crew gathered at the trucks and equipment, the only easy shade. Gussie reached up and knocked on her truck window, called to Anne, but Anne wasn't there. So Gussie slid down against a tire, dug into her lunch. The girl would return, or she would miss the meal. Then Gussie saw Anne along the highway at the next rise. Anne looked west. Automobiles passed at slow intervals.

From that rise, there was a view of the Wind River Range, the snowy peaks in cloud. No view yet of Lander, the city on the Popo Agie. Lander was cluttered with people, storefronts, rail line and station. Who knew but a hundred people a day might step from the train, take a room at the Noble Hotel, book a coach to Yellowstone. Northeast of Lander, it was rich land, or so Gussie had heard, land thick with tame hay, five tons of alfalfa per acre, sunflowers, peas and rape, apples in orchards, buffalo berries, wild cherries, green pears, raspberries, currants. Farther, at the Little Wind River, halfway to the big Wind River itself, the Shoshones danced their holy steps at Fort Washakie, listened for the beat of other steps on other paths, sang the sun from the clouds, sang of long rain on the tall-grass plain, and the wickiup in the grove. Gussie wanted to linger at the edge of those circles, but there was no admission for whites. She wanted to judge the language and dreams, see if any of it had come to her through her blood, see if the eyes were as dark as Brud's, if there was a map to these particular wilds, a trail she could follow to a warm spring, a corral, a cabin.

Dozy in the heat, Gussie watched the distance. Antelope wandered the plain. An automobile passed, dipped through the draw, continued west, approached Anne, stopped at the crest of the rise. Anne backed away into sage and rabbitbrush—her trousers and shirt were as faded as the brush, her hat a dark crumpled blob. From the automobile climbed two women in long slender dresses. They pinned on straw hats against the sun. One pulled a large black camera from the trunk, the gangly tripod tangling with her legs. The women seemed reluctant to take a full step off the road, so they tried to coax Anne to come closer, but Anne didn't move. Finally, one of the women just leapt into the brush herself—her giddy laugh came down the wind—took Anne's arm and held the girl tight against her side. The second woman set up the camera, held her hand aloft, took the photograph. Then they left Anne, returned their camera to the trunk, climbed into the automobile, and disappeared over the rise toward Lander. They took with them a negative of a lovely woman in a yellow dress, a shock of sagebrush, cloudless sky, the woman gripping the arm of a girl in trousers, her face shadowed by the crumpled brim of her hat, and a backdrop of river, hills, antelope.

Anne turned away, walked back along the road toward the crew. She seemed to struggle against heat and gravity—her boots scuffed the road, her head lolled forward, turned side to side. Slowly she passed down the gauntlet of the resting crew, and the men made their usual jokes.

"If you're bored, we got extra shovels."

"I don't think she's much for work."

"Ain't it work to wait all day on your mama?"

"She's a girl what's got a delicate sense."

"We gots a extra shovel."

"I told her that."

Anne kept to her pace, the stiff flick of her fingers the only sign that she heard them at all. Beside Gussie, she sat heavily, reached into the lunch pail and pulled out a baked apple, unwound the wax paper, took a bite, wiped a sugary drip from her chin. Her legs stretched out as far as the sunlight.

"You nearly got carried off on someone else's holiday," Gussie said.

"They're going to Yellowstone Park. How far is that?"

"You just follow this highway. It's far, but not too far. Colter's Hell. Boiling water splashing all over. That's what I hear."

"They said it's supposed to be magical. It's not as if Crooks Mountain is heaven."

"No. Of course not."

"You have something to say against every place that's not here. Or not Ravenglass."

"Maybe I do. I'm sorry."

"You're not sorry."

"Maybe I'm not." Gussie took a long drink from her canteen. The Crooks Mountain water left its metal tang on her lips—she thought she hadn't really tasted it for years, the water distilled through this land, endless seasons, rainfall, snow. She looped Anne's arm, just as the woman from the automobile had. "I thought they were going to take you."

"They had room in their automobile. They invited me. I could've gone."

"You didn't even want your photograph taken. I don't think you're going to run off with strangers."

"That's exactly what you think I'm going to do. Else I wouldn't be here with you. I'd be home, keeping Arthur company, doing the work that needs to be done for him and all of us."

"Seems doubtful."

"Do you think I would ride down off Crooks Mountain while you're at work, that I'd find someone to rescue me?"

"Yes, I suppose I do."

"Those ladies were traveling alone, just for the adventure. They were not much older than I, yet they talked to me as if I were an imbecile. Look at me. I do not appear to be a young woman of intelligence or refinement."

"If it's important to you, I could buy you a dress."

"With what money? We have nothing. And what good is a dress? I'd ruin it in a week out here."

"I know. I've ruined a dress or two."

"I'm seventeen."

"What do you need?"

"I don't know." She finished the baked apple carefully, licked the tip of each finger. She rose to her feet, bent down and pushed Gussie's hat off, kissed her mother on her square brow, replaced the hat, leveled it, smoothed the brim. "I don't know," she said. "I love you, Gussie."

"Thank you," Gussie said, and she looked up at Anne, the girl tall against the first high scudding clouds, a real smile on her pale face. "I love you too, Anne."

"You worry about me."

"I love you." Gussie held her hand out, and Anne took it, helped her to her feet. The crew was wandering back toward the bridge. Gussie and Anne fell in line. "And I worry."

"I'm a smart girl."

"I was too."

They laughed. Gussie joined the crew, and Anne kept walking along the highway, then cut down to the fields. Into afternoon, the crew kicked at the stones, stooped to inspect the sand, the deposits, dug out the remnants of battered beams. Finally, Gussie stepped away from the forms she'd set, made room for the men with the concrete. She sat on a stack of lumber, rested, looked toward the Sweetwater River.

Antelope had come closer, into the grass between road and river. Anne was in that grass too. Those sleek animals moved toward her, their hooked black horns punctuating the acres. Anne waited for the antelope. She was almost as invisible as an antelope—the tan cloth, the white cloth, the black hat. The big buck was twenty feet from her. She held out her hand, a fistful of grass, a doomed gesture. The buck raised his head, shook his horns, did a little jump. And then the antelope all turned in a brilliant silent move and flashed toward the river. And Anne ran, fast in their wake, made for the willows, weightless strides. If she shouted, if she sang, her voice was lost to Gussie. Anne disappeared into the willows, just a flash of her white shirt among the first branches.

Gussie didn't move. Heat rose in lines. Sun sparkled on the Sweetwater.

SIX

The Pinnacles

Gussie carried what she needed for a trip of a thousand miles—clothes in a satchel, her final road crew pay in her pocket. She traveled in a succession of automobiles. The agents at the Lander rail station couldn't answer her questions, weren't certain if they'd seen Anne. She continued northwest, the hayfields and orchards, brushy ridges, into Fort Washakie, the Indian offices. She stared at the faces of the Shoshone—the dark eyes, dry lips, skin like a clue to the arc of the sun. For them, she was sure, the notches in the horizon were like a language, a compass, and she thought of Brud's stride, the distances he could travel where even she couldn't follow, the miles he had lived beyond the borders of the woods she'd known.

Gussie caught another ride. The highway spanned the Little Wind River, rose with the bare hills, descended through a labyrinth of broken rocks and undercut rims and blind canyons, until the green plain of the Wind River was laid out ahead, the bright tangled river. She was left standing at a crossroads—turn east to Riverton, or turn west up the valley to the verging of the Wind River Range and the Absarokas, to Togwotee Pass, to the farther views, the geysers and peaks, on out of Wyoming. West seemed the logical direction. She turned, walked along the highway.

Afternoon blew in—distant squalls and dust devils. Soon she heard an engine approaching, and she stopped, looked back. Here came an apparition of rusty metal that just barely escaped from the dust it kicked up. The cab was dark, appeared vacant. She raised a hand, waved vaguely, and the truck squealed, chugged, stopped dead. She walked back, climbed up on the running board, peered inside. A small man sat behind the wheel, worked at the ignition. Gussie leaned farther in and said, "Excuse me, sir."

He turned, looked at her. She tried to make him out. At first, his jaw appeared silver—it was a few days of whiskers. His eyebrows swept wildly above his narrow squinted eyes. He was rumpled, tiny, ancient. He tilted his head a bit, turned to the choke, his fingers shaking until he got a good grip. In a deliberate choreography of hands and feet, he brought the engine back to life. Holding high to the wheel, he pulled himself up straight enough to see forward. Then he just sat there.

"Sir?" Gussie said. "Can you give me a ride?"

"Ain't I stopped for that reason?"

She opened the door, climbed in, and they rode west together. She shifted on the seat, failed to avoid the sharp springs through the rotting fabric.

"Not a worthy chariot," the man said.

"It's fine."

"It's not. But see how fast we fly."

The truck crept forward. The highway clung to the contours of the hills, above the green plain, below the precipitous range and its black defiles, stark-lit cliffs. A butte stood north of the river, a hazy sentinel against a hazier distance. Gradually the butte sharpened— flat on the top, like a beheaded pyramid, but much older than the most ancient monument, its sides striped with layers of time and carved deep with channels, folds, erosion.

"Crowheart Butte," the man said, without looking away from the road. "Up on top, a chief ate another chief's heart. That was the end of that particular battle."

"What about their tribes and warriors?"

"You going to keep fighting if you seen one man eat another man's heart?"

"I follow your point."

The butte drew past. The highway dipped into a broad draw, and the sage flats gave briefly to humps of thick grass, willows, a creek. There, beneath a lone cottonwood, a ranch settled—one-window cabin, fences set out around a long shed, a huge bull in the dirt. Black dots of heifers far up the creek. The road wound the next hillside.

"That place weren't there," the man said. "I don't remember it. You know who got that place?"

"No, sir." She looked back through the cracked oval window, saw the spread laid out like a map, the trails threading the acres—game trails or cattle trails or both. And a spot of red, a half-barrel planted with flowers—geraniums?—and a bench beneath the tree. The road crested the lip, and Gussie turned forward again. Miles of vacant open, with the foothills rising closer. "I'm just on my way through."

"No. You're not."

"I'm following someone."

He nodded. "I know all about that."

"How could you know? You and me haven't ever met."

"Myself, I never had any luck. If I looked for someone, I was sure not to find 'em. You see . . ." He adjusted himself taller in the seat, let off enough on the gas that it seemed the wind would stop the truck's progress altogether. He scanned the road ahead, the hills, the river bottom. A succession of automobiles approached from the west, and, as each passed, the man's knuckles went white on the wheel and his eyes nearly shut. "There," he said, and he raised a finger, pointed ahead. His foot pressed, the truck accelerated, the rattling chassis tested its sounds against the wind.

"Sir?" Gussie said. "Can I help you some way?"

He kept driving, probably didn't hear her, another quarter mile or more, and then he released the accelerator, pulled his feet back beneath the seat, coasted off into the stony brush. The truck bucked and died, stopped short.

"You don't have any brakes?" Gussie said.

"Just want to keep them new." He opened the door, slid to the ground, shut the door. Only the top of his head showed through the open window. "Come along, little lady." He moved around the front of the truck, angled northwest, in the general direction of the river.

Gussie waited. The man took healthy strides, winding among the sage, prickly pear, anthills. His head turned side to side, he shaded his eyes, stopped as a gust of wind tightened his clothing around his limbs, torso—he was no more than a collection of bones, a flip of fine gray hair. The wind died to its usual steady whip, and he brushed the dust from his shoulders, continued. He seemed to be walking someplace particular. Gussie couldn't see anything but distance. She slid down from the truck, followed.

His footprints in the sandy soil had already drifted away. Hurrying, she tried to take the steps she'd seen him take, to weave the spiny cactus paddles and dead fingers of sage, and then she found herself beside him, and he reached and took her hand, such a light, hollow touch, and they walked together. Gussie saw that his boots barely held to their soles, that his trousers were belted with a rope of plaited horsehair.

"Where are we going?" she said. "Sir?"

"Walker."

"Yes, we're walking, and you're very good at it. But do you have something in mind?"

"No—*I'm* Walker. My name."

"Gussie."

"You're looking for someone, Gussie."

"She's not out here."

"Probably not. But I lost someone here. Maybe we can put our minds together."

"When did you lose this fellow?"

"It was a girl, a lovely girl. It's been a while. When did you lose yours?"

"Two days ago."

Walker stopped, pulled Gussie to face him. And she saw him clearly in the bright sun—whoever he had lost, however long it had been, he wouldn't forget for a single minute of the time he had left to him. His face was ashen, deeply lined, the bones holding the tension of the skin. She raised her hand, touched him on the brow, on the chin, felt his warmth, and she touched her own face, felt the soft padding of her cheeks, the spongy point of her nose, the tightening of her eyes, quiver of lashes. Two days only, since she'd lost Anne. She might never find her. No way of knowing if she was even on the right trail. She closed her eyes hard, and she saw dark red and sun spots and nothing certain.

◆ ◆ ◆

On her last day with the Sweetwater road crew, as the afternoon cooled toward evening, thunderheads had sailed past to the north and south, but there on the highway the sunlight was undisturbed. The crew had gone about packing away the tools, adjusting the flags that led traffic around the work site, checking again the concrete in its wooden forms. She laid her hand on the curing concrete, and it was warm to the touch, with the slightest give, deceptive—soon the forms would be pried free, and the bridge would span the draw, stand there for decades, still stand even after the road had been moved to a different grade, leaving a structure that served only to link one square of desert to another, until finally the draw would channel enough time and boulders to carry that bit of construction away, bury it in strata that eons might not disturb.

The crew walked back toward the vehicles, and Gussie came along behind. She was hungry, wondered if Arthur had prepared supper, but she was sure he hadn't. She thought of Arthur far down the ranch road in the lodgepole pines, at the point from which a man could watch the next mile of the road descend the mountain and disappear into Crooks Gap. There had still been road dust on the air, the federal vehicles so freshly departed that their engines still echoed against the house and the slopes behind. There Arthur had stood until dusk caught in the pines, until there was little of the view left but dark patches of trees, lighter stretches of rock, and the bulk of Sheep Mountain swallowed by the grander rise of Green Mountain. Maybe Arthur replayed the moment when the agents first climbed from the vehicles, the moment when Charlie St. George said, "It's all mine. I'm the one you've come for. These others couldn't distill anything stronger than water. They stayed out of the business. They're ranchers only," the moment when Charlie gave them each a quick hug, saying to Anne, "Sweetheart, there's more to learn," saying to Gussie, "I don't hold you to anything," saying to Arthur, "I don't go for long—I'll return." Maybe Arthur waited for those vehicles to turn back, for the lights to swing around the switchbacks, illuminate the pines in muddled sweeps of shadow and light. But nothing stirred in the miles below.

Finally, when the stars had turned and sparkled and dimmed in a scrim of cloud, when the silence of dead night had rendered the mountain small and alone, Arthur had come up the road, entered into the house where Gussie and Anne waited with hot cider and shepherd's pie. He was stiff with cold, couldn't seem to turn to close the door, to step farther into the warmth. Gussie and Anne brought him in beside the stove, fed him, rubbed his shoulders. Gussie thought then that not even cold could ever make her that numb. Arthur was a fragile man, more fragile than she had ever guessed. Slowly his ears flushed with color, his angles relaxed, he slumped forward.

Gussie had sent Anne away, stoked the stove, took Arthur into the sleeping alcove, sat him on his bed, stripped off his clothes, the fabric still icy in the weave. There he was, naked as a newt, his arms wiry, nipples pink and tiny, downy hair catching the lantern light, and his penis cradled at the crux of his muscled legs. She couldn't stop looking at him—he was the man she might have been, would never be. Maybe he was stronger than she was, could lift more, but she was smarter, could devise a way to lift whatever needed moving. His skin was raised with goose bumps even as he shrank in on himself. She had no desire to touch him, to kiss him, to pull him to her. Somehow it seemed that she would be touching the wrong sex.

Arthur looked up at her. He was waiting for something. His eyes were wide, blank. She pushed him back onto the bed, got him under the covers, and his eyes closed. That was good—he would awake with a fresher take, back to himself, back to the work at hand, practical things. But she couldn't leave him yet, not with only the single blanket and the house bound to get bitter before dawn no matter how hot she stoked the fire. She turned from him, and there was Charlie's bed within reach. She pulled from Charlie's bed the sheets, blanket, pillow, and she covered Arthur with Charlie's layers, and she tucked Charlie's pillow between Arthur and the wall, where cold was certain to find its way through cracks in the chinking.

Arthur was deep now in the bed. She leaned closer over him, heard his slow whistling breath, placed her palm on his brow. He was warm. She kissed him lightly on the cheek, straightened the heavy covers across his neck. Asleep, he said, "I'm asleep, Charlie St. George. See you in the morning." Gussie had thought often of the particular quality of his voice, then, his mouth misshapen by the pressure of the pillow, his lips caught in the cloth, his neck restricted by the weight of sleep, the softness of the sounds as if he had known the listener would recognize the words simply by tone and shape.

Gussie continued along behind the Sweetwater road crew. No supper would be waiting at the ranch. She thought her way through the supplies, planned a meal of onions browned in a skillet, dried beef softened in a sauce of butter and flour, coffee, biscuits. Arthur and Anne would wait at the table. And then, as Gussie cleaned up the dishes, Arthur might place a recording on the Victrola, Anne might toy again with her plan to read another chapter in the chemistry textbook.

The crew all separated toward the various vehicles, and Gussie stepped up to her truck, opened the door and tossed in her gear, then stepped back and scanned the surrounding acres for Anne. The girl was nowhere in sight. Gussie walked to the rear of the truck, climbed up onto the bumper, looked again, but the higher vantage made no difference. She cupped a funnel of her hands at her lips, called, "Anne . . . Anne . . . I'm going." No echo. No answer. Then the sound of the other vehicles starting, the grinding of gears, crunch of tires on gravel. In a minute, Gussie would be alone. She looked again, up the hill, off toward the Sweetwater, but if Anne was there she had blended into the evening colors, cast no shadow. So, before the crew could escape, Gussie jumped down into the road, stopped everyone.

"I saw her east," one man said.

"Seems she was up the hill, that way," another said.

"Wading in the Sweetwater."

"Talking to travelers."

With the vehicles all parked again, the crew stood together awhile, looking off west into the sun, looking east down the line of their own lengthening shadows, a gaggle of sweaty, exhausted men, with Gussie at the center. She saw their torn trousers, their frayed shirts. She felt their hands on her shoulders and back, a pat or rub, as they talked of what might be done.

◆ ◆ ◆

Gussie and Walker made their way farther, caught an animal trail, and Gussie went ahead, down the narrow line, reaching her hand back to Walker's hand, bringing him along. Over the lip of the floodplain, angling slowly down the slope pocked with river rock, onto the water-smoothed bottom. The trail continued, no doubt would lead to the water in the riverbed. Tall willow brush. Cottonwoods farther toward the river.

They stopped in a clearing thick with bunchgrass. "This is the place I wanted to find," Walker said. The willows were half dead branches, half fresh shiny limbs with long leaves. Birds chattered, circled, the flutter of wings. The air flowed above the willow thickets—here on the ground the air was still, the slow circling of black flies, the jump and crackle of grasshoppers—but the river, out of sight beyond the ranks of willows, seemed to carry wind along with its cold sound. High cottonwood leaves whipped on their loose stems. Magpies took the gaps among the trees.

"Used to be eagles," Walker said. "Don't see any today."

"If we wait long enough, we'll see an eagle, maybe."

"I waited for three days. Yes, if I remember, three days."

"For eagles?"

"No, Gussie. For the girl I lost. Are you with me here?"

"Yes, sir. Sorry." Still, she looked at the sky.

He pulled at her hand, and gradually they lowered themselves onto the grass. It was warm in the sun. The grass, stiff and sharp, made a substantial cushion. Gussie sat straight above her crossed legs. Walker pointed, and Gussie looked up along his direction. The Wind River Range stood like a battlement, unbroken, unbreakable, building its own storms.

"She went in there," he said, "into them mountains. I waited here. She didn't come back."

"So you followed?"

"I didn't know the way into the mountains."

"Did she say she'd come back?"

"Yes. Could be I didn't wait long enough. Could be she didn't know where to find me. But how long can a boy wait? I had to find myself a place to live. I found a place. I lived. Even through winter, and lots more winters, I lived. My own place."

"What happened, Walker? Why'd she go into the mountains?"

"There was a stolen horse. There was some people who wanted it back. And they wanted *her* back. She was not old, not at all. She was a girl, actually. From beside the Black Sea. The Circassian girl. Such a sweet thing. She would've lived with me."

"Was she your wife?"

"No. Nothing like that. She just liked the thought I was going up this valley. She liked I would be the first man to settle this valley, though I wasn't hardly a man, and I didn't know yet how to find the gear and game to help me survive."

"When?" Gussie said. "When did you lose her?"

"Oh, Gussie, it's been a few years, since 1871, I think." He scratched his head, laughed, looked away from the mountains, looked at Gussie, his eyes clouded with tears. "I guess she's not coming back. I guess there ain't nothing to do about it. Sixty-four years past? If she's not dead, I hope she's in a fine place of her own, 'cause if she is dead, there ain't a nice place in all the stars could hold all the sin she did in just the weeks I knowed her. And I ain't looking forward to dying, too, 'cause I'm worse than her."

◆ ◆ ◆

Gussie awoke, sat up, looked at Walker where he lay beside her, sleep still fluttering his eyes, gapping his lips. Evening had drained down from the high, lit peaks, the sailing clouds, and settled in the floodplain. Walker might have been a handsome man in his day, though a bit on the petite side. In the silver-gray of his hair a few strands of black lurked. He startled, his hand went to his throat, his eyes slitted open, looked straight up to the sky, a moment of focus, then swung sharply to Gussie.

"What you got us into?" he said, and he sat up, tried to jump to his feet, but his muscles wouldn't do the work. His head snapped around at the view, and then abruptly he calmed and settled, smiled at Gussie. "Oh," he said. "Thought I was someplace particular for a second, then I saw that I was just where I thought I was."

"That's happened to me, once or twice. Only I wake and think I'm home, but then I don't know which home."

"Tell me, Gussie, about this person you've lost."

"Ain't a person—it's my girl."

"Goddamn. A baby?"

"My girl is seventeen."

"Can't be."

"I know. But that's the truth."

"She run off?"

"Yes, sir."

"And here I've got you napping when you're in a rush to follow."

"Don't know which way she went." She tried to do the math on sixty-four years, tried to imagine the thousands of routes that could start from the bank of the Sweetwater River. It could take ten times sixty-four years to search out all the possibilities. Would Anne turn east or west, shade her eyes from sunrise or sunset? Would she head toward cold or heat? What had Charlie St. George told her of all the places he'd been or the places he wished he had gone? Anne might have picked a destination years ago, as soon as she could think of leaving, and maybe Anne had even talked to Gussie of directions and desires, though Gussie couldn't remember. Gussie realized that she was just as likely to find Anne by standing still and waiting for Anne to circle around again. And maybe that was why Leota had never come after Gussie—Leota waited in one place until the day Gussie would turn back. Was it the duty of the one who had left to return to the one left behind, no matter the miles or the years between? As long as Anne was safe, Gussie thought, that was all that mattered, and she knew her girl was safe because she was Gussie's daughter, and hadn't Gussie always found a way to survive? "My girl could be a mile from here," Gussie said, "or she could be long gone."

"I'm guessing you don't got a plan, right?"

"No, sir, I don't. I haven't really got it straight in my head yet."

"And you don't got a sense that time lost will be fatal to your pursuit?"

"Maybe it was already too late yesterday or last week or ten years ago."

"Then let's stay here tonight. I'd like to. Will you stay?"

"It's the only offer I have at the moment."

"I stayed here once. It's quite passable. This is most likely the last time I'll be here—every sixty-odd years. I might not last another sixty. I got some food for us, and some matches. I never know if I won't make it home, so I always have to be ready."

He rose to his feet, reached into his ragged pockets, and produced a box of matches, a handful of jerky, some dried fruit that looked to be apples or pears. He dropped his supplies onto the bunchgrass at his feet. Gussie stood up beside him, searched her pockets, came out with three flattened biscuits, some shattered sticks of hard candy, a tin of sardines, and a box of matches the twin of Walker's. She added it all to the cache.

"I like you, Gussie," he said. "You remind me of me."

"I'd say you remind me of me too, sir, if you wouldn't take it unkindly."

"How could I?"

They looked straight at each other, looked each other up and down. They were a pair—nearly the same height, same shape, clothes the color of the land, cloth torn by brush and splinters and time, hair cut shortish, tangled. Low down their legs, their dungarees had browned with Wyoming dust. They smiled, shrugged, and Walker held out his hand, and Gussie took it, and they shook on some sort of final greeting.

"Let's get to work," Walker said. "Soon as the light goes, the real cold comes."

And when the sunset bled down into the horizon, the light of their fire in its nest of stones set the willows into ghostly motion. Lightning flashed over the Big Horns to the north, too distant for more than a murmur of thunder to mix with the river flow, the coyote yip, the pop of dry willow and cottonwood. They finished their supper, dropped the sardine tin into the fire, watched the heat blacken the metal, sizzle the oil. Walker laid on more wood from the stack of fuel they'd gathered. The fire threw plenty of heat.

"It was this time of year," Walker said. "Summer."

"You had a fire?"

"Couldn't. Had to stay secret, in case those men came back around."

"They were too much for you to handle?"

"Too much for three of me to handle, 'less I had dynamite and a cannon. But I didn't. Just me and my mule and a rifle."

"No one to help you, not anywhere? No law?"

"No law. I was alone. Listen, now. Look around. It was like this, nothing at all but animal trails, Indian trails, no ranches, nothing, no fancy highway, no town. Who would help me? A boy has to help himself."

"But the Circassian girl."

"I know." He squinted against a shift of smoke, held his palms out flat toward the flames. "Last I saw her was on the back of the gold horse, quick, then gone. And in all the miles I gone since, and with all the ladies I loved and lost, and with all the children I raised, the sweet girls and the boys, and one of them dead too soon, his face white in the coffin, still and all I see the one I knew the least and I grieve that I never found her again. If there was still tracks, I'd go now and find her, but there ain't tracks except in my mind, my waking mind sometimes and my dreaming mind regular." He withdrew his hands from the bright heat, rubbed them together, crossed his arms tight, let his head fall forward, as if he'd nodded off.

But then he talked on, the flames rising with each new branch added, the coals a liquid orange. He told her of the valley, the Wind River, the town. *F. A. Welty's—General Merchandise.* Cattlemen. Wyoming Tie and Timber. And then, years ago, the ranches started to take guests, called them "dudes." The work Walker had done to his place had paid off, his ranch on the lake in a valley of the range. On a good summer day, until lately, his valley was alive with echoes, the horses trailing behind the wrangler, the riders laughing, the canoes on the lake, the axe to the firewood, the waterfall a blaze of high sound. He'd made a paying game of everything that had nearly killed him when he was new to the upper country, when he was alone.

He knew this land better than almost anyone could ever know it again, seeing as how he'd learned it from one who had been born right out of the granite peaks and the glacial lakes the color of milk. That had been the Sheepeater girl, whom he'd named Mary, she who dressed him in brain-softened skins to keep him safe through winter, she who led him close enough to slay an elk with a shot from the ramshorn bow—together they had slit the animal's belly, spilled the blood onto the snow, eaten the heart—she who had left him of a sudden as if he'd chased her away, and he hadn't known what he'd done wrong or how to find her once she was gone.

And his wife, Eugenia, orphan girl found in a thicket, who calmly told of the pursuit and slaughter of her family by renegades. Eugenia gave him his five children, sat with him in the lodge above the lake, and they shared a sip of whiskey, remembered a trek across the range when rain fell through darkness and the cliffs broke and tumbled like the endgame of some godless battle. She died even before the first schoolhouse was built in the valley, no mother left to lead the five young ones through their lessons, no mother left to bundle them through the snow to the black lake and the hole in the ice and the string, hook, bait, no wife to lie with Walker in the bed beneath the window. Eugenia dead before there was any town to speak of at the confluence of Wind River and Horse Creek, no town yet where he could take her for a stroll, a meal, a dance, so that others might see her pale neck, her small hands. He buried her on the western slope above the lake, where she had liked to lie out in the fireweed on a summer day, buried her in a box of pine he'd cut, planed, joined, and on the grave he placed jagged bits of scree because she was always sharp enough to cut.

Eugenia had made of the ranch a working concern, had named the place the EA Ranch—*E* for Eugenia, *A* for Walker's family name, *Avary*—and he was fine with the name because there would have been no ranch but for her. And now it was a ranch without her. At evening, when cold filled his small valley, and the lake was calm, the air still, only the hiss of the waterfall, a constant drift of woodsmoke, starlight, when a huge moon tipped over the cliff and flooded the valley, moonlight on his skin, he wondered if he would always pass through that half-light, if he would ever see the truth of things in daylight, clear, crisp, if he would ever put together the story of his travels so that he could understand where he had been headed, where he had arrived. His children asleep in their bunks— a gathering of small beauty. Walker would sit on his bed and wait. Eventually, dawn would brighten the window, the valley would inch toward the sun, the young ones would stir.

Gussie tried to remember if there would be a moon tonight, tried to taste the air for coming rain—she tasted only smoke, saw only Walker Avary close his eyes, tighten his lips—tried to consider whether she would ever gain what Walker had lost. Maybe she was too far into her years, maybe she'd already lived her life. She had owned her part of the ranch on Crooks Mountain, had spent the night with lovers of varied skills, if such passing men could be called lovers—they were no more than that—and she'd raised a child, a single child. Already, Anne might have moved out from under this sky, might sleep in the shadow of different stars. Gussie wished she could see Anne at that moment, read her dreams, her memories. And Gussie wished she could remember her own first nights away, and reach farther back to Leota, hear Leota tell of her journey to Ravenglass, the first dream in the cabin in the red pines, hear Leota tell of the first night in Greeley, the first night with Frank Locke, the first night without Gussie.

Walker stood up from the edge of the fire circle. The smoke curled around him and moved on toward the willows, his shadow on the surface of the smoke, breaking apart. He seemed almost tall, almost young—slender and unsure. He dug his hands into his pockets, shrugged his shoulders high, looked around into the night. Turning, he took a few uneasy steps away, until he found his balance, and then he was striding into the far edge of the firelight, as if he'd found a trail.

Gussie jumped to her feet, left the warmth, followed Walker

Avary into the cold air toward the Wind River. Soon she moved past the light, lost sight of him—for a moment she thought she was alone, thought she'd always been alone beside the campfire on the floodplain—but she heard his steps, and she hurried to bring his steps closer, to touch his arm, hear his voice, this stranger. She might lose the fire, lose the highway, lose Walker's truck where her satchel waited on the seat, lose her way in the willow thickets where deer might lurk, where songbirds nested and night birds hunted their shivering prey, where the coyote hid from the wolf, but she wanted the man's heat, his story.

The river swept a current of humid air through the willows, through the cottonwood branches. She heard the leaves in the sky. The dry grass drawing across her legs. The soil going from dust to almost pure sand beneath her feet. And she thought she could hear the temperature of the river water—a density drawn from snow and altitude, somewhere in the range, the peaks, the hidden valleys, maybe Walker's own valley with its long lake, its black ice, its drifts that turned the daylight blue. And then she came to where the ground dropped away, and she felt the air open, and she caught her balance.

Here she was in the cold rush of sound. If there was a far side to the open, it seemed to be in the stars. She didn't move. Slowly a shape rose in the lower stars—the far cottonwoods, the farther line of the Big Horn Range connecting the clouds of treetops—and then the far north edge of the earth, beyond which she'd never thought to travel. And then she saw the river. Impossibly small reflections of stars on the water—the dips and eddies drew the heavens into new patterns, always shifting a fraction downstream. Maybe she had left all she knew behind—maybe she could step forward now and finally fall into the sky.

Walker was beside her. He placed his hand on her back. "This is the Wind River," he said. "Taste it." He took hold of her elbow, and they stepped down the bank. He guided her until they stood beside the flow, and he helped her kneel on the stones, took her wrist and plunged her hand into the water.

She shook her wrist free of his hold, cupped her palm, raised a bit of water to her lips, tasted it. It numbed her tongue, killed the flavors of their supper, the salts and stringy fiber. She'd known water like this before, the Big Thompson that nearly stopped her heart. She tipped back, sat on the bank, felt the night chill her bones. Pulling off her boots and socks, she stretched out her legs, let her feet submerge.

Something brushed against her skin, could have been a filament of green waving loosely or a fingerling adrift in sleep. And the bottom rocks were smooth and slick—she felt the contours, the rounded cobbles like hills, the patches of sand like plains and valleys. Slowly she mapped out the arc of riverbed that she could reach, and then her feet went numb, and she could feel nothing but the release of pain from the miles she'd walked. That was good, the cold, the absence. Walker also removed his boots and submerged his feet in the Wind River, but if it was his feet or the current that pushed at her, she couldn't tell. Then he took her hand, held it in both of his.

"I saw my son die," he said, and for a long minute he said nothing more. But finally he started again, close against Gussie, his voice a whisper as steady as the water. "I remember the bright grass in the sun, and the snow still in the shadows of the trees. It was spring. I waited for Tom where the road leaves the lake and heads into the woods, toward the Wind River. Tom was my son. He was sixteen. Had learned everything Eugenia had taught him and more than I could ever teach. We'd named him for Eugenia's lost brother, though I hope that weren't what made his luck.

"When he was a boy, he liked to sit on the rocks by the waterfall and breathe the water out of the air. He said it made him strong, but he never said how. He had his own mind. In winter, you would've took him for a Sheepeater Indian—he had on all my old skins, and what he couldn't find to fit he made for himself. Off he'd go into the coldest day. He had the Sheepeater bow. He had his own arrows and chipped his own points. I could never chip a point, just got a broken scrap of obsidian. He knew how to go farther with anything he learned, and he knew how to learn things himself. He had his brother and sisters reading and doing their arithmetic soon as he figured I wasn't a teacher. He was a comely boy, and smart. I wondered how he'd ever come from me. But there was Eugenia in him too, and she was not a woman to be stopped.

"Tom said we couldn't wait for commerce to find its way to us— we had to bring it here ourselves. Wouldn't city people like to wake of a morning and look out at the lake? Wouldn't a person like to ride past the waterfall and follow the creek and see where the water started? He wanted to build guest cabins, and I remembered that I'd thought of that too, when I was new to the valley. Tom sat me at the table and showed me the plans he'd drawn. He talked such a good story about how it would all come to be.

"So I was waiting for Tom where the road came up from the woods. I could hear the wagon and Tom's call to the horses. Tom had cut logs from up the DuNoir, good logs. Once I heard him coming, I went back over to the lodge, I don't know why, just to wait with the younger ones in the sun. They built cities of sticks and pinecones, as Tom had showed them.

"First I seen just the colors moving in the trees. Then I seen Tom's red coat. Then his face and his hands. And the reins. And the horses. Then the wagon stacked with the logs. The yellow pitchy ends of the wood and the black bark. Then out into the sun, and Tom with a smile and a wave like he'd already finished all the building and was proud of his work. That is the smile I remember.

"I don't know what kind of gods could make the Wind River Range that steep and sharp. In my valley, the water pours into the lake through a tight waterfall, and at the outlet the water cuts down into a channel, all the boulders dug up by the flow. Crossing that creek is always rough, even on foot.

"Tom drove the wagon up from the woods and came to the creek, and there he slowed the horses and talked to them and used the brake, and the wagon rocked on the way down the creek bank, it was steep, and Tom tried to be steady, but the weight of the logs would not slow, would not hold inside the ropes, and they started to slide. I ran. Tom was down beside the wagon, his feet in the water, and he held the ends of the ropes, and onto him came the logs like they had no weight at all, they just tumbled like sticks, and I don't think there was any sound till they settled and Tom was gone, and then I heard my splashing in the goddamned creek and the rattle of the wagon going on without a driver, on up toward the place where the cabins would be built."

Walker released Gussie's hand, and she felt the sudden chill of her skin where he had pressed her. Up against the stars, he stood, and then he took a few steps out into the water. Gussie rose, stood with him at the slow edge, where the detritus might turn and swirl upstream, lose its momentum.

"And still," Walker Avary said, "after that and more, I still see the Circassian girl when I close my eyes."

◆ ◆ ◆

Late into the night, Gussie awoke to the crackle of the fire. She sat up, looked down into the sticks and flames, to the coals. She had been dreaming of Anne, she thought, though now she'd lost whatever it had been. She was unsure even if it was still the same night on which she'd drifted off to the sound of Walker Avary's slow whistle, his words to an old song—*long, long trail* . . .

He wasn't beside the fire. She looked into the reach of the light. He was off toward a gap in the willows, looking on past the end of his shadow toward the Wind River Range and the cutout patterns of stars. His hands were deep in his pockets, and he swayed a bit, kept looking. She tried to see what he saw, to attach to the darkness the stories he had told, but it wasn't clear to her, still too fresh. She rose, walked to his side, looked where he looked. He circled her waist with his arm, pulled her hip to his hip, held her, his pulse shaking his grip.

"There," he said, and he pointed to the darkness where the range stood. "I found it. Where the stars fall into the canyon, there, she went out of sight. I think this is where I stood when I waited for her."

"You knew she wouldn't come back."

"But still, you have to wait and look and go through it all. Could you find where you last saw your girl?"

"I saw where she went into the willows toward the Sweetwater River. I went to that spot at sunset. The road crew looked up and down the floodplain. They shouted her name—something beautiful about that sound—her name in the air, and the birds in the brush, the birds' songs and the men's calls. It kept on till dark. Then we got in our trucks and drove off. And I planned to follow her."

"No plan, if you don't know where to go."

"I started the next day—that's today, this morning. Guessed she'd go west. Asked people if they'd seen her."

"You don't think she was gone temporary?"

"I knew she wouldn't come back."

"What'll you do now?"

"Arthur said he'd sell off the place if we're all going away. He'll go to Kansas. So that's the end of that. I won't go back. He was in the dark when I got home. I lit the lanterns and stove, and I got us some supper. It was as good a meal as I could make with what was left. We had the last of the sausage, and the potatoes and onions, and a bowl of beans with brown sugar, and we ate till there was nothing more.

"Then we went out into the dark. We had been up and down the trails over the years, and we knew them without seeing because we'd made the trails ourselves. Then we went up where there ain't hardly a trail at all. We get to the tree we knew on the ridge, we feel down around the roots and find the slate, slide it off, reach into the crate, and we each take a bottle and keep climbing the mountain until the trees are below and there's nothing but sky and star. Then we drink for a while and don't talk.

"Charlie St. George could've made hooch out of sagebrush, and it would taste like dew. The bottle I pulled from the last of the stash was loganberry, but only a breath of the fruit. It didn't burn my throat—it just heated me. I thought maybe I could drink until I slept, and Arthur would drink until he slept beside me, and we'd wake up together in the dawn. Then we could help each other up, throw the bottles far down Crooks Mountain to see them crack, laugh at the fun of wrecking something, walk down the mountain to the house, find Charlie St. George and Anne Fisher on the bench in the sun by the door. I thought I could drink enough to bring them back, for me and Arthur, or drink enough to dream it. But that perfect liquor couldn't do any magic. Never could."

Walker rubbed her arm, turned her from the dark view, led her back to the fire. There, with the fire bright on their faces, they looked at each other across the heat. The old man. The young woman. In the willow thickets. In the plain deep among ranges. In the cold air flowing with the Wind River.

◆ ◆ ◆

Five years passed, and Gussie didn't stray far from the Wind River Valley. She lived on Walker Avary's ranch, learned to lead a pack train, to trace the range from lake to lake. She crossed the sharp runs of glacial water, heard snow fill the branches, dozed in fireweed. At summer altitude, after a long twisting ascent, she led a string of mules and saddle horses into a campsite where the stock could graze among the trees, where the gray cliffs turned gold at the end of sunset. The dudes trusted Gussie to navigate the sheer trails, to set the tents square, to roast the corn and potatoes.

At the campfire, the night chill pushed them all closer to the heat. A dude might have brought a harmonica or guitar. The group might sing the songs they all knew, something of the old West, a lonesome cowboy, *bury me not,* and then the music stopped and the darkness and dead echoes crowded around, the thought of trout cruising the depths of the unseen lake, and they hardly dared breathe in the sudden startling solitude of the camp, the intense hiss of the fire.

They turned to Gussie, watched her, waited for a story. They assumed that she had lived in the Wind River Range from birth, though she knew only what she'd gleaned from Walker. As if she'd blazed these trails herself, as if she remembered the first slow wander into unexplored canyons, the ancient tools in stone shelters, as if it were she who had slept in this upper country before roads or laws, she told them of the wickiup beside the skunk cabbage marsh, the thermal pools where the whole dark underside of the earth bubbled up.

The dudes marveled at how Gussie could survive in such a rare corner of the globe, at how anyone could leave such a place once they'd camped its isolated valleys. Gussie asked them about their homes, the trees, the cycle of seasons. She asked of the rivers, the steepness of the hills, the relics, roads. Rarely could they tell her much, and if she pushed them for more they would fall silent, lean closer to the flames, adjust the logs.

Gussie lay awake in her tent, heard the stragglers whispering at the fire, the horses nickering at imagined dangers. And then she ran through each dude's particulars of place and distance, tried to construct a home, a sound of wind or rain. She placed Anne in those far towns, imagined Anne with the dude, tried to hear their conversation, tried to see them pass on the street, touch each other on the arm or shoulder. Gussie thought that if she could picture Anne with one of these strangers, then Anne wouldn't be alone. But as the years passed, Gussie was busy with her work on the EA Ranch, and she lost track of the imagined Anne, confused the miles, the states, the roar of sea or train. Each week during summer, she square-danced at the tavern in town—a tourist gathering, Gussie in her trousers and boots. Occasionally she saw a young woman take a promenade in a square, a young woman of a certain height and grace, and she'd think of Anne, wonder what Anne would say if she released her partner, turned from the square, approached her mother, took her hand.

Walker died as he slept—she found him, a small ripple of a man beneath blankets, deep in the sag of the ancient sawdust mattress. Walker's second son, Jimmy, a smart man with bandy legs, a man who'd never needed her help, allowed Gussie to dig beside him at the grave, and they lowered the box beside Eugenia on the slope above the lake. Walker's three daughters and Jimmy, all the various family, all the townspeople who knew that Walker had been there far longer than anyone could remember, that either by plan or by accident he'd crafted some important part of the upper country, they all stood at his grave and talked of what they knew of him, what they remembered, but no one seemed sure.

Later, after the others had retreated from the cooling evening, Gussie stood at the grave alone, watched the valley descend from the high clouds and brightening horns of a young moon. She thought of all she knew of Walker's travels and losses, and she wondered how any of the souls he had lost in his life might find him now. She cried out, and her echoes caught in the bowl of the cliffs and spun down on themselves, into silence.

She left the EA Ranch, walked down the road, through the woods, out of the range to the Wind River. For now she turned upriver, along the road toward Togwotee Pass, the way she'd been headed the day she met Walker. And that evening, nearly at the summit of the pass, she floated in a canoe on Brooks Lake. All over the lake, canoes drifted. The moon had brightened. The stars fell into place, ridiculously bright even in the blaze of moonlight. A celebration of the Fourth of July at the Diamond G lodge, there on the shore of the lake. No dudes this week, though a dozen were expected the next week. So the crew all ate steak and taters, all took to the lake in the ranch's flotilla of canoes, all let the night breeze move the craft where it would. A person might chart the path of each canoe, might learn something of the lake's currents, of the way the mountains guided the wind, but that night not a soul cared about reasons, patterns. They felt the weight of their bellies. They felt the beer like a warm scrim behind their eyes. And Gussie, taken in by the crew, fed and satiated, lay in the bottom of the canoe and let it rock her, let the banded, ruined cliffs come in and out of view, let the sound of water against hull set the tempo of her breath and heart.

Here was a ranch hand named Allen, also in the bottom of Gussie's canoe, also watching the sky, the cliffs, also adrift in the currents of voices. Maybe one day Gussie and Allen would talk the way old friends talk, where everything uttered is somehow part of a memory. But for now they were silent. Other voices carried from other vessels.

". . . up into Five Pockets with some tenderfeet."

"Absaroka Range is grizzly heaven."

"Be on watch for a grizzly sow, guards her cub."

"Shame to kill something just wants to raise a cub."

"Think the Indians could bother a grizzly?"

"Indians got arrows."

"Bears got claws and fangs."

Gussie reached up, took hold of the gunwales, settled on the seat. With the paddle, she turned the canoe in wide circles. The Diamond G lodge was lit like a beacon on the shore—such a sturdy log structure might stand for a few hundred years, until a wayward spark took it down.

From her spot adrift, coming around again, she saw someone move on the road, in from the trees, another person taking the route Gussie had taken that day, up toward the pass, though this traveler might have been planning to continue on over Togwotee, on to someone waiting or a job or an adventure somewhere past the Snake. Gussie tried to focus on the figure in the moonlight, but the distance was too great, the colors washed to gray. She dipped the paddle, took long strokes toward shore.

"Where you taking us?" Allen said, climbing to his seat.

"Trying to get a good look over there."

"Look at what?"

"Look at that person, see who it is."

"Where you looking?"

"There. Ahead. By the trees. On the road. Near the lodge."

"I don't see nothing."

"I've always had good eyes," she said. But now she wasn't sure of what she saw. What had been a figure walking steadily, someone with a gait that seemed familiar, was now a hazy shift that she couldn't really see if she looked directly at it. So she looked ahead of where she thought it was, or she looked behind, and then she could see the movement at the edge of her focus. She paddled harder, wished for daylight.

"You taking us in to shore?" Allen said.

"What do you think I'm doing?"

She ran the canoe up onto the lakeshore, full speed, and climbed past Allen, jumped onto the sandy ground. Now, what she thought she'd seen had taken the turn of the road toward the lodge, and the shape moved in line with the shadows of the ruts. She ran through the grass, the woody scrub, onto the road, followed the steps she'd taken that afternoon. There, ahead, the shadow moved into the greater shadow of the lodge, and maybe the lodge door opened a second, and firelight or lantern light flashed and disappeared.

Gussie ran, as fast as she could remember running, felt in her legs the past years on Walker Avary's ranch, the miles she'd ridden, the passes she'd crossed, the wend of the narrow ways at altitude, the sound of Walker's voice as he laid out the day's map, drew the range in the air. She remembered most clearly the things they hadn't talked about since the day they first met. At night on his ranch, they sat on the stoop and watched the lake, smoked a bowl of cherry tobacco, passing the pipe back and forth. And in the gaps between the sizzle of the draw, the hiss of smoke, they heard the far waterfall like the eternal flow of lifeblood, and they saw the lights of the cabins in the pine eaves, heard the voices like bells or birds or fire, mother to child, man to wife. Finally the lights would extinguish, and Walker would rise, step back into his lodge, shut the door silently as if there were someone inside he might disturb. Gussie might wait a long while on the stoop, wait until all internal sounds were gone and all that was left was external, the passage of the night. She thought that Walker was asleep, that he could no longer control where memory took him. She rose, left Walker to the empty volume of his old lodge, the logs of his own cutting, the space sealed from the wilds by his own skill. In her cabin beyond the corral, each night, she wrapped the blankets tight and held her eyes open as long as she could, sometimes straight through to dawn. She'd always rather face the tears of dry, tired eyes than enter back into all the places she had traveled, all the people she had known.

Up from Brooks Lake, along the road, Gussie ran. Whoever it was who traveled in moonlight was already inside the Diamond G lodge. Such a beautiful structure. She left the road, followed the path, in through the door. Heat from the tall fireplace. Shadows of beams and antlers high across the ceiling. And the sudden arrest of motion set her to shaking, as if she'd carried the chill of the darkness and the lake inside with her. She advanced, sat on the hearth, let the fire tighten her skin, calm her. She looked around. It was a fine room, lined with log furniture, leather, Indian blankets. As close to a palace as a mountain ranch might conjure. And here she was. They'd fed her, sung their songs, floated her on the lake beneath the Pinnacles, the immense and ruined cliffs that walled the Diamond G and the lake from the mysteries and ghosts of the Absaroka Range to the north. She could sit here, alone in the lodge, until they all came in from the aimless regatta, until the liquor began to flow again, and someone would try to kiss her, and someone would offer her a job, and someone would start the music.

The door opened. Allen came in. He'd followed her from the lake. He crossed the room and sat beside her on the hearth. She could feel the cold from his shirt and trousers.

"Wanted to see if you were alright," he said.

"I'm okay."

"I know your friend is dead, recent."

"Walker Avary."

"You got someplace to settle now?"

"No place particular. But the Wind River Valley has been good enough to me."

"You'll stay."

"I've got no other plan."

"Who'd you see on the road?"

"No one I couldn't see right now if I closed my eyes."

DuNoir

Gussie awoke. No light at the window above the bed. No stars. Cold sank from the panes. At this hour, the air was calm, no sound of wing or hoof. She would have inched the blankets higher, looked for a way back into sleep, would have searched again for all she couldn't find, but she'd already slept enough.

She rose, pulled on her clothes, lit the lanterns. Brightness closed the cabin in on itself, no view past the reflections in the panes. Stove lit, kettle and fry pan hooked down from above, eggs and bacon set to the heat. At the table, she laid out her meal, sat and ate. She waited for dawn to swamp the lantern light. When the first gray came into the window, she returned the dishes to the counter, pulled on her coat, stepped outside.

Even August couldn't completely banish the constant underlayer of winter. The DuNoir Valley was wet with dew, heavy with fog. Gussie followed the path to the gate, stood on the bars of the cattle guard and scanned the road. North, above the fog, the Ramshorn anchored the first wall of the Absaroka Range. The peak would soon draw sunlight along its edges. Up the road, squat and bulky in its grove of aspens, was Dr. Morgan's house. The owner of these acres, Dr. Morgan had left the day before, driving back east with Dr. Janvier, not to return until next year—late spring, maybe early summer—to walk his fence lines, to sit on his porch and watch the sunset sink into the peaks.

Earlier that year, late May, Gussie had been working an odd job in a field along the Wind River. Slowly she'd dug around in an irrigation ditch, clearing mud from the gates. Finally she tested the ditch—it held the flow, didn't leak, sent river water out through the hay fields. Then she heard someone yelling, looked around for trouble. Up at the road, a man stood beside his long green sedan. Steam billowed from beneath the hood. "You," the man shouted, "help me. I have mechanical difficulties." And an hour later, after Gussie had tinkered with the engine but really just added water to the radiator, she was riding along with that man, Dr. Morgan, and his rangy brunette woman friend, Dr. Janvier, on their way up the Wind River Valley, angling off into the DuNoir Valley, to the man's new property. There Gussie stayed the night, and there she had stayed the summer, as Dr. Morgan's caretaker, watchman, handyman, nanny to a finicky band of Texas longhorns.

Through June and July, after Dr. Janvier was called east for business, Dr. Morgan would sit on his porch and drink vodka over ice, and Gussie would sit and drink with him, take another glass when he offered, the drink sharp and thick with cold. As the last high daylight flowed on the surface of DuNoir Creek, Dr. Morgan told Gussie of the books he'd read as a child. Even as the streetcar rattled his bedroom window, he had dreamed trails through pine forest, his first taste of antelope, the brushy hills, the badlands.

"You must think me a frivolous man," Dr. Morgan said. "You must think I'm playing at this valley, that it's nothing but a fancy, that I don't understand what I have."

"I don't think that," Gussie said. "I think you set out to get what you wanted, and what you wanted was something beautiful."

"Maybe."

They drank some more. Darkness finally settled across the view. Far down the DuNoir, at the Wind River, lights passed slowly on the highway, too far away for sound.

"It was just a chance that I wound up here," Gussie said.

"Do you want to be here?"

"Yes, sir."

"Where else would you be?"

"That's what I wonder."

"You could take some time this fall and travel wherever you desire, take care of any business you might have."

"Thank you, but I can't think of where I'd go."

This was easy, this life in the DuNoir Valley. She had her cabin with a good stove. A truck and trailer. A fine paint horse chosen from the fields east of Riverton. She charged ranch supplies to an account at Welty's General Store, and Dr. Morgan ran her a line of credit for whatever she needed for herself, for her cabin, to get herself settled. All she had to do was improve the ranch—she could follow Dr. Morgan's instructions or make up her own mind. She started replacing the rotting fence posts. She irrigated. She had her boys come out from town to replace the roof on the granary. Why leave?

Seven years ago, if Walker Avary hadn't stopped her, she might have traveled past the DuNoir without noticing the stretch of green, the meandering creek, the Ramshorn. She would have continued over Togwotee Pass, down to the Snake River, taken a turn toward Montana, Idaho, Utah. She could no longer find that trail—seven years—couldn't imagine how she would pick herself up, what she would carry with her, how she would start, how the road would jolt her knees, how many miles she'd cover the first day, how cold the first night, and the next day. Anne might have her own child now. Anne might look out on narrow alleys, smell the oily exhaust, hear a trolley clatter on the street. Or Anne in a mountain town with ruts in the road, spattered mud on the gates, and the circling heights, the bristly tracts of spruce and fir. How had Anne's face thinned? How had her voice changed?

Early August, Dr. Janvier had returned to help Dr. Morgan pack up for the season. The last night before they left the DuNoir, Dr. Janvier insisted that Gussie join her and Dr. Morgan on the porch. Dr. Janvier was a quiet woman, a medical researcher, had discovered answers to questions Dr. Morgan hadn't even thought to ask. The three of them sat there in the dark, all drank their share, silent for an hour. The valley was long gone in deep night, nothing but the impression of space and possibility beyond the porch railing. Animals forced their way through the valley with the sound of breaking branches, splashing creek, fallen rock—moose, porcupine, elk, coyote, grizzly, the idiot cattle. Gussie looked back toward the windows—there was hardly a shade of difference between inside and outside, both vulnerable to the passage of time and season.

Dr. Janvier stirred, made her way to the door, said, "Maybe you can help me, Augusta." The two women entered the house, found matches, illuminated the rooms on their way to the kitchen. They gathered the makings of a cold supper. "You've already done a great deal of work this summer," Dr. Janvier said. "The property is much improved. Dr. Morgan told me how impressed he's been with your skill and focus."

"I'm paid for the hours I put in," Gussie said.

"It's just that Dr. Morgan loves it out here, it's such an escape for him, and you've made it all easy. I couldn't complete a fraction of the work you've done, not in a dozen years."

"No one would ask you to work a ranch."

"All I'm saying is that I'm glad we found you. I admire you, Augusta." She rubbed Gussie's shoulder, then carried a platter of chicken from the kitchen to the dining room.

Gussie watched Dr. Janvier lay the platter on the dining table, pull plates and utensils from the sideboard, set Dr. Morgan's place at the head, set places to either side. The woman's hands moved smoothly, shifting the items on the table until it all precisely matched whatever sense of order she carried in her thoughts. A lovely woman, the candlelight blushing her neck. "You may bring in the rest of the food, Miss Locke," she said, and she walked away through the rooms.

Gussie brought out the sliced tomatoes, bread, returned for the wine and water. She tried to complete the pattern that Dr. Janvier had started. In that room with its high rafters, shadows, the paintings askew on the log walls, Gussie waited at the sideboard, unsure of which chair was intended for her. Then the slap of the screen door, and she saw the couple pause in the living room.

Dr. Morgan, in his pearl-buttoned shirt, leather vest, brown slacks, tall clean ten gallon, was the picture of pretend Western. He stopped, turned to Dr. Janvier. They stood eye to eye, touched lips, no great show to it. She took his hand, and they stumbled a bit, came into the dining room. Dr. Morgan pulled out the left-hand chair for Dr. Janvier, and she stepped in front of the chair, took her seat. She sat still, her hands flat on the tabletop.

Gussie wanted to remain where she was, out of the flow of affection. She had nothing to add. She didn't belong with these people, yet she had a certain backward pride for them, as if she'd had something to do with their accomplishments, though their lives were largely mysterious to her. She knew that they were somehow proud of her, and it embarrassed her to think that they probably felt they had rescued her from a life of odd jobs and bunkhouse living. What did they know of her life? Perhaps she was their pet.

Dr. Morgan pulled out the right-hand chair, and Gussie came forward, allowed him to slide the chair under her. She laid her hands flat on the tabletop, a mirror of Dr. Janvier, though she couldn't look at the woman's eyes, didn't want to know the expression. Dr. Morgan sat at the head of the table, reached and laid a broad soft hand on Dr. Janvier's hand, on Gussie's hand.

"Final supper of a wonderful summer," he said. "Couldn't be

more pleased. Thank you both. This seems like home." He released their hands, poured the wine, offered a toast. "To the DuNoir."

They all repeated "To the DuNoir," drank the sweet red wine. The room, the house, paused for a moment—if candlelight can make a sound, candlelight was the only sound, a sound like the luxuriant slowness of time. Gussie had heard the sound of splendid light before, a night in Mr. Foster's parlor when she had fallen asleep in a supple armchair, Anne in her lap, awoke to confusion, and then she knew where she was, she saw the vivid yellow light on her hands, she felt almost ready to call Mr. Foster's house home, and it seemed the light was the same tone as her dreams. And she remembered a Ravenglass summer night, her bed on the sleeping porch, the light from the window high in the door that led to the house, the unsteady but constant light, a light that might gutter out but wouldn't, and at some point a shadow moved through the light, a shape of some part of Leota fluid across the ceiling, against the pane, then nothing else, no disturbance, so Gussie slid from her blankets and cracked the door open, saw the slip of light cut down across her chest, warm her ankle, and she turned her eyes away, held her ear to the light, such a sound of solitary waiting, of attentiveness, of the long night passing, Leota's inhalations and exhalations as evanescent as the air drawn up through the flame, as timeless.

Dr. Morgan helped himself from the platters, then served Gussie and Dr. Janvier. They all set to eating. Dr. Morgan and Dr. Janvier talked of their research, their fears for the war, the hour of their departure in the morning. And when the food was gone, when the bottle of wine returned to the tabletop with a hollow clunk, Dr. Morgan took Dr. Janvier's hand again, held it loosely. Then he turned to Gussie—she clasped her hands tight in her lap—but he only pointed at her.

"Augusta Locke," he said.

"Yes, sir?"

"I hope you will consider this valley your home."

She looked away, couldn't watch his slack mouth. She knew where liquor could take a person. She didn't want Dr. Morgan's pity.

"To that end, my dear," he said, "I'd like to reward you if you stay, entice you to stay. I'll draw up the papers for you to sign, if you agree."

"Agree to what?"

"To making the DuNoir your home. Stick with me through the years—perhaps ten years minimum—keep improving the place, and you'll earn your cabin and five acres. No homestead to file. No proving up. No lease. Yours in appreciation."

She couldn't think. She looked down at her plate, the white surface streaked with oil, tomato seeds. She looked at the candle flames, ablaze, unruly. She looked at Dr. Janvier, the woman's square shoulders in her crisp white shirt, the thin silver band of her turquoise bracelet, her fingers entwined with Dr. Morgan's. Dr. Janvier would marry him if he asked, but times were not good for marriage, not with the war, the threats east and west, and what good was marriage, anyway, destined to end one way or another. Later, when Gussie retired to her cabin, these two would bank a fire on the hearth, douse the lights, sit together until the heat faded.

She looked at Dr. Morgan. She read pity in his bleary eyes. He seemed to watch for a sign that she would break down.

"I lost my husband," Gussie said. "He went to war."

Dr. Janvier leaned back in her chair, let out a breath.

"I lost my daughter," Gussie said.

Dr. Morgan released Dr. Janvier's hand, stood, came around behind Gussie, placed his hands on her shoulders, kissed the top of her head, a kiss full of the sleepiness of the hour. "You poor thing," he said.

Dr. Janvier stretched a hand toward Gussie, left the hand suspended in the space between them, said, "I'm surprised. I'm sad. I didn't know."

And Gussie felt the churn of vodka and wine in her belly, the spasms in her throat, and she wanted to dodge from beneath Dr. Morgan's grip, wanted to take back what she'd said, but she was crying, gulping breaths, forward over her plate, already unsure of why she'd spoken. The doctors tried to soothe her, asked about her lost family, lifted her from her chair and led her to a seat beside the hearth, lit a fire, fed her slow sips of brandy, but even the burn of the liquor couldn't clear her thoughts. She looked at the fire—the logs crumbled into each other.

The woman knelt before Gussie, hands on Gussie's knees. The woman was talking on and on, and for a while Gussie didn't know who the woman was or what she was saying. Was this woman Gussie's mother? Sister? The high white forehead. The little cowlick of the right eyebrow. The cascade of gold-brown hair that curled lazily at the shoulders. A flat wall of teeth. And the hands resting on Gussie's knees—the long fingers that seemed to have no strength, maybe no real skill, and the pink nails tipped with white crescents, a sharpness there at the end. Gussie's own hands rested, also, on the dusty legs of her dungarees, her fingers scraped and scabbed from her work on the buck-and-pole fence. Yes, the fence, she saw herself in the willows along the creek, saw the poles span the water, and the ripples of sand along the bottom of the flow, and rocks that caught and whitened the icy water and downstream the water ouzel that perched its plump body on the peak of a boulder, oiled its feathers, sang a long succession of notes, repeated the pattern, walked down the boulder and entered a bubbling eddy, and then Gussie saw the ouzel walking beneath clearer water, searching for something, wings working through the cold, then back up the boulder, into the air, and, above, Gussie saw the woman on the far bank, the beautiful tall woman in her riding clothes, slick black boots, jodhpurs, the tailored jacket, a woman like a painting of another life, the same woman afloat on the surface of the creek, and Gussie thought that if she knew anything of myth this woman would be high on her horse, passing in and out of daylight, starlight, there on the surface of DuNoir Creek, a being of beauty and speed and wisdom, and the woman spoke, and the water ouzel startled, took to the air but stayed low, followed the cut of the creek, the highway of cooler space through the willows, out of sight, downstream. The ouzel could follow that highway from confluence to confluence to the far curve of the ocean where the blue merged with the sky.

But here, in firelight, the woman knelt before Gussie, and Gussie heard her voice—*anything I can get you, anyone you'd like to see, there's nothing to worry about, you're in a safe place with people who care for you, dry your tears and think of all you have, dear Miss Locke, and how you can forget whatever worries you might have had about your future life, all is taken care of, the answer to your prayers, if you pray, I don't pray, what god could have put the world into such a state, what god but a mocking god, there are fine earthly creatures who are upstanding and generous in spite of their frailties, and Dr. Morgan is one such* . . . This was Dr. Janvier. Of course.

There seemed a great distance between Gussie and Dr. Janvier. Gussie recognized nothing of herself in this woman. How could she say *the answer to your prayers* if she hadn't known Gussie more than a few weeks? Gussie tried to rise from the chair, but Dr. Janvier's hands were suddenly heavy on her knees. And then Dr. Morgan was behind Dr. Janvier, his hands on her shoulders, and he brought his lips to Dr. Janvier's ear, the brush of lips on the white curve of the ear, and he breathed words to her that Gussie couldn't hear, she saw only the shape of his hands on Dr. Janvier's starched white blouse, the pressure of his hands as if he'd memorized the hidden bones, knew what the bones would feel. He whispered to the woman, and the woman's eyes pulsed, a sleepy pulse that slowly shuttered her lids.

Then Dr. Janvier rose, stood with Dr. Morgan, and they hugged a moment as if they each needed comforting. Dr. Morgan took Gussie's arm, lifted her to her feet. "You're a bit overwhelmed, Augusta," he said. "Nothing a good sleep can't cure. Dr. Janvier will take you to your bed and see that you get to sleep. In the morning you'll know what to do and how to thank me."

Dr. Janvier led Gussie through the darkness, to the cabin, lit the lanterns. Gussie allowed herself to be disrobed, stood there in her nakedness in the cold, still room, held up her arms for her night-shirt, sat on the edge of her bed, lay down under Dr. Janvier's urging, felt the mattress, the sheets and blankets. Dr. Janvier extinguished the lanterns, found the bed again, sat beside Gussie's hip, rubbed Gussie's shoulders.

Gussie saw the vague silvering of the window, the black void of the woman's shape. Closing her eyes, Gussie tried to feel only the slow massage across her shoulders, the hazy warmth stirring her blood. Such a strange sensation, nearly forgotten. She tried to bring to mind the last person who had touched her, cared for her, but she couldn't find the image. Behind her eyes, in the darkness, she could see nothing but blank white, no Anne Fisher, no Jack Fisher, no Charlie St. George or Mr. Foster or Arthur Tooley or Walker Avary, no one she'd known, no move of lips, turn of wrists, no word. The blank white burned on, unbroken. Finally she slept. Dreamless sleep.

At dawn, she awoke to an empty cabin. She heard voices, smelled woodsmoke. The salty tightness of her cheeks, nostrils. She almost couldn't remember what had happened to her, unsure of what she had said and what she had forgotten. She thought a minute, drew to mind those she had known—they floated far away but clear, until they lost focus in the fields, hills.

She dressed, came out from her cabin. Followed the path around to the road. The small figures of the doctors dropped their luggage at the sedan, waved at Gussie, waited arm in arm as she approached. Clouds of breath as they greeted each other.

"You'll be okay now, Augusta?" Dr. Janvier said.

"I will."

"You slept well, thought about your future?" Dr. Morgan said.

"I did. I don't know what was wrong."

"Understandable," Dr. Morgan said. "I'll send the papers. Please sign them. Return them to me."

"Glad to see you're feeling better," Dr. Janvier said. "Don't worry about a thing."

Then the long green sedan had made its way down the DuNoir road, quickly shrinking to a sparkle of sunlight, quickly lost to sight and sound.

And now, a day later, the morning's fog was burning off the hills, but it still settled in the valley. Gussie stepped out into the road. All tracks had been washed away by rain in the night. She turned around slowly. Back down in the fog, her cabin was lost, its red roof and leaning stovepipe. She thought that she could almost hear the fog move, opening views, blocking views, breathing. Might be the sound of the creek, but she couldn't see the water. Dr. Morgan's house disappeared.

Something moved on the road, beyond the house. Where the fog draped the edge of the aspen grove, the sound of steps matched suddenly with movement, color, and for a second the apparition could have been man or beast, but then it was clearly Gardelle Jankirk striding down the road. He was always heading somewhere, could be found at any time of day or night on a road or trail, leaving or returning to the Wyoming Tie and Timber operation on Warm Springs Mountain. How he ever got any work done she couldn't know. She wondered if he'd ever find what he was looking for in these mountains.

"Halloo, Miss Locke," he called, waving like a fool. He sped up, nearly ran. "Great to see you. Didn't expect to see anyone this morning. But it's always nice. Nice to see you." He came up in a rush, took her in a hug not quite robbed of momentum, and they teetered, staggered, shuffled in across the cattle guard, onto the path. "Don't mind if I do," he said, untangling himself from her, taking her hand, leading her on toward her cabin. "It was cold last night. Coffee would do the trick."

"Can I offer you some coffee?" she said, her hand in his icy grip.

"Didn't you already offer?"

"Nope." She pulled her hand from his. "I didn't say nothing. Come along." She moved ahead, and he followed.

They sat at her table, circled their tin cups of hot coffee until their fingers thawed. They both looked out the window, into the fog, where light swirled and the brush came and went.

He tapped at the window, pointed. "I see a brown pelican," he said. "There, to the left. You see it?"

"Nope. Don't see it. Not a native species, I think. An unlikely occasional. But, there . . . a Chilean flamingo . . . no, sorry . . ."

"A violet-crowned hummingbird. Ah, hmm . . ."

"Bird of paradise?"

"Sure." He reached across the table, patted the back of her hand. She looked at him, smiled. "You got anything to eat?" he said. "Coffee don't quite make it after the miles I covered."

She slid the fry pan back onto the stove, got some bacon sizzling. Then the eggs went into the grease. From a loaf in the bread box she cut a slice. She watched her hands as she worked, tracked the set of her shoulders, felt the twinge in her back as she lifted the pan from the heat. She did not move in this manner when she was alone—there was something fluid in the way she cooked for Gardelle Jankirk, as if she planned each action ahead of time. She didn't recognize what she was doing, but then she saw the way she touched her fingers to the hand towel, the flick of the spatula, the way she turned the plate slightly as she laid it on the table, and she saw Leota.

Leota turning from the stove, her brow flushed with heat. Leota crossing the room, leaning close behind Gussie—her arm brushes Gussie's shoulder as she lowers the plate to the table—and Gussie feels Leota's breath on her ear, her neck, moving her hair. Then the meal, arranged in neat portions, and as Gussie mixes the edges of the food, tastes different combinations, Leota moves about the room, seems to follow where her hands lead, touches a wooden spoon, tightens the lid of a jar, rinses glasses in the sink, pokes again at the food on the stove, straightens the curtains, crushes a mosquito between thumb and finger, pulls out the chair opposite Gussie and sits. Leota crosses her hands on the table in the spot where her plate should be, her slender hands just a bit pink from the work she has done that evening, and she leans forward a fraction, gazes at Gussie but not into Gussie's eyes, seems to take inventory of her daughter before she says, "How is your food, Augusta?" and then stands before Gussie can answer. Gussie watches her mother turn the pots on the stove until all the handles align again in a new direction. Leota places her hands on her hips, seems to push down, as if she tries to hold herself from floating away.

And Gussie remembered Anne, thought of light through the Crooks Mountain window, light radiant in the girl's hair, Anne waiting with her hands flat on the tabletop, framing the spot where the plate would land. Cared for, Anne must have memorized the patterns that Gussie moved through, must have come to know them even though Gussie herself did it all without thinking.

Gussie sat across from Gardelle, watched him eat. "Good enough?" she said.

"Plenty good enough. Thank you."

"I got food to share for anyone who passes by. Just happens that you always pass by at mealtime, wherever I happen to be living."

He laughed. "I like that you invite me in instead of chase me off."

"Is there anyone I'd chase off?"

"Anyone you wouldn't invite in?"

"I'd even invite in the likes of you."

"So . . . we're talking in circles."

"Back to where we started. I'm serving and you're taking. Maybe some day you'll give me something in return." She smiled at him, and he nodded and smiled back. She was content just that he ate her cooking without complaint, even showed real desire for what she could produce, and he could eat in silence for all she cared, because she liked to hear the creak of his chair, the grind of his teeth. But he was rarely silent, rarely serious, and their talk fell to its usual pattern. "Where you been walking?" she said.

"Up to the Ramshorn," he said. "Slept up there. I need help with a bird I saw. You can help me? Sounded like this." He buzzed, metallic, and clicked.

"Nighthawk?"

"Not a nighthawk." He buzzed again and whistled, short beats.

"Meadowlark?"

"Listen." He hummed, the sound rattling his nostrils. Then he went quiet.

The window groaned with the beginning of a breeze. The morning fog tattered, blue sky above green leaves.

"I was fighting my way over dead-fall trees," he said. "A creek was ahead in the gaps. The call was somewhere in the sound of a waterfall. I kept following." He cawed softly.

"Coot?"

He whispered, "Tik-tik-tik."

"Sandhill?"

"I got into a tight place, not hardly any light, and I went along the creek, ferns and all, you know the kind of place. You get so far off the trail that you don't know if you'll find a trail to bring you back out. The bird called." He let out a long, sad, falling whistle. "Where the water fell to a pool, the bird was flying around like it was trapped. I can't tell you what it was. Plumage—purple, green. Claws trying to get hold on the wet rocks, then it flapped up again. I got close—it didn't bother with me, like it knew I was harmless. You know I'm harmless, don't you? I saw its yellow eye with a red lid. I saw its speckled pinfeathers. It had a split tongue and a blue bill." He made a vague hiss. "Maybe you can tell me what it was?" He watched her without blinking, his face hard and sober.

"I don't know what it was," Gussie said, "but it was a strange dream. Beautiful. As usual."

"Yes. I see." He nodded, took his fork and pretended to write on his plate. "Unidentified dreamlike chimera."

"Wish I'd seen it."

"I'm sure you've seen it."

"I'll see it next time." She stood, came around behind him, leaned in to take his plate, smelled the miles he'd walked, the damp and dust. To be this far down the DuNoir at this early hour, maybe he had let himself into Dr. Morgan's house, slept on the feather bed. She took his plate to the sink. "You haven't been letting yourself into places you shouldn't, have you?" she said.

"Plenty of places to be without going someplace you don't ought to be. I ain't a trespasser. *Thou shalt not trespass.* Didn't someone say that once?"

"I said it." She would check the doctor's house later. "Do you ever sleep in your own bed?"

"What are you implying?"

"I see you around."

"And you sneak strange men into your place for breakfast. What'll the cows say?"

"I just want to know that you're alright."

"I've ate a good breakfast. I've enjoyed some time with you. What else?"

"Nothing else," she said.

"What?"

"I want to know that you ain't walking around all the time just because you don't know where to stop. That you got some idea of where you're headed."

"Why do you want to know that?"

"I worry about you."

"Alright. I'm headed right here some days, not only when I want some cooking. You're my friend, ain't you, missus? And I go up Warm Springs when I need the work to pay for my walking boots. The trails in the Winds got some good lonely camps and golden trout. Absarokas got all the ghosts and lost time and odd birds. You seen as many odd birds as me, I bet, with all your years in this territory. Good enough? That what you want to know?"

"Do you wish you had a place to stay?"

"I ain't picky."

"Wish you had someone?"

"I'm pretty likable. I'm not worried. Should I be worried, missus?"

"No, you're right. You'll be fine." She came forward, patted him on the back. "Let's go." She walked out the door, and he followed. They left behind the closeness of the cabin, the leaking woodstove, scent of smoked game. The morning had gone from fog to baking clarity. There was barely a hint of moisture on the air.

Gardelle had slept in her cabin in the DuNoir more than once that summer. Stopped by in the evening, watched her put together elk stew, potato pancakes. Their talk always went back outside, into the summer dust. A storm might blow through, rattle the door, and in the lulls of their talk they heard the mountains fill with the roaring night. It was unreliable, the weather—storms came and went, lowered from the pass, filled the lowlands, gained speed toward the plains, moved on, or the days could be parched and crisp. She would put Gardelle up in the storage loft above her bed, lay out some blankets for him. The wind brushed the aspens against the roof. The aspens were grizzly scarred, cold to the touch even on the hottest day, they were trash trees, quick to burn, liquid shade. Did Gardelle know that? He slept up in the sound. The loft strained each time he shifted—he was too big a man for that loft, too big a man for a nest in the eaves.

Gussie trailed behind Gardelle on the path to the road. She tipped the brim of her hat lower against the sun. He stretched his arms high, worked the kinks out of his neck. His dungarees were worn nearly through in the seat, and the blush of his red long johns showed through the threads. He needed a sweetheart to patch the hole, protect his dignity. Gussie could do the work; she'd become proficient with a needle during her days in the hotel laundry.

Gardelle was ten or fifteen years Gussie's junior. He might yet break out of his drifting. If she decided that he should live with her, that there was room in her cabin for a man smitten with birds, she would have to make a direct invitation, and, if he accepted, she'd learn the scent at the hollow of his neck, the rough pads of his fingertips. He was handsome enough—lanky, well muscled. If not for the snaggle of his teeth, his tidy mustache might have made him a bit of a dandy. Over her years in the upper country, Gussie had paired off once with a square dancer from Cody, a few times with a hunting guide from Butte, but she'd mostly spent solitary nights, the odd Saturday drinking in the tavern with her fire crew volunteers. Lately Gardelle was the only man she'd considered touching, but if she stared at him too long, if she found herself going a bit soft in the head as she fried him a steak, tipped whiskey into his coffee, he laughed, and she laughed too. They were friends.

Gardelle didn't look back as he stepped across the cattle guard and headed down the DuNoir road, toward the Wind River. "I'll see you soon, missus," he said.

"When you're hungry."

"I'm always hungry."

He kept walking, stepped up from the rut to the grass when things got muddy. His stride was steady, even.

Gussie waited until he was small in the distance, and then she turned back, followed the path. That day, she would finish closing down Dr. Morgan's house. Shutters to block the windows. Caps for the chimneys. The kitchen might still be stacked with dishes to be cleaned and put away. The bed linens to wash and iron.

She entered her cabin. At the table, she sat in Gardelle's chair. From that vantage, she looked straight at her bed and its snag of graying sheets and wool. She would wash her linens along with the doctors'—she wondered what would mix in the water.

Gardelle was a sweet man, not much for conflict or reality. What had he thought when he looked at her bed? Maybe the rumpled bed seemed a challenge, the blanket thrown to the foot, the pillow askew. She could tell him that the cabin was to be hers, if she would sign the papers, do Dr. Morgan's work. And then Gardelle would tip back in his chair, look around. The cabin was already a good fifty years old, well settled in its spot, the trees grown up past the eaves. A bachelor pioneer had settled here, brought the logs down from the Absarokas, fitted the walls, chinked the gaps. How many weeks or months would that bachelor have gone without laying eyes on another human soul? Gussie knew the mountain winters. From the cabin's windows, the whiteness of the world would be blinding at midday, the paths buried, the creek silent. And toward evening, the drifts would fade to gray, then a murky violet, then disappear. And it was that final cold darkness that Gardelle would think of when he saw her bed, felt the walls around him, considered Gussie. She was likable enough. She was skilled at a whole list of tasks. She was up in years, always alone. Why not Gardelle? Why not any of the men she'd known, loved, never really known?

She missed each man. She hardly had a single full name to write on a piece of paper, to trace if she thought she might like to see a man again, to match a face to her memory. Would she have to close her eyes, touch his lips, to know him? Whoever he was, he didn't love her. He might not remember her. He might be dead in the war. He might never have told anyone of the night he lay with her, or he might have told the tale with the tenderness left out.

She sat at the table, in Gardelle's chair, in her home, in the DuNoir Valley. The grease had gone white on his plate. The pepper made a little trail beyond the hardened egg. She lifted the plate, placed it on the counter, returned to the table. It was still early morning. The sky was pale along the blocky horizon, rising to a clean blue, cloudless. She could see the notches that led west and north from the DuNoir Valley—animal trails and pack trails toward the Pinnacles or up Frozen Lake Creek, around the Ramshorn, toward Wall Mountain, Shoshone Plateau, into the heart of the Absaroka Range. All summer, she hadn't seen anyone come into the

DuNoir from those passes. She might be completely alone. But for all she could see from the seat beside the window, whole trains of people could be passing through the forest, streaming in from the valleys and eroded monuments north. Actually, she could see very little from the window—willow, fence, elevation.

From the sill she took down some animal bones and a potsherd she had dug from the sand along the creek. She laid out the bones on the table, tried to arrange them into something, but she'd never been able to make a creature of them. Could be ferret, picket-pin, young porcupine. No skull, no complete limb. Just the long articulations, the fragments of knobby spine. From among the bones she plucked the potsherd. Even though the sherd was small on her palm, it seemed somehow complete. Easy enough to imagine the full curve of the pot and what it might have held—mountain berries, roots, pemmican. The pot was just an implement, could be put to use, could be cherished or discarded.

She heard a sound, looked out the window, saw nothing, went outside. No storm clouds in the air, it wasn't thunder, and the sound continued, droned. She walked down through the willows, climbed the fence, walked into the middle of a pasture. The view opened all around. The sound went on, separate, deeper than the sound of the creek. She saw no vehicle on the road. Far toward the corral, the longhorns dozed in the early heat. No one at Dr. Morgan's porch, no smoke at the chimneys. And she could see all the way down the pale line of the DuNoir road to the Wind River. Gardelle was gone—no sight of him across the miles. She was alone in the valley, with the walls of the ranges holding her, holding that odd resonant sound.

She scanned for the focus of the sound, and then she saw a silver airplane approaching from far down the Wind River Valley. The airplane seemed to be moving too slowly to stay aloft. She couldn't judge its distance, couldn't pull the plane cleanly from the sagebrush foothills it ran against. Its shadow fleeted across the hills, then it flew up the DuNoir. Four engines, massive. Flat wings that held the air. It started a broad turn, as broad as the DuNoir would allow, and she watched it circle her, saw the windows, the turrets, the bristle of guns, it was low, saw the men holding their faces to the view. The bomber against the wooded slopes of the Ramshorn—silver against pine and high snow.

Glacier Trail

The bomber completed its turn, and its shadow dove off the flanks of the Ramshorn, dove back into the DuNoir Valley, through the aspens, across the fences, into the pastures. And there Gussie waited, saw the shadow approach, its breadth and weight. She was grounded in the slender wheatgrass, wild rye, the earth cold beneath her soles. The shadow bore down, the silver craft soared, armor and armament as bright as air.

She knew they could see her if they cared to look. She waved her hat in a high, broad arc. The bomber drew its shade onto her, and in that moment she saw the shape of wing and speed in a brilliant halo, and the next moment the sun blazed again, hot on her face, and the craft was silver again, the men watching her from their turrets, perches. Somehow she saw each face, held the shape of each face in the sun-dazzle behind her eyes. The bomber chased its own roaring vibration away, descended the Wind River Valley, and then it flew silent against the foothills.

She placed her hat on her head, hugged herself. Quickly seen, quickly gone, the men might already have forgotten her acres, her red roof in the clouded leaves, the creek a stroke of early blue, the trails laid across the valley. The trails continued on through the upper country, followed the canyons, ridges. Now the bomber rushed above the Wind River, the cold watercourse.

Other trails had brought those men to the high country air. Each man had left a family. Each had chosen to fight this war, or the war had laid itself across his path. Each had loved someone, left someone. Each had heard the friction of his soles on sandy ground. Each had felt the weightless soar, the bottomless dive, the monstrous power that might shake him to bones before he reached his target.

She watched as the bomber rolled left and right, searched out the badlands that hemmed the town, reached up into the Wind River Range. The bomber took a gleaming turn around Whiskey Mountain and was gone from sight. Did it follow the Trail Lake road? Was it looking for an escape back to the air base in Idaho? Idaho was west, not south onto the spine of the Winds. Something held the craft low—it couldn't rise high enough to clear the range.

Gussie waited, watched, imagined how the bomber cruised, the props pulling at the thinning air, its sound huge on the surface of Torrey Lake, Ring Lake, Trail Lake. The road gave out to sagebrush, spruce forest, pine, and the wanders of Torrey Creek. The men leaned to the windows. The vibration was as huge as silence. Below, birds fell away, fell back, flipped their wings above the trees. The sheerest stone faces had slumped. Water plummeted, slipped away. The bomber climbed. The cliffs climbed. A streak of steep water broke against boulders, the cool mist a prism in the summer heat.

She watched long after the bomber entered the mountains, until a slender line of smoke started up, black and distant. And then she lost balance, lost sight, felt near to suffocating. She hadn't felt such heat, such a pure dry beat of the sun, since the Red Desert. It was as if the sun went white, filled the sky, burned away the shape of the land. Only white—all she could see. She stumbled, found herself flat on her back in the pasture. She looked up into emptiness, into the heat of August 1943.

Once, in Colorado, she had walked all day under a hot summer sky, and she came to a stretch of land where she lost sight of the mountains altogether, and she turned with the roads, followed where they took her, and with the sun centered overhead she lost direction, and any way she turned could have been toward home or away. At long intervals she passed a drive that cut off from the road, headed straight for a copse of wind-warped trees, a house, a barn, the whip of windmill blades. At each drive she stood awhile, tried to see what was at the windows of the farmhouse, what was on the porch. She saw no one, but she thought that someone in the house might see her stopping there, wonder where she was headed or if she was someone familiar. And if she turned in past the gate, if she made her way along the drive, came into the shade and calm air of the trees, if she stopped at the porch step, stood there long enough, someone might come to the door, open it, see her standing there with the unbroken miles at her back. Who would welcome her? Who would know her?

Gussie tried to remember the faces from the bomber, afraid she'd already lost them. She tried to reconstruct what she had seen—the brows, the eyes, the sheared hair. One man was pale as salt. One man had a black mustache, she was sure. One had narrow eyes, a hand pressed to the glass. She was the last to see them. No other soul would have seen those faces after they fled the DuNoir, before they entered the Winds. No one could have seen them as clearly as she. They were handsome, surely. They were beautiful.

And then she saw Anne, clear as day. Anne Fisher. Gussie's girl, a tall woman now, with the slow stride of beauty. If only she could see her girl again, Gussie thought. If only she could know her girl as a woman. Such a hollow longing, without shape or hope. Anne would stop where a creek slid among roots, lean against a white trunk, watch the turn of the water. Off in the trees the men would circle, fragments cut by the white trunks. Perhaps one of the men had known Anne, had touched Anne lightly on the shoulder, had run a finger along her jaw. Which man was it? Anne would wait for him to return.

Gussie sat up. The line of smoke beyond Whiskey Mountain had barely grown—a black exclamation, shapely and clean edged. She had been there only a minute or two. She rose directly, no hesitation, across the pastures, to the barn. Her volunteer fire crew would be waiting in town. She gathered her gear, hitched the horse trailer to the truck, loaded her new-shod paint.

◆ ◆ ◆

Gussie drove past the red bluff, into town. The sudden rows of buildings and leafy trees seemed like a city after the vast DuNoir. She passed Welty's, the Rustic Pine. People tipped their hats with a certain solemnity, knowing the work that had to be done. At the Community House, her crew waved her up to the boardwalk. She climbed down among them. Circling her, pulling her toward the gear, they didn't hardly give her a moment to breathe.

It's true that war takes the best. Here was Cootie, worked part-time as a ranger to make up for the wartime lack of men, eyesight half gone, but he could tell a forest or a grizzly when he saw it. Here was King, who'd homesteaded on Tappan Creek, dug ditches to bring water to the fields below Battram Mountain, cleared the sage and rabbitbrush, set wheat in the badland outwash, ran a herd of gaunt dairy cows. And Hutchinson Park, a Rhode Island boy, a year of college, a life of doctors, bad lungs, sent west for the air, big now with muscle and gaining a ruddy tan and a new accent. And Buddy, always digging through hillsides, slicing lengths of petrified forest, polishing dinosaur bone, ancient shells, and he drove dudes to the ranches when the ranches were open.

Hutchinson placed his arm around Gussie's shoulder, pulled her into the shade of the Community House. She looked up at him, the young face. He was unshaven, smelled of hay and horse, his eyes red. She thought of him asleep in his cabin along Horse Creek, and how he might have rolled over at the sound of the bomber flying up the Wind River, how the drone disappeared again into the drone of Horse Creek, and he sank back into dreams, until the bomber returned, the sound grinding the morning, and he rose, quick to the door, outside to stand in the yard and look up, follow the flight, judge the path into the range, see the smoke rise from silence.

"What are we doing?" Hutch said. "What can we do?"

"You know how to ride a horse," she said. "You know how to contain a fire."

"What'll we see when we get there?"

"I can't say."

"You won't say."

"I don't know what we'll find."

"I've got to know."

"Don't think about it," she said. Hutch's face against the range and the sky, his scruffy chin, oily nose. She laid his features against the faces she'd seen in the bomber. Eye to eye, chin to chin. To think of Hutch carried off through the air. To think of those who waited for his return. His mother might not know him, changed now from what he'd been when he left home. "Let's go," Gussie said. "We're too late already."

She pulled Hutch back into the sun, pushed him on toward his truck. He walked away—his narrow hips, long legs, the square slap of his boots on the boardwalk. He might be a stranger. But then, if he glanced back, she'd know his small ears, his lips in their tight thin line.

Gussie got Cootie's horse into her trailer, Cootie climbed into the cab with her, and she started off, leading the parade of three trucks and horse trailers toward the edge of town. They passed the last house, continued along the river, turned at Jakey's Fork. Climbing the soft foothills, over the moraine, through gardens of huge boulders, patches of aspen, pine, they drove far up, entered the Torrey Creek drainage. The badlands sank far behind, far below. They followed the valley, passed Torrey Lake and the Boardman cabins, passed Ring Lake, passed the camp at Trail Lake. Bare rock high above, endless mats of evergreen, and the barren avalanche funnels.

Finally they stopped at the Glacier trailhead, a drive of an hour that the bomber had covered in seconds. They brought out the pack mules and horses, set to loading the gear. Gussie had the shovels, axes, water cans. Cootie came out of the truck with grain for the stock. King had thrown together food for a few days' bivouac. Buddy folded the tarp and blankets into the panniers. And Hutch held the medical kit, placed it in the last pannier, and buckled the canvas flap closed.

Hutch looked at the sky. "It's only eleven o'clock," he said. "If nothing else, we'll get there in daylight."

"They'll need more than us," Buddy said.

"We've got our job," Gussie said.

They all turned to mount up. Hutch gave Gussie a boost. Then he just stood there. She looked at the stained brim of his hat, his fingers tracing the stitchery of her worn-out boot, the sweat that had already pasted his shirt to his chest. The others rode off a ways toward the Glacier Trail, but still Hutch didn't turn to his own mount, didn't take up the lead of the second mule. His hands shook, the slightest tremor. Could be lack of sleep, or too much drink, though she remembered that he didn't drink despite the ribbing he took at the tavern. Could be something of his old illness, something he thought he'd left behind. She reached to his shoulder, laid her hand there, saw that she shook too, thought she might have caught it from his pulse. Here was his damp warmth beneath her hand. Here was this boy not as old as her own lost daughter. He wanted her to wait with him a moment, to breathe the dry heat before the long rush up the trail. What had brought him to this point? How many turns?

Gussie gripped his shoulder, a quick squeeze, and released him, laid her hand on his cheek, the soft skin in the scratch of beard. He was alone with her, the others halfway to the first switchback. She wanted to remove his hat, stroke his pale forehead. She wanted to cry, though tears might keep her from the task at hand. She wanted to ask him what he feared, though it was probably better not to know. So she stared into his dry eyes, and he held the stare, unblinking. For an endless minute they held each other against the wrong decision. And then Gussie pulled her hand from the warmth of his skin, she tipped her head toward his horse, shrugged, smiled.

"You best hurry," she said. "Soon they'll be gone from sight."

He broke from her, ran to his horse, and then he was up, the rope in his hand, leading the pack mule onto the trail. There by the trucks, Gussie sat her paint. Hutch looked back, shouted, "Come along, Augusta. Ride with me."

"I'll take up the rear," she said, "to keep you boys from turning tail."

Hutch laughed, brought the mule in tighter, urged his mount in fast pursuit. The others slowed for his approach.

Gussie let the trail sounds recede. She inhaled the mountain air, tasted gasoline, pitch, sagebrush, dust, horse, leather, the things of her life. How had the war come to her? The sun was hot on her shoulders. Hutch had nearly caught up to the others. The crew would soon enter among the pink granite knobs, would soon pass into the woods above. She drew the reins loosely through her fingers, closed her eyes. She heard ravens—no unidentified dreamlike chimeras, these birds. Their song, if it could be called a song, was the rough call of her memory. She opened her eyes.

It was no memory. Close at hand in the aspens, a dozen ravens hopped the branches, watched her. They were pure black until they spread their wings and took air to another tree, and then they weren't black at all. Maybe it was her angle toward the sun, maybe it was the edge of dizziness as she followed their moves, but instead of black she saw the colors inside the black—blue of dusk, red and gray of the badlands, yellow of a scarred pine, bleached turquoise of hooded bone lichen, mute white of sharp-toothed angelica, spotted purple of the coralroot, snowy green of the mountain death-camas. She tried to blink the ravens back into black, but they flashed, flew, called, waited. Waited for what? She didn't want to think.

She turned her eyes to the ground, urged her paint forward, listened to the complaint of leather, her horse's huffing breath. And the sound of wings came close, and she caught the brim of her hat lower, leaned into the first incline. Soon she entered the stretch of pink granite, huge glacier-scoured knobs. Black shadows cut the trail, gliding, and she heard the calls scatter into the woods as she entered from stone to shade. The ravens paced her, out of sight, above and below.

She laid her heels to her paint, made haste. She thought she might have lost the crew already, though there was only one way up this mountain. She thought she hadn't seen them enter these woods, though she followed their prints, passed the fresh droppings. She thought it might be raven mimicry she heard, that there were no men ahead, no horses or mules, the ravens making the dull knocks of hooves on stone, but she heard a man's voice, could be King, speaking words beyond even a raven's skill—"How the hell will we find this nightmare?" So she kept riding.

The trail switched back and forth among fir, spruce, wiry arms of limber pine. Sometimes she saw the crew far ahead, just as they turned at the next switchback, and it was Hutch who waved his hat at her before he disappeared. Her paint stumbled against the steepness. Gussie didn't seem to be gaining ground.

At each turn, the view opened. Far away, past Torrey Rim, the Absaroka Range took the northwest, the distance like a faint drag of charcoal. Cliff shadows swung to meet the trail, swung away. East Torrey Creek came in and out of sight, veered off. Now the trail climbed the first slopes of Arrow Mountain, exposed to the sky. The crew, a half mile ahead, strung out toward Goat Flat. She stopped, drank long gulps from her canteen.

From that vantage, she was certain she had chosen the correct trail. There were still no clouds in the sky, just the smoke rising above the glaciated valley to the right, a cleft of granite where East Torrey Creek meandered. Soon the crew would have to cut down from the Glacier Trail, into that valley, and then they might see the flames in the smoke.

She studied the smoke. Something jagged swirled in the uprush. She didn't know enough to distinguish a fuel fire from a forest fire, didn't know what might burn into ragged sheets and fly that loosely, distinct from the currents of the smoke. Then she saw what it was—her ravens had flown ahead, and they weren't in the smoke, they were in the middle air between her and the smoke, looping in a column high above her boys, pacing their progress. She heard the ravens' calls, and she gave her paint a kick, leapt forward. She didn't trust the ravens, though she didn't know what kind of trouble they could conjure, knew only their desires, knew only what she had seen in the miles beyond Ravenglass.

She could feel the shape of a raven's voice on her lips, in her throat, the curious strain. She wouldn't dare make the sound now, unsure of what it would mean. She had never learned the language of the Wyoming ravens, never tested their calls, never found their roosts, didn't know if the young ravens mobbed together in the trees at night, and which trees, and where the nests were, and what they ate. She'd never followed them, as if they were an entirely dif- ferent creature, though they were ravens, they carried the heavy sharp black bill, the talons, the wide-ranging beat of wing.

She thought of the ravens in the stands of black spruce north of Ravenglass. She thought of Brud running among the thin rattling trunks. She thought of the ravens startling at his passage, the black birds huge on the air, sharp in his wake. She didn't know if Brud was alive. She didn't know where he traveled. She didn't know if, even now, after thirty years, he circled back to Ravenglass, if he troubled the edge of town.

At dusk, at the fringes of Ravenglass, she had seen the ravens come in, and she'd followed as they landed on the roofs, lined the fences. They tasted smoke on the air, the scent of roasting chicken, lamb, steer, fish. She saw the neat squares of the lit windows float- ing all around, and the shapes passing inside, the platters, the flames and reflection. The ravens hopped their perches, turned their heads to the side, took a glide down to the cooling ground. There they found the leavings in the bins, picked among the bones, the peels, the skin and tendon, the fruit opened to the soft cup of seeds, the spoiling butter. They kept their calls soft in their throats. They kept their eyes on their work until they flew up into the last of the evening and found their way home.

And the day the ravens mobbed the cedars, watched her, and when she walked one direction they called and moved another direction, and she turned, and they called, and she turned, until finally she was following them as they flew on ahead. They stopped, and she came up beneath them, and they no longer seemed to notice her, they just sat quietly in the trees and looked ahead. She walked on, found a deer dead on the fallen needles. It wasn't a kill, not that she could see. It hadn't been shot or brought down through force. It was just lying on its side, the unbroken brown of its fur, the legs straight, the neck oddly twisted. She turned to the ravens. "What?" she said. They called, a whole chorus in the branches, a whole flock of the same sound. They were strong, but not strong enough. The hide was thick. They were hungry. With a sharp stone, she sawed through the breast of the deer, sawed down the belly, peeled open the hide to the fat and muscle and organs, rolled the deer onto its back, cracked the legs open, cut the throat, laid out the structure. And she left. And the ravens remained behind. She would have stayed with them, but they would not have fed on the carcass with her there. They knew her. They feared her.

There had been deaths in Ravenglass, a cemetery in a pasture of shorn grass, the procession of the black wagon with the single black horse, and Gussie wondered if the ravens had followed that wagon, knowing that death was carried there, if they knew the shape of the deceased by the smell of his death. But then, each time, the death was buried out of reach, and the ravens must have learned the pattern.

In Wyoming, in Rawlins, she had watched the funeral of a boy killed in the Great War. There had been nothing to see but the box, the flag, and the mourners. She'd thought of how he'd died, and how long he might have lain unnoticed, and how his face might have been turned from the sky, so that his cheek and the tip of his nose touched the earth. As he lay there, if he'd lived for even a few seconds, his entire world would have been the blades of grass, and the spider with its dance of legs and silk, and the down and pollen drifted from above, and the textures of moisture and dryness, and the roots, and the creatures no more than specks of red feeding on the loam, the sheaths of stem and bud, the spore and petal, the grove of fungus on the sandy scraps of boulder. It was all too beautiful to comprehend.

The crew cut down off the Glacier Trail and continued out of sight—they had seen how the Glacier Trail headed toward the wrong valley. Gussie rode on, and the ravens continued, sinking against the smoke, following her boys' progress. Gussie came to the spot where the crew had left the trail, and she turned her paint and headed down. Still a good two miles to the rising smoke. Her crew was already far below, almost to the valley floor, and in the middle distance she saw the ravens, and she saw her crew as the ravens saw them, how slowly the horses moved across the gray and green vastness. Wherever the men traveled, the ravens could follow. The birds flew ahead, circled back, the defiles of the range no more than channels for wind, cradles for clouds. Whichever way the creeks drained, whichever direction the trails scratched, the Wind River Range was no real obstacle to the sky, the peaks barely rising into the lowest sink of the immense blue.

Gussie came down into the valley. If the crew had found a new trail, she couldn't see it. She followed in their general direction, eventually picked up their tracks. East Torrey Creek was slower here, deep in the valley. Ahead, the granite walls narrowed, and through the gap the peaks and snow shone. Here, it was scrubby, the ground heavy with water. She looked up. The crew waited at the eaves of a spruce forest, a gloomy break in all the sheer light. She slogged in through the marshy grass, stopped with the boys.

They all sat in silence. The sounds of the valley scattered on the afternoon sun. Water running in the creek. Crackle of heated granite. The stock settling. A snapping or a rush—something constant.

She looked up into the fringes of the trees, looked for the ravens, didn't see them there or in the sky. Then she realized what it was she heard—it was the fire making its own wind. She looked at the set of her crew, their slump in the saddle, and knew that they heard it too.

"If we're going to be any good at all," she said, "we've got to do what we've been trained to do."

"We ain't really all that good," King said.

"Never have been," Cootie said.

"We've got a duty," she said. "We've got a reputation to maintain."

"How could anyone think any more poorly of us than they already do?" Buddy said.

Hutch wasn't speaking. He looked at Gussie, seemed to be thinking of how to get himself moving.

"We're going," Gussie said, and she urged her paint forward, touched each man as she passed, came up to Hutchinson and paused, laid her hand on his, extracted the lead rope from his fist—he didn't resist—and she continued into the forest with Hutch's mule in tow. The crew followed. No one spoke.

If there had ever been a trail in that forest, it was drifted beneath fallen needles, hidden by fern, downed trunks, mats of Solomon-plume and twisted-stalk, red berries already set. The crew was closed in now, with the hoof falls sharp and dense, the valley gone. Gussie wove among the trunks, ducked from the sharp branches, drapery of lichen. The mule kept no tension on the lead, right in step with the paint. Gussie looked up. There was only sky. No smoke to be seen through the screen of trunk and limb.

Could be the forest north of Ravenglass, she thought, could be anywhere but this valley. She thought she could hear each breath coming up behind her, could separate the sound of each man, could separate the stock. This forest could continue, and she could keep weaving, looking for a passage, and the men could continue to follow, and that would be alright. There was no wind here, seemed almost to be no air, but above the branches the air must move. She thought she heard something passing, looked up again, looked for ravens on the wing, and there might have been something black moving high above the canopy, but she couldn't be sure. And when she led the crew out of the forest, back into the open, she looked first for the ravens, and she didn't see them, not in the sky, not in the smoke, not at the waterfall that blasted white, just ahead.

They approached along the creek. The air misted. They looked up the sluice of water, slick black rocks. The mist tasted of kerosene. Gussie tried not to inhale. Far up the slope, a few hundred feet, the flames seemed to rise from the tumbling water, a nexus where the blaze sent a white rush up and the creek sent a white rush down. For all the waterfall's power and chill, it seemed reedy and fragile beneath the column of smoke.

The crew came up around her. They sat their horses in the mist, wiped the oily water from their eyes. "How do you intend to get up there?" King said.

"We might have to leave the animals," Gussie said, but she urged her paint on past the falls, past an upheaval of boulders, and over the next half mile she found a way up, and then they gathered close again at the top of the falls.

Across the creek, the flames had blackened a huge rift of granite. The fire had blasted up a stone passage, away from the wreckage, the fuel nearly spent. Above, the forest crackled. Here, the fire had mostly burned itself out. Embers slid down the long sheets of aluminum, showers of light in the warp of the metal. The fouled creek rushed to cleanse itself.

Below, the valley ran south toward the divide—cliffs and ridges, snow and sharpness. Storm clouds rose above the highest peaks, farther in. Gussie hoped for a cold storm to douse it all.

She dismounted, and the crew followed in silence. They secured their stock, assembled their gear. Then they started out, Gussie in the lead. She passed along the creek, across from the wreckage, scanned only enough to see that there was nothing to be done, the boys all lost, a scene too bleak to take hold in her thoughts. They slipped over the boulders, the slurry of ash, into the near edge of a blackened grove. This wasn't anything they could handle—they were more of a brushfire crew. At their feet, the earth was a sheet of seething coals. Farther, trees burst with orange heat. The branches swayed, twisted in the sparking wind. Gussie could feel the air drawn from her lungs, and she dared not speak for fear her words would add fuel.

At the margin, where the green gave to black, the crew turned the earth over onto the coals. Slowly they worked their way in from the edge, left behind the white roots, the sad leaf. They hacked at the shattered trees, saw them crumble beneath the blade. The heat rose through their soles. Still, the fire pulled the air across them. It seemed to Gussie that if she lost focus for a moment she'd be lifted, carried through the spectral forest, fed to the immensity of flame and destruction. The fire was moving away. The crew wouldn't catch it, couldn't get close to what mattered.

Gussie dropped her shovel. The long handle sank in a cloud of ash. She didn't reach for it—it could burn away before she'd take it up again. Her crew continued. She watched their backs bent at the work, their small forms shuffling forward, scratching at the mountain.

She turned, felt the air fresh against her face. She made her way back out, stopped on solid ground, the crushed sedges. The storm clouds had crept over. Lightning struck the summits. The veil of approaching rain. Let it come down—the rain too would be swallowed up in heat.

She descended carefully, slick steps, and came to a spot where she looked directly down on the B-17. The wings were still beautiful. The tail was tall. The turrets, even in their ruin, were strange and glorious. "Training mission," King had said. "Should be ten crew, maybe. Poor kids." Here on the verge of the sky, near to escaping, beside the fast water, the bodies curled. There were eight that she could see, laid along the split center of the craft. It seemed almost that the bomber had broken through the surface of the mountain. Gussie saw girders and underbelly, an open door.

She continued down until she was level again with the wreckage, across the creek. Fresh wind came in advance of the rain, and the smoke fought and swirled. And there, as the rain began, she saw the ravens silent on the brink of the rift. They watched her. They tipped their heads back and opened their heavy bills and took in the stinging cold water.

Gussie crossed the creek on the backs of boulders, walked around the wreckage, past the engines, props, toward the ravens. She couldn't get close enough to them. Against the rain, she could barely hold her eyes open as she looked up, their black shapes against the black storm, the smoke and soot and heat. "What do you want?" Gussie shouted. The ravens looked at her, looked at the wreckage. They spread their wings, let the rain wash over them. "What? I can't do what you want me to do." They all looked at her, the black eyes. "What do you want me to do?"

She spun away, leaned back against the rocks, felt the massive granite that held it all aloft. Even against fire, the deep cold would soon reassert itself. Nearly at Gussie's feet, a boy stretched on his back in scorched swamp laurel, the blossoms like dry fists. His face was dusted with ash. She crouched beside the body, spread the rain across his hands and brow, washed his skin. She straightened his uniform, arranged the cloth to obscure the wounds.

Gussie made her way among the tattered sheets of metal, and as the rain passed over, she crouched at each body and tried to see who it had been. She was chilled from the rain, her hands shaking. She tried to make out a name on each uniform, each dog tag, and if she found a name she said it aloud. Some of the names were strange on her tongue, but she didn't think it mattered how she pronounced them. *Purgatorio. DeVilliers. Eliason.* Three of the names were familiar, and, as she said them, she thought of the person she had known with that name.

There had been a namesake boy, Amoretti, who fished the slow pools in the DuNoir through summer, who didn't seem to care what he pulled from the water as long as he was out in the deep thickets. Gussie would see him there in the distance, his fly pole flicking and sending out long arcs of line, and occasionally he'd see her and raise his hat a bit off his head. Once, when a fierce rain blew through, she invited him in to warm himself, and she took his wet clothes, draped them about the stove, and wrapped him in a blanket. He hadn't had much to say, just a few words about his sisters and their troubles, about the horse he hoped to have ready for elk season. Mostly they sat in the steaming scent of his clothes, and they watched the clouds clear away, and then the view was a strange brightness of wet leaves, stark sky. When the boy rose to dress, when he dropped his blanket, Gussie didn't look away and he didn't seem to notice, not after a life lived with family underfoot in a two-room house. She remembered the protrusions of his bones, the brown of his face and hands, his scrawny legs, gnarled feet, patches of bloody mosquito bites, black fur under his arms and at his crotch. It didn't look as though he shaved his chin yet, or maybe he would never have much to shave. As he bent to pull on his socks, he glanced at her, and she didn't glance away, and something in the corner of his eyes told her he knew he was a lovely shy handsome boy though he didn't yet know what to do with that knowledge. "Thank you, Miz Locke," he said when he'd dressed. "I sure do appreciate the heat." She hadn't asked him to stay for supper, and she knew she'd done right when she saw him run off through the sparkling wet field. He leapt and spun, joyous. She wondered at the control it must have taken for him to sit politely, naked in a blanket, and wait. Left on his own, he would have walked home in the grip of wet wool, and maybe he would have preferred it that way.

And there had been a namesake boy, Murdock, found in the lobby of the Brunswick Hotel. Late night, Gussie awoke to the far echo of an eastbound train, or was it a dream of travel that jolted her? She stood over Anne's crib, leaned far in, just to taste the air the girl cycled. And she held her hand near the small head, let the heat float up against her palm. She left Anne there, the girl asleep, and walked out through the halls, stretched her nervous legs, descended. The parlor waited at the end of a long hall—a single dim bulb burned above the locked door, sent jungle shadows beyond the potted palms. She liked to think that this late-night parlor wasn't stationary, that it could travel the territories in the wake of the transcontinental trains. She stood at the door, leaned her forehead against her own reflection. Then she heard a certain tightness of breath, small, and she turned away from herself. In a deep corner of the parlor, a young man leaned as far out of the light as he could get without disappearing. "You aren't a guest," she said. "No," he said. "That's alright," she said, "but how did you open the door?" "Locks are for people who don't try." She sat with him in the palm shadows. He was a thousand miles from home, though he wouldn't say where that home was. He had no money, but his father worked for the railroad, so he had free travel. Opening his small satchel, he laid out the gear he needed for a month or more on the rails—a change of clothes, knife and spoon, cup, matches, moleskine notebook, pencils, flask, Shakespeare's sonnets. He flipped to the notebook's back inside cover, and from a pocket there he pulled a photograph of a dark bungalow beneath huge elms, a sad horse hitched to the porch rail. "Each time I travel," he said, "I know I've gone far enough when I miss my home. Till that moment, I'm free to do what I please." "And what do you please?" she said. "Miles," he said, "and a warm place to sleep, and a good meal once a day. But the meal has to be given free, so I have a bit of a challenge." He smiled, a tired squint, and returned his belongings to the satchel. He asked her of her life, pushed her for odd details—color of the blanket on her childhood bed, type of flowers on a spring table, scent that evoked mother, most stars on a winter night, song she'd never forget, second kiss. She kept building on her answers, until she'd taken him into the old house in the red pines, and a cold rain was falling beyond the windows, the soft rush on the roof, the stove hot, sound of roiling steam from the kitchen, the lanterns unlit, a gray endless closeness. A freight train whistle shook the hotel, moved on. Gussie said, "Are you hungry?" They laughed, tried to suppress the sound. Gussie took up his satchel, led him to the kitchen, turned on the light over the table, laid out a meal. The next morning, she saw Murdock on the platform at the station. He sat on a bench, leaned against the sunny wall, wrote in his notebook.

And there had been a namesake boy, Pickett, in the Red Desert. Gussie and Anne had driven north, and ahead they saw a horse, thought it was a wild horse, but it walked right for them, spooked off at the last moment. It was no wild horse—its back was marked with sweat and saddle sores. No way they could catch it, but its tracks seemed to come from the notch they had aimed for, so they used the tracks as a trail, hoping for an answer. They came through the notch at sunset, and in the streaks of shadow that laddered across the plain they saw a white square and a speck of fire. They kept on. As the high gray sky finally washed away in a wave of stars, they pulled up to the camp, to the fire dying in its pit. They climbed down from the wagon, looked about. No one. So they tipped open the door to the white canvas tent, and in there lay a boy, Pickett, stuck in the desert with a fever. Gussie sat with the boy as Anne built up the fire with sage branches, brought water, bread, set to heating some soup. And then they brought Pickett out from his tent, propped him by the fire, fed him. When Pickett could eat no more, Gussie and Anne ate their own supper. It was his horse they had seen, probably headed back to the barn in Green River City. Pickett had been headed toward Cody, and had gotten off track, his fever killing his sense of direction. So he'd thought he'd rest for a day, but the day had grown to a week, and he hadn't had a sip of water for three days. "Now that we found you, you'll be fine," Anne said, "but if we didn't find you, I don't think you would live." "And I thought," Pickett said, "that I could have picked a more hospitable place to die." "The Red Desert is not hospitable," Gussie said. They brought out some pillows from the wagon, more blankets, made him snug. And then he fell asleep, and they watched him. His body took the water they'd given him and beaded his skin with sweat. They patted his brow with a soft cloth. Anne tended the fire. The dry sagebrush roared and sparked. Pickett lost all the food they'd fed him, and they cleaned his chin, changed his shirt. Gussie laid her ear to his breast, listened, but she didn't know what she should hear. His heart seemed fluttery. "He might not make it," Gussie said. "We'll take him to town, and he'll get better," Anne said. "We can't ride through the dark," Gussie said, "and he might not make it to morning. Maybe we're a day late, or maybe just a few hours." Anne walked away, came back with more sagebrush, built the fire until it stood tall. She paced, held her hands up into the smoke, swayed, sang songs she barely knew. . . . *all you melancholy folks wherever you may be* . . . Gussie watched the strange small figure wavering in smoke and heat. And then she heard Pickett rustle the blankets. His eyes were open. He watched the fire, watched Anne. "I've seen such lovely things, ma'am," he said, "and this is lovely too. She's a sprite, I think." He asked about Anne, and Gussie told all she could remember, of the first sight of the girl's hands, of the silk hair, of Anne's gathering of buttons and thimbles, Anne's first song, and Gussie's pursuit of the infant girl through the Wyoming snow. He kept watching the dance, and slowly as she spoke Gussie doled him sips of water. And then, perhaps driven by Anne's steps on the hollow world, a huge moon rose beyond the fire, the miles went bright with silver light, and Anne came around the fire, took down Pickett's tent, put all his gear in the wagon, brought the horses up and had Gussie attach the harness. They helped Pickett to the wagon, got him settled in back. "You stay with him," Anne said, "and I'll drive till the morning. Of course, the moon would come." Through the night, they rode south toward the Lincoln Highway, toward Rawlins. The inside of the wagon was bright with the moonlit squares of window.

In the wreckage of the bomber, in the rift of East Torrey Creek, in the last burst of the passing rain, in the rare altitude of the Wind River Range, in the presence of a dozen ravens, Gussie moved among the bodies. The grim spectacle of it all didn't stop her—layers of skin, fibers of muscle, cold white bone. She was faithful. She continued. She found eleven dead, looked into the glazed eyes, the new faces just barely made. She did not refuse to pacify the wounds with a soothing touch. With a sudden deep ache, she realized that, if her death could have kept the craft aloft, she would have died for these boys.

She set the boys cleanly in her mind, she would not forget their paleness, and if called upon one day she would repeat what she had seen, tell of the steepness of the granite rift, the drum taps of thunder moving over, the rain washing the precious skin. And she'd tell of the morning, and the faces that soared above her earthbound form. For her, the bomber would circle forever between the walls of the DuNoir, and she would remember the faces she'd seen.

◆ ◆ ◆

When Hutchinson found her, she was in the tail section. She looked up when he touched her shoulder. He was very beautiful and very young. She took his hand, pulled him down to crouch beside her. Rainwater dripped from the split aluminum skin above, closed them from the bright afternoon, the splendid sun.

"Come with me, Augusta," he said. "We're done."

She looked at his blackened hands, the scrapes, dried blood. "What about the fire?" she said.

"They're grateful. They'll take over. We're in the way."

She looked out from the metal alcove. A whole big crew of firefighters from the reservation was moving up along the creek, past the wreckage, toward the flames. They were tall, serious, grim, walking as if the terrain were nothing. Their uniforms were creased with use, dusted with the trail. A string of horses followed, frothed with sweat but undaunted, loaded with gear. The wrangler spun on his bay, shouted gutturals at the horses, rode on over the rocks, into the rift, and the smoke swirled and turned all the movement gray.

Gussie followed Hutch out from the wreckage. Across the creek, her boys waited, gathered beneath a thicket of stunted pines. The branches reached down around them—twisted wood, bursts of green. And in the branches above the boys' heads, the ravens perched, also waited.

She sat with her crew, accepted the food they offered, relaxed into the shelter of the pines. They all watched the scene. The reservation crew swarmed up the ridge, cut off the fire's advance. They dug around the wreckage, probing for embers. They gathered the bodies, laid them in a line beside the plunging creek, covered the bodies with a tarp.

"We could've done something with the dead," Gussie said.

"We did fine," King said.

"We're not much of a crew," Buddy said.

"We did fine," King said again.

"I just meant that we're only five," Buddy said.

"And those five are us," Cootie said.

"You did enough," Hutch said. "No one's going to say different." He rubbed Gussie's knee, passed her a canteen.

Gussie took a long swallow of water, lay back, felt the mountain press her spine. The ravens were against the sky, their blackness at cross angles to the branches. They preened, sharpened their bills on the wood, plucked scraps of lichen, dropped them. A slow rain of debris. Gussie pulled a scrap off her cheek, held it to the light, brought it close. Delicate strands of red, brown, and yellow— horsehair lichen. The Sheepeater girl had shown Walker Avary how to gather the lichen, wash it, roast it in a pit with roots and onions, pat it into cakes, dry the cakes. Later, when the snow was deep, the Sheepeater girl had shown him how to boil the cakes with elk meat, dried berries, roots stored in a hole beneath a rock. Walker Avary had demonstrated the whole process for Gussie. They'd shared a few of the cakes on a bitter winter day, found them hard to chew, washed them down with whiskey, smothered them in jam and butter and brown sugar, finally could no longer find the cakes beneath the dressings, and they laughed, drank some more, boiled more cakes, tried to eat them. "Lichen is only if you're starving or near death," Walker had said. Gussie picked up more of the falling shreds of lichen, pushed them into her pocket. She wouldn't be eating lichen today.

A half-hour later, they saw an army crew move at great speed along the flank of Arrow Mountain, dive down the slope, take the valley as if it were a dry road, disappear below the falls, rush up suddenly along the white water. These new arrivals left the fire to the reservation crew, moved in on the wreckage and the bodies. Soon they'd placed the bodies in bags, labeled them, and then they began to pry around the bomber.

The ravens hopped into flight, took loops over the wreckage, flew up the slope and looked down on the flames. And then the ravens came gliding back toward Gussie and her boys, and the ravens called to each other, alighted a moment on their perches again, made a racket, flew along the ridge.

Gussie got to her feet, walked through the trees, watched the ravens. They flew in circles, toyed with each other, landed, jumped about on the rocks, farther up the valley, farther into the range. "What do you want?" Gussie shouted. The ravens all looked at her a moment, then turned their attention back to the rocks and the distance.

Hutch came up from behind, handed her a jacket, helped her slip it on. "We're packing," he said.

"I'm not ready."

"We've packed your gear."

"I'm not ready to go back."

"What do you have in mind?"

"What's up this valley?"

"You need a good night's sleep, Augusta."

"What's up at those peaks and snow?"

"I'll ask." He left her, returned in a few minutes. "We'll go where you want to go. We have provisions."

"I'm not hungry."

"Cootie says we'll camp at Henton Lake," Hutch said. "Three more easy miles."

◆ ◆ ◆

Gussie rode along behind the crew. During her years with Walker Avary, she had traveled all through the Wind River Range, followed the trails to glaciers and sheer walls, traced the divide to lost lakes, forlorn peaks, found bleached bones, miles of bare stone, but she had never followed a canyon as rare and lonely as this. East Torrey Creek meandered, and to each side water fell from the vast, hidden expanses of Middle Mountain and Goat Flat. The music of white water in its descent through breaks in the cliffs, and the deep murmur when the water slowed into marshy reaches. There was no trail. The crew spread out across the valley floor. Each found his own way—no real turning to be done. Even the sunlight seemed to be captured, funneled toward the high, stark snowfields and the Continental Divide.

Gussie's ravens took the full air in the valley. They tipped their wings, searched out the shadows, the rims, took diving falls, rolls and half-rolls, always far ahead, always within sight, their calls mixed with light and water. The ravens could have caught a thermal, drifted high, until the valley was a scratch on the northern slope of the range and the creek was a flat thread. The ravens could have risen high enough to view the farther ranges, the plains and safe roosts, the towns and rails. Still, the ravens stayed ahead, constant, braiding their airy trails.

The crew slowed when the valley steepened, and they all came together, back into a line. Ahead, they could see where the narrow way opened. "That's going to be Henton Lake," King said.

"After what we seen this day," Cootie said, "we maybe could name this valley and lake for the honor of the lost. I got some pull with the Forest Service, though you might not believe it."

"B-17 Lake?" King said.

"Fire Basin?" Buddy said.

"Should be something to help people remember," Hutch said, "though I doubt many know who 'Henton' was or what he meant."

They leaned into the incline, wove among the boulders, followed the noisy creek, and then the basin opened. They fell silent again, bitter smoke in the fabric, but a cloud of sound paced them—the knock of stone, creak of leather. The lake stretched away, the surface chopped white in a breeze. Air so clear that it seemed to have no scent. Across the lake, the valley cradled a dark forest, and, beyond, a massive pyramid of a mountain cut by late afternoon shadows, and then the granite and glaciers continued into the horizon. King led the crew down to the water's edge, and they wandered along, and then he dismounted and led his horse on foot, and the others followed suit. No sign of a trail, no fire circle, no axe mark on trunk or branch. The breeze died away, and the lake opened into the sky, the peak pointing the way into the reflected world.

They stopped beside a stand of pine, a good place to camp—open ground, open air, the lakeshore running through boulders and dark sand. Not a single fish rose across the whole expanse of the lake—a strange calm, unnatural—maybe the lake was barren. Gussie let Hutch take her paint—"You take a minute or two," Hutch said—and she walked on along the shore, stopped in a line of spindly pines, sat on a log, watched the basin.

There were ghostly dark streaks on the cliff faces. The sun was falling toward sunset. She heard the crew at their work, unsaddling the horses, unpacking the mules. Then the dig of a shovel, the thump of dropped rocks—a fire circle. The strike of hatchet on deadfall wood. And the voices.

"Is this the first second we got to stop and think since we first heard those bomber engines?"

"All I'm thinking about is what King packed for supper."

"Pass the whiskey."

"Don't start singing."

"As if we ain't had enough smoke for one day, here we go."

The crackle of flame could be such a heartening sound. Gussie felt the first chill, the dampness of her clothes. These men, this crew, boys she had known no more than a few years, she could not imagine losing. She loved them, loved their every failing, their every joke, and if she could sit with them and no others over her remaining years, that would be a lucky thing. But there were many others she loved. Hand touching hand. A shared drink. Voices around a fire. The long span of winter nights. Smoke in the old canvas walls of a tent. Why had she not realized that she loved these men?

She heard a soft rush from behind, she ducked, unsure of what might strike her, but it was ravens flying, her ravens, heading out from the shore to those twin skies of the lake. Multiplied, the ravens looped against themselves, played in space, in the basin silent but for the crew at their fire, the voices, the wood crackling, and the ravens' calls, sounds that set out the world, echoed with each stand of pine, wall of granite. Up they went, spiraling together. They might plummet again, catch themselves just above the water, call each to each, cruise the dusk, roost together in a grove, their sleeping black heat and wit gathered close, but Gussie watched their ascent, and they didn't turn back. The last light was high at the center of the sky, that same light suspended in the undefined lake. The ravens disappeared into that light, and the stars filled in, the Milky Way snaking the black gap between cliff and cliff, between shore and shore.

Hutch called from the camp—"Augusta, we have supper." She smiled, rose from the log, fought her tired legs, kept along beside the cold lake, a sink draining the last remnant of heat. She walked through a patch of boulders—the granite scratched at her trousers. She didn't know the place, didn't know what she was following. The dark night. There was just plant and stone. Only the highest reaches of the valley were definite, where rock touched star, and she was deep below the sky.

She heard how fiercely the fire ate through the dry wood. The men stood watching her, or they watched the space where she stood. They leaned together in the white rush, all muddled with the smoke. Cootie dropped a pile of branches onto the fire—ragged flames and a roar of sparks.

"Come in," Hutch said.

She walked forward, into the heat. They made room for her on the logs they'd laid in for benches, and she sat between Hutch and King. They ate a stew of chipped beef, carrots, potatoes. They passed the whiskey around the circle, and after a long swallow Cootie began to sing, straight through to the end of "The Pecos River Queen."

. . . For he told her he would gladly risk all dangers for her sake
But the puncher wouldn't follow so she's still without a mate.

They all heaved a sigh at the sadness of Patty Moorhead. Cootie had a pleasant singing voice, a quavering tenor. He sang a few more songs, and no one sang along, all wanting to hear him pure.

. . . he said he'd had to leave his home . . .
. . . this little adobe casa on the plains . . .
. . . beware of the cowboy who swings the rawhide . . .

Then silence all around, and they waited for the whiskey fog to clear. Gussie watched the stars, watched the firelight on the men's faces. There was something final about this camp, as if, even if they'd wanted, they could not have continued. Quietly, as they fed twigs onto the flames, they began to speak of the mountain sheep they'd scattered just beyond the bridge, the ration of beer that never made it to town, the failings of the high school basketball team, the last wolf, the bald eagles nesting at Bull Lake, and the tie run, the fresh-cut railroad ties rocketing the sluice down Warm Springs Canyon, the ties clogging the Wind River, the German prisoners of war scaling the bristling heaps of ties, wielding long grappling hooks, working the tie run shoulder to shoulder with the Swedes, too few Swedes to work it alone, what with the war, and the shouts as the clogs broke free and started to move. They all warmed their hands above the fire, they all drank from the canteen, they all tried to figure how that mass of ties spared a single trout in the Wind River, the weight of severed trees crashing and flowing with the river's high rush. They took themselves beneath the water, where sound is drowned, where scent is dissolved, they slicked through the green flowing tendrils as the blackness loomed, they wedged themselves between round boulders, they sank into deep holes where the current is a memory, where sediment softens the bed, they sensed the other fish around them, suspended and alone, and then they stopped.

They heard the faint echo of hooves from the head of the valley, a far echo, and they all listened, frozen.

"I don't like the sound of that," Buddy said.

"We're supposed to be alone," Hutch said.

"There's a lot of fresh souls on the loose," Gussie said.

They went quiet. Gussie waited with the men, the campfire settling into its own orange death, the hoof falls close. Whoever or whatever it was that approached, it might move on and leave them to their stories. The dark world was cut off beyond the reach of the firelight. But a man rode in. His shadow angled against the pines and lost its shape in the branches. His long legs nearly buckled when he swung down. He caught his balance, reins in hand. They all looked up at him, skinny, six feet tall, his horse a roan monster frosted with sweat.

He removed his hat. Gussie knew him. She hadn't seen Jack Fisher for nearly twenty-six years, when she was fourteen and he was sweet and new. Now he had a mustache, a meager droop. Still the deep-set eyes, pale green, and his white forehead creased by his hat, the skin stained with mountain dust, the stain like an unformed thought. He looked them over. "You men," he said, and he dropped the reins. His horse came forward against him, nuzzled his back, hid its eyes from the light. "You men been digging through something. I know a bit about fire. You finished your work yet? I saw smoke, north, saw it all day. You ain't run off the job, have you?"

No one spoke. Gussie saw their black hands, their faces as if they'd risen from a mine. She felt coal oil in the pockets of her lungs. And she saw the trousers she wore, ragged at the knees, shiny where they'd rubbed the saddle, and her boots crumpled from wear, mud on the stitching, and the sleeves of her canvas jacket cracked from the bend of her arms. All infused with smoke— fuel and pine and death. She tugged on the neckerchief knotted at her throat. She touched a finger to the brim of her hat.

He couldn't recognize her—not like this. But here he was, alive. She stood up from her place with the men. "Jack Fisher," she said. She brushed her hat back, let it fall.

He studied her as if waiting for the firelight to accumulate and break through her surface. And then he too dropped his hat, dusted his palms on his shirt, took a step in among the men's legs, and he reached a hand as if to take her hand, but instead he laid his hand full on the side of her face. "Augusta Locke," he said.

SEVEN

Bomber Basin

Flat back against the cliff, Gussie held to her great-granddaughter, Laurel. The girl's hand was twisted behind, anchored to the crevice where the black rosy finches kept cover. The afternoon had tipped toward evening. For all the brilliance of the sun off the snowfield, the light had grown cool. Gussie looked for the coming dusk, felt the closeness of Laurel, this lovely girl straight against her side. Any minute, Jack Fisher would arrive.

Gussie wondered if it was best to send Laurel back down to camp to help her father with supper, and Gussie would wait here, alone, and watch what developed. Or maybe it was best for Gussie to greet Jack first, to step forward from the smoky camp, take the reins of his horse, allow Jack to shake the miles from his legs. And then she would step aside, urge him on into camp, Hayden and Laurel standing beyond the fire, waiting to engage this gray apparition from Gussie's past.

When Jack Fisher had ridden into the valley on the breath of ghosts and disaster, when he had found Gussie in the camp beside the lake, forty-three years ago, he'd laid his rough hand on her face for a long minute, as if waiting for her heat to penetrate his hide, to prove that she was not some specter caught in the Wind River night. Then he'd settled in with the crew, Gussie at his side, ate the meal they offered. He'd been riding along the spine of the Winds, scouting routes—he wanted fresh destinations when the dudes returned after the war, if the war ever ended. He'd come up to a pass, nothing more than a bighorn trail across chips of stone, and the view opened north, and he saw the smoke. That was in the morning, and it had taken him all day to find his way from the pass to this lake—a tortuous trail from drainage to drainage, over stair-stepped ridges, around undiscovered lakes.

"What's this lake called?" he said. "If you tell me it's 'Last Step Before Hell Lake,' I won't be surprised."

"This is Henton Lake," King said, "but we're going to rename it."

"We'll take your idea under consideration," Cootie said.

Jack laughed. He seemed comfortable in the haze of smoke and liquor—he might have been with the crew always. Still, though, he was a stranger, and he was keen and strong, and his horse looked like a beast out of legend, a roan monster with a proud neck and hooves like boulders. The crew watched Jack as if they half expected him to dissolve in the woodsmoke, to flicker out, to leave only the echo of his laugh.

He told a story of his old days firefighting in the north woods toward Canada, the horizon bleeding into flame and black, and when he'd seen the column of smoke that morning, he'd thought it wasn't much of anything, that he could probably do someone a favor by riding over and dousing it himself. But now that he'd seen the crew's faces, seen the strain and bruises, he knew that the granite maze of the Wind River Range had held him back for a reason: he'd already seen enough death for one life.

He told them of the Great War, the miles he covered under rain, snow, the sleepless dark opened by flame, distance, unreachable heat, the trail of cavalry among the trees, the arc of stars and moon. A point came when he couldn't tell shadow from shape, couldn't guess if the man lying beside him was dead or alive, even for the man's lively gaze, even for the man's breathing, his voice, his wretched cough. How quickly he took in his comrades' faces, scents, songs, memories, how quickly he lost what he thought he'd never forget. The wounded. The dying. The cut lip and broken tooth. The abrupt limb. The antiseptic nurses, the gods and goddesses. The salve, the loving touch, the ruined face, the shroud of gauze.

He told the crew of his landing in New York, a lone man without family or sweetheart, the motorcycle he bought surplus from the army, and the whole country opening west. The road inclined toward the Rocky Mountains. Then a day when the peaks finally soared into a white-blue sky, and he followed a section road, came in along a river, found Greeley again. "I remembered the name 'Augusta Locke.'" He asked around, learned that Frank Locke had died in the influenza epidemic, and Leota Locke had sold off the gentleman's farm, left the county, no word of where she'd traveled, no way to know if she was still alive.

• • •

Until the end of her own life, for all the years after the night on which she first learned of Leota's fate—or learned that she would never know Leota's fate—Gussie worked at creating a final story for Leota. Although the details expanded over the years, the story always started north of Ravenglass.

The ridges held the wind, rain, loon's call, ancient buried camps. Gussie followed the shallow channels, only her dreams of Brud's black speed to guide her. Leota must have shared those dreams. After miles of cedar, birch, silent dark, Gussie came to a far northern basin, a lake perched at the boundary between known and unknown. A pink sunset, and the calm gray water. Far out a small island bristled with a dozen tall Norway pines. When the sunset faded, Gussie saw a light on the shore, and she knew she had found Leota.

Squared to the lake and the long view, screened by paper birch, the solid-built cottage held to its patch of rocky ground. Gussie walked up onto the covered porch, to the door. She could never quite imagine the moment when the door opened, when Leota would stand within reach. But Gussie could skip that moment, move forward through the summer months, alone with Leota.

Side by side on the porch, they counted the minutes by the swelling of the stars, the slow accumulation of infinitesimal light. On through the seasons, they watched the wolves lope along the lakeshore, an eagle chased by ravens. Sometimes they heard a passage in the night that they couldn't identify, and at dawn they circled the cottage, walked the lakeshore, traced the trails, searched for a fresh track, a strand of hair, feather, anything to tell them that they didn't need to look any farther, that it had only been a black bear, a white-tailed deer, that it hadn't been Brud.

The winter nights were boundless. Gussie stoked the fire, helped Leota to her bed, laid her hand on Leota's brow.

Leota looked up at her daughter. "Where have you been, Augusta?"

"I've been right here," Gussie said.

"But where did you go?"

Gussie climbed up onto the bed, lay beside Leota, their heads on the pillow. Gussie told Leota the story of her travels, the Laramie Plain in a lightning storm, Rawlins snow, Crooks Mountain in summer, the Wind River, the DuNoir, the sound of approaching flight.

"Where have you been?" Leota said again.

Gussie told her of the faces she remembered, the quality of each voice, the men who leaned across the cab of a truck to open the passenger door, and the faces looking up from the blazing starkness of firelight.

"That's not what I want to know," Leota said.

"What, then?"

"Take me outside."

"It's too cold."

"I want to feel the air in my lungs. I want to see the lake."

So Gussie helped Leota rise from the bed, took up all the covers, gathered some skins, and they settled together on the porch, wrapped in a cocoon of wool, deer, bear, fox, moose. That day was the winter solstice. That night was a full moon, huge and cold. The lake had frozen deep, the black ice mute beneath a layer of snow—such a spectacular flatness in a land of hills. Far out the island floated on its moon shadow, the island with its grove of Norway

*pines like stiff feathers, the island too perfect to survive, liable to be caught up
by the soaring moon, carried off into the stars.*

*Gussie could feel Leota's small heat against her side, a failing heat. Each
breath diminished Leota, her lungs closing themselves down from the cold.
Gussie circled Leota in her arms, somehow thought that holding her tighter
would keep her from breaking.*

*Gussie pressed her lips to Leota's cheek, felt that splendid ashen skin losing
heat. She pulled them deeper into the cocoon, away from the view, and the
white glow followed. Leota's face was glazed with moon. Gussie placed her
lips at Leota's ear, whispered the answer to Leota's question.*

*Gussie told Leota of Anne, of the girl's first steps alone in the Red Desert.
Anne had worked out a stride for herself—a few hell-bent steps, then a pause
to catch balance, to scan ahead. Among the sagebrush the girl moved west,
chasing her shadow. Then Gussie looked again and the girl was gone. Gussie
followed the girl's small prints. Ahead, a darkness opened—a gully to channel
the rare water from dry to dry. It had rained last night. Gussie ran, came up
short, sent a cascade of grit into the gully, the dim fold with the line of muddy
reflection. Anne was at the water, painting herself with red clay, and she
turned her head, smiled, the muddy hand beckoning Gussie down from the
sky. And then Anne painted the silky clay on Gussie's skin, until mother and
daughter were the same.*

*Leota turned her head as if to kiss her child, but the motion continued, the
head tilted back, the throat washed with moon, a defiant chin. "Augusta," she
said, the lips without color. And then the face went stony. Gussie's arms
reached around until her fingers touched her own sides.*

✦ ✦ ✦

In Bomber Basin, Laurel was steady, smelled of horse and trail, of
strawberry. "We're a long way up," Laurel said, "especially if we
have to go back down." The black rosy finches made their small
sounds, then let loose a string of sudden notes. Gussie released her
hold on Laurel's arm, turned to look into the crevice, thought the
notes might illuminate the nest, thought the finches might emerge

in a shock of wing and beak. She recoiled. Then she saw only sky, and she was sliding away on the snowfield. She heard the scour of large crystals, the ice that sped her into the sink of gravity, until something struck her shoulder and she stopped.

She looked up into a lake, down into the sky. There was a dizzy pressure behind her eyes. She tried to focus. She heard a girl's voice calling her name, a sweet voice. She heard soft footsteps, or the pulse of wings. Nothing flew in the sky, nothing moved beside the lake, not that she could see. She couldn't attach the steps or wingbeats to anything. And then she knew the sound—it was her own heartbeat centered between her ears—and she knew that she could be near death.

She didn't move. She didn't cry for help. Who could help her? She couldn't even tell for sure where she'd landed. She feared she'd already been lying there too long, though she couldn't remember what she might have missed.

"Let's see what happened," a girl said. "If I get a good hold of you, you won't slide away."

Gussie looked up—or looked down. This young voice, this slim shape, stood against the sky. "I think I've hurt myself," Gussie said. "Think you can help me?" Her shoulder throbbed. The whole back side of her body was numb. Her neck was wet. Her ears burned.

"When we get all the snow out of your collar," the girl said, "I'm sure we'll find that you're just cold and uncomfortable." She took hold of Gussie's shoulders—a pain that made Gussie cry out—but the girl kept working until she had Gussie sitting up and turned around, legs pointing down the slope. And then the girl dug her fingers into Gussie's collar, into her ears, dusted lightly at her shoulders and arms, cleared away the snow. She bent there, looked directly into Gussie's eyes, said, "I'm sorry I let you fall."

"You let me?" Gussie looked past the girl. They were high on the wall of an alpine basin. Afternoon was failing—the light angled in long cooling lines. The lake was smooth, waiting for something to break its surface, the lake a pale scoured blue—Bomber Lake, of course. And this girl—Gussie looked at her closely—could have been Leota, could have been Anne, she was such a pretty thing, but it was Laurel. "How did you let me fall?"

"I wasn't holding tight enough. You got free."

"I'm like that."

"To your feet." She took Gussie under the arms, hoisted her up, held her steady, inspected her. "I don't see any blood."

"Bloodless."

"Your eyes look normal."

"These eyes are normal?"

"What's your name?"

"Augusta Tornig."

"Tornig?"

"That was my name. Should have stuck with it. It might have taken me somewhere else."

"You don't want to be here?"

A rush of heat or love knocked her unsteady. "Oh, honey . . ." She tried to reach for the girl, to touch her face, but her shoulder made an audible snap, and she froze, arms extended. "Shit, shit, shit. I've damaged myself."

"Yes. Your shoulder. I think it's a bruise, maybe. Not dislocated."

"How do you know?"

"Lifeguard training." She came up level with Gussie, locked her arm around Gussie's waist, and started them sidestepping toward the edge of the snowfield. "I knew better than to let you follow those black rosy finches."

"Lifeguards know about finches?"

"I haven't finished the class. How's your heart?"

"Can't turn off the sound."

"We'll go slow."

And slow they went. Off the snow, onto the scree, the gradual transfer from boulder to boulder. Each step jolted Gussie's shoulder, but she forced her breathing to run steady, even. Something about the pain made the descent an adventure, with the girl holding her tight, the scowl on the girl's face, the constant tiny shifts of balance, the intense closeness. They reached level ground, and already Gussie missed the steepness. Here the trail through the dense mats of shrub was too narrow for them to walk side by side, so they fell into a complicated dance, Gussie shuffling ahead, Laurel shuffling behind, her hands on Gussie's hips.

Hayden waved from the camp across the lake. Smoke layered among the whitebark pines. "You girls having fun?" he shouted.

"Gussie's hurt herself," Laurel called.

"Poor old Granny," Gussie said. "I'm fine." But she wasn't—the pain in her shoulder had stiffened down her side. She began to feel that her left knee was hinged backward.

"I'll start something hot," Hayden said. "Or do you want cold? Or do we need to evacuate?" He looked around, seemed to judge the sky. "Too late? What?"

"I'm fine," Gussie said, as much volume as she could push from her lungs, but the pain stopped her. And there was Laurel's calm breath against the back of her neck. She looked down, saw how Laurel's hands sat on her hips as if they were her own hands propped there, a casual pose, but the girl's small hands wouldn't let her take a wrong step. "We'll lap the lake a few times," Gussie said softly, "until we figure out how to walk together."

"Soup," Laurel called to Hayden.

◆ ◆ ◆

Gussie was wrapped tight on a narrow bed. From what she could tell, she was lying on her back, looking up into darkness. If she had somehow gone blind, she would be miserable. There were plenty of things in her life that she was glad she'd only seen once—a grizzly dragging a moose calf from a thicket, or fire rising through a schoolhouse roof, or the remains of the men who'd fallen with the B-17. And if she could go blind to these certain memories, she would, as long as she could still remember the first time she saw Laurel and

Hayden step from the car on the DuNoir road, as long as she could always see clearly their familiar faces, the faces of strangers stepped from her oldest dreams, faces that called up the Jack Fisher she remembered, called up Brud and Leota in the Minnesota light, as long as she retained enough sight to see Laurel dozing in aspen shade, to see Hayden recoil from bacon spitting in a fry pan, to see Laurel and Hayden greet the man they didn't know—Jack Fisher. They would recognize Jack, just as she had recognized them. And Jack would feel as she had felt—these two young people, father and daughter, were so dear and familiar that it would nearly knock him dumb and blind.

She was not blind. She saw shadows in murky light. She fought to sit up. She wasn't too tightly bound, but her shoulder was weak with pain, and she remembered her injury. Then she knew she was in the tent, on her cot, put there by Laurel to slow her heart. The bruise, a dark pool on Gussie's skin, had worried the girl.

The light on the old canvas walls was the fire in the stone circle. The shadows were the pine branches. And the sound of Bomber Basin in cold darkness, the water that carved the cliffs, the wind advancing until it shook the tent, and voices at the nearby crackling fire. Voices.

She forced through the pain, got herself out of the sleeping bag, feet on the ground. She was in pajamas, stocking feet, the chill night air caught in the tent, the close sound of her breathing, the strain of the cot in rhythm with her pulse, her pulse a hot point in her shoulder. She stood, waited. The voices had stopped. Then they started again, in and out.

A man's voice. Jack Fisher. ". . . in over the pass, as I'd done once . . ."

Another man. Hayden. "We came up the Glacier Trail."

A girl. Laurel. "Out from California."

"Point Reyes, north of San Francisco," Hayden said.

"We got to the lake after noon," the girl said.

"No question but this is a rare place to wind up, all the way from

California," Jack said. "I hope your trail wasn't as rough as mine. I still feel the jolts in my spine. I'm too old for this range, too old by fifty years."

"Bourbon?"

"Thank you, Hayden. Yes, please. I appreciate it. Youth serum. And the stroganoff was expertly reconstituted and heated, Laurel. I seem to have timed my arrival pretty good."

With a shiver, Gussie was fully awake. She'd slept past the start of it, when the first words would shape all that followed. She didn't know how far they'd gone. She threw herself forward, searched on the ground, found some boots, not hers, pulled them on. A blanket around her shoulders, a quick breath to ready herself, and she was outside.

The cold hit her lungs. She stopped. The stars were thick in the pine branches, sharp along the towering horizon. Smoke drifted toward her, and inside the smoke the fire seemed intensely bright, carving shadows. There were three people there—Hayden, Laurel, and Jack.

The three circled the flames, passed cups and a flask, and Laurel screwed the flask open, smelled the contents, shuddered, passed it on. The men filled their cups, Hayden looked up at Jack, they nodded, drank, filled again, drank. Then, in silence, they all bent to the dinner gear—dishes washed and dried, food gathered into the bivy sack. Hayden lit a flashlight, started off to hang the sack in a distant tree, keep it safe from bears.

Jack and Laurel sat alone together beside the fire. They held their palms up flat toward the heat. Gussie watched them, waited to hear what they would say, to guess what they'd already said.

"I called this place 'Hell Lake' once," Jack said, "but it doesn't seem like the end of the world now."

"To me it seems like a hundred miles from anywhere," Laurel said. "Too far to ride for help if we need help fast."

"But you said Gussie is okay for the night, so it ain't really the problem it could've been."

"How long would it take to ride out the way you came in?"

"With the pain I've got in my back, I might never make it out. Half the time there ain't a trail at all. Maybe if you'd lend me your bourbon to numb my bones. It might've been a mistake to make this trip at all. Two days in a saddle is too much for me. And if I hadn't said yes to your friend Gussie, she'd be home and safe. You've seen her place in the DuNoir? As sweet a valley as I ever saw. She has special luck, no question. She has her life all figured out. You've seen her cabin?"

"My dad and I bunk with her. I like the DuNoir enough to live there permanently, I think. Don't know what Dad would say to that, but he's calmed down a lot since we got here."

"Before you send for your boxes and cats, young lady, wait till you see a winter in the DuNoir. You can get buried to your neck from just one storm."

"Oh, we've been with Gussie since most of last winter. I'd never lived in snow before I came to Wyoming, but I liked it. I got a snowmobile ride down to the highway most days to catch the schoolbus."

They went quiet. Seconds passed. Then Jack said, "I don't think I followed what you said. I'm tired. You been living with Augusta Locke?"

"Yes."

"You're on hard times of some sort?"

"My mother passed away . . ."

"Oh, sweetheart . . ."

". . . so Dad took custody, and we figured out what to do, and we said we'd finally go looking for Gussie. We'd heard stories about her. She was right in the phone book. Anyone could have found her—it's not like we inherited her special luck or anything."

"So . . . Augusta Locke took you and Hayden in because . . . not that I doubt she would take someone in . . . but her cabin is close quarters, even for family . . . she took you in because . . ."

"Because we're family."

"You're a family, you and Hayden . . ."

"We're her family."

"She's your aunt or something?"

"My grandmother Anne is her daughter."

"No."

"Anne Fisher . . ."

"Fisher . . ."

Quiet again. Hayden walked back into the firelight, sat with them, tossed more wood onto the flames. "What're you guys thinking about?" Hayden said.

"I told Jack that Gussie is my great-grandmother."

"Yes," Hayden said.

"And I was getting ready to say that can't be so," Jack said, "because I've known Augusta Locke since she was young, and she doesn't have children, but you said 'Anne Fisher,' and I'm Jack Fisher, and I know there ain't any extra Fishers loose in the world, not that I could claim, but I'm sort of losing the thread here."

"More bourbon?" Hayden said.

"Couldn't hurt."

"Then we'll run the math. For you to be my grandfather . . ."

"Can't be," Jack said.

"Could be. Why not?"

"How could I be almost dead and not know I had an extra child?"

• • •

The night Gussie found Jack Fisher again, 1943, after hours of talk and whiskey, after the fire had eaten through armloads of bleached sticks, after a final stretch of silence, the crew began to look off into darkness, look toward sleep.

"I'm not ready for the future to begin," King said, "but I've got to shut my eyes." He stood, bent forward, gave his knees a good rub.

"Soon as you step away from the firelight," Buddy said, "it's too dark to tell if your own eyes are open or closed." He held out his hand for help, and King pulled him to his feet.

"I think we all drifted off," Hutch said. He rose, laced his fingers over his belly. "I hope I don't dream. I hope you old grizzlies don't snore."

"We can't leave the fire burning," Cootie said, and he glanced at Gussie as he stood up. The crew all backed a step away. "Mr. Fisher, you going to help our Gussie douse the fire?" Cootie said. "Don't let it spread. We don't have it in us to fight any more fire."

"If everyone's turning in," Jack said, "I'll stay here and wait for the fire to die. Don't worry about it."

"I know how to stir the coals," Gussie said. "You boys go on. You earned your sleep."

The crew turned away, passed beyond the faint light. Then the sounds of the gear dug through, arranged, some dry coughing, silence. If one of the boys lay awake, still roused by the hazards of the day, his vigil would be more in his mind than in the blind night of the granite basin. Whatever moved in the camp and beyond, whatever scraped on rock, whatever he heard he would shape to his fears, until he raised his hand against the stars to shield himself.

Gussie and Jack were alone together, nearly touching at the elbow. The fire had settled into a flat orange battlefield crawling with blue flame. Jack reached for the remaining scraps from the woodpile, laid the twigs onto the coals. Spots of brighter flame started up.

Gussie looked up at Jack Fisher. The brim of his hat caught warm light against the sky. She looked at his wrists, the grime of the long ride. She looked at his ears, neck, the set of his hips, long angle of his legs, tried to make a whole man out of what she saw and what she'd forgotten. She had lost his shape too many miles ago, hadn't been able to separate him cleanly from the other men she'd known. He was a stranger, but she thought that she almost knew him well. She'd created his story over the years, given him wounds, imagined his loves, saved him from suffering, and inside his story she'd marked her own desires, recalled drunken nights and a stranger's kiss. She'd always known that she would never find him again, but here he was. Maybe she'd done something to send him away, or maybe she'd done something to bring him back. His jaw was rough with stubble, gray mixed with the dark. He had turned into a rugged man, the slim white line of a scar on his cheek.

Jack glanced down at her, a sidelong dart of his eyes, a hint of smile or smirk, and then he looked back to the fire. In that flicker, Gussie saw Anne, her way of taking in a scene, judging it, retreating into her thoughts. And she saw more than just Anne's manner. Male against female, ruddy against fair, still there was a strong resemblance between father and daughter. Jack was handsome—a surprise, coming from that wiry boy. The light edged along his cheekbones. He touched a finger to his lips, traced down his chin, down his throat.

She wanted to trace him too, to feel the planes of his face, the jut of his nose, and then she'd know how much of Anne was there. Jack had changed a lot since Estes Park. Anne must have changed too—the girl had lived a quarter century already. Whatever countryside she'd faced each day had molded her, controlled the squint of her gaze. Jack had faced the western sun all these years, the distances that required a long hard stare. Anne and Jack, daughter and father—maybe they'd matured into an unmistakable pair. Where was Gussie in that mixture? What would Jack think if he looked from mother to daughter? But Anne was far away, not to be found. There was no danger that Jack would settle Gussie and Anne at his sides, work two mirrors, gauge the profiles, see Gussie clearly for the first time. She was an unshaped muddle, an awkward woman.

Jack looked again at Gussie, kept looking, going from eye to eye, to her mouth, down her arms. "That baptism dress you wore," he said. "I thought it was the finest I'd seen. I'm not much for womanly things, but that white dress gave me a hollow in my stomach like I ain't felt too many times in my life. And then I find that dress all folded in my duffle where you put it, and I had to figure what to do with it. I can't toss it away, because that wouldn't be fair to the one who made it. I was going to the army camp the next day, and I got the dress on the bed in the hotel where they got us all staying, and I'm thinking I'll cry 'cause I'm just soft enough in the head to cry over something like that. Can you see a man ready to go to war, with his mind all mush?

"The hotel had the families of some of the boys staying too, so I go into the hall with the dress, and I go door to door, looking in to see who is there. Found a girl no more than twelve years old, maybe not even that, but she's tall and really sweet as a cornflower. I ask her mama if the girl might want the dress. The mama seems like maybe I'm a seducer, but the girl comes over and takes the dress and holds it up to her shoulders. Then she kicks around the room and out into the hall. She's having fun with the way it catches in her legs. She's stopping to let it settle down. I can see that she ain't going to ever get rid of that dress, and then she tells me so.

" 'This is for more than just Sundays, isn't it, sir?' she says. 'I'm going to be a beautiful lady.'

"Then her brother comes into the hall, and he sees her and smiles big and tells her to go and put it on, and she does, and she comes out into the hall again, and the brother laughs at what a woman his sister has become. The other boys come out and laugh too, such a sweet thing to see. To think the world could go dark in a few weeks, far away in the battles, and this girl, this beautiful young lady in the fine white dress, will be lost to sight.

"The girl said, 'Thank you,' and I thought that she was already a different person, and she already knew that the world was hard and that she'd probably lose much more in life than she would gain, because she could guess that under all the laughs and compliments the boys were sad and scared and afraid to turn away. I don't doubt that that girl wore the dress on more than one particular occasion, and that she was a beautiful lady, and that she felt a little melancholy when she remembered where she was when she received that gift, not knowing if I who'd given it to her was still alive, or thinking of her brother now dead or maimed or shell-shocked, or remembering all the boys in the hall of the hotel before they left for war. Then she might have given that dress to her own daughter. Think of a mother giving such a gift, and telling such a story of the getting of the gift, and the daughter holding it up to her shoulders and thinking that now she had hope of becoming as lovely and loved as her mother."

"Do you know who the girl was?" Gussie said. "Do you have her name?"

"I don't."

"I wish you'd kept it, not handed it away."

"I would've, but what could I do? Sail to war with it? Wave it like a flag? A white flag? I wasn't planning to give up. And I wasn't going to forget it, anyway, which is all that matters, ain't it? I found someone who'd appreciate it. It was nice. You don't need to worry. It was a good end."

"It was for a daughter."

"I know."

"It was for you to give."

"I did."

"For a daughter."

"I only have sons. Do you have children of your own?"

"You have sons?"

"Two. Good boys, I hope. I'm working on making them worthy." He exhaled a long, tight breath. His face was flushed from talking, from remembering, from the rocky trek he'd made, and the whiskey, the shift from the failing heat of the fire to the waiting chill of altitude.

He was a good man, Gussie thought, more than good enough for Wyoming. She had met a whole slew of gentlemen in this territory who looked only to dig out a bit of gold and then move on. But Jack Fisher had dug in for the summers and winters on his acres near Cora, south of the range. From what he'd said, he ran cattle in the fields among the willow brakes, guided dudes into the Winds, outfitted for the hunters who came west looking for elk, bear, bighorn, deer, antelope, did whatever brought in money. From the vantage of his ranch, the Wind River peaks ran southeast, a jagged wall of gray granite, and he saw the sun go from pink to white on the stone. He could have feared the peaks, the gray taken by rain or snow, swallowed in clouds or small in the morning clarity. He didn't fear what he'd come to know well. For all the shattered defiles, all the blind cliffs and snowbound cirques, he'd always found a way around or through. Riding the highest ridges, feeling gravity work at each stone his horse kicked loose, he saw the strings of lakes far below, and he knew there were trout to pull from the water, there were camps to be made among the boulders and stands of pine, and when the moon came into the night above the camp the light was white as silver, and the range was full of danger and echoes and snow and voices.

Somehow, in her years outfitting through the range for Walker Avary or following the roads for Mr. Foster, Gussie hadn't found Jack. She'd been to Cora, driven the wagon up to the single line of storefronts, the post office, climbed down with Anne, entered in from the gritty wind, made purchases as the day grew dark and hail battered the roof. There they waited in the Cora Store. Across the road, the trees shivered, scraps of leaf falling. If Jack Fisher had ridden up then, jumped to the ground, run in through the doorway, stopped full and wet in the greenish light, the roar of the storm swirling around the building, he would have found Augusta Locke and Anne Fisher at the window, Gussie with a cup of coffee sheltered in her hands, the girl working on a crystal of rock candy.

Anne had been small then, delicate, an unlikely girl in the rough country. She would not yet have grown as high as Jack's waist. Her chin could rest on the windowsill, the light running with lines of water. Jack would pick out his supplies, some treats for his boys. When he turned back toward the door, he'd see Gussie and Anne against the trailing edge of the storm. Jack thought there was something familiar about the woman. As he approached, Anne turned from the view, looked up at him. He stopped. This girl was every bit the girl who would be his daughter if he was ever lucky enough to have a daughter. He saw his own eyes, his own nose. He wanted to replace the rock candy she'd nearly finished, buy her an apple, a ribbon.

He had a room for her in his home north of Cora. He might hold her on his hip, walk out beyond the fence, take her to where the willows blocked the ranch and the birds swarmed. She might lean far back within his hold, look him over. Then she'd reach some sort of a judgment, a hint of a smile, and she'd bring herself back up, lay her head on his shoulder. If Gussie had been tall enough, she would have seen Anne's lips resting against Jack Fisher's wind-chapped neck.

Gussie reached for a water jug, screwed it open, and poured from a height. In the splash and hiss, the coals gave out. Then it was darkness, blindness, Gussie and Jack alone. The heat evaporated. No sound from the crew.

Jack stood up—he cut across the Milky Way. Gussie rose too. Jack stumbled a bit, toward the lake, and she followed. Her boots dragged through the kinnikinnick, stubbed the boulders, but still she could see the shift of Jack's darkness ahead, and then they stood together on the shore. The lake sent calm swells against the gravel, sand, the granite rim of the bowl. Wet cold sank into Gussie's lungs, tightened her chest, iced her veins, until she thought her breathing had stopped, and she let loose a violent cough, a gulping intake. The sound flew around the basin, up onto the slopes, the cliffs, the snow, and came back in broken echoes, a whole valley full of her struggle. Jack patted her on the back, she cleared her throat into silence, calmed, and he placed his arm around her shoulders, pulled her to his side.

"I been in Cora now almost twenty-five years," he said. "I have my sons, Virgil and Jason. They've gone off to the war. They write to me. *Dear dear Papa, I miss you and the ranch. Have you fixed the loafing shed? Have you got the stovepipe to draw clean? I know you have too much to do. Don't worry. I been planning the improvements. When I get ready to ship home, I'll send a supply list. I'll get right to work. You just keep everything from blowing away until I see the place again.*

"They're smart like their mother. They got their handsome looks from her, thank goodness. She came out from Delaware for a summer, the summer I married her, and she stayed as long as she still loved it here, and then she went back east. 'The boys are your boys,' she said, 'and the ranch is your ranch, and I can't claim any of it.' I couldn't argue with her. She'd been waiting till the boys could care for themselves. I'm alone on my acres. Just my ranch hand, and he does most of the work since my boys been gone. I think about all the places I been in my life and how I ended up in Cora.

"How did you end up in this part of Wyoming, Gussie? You got a place to live? You got a husband or someone to keep you happy or keep you busy? I like to think that after all these years since I knew you, and all these miles we followed before we got ourselves to this spot, here by this exact lake, that we both found what we wanted. What did you find?"

Gussie stood with Jack, the weight of his arm around her. How long would they stand there, the lake pulsing against the shore, the stars flowing? Were they friends? Were they even acquainted? Winters separated them, and summers. She couldn't tell him of the frost on the Red Desert, the steaming breath of Anne sleeping beside her in the wagon, the turn of Anne's head as she walked into the lengthening shadows, the sun's heat turning the girl's skin pink. She couldn't tell him of her own long nights, the open roads, the wait as the stars made their circuit. And what could he know of Anne, even if Gussie told him all she could remember? Each question he asked would alter her own memory. Each question would somehow accuse her. And he'd look at Gussie through long silences, study her face, touch his own chin with a finger, try to form the girl's image, try to shape the girl's voice, the girl's reason for leaving.

"I have a cabin in the DuNoir Valley," Gussie said. "I look down the valley to the Wind River Range, though my view is not as impressive as your view from Cora must be. I've lived in the upper country long enough to have a whole list of people I know by sight and name, and some of them I love and I'd miss them if they went away."

"Some of them," he said. "And others wouldn't be missed. I know how that is. And then you think about who might miss you yourself, and if there are people outside the territory who think about you kindly or wonder how you're getting along."

"I wonder the same thing."

"And then I wonder if my real home is somewhere else, and I just don't know it. But how could I ever know the answer? You wind up where you wind up, good or bad. It's been mostly good for me."

"And for me."

"That's all I need to hear."

The night continued, grew colder, and Gussie and Jack found their way back through camp to the gear, and before long they had each found a space among the crew, down into the layers of bedroll, and they all slept the sleep of miles and smoke and loss and altitude. The dark breeze barely found them there. Fragments of glacier-grind and sloughed petal drifted across them, and they inhaled a few molecules, didn't know what passed through them, what crawled beneath them in dark tunnels, what gathered crumbs at the fire circle, what else slept in the basin and waited for dawn.

The sun rose on an empty sky, only a vague mist to the north where yesterday the fire had blazed. The night's cold was quickly lost. The lake was smooth. Sound echoed everywhere, birds at the trees, the snow, and the crack of dry wood, the new flames, clatter of metal pots, horses knocking stone with their metal shoes.

Jack Fisher rode out of the range with the crew, circling around by way of Upper Ross Lake, Ross Lake, and Whiskey Mountain. In town, the Rustic Pine gave the crew a steak dinner on their return, though none of the boys felt they deserved any special notice, and Jack wouldn't attend at all, having just stumbled across the crew after their work was done, his good firefighting intentions irrelevant. Instead, Jack sat at the bar in the Branding Iron Club and drank. Gussie found him asleep on the bank of Horse Creek in the morning, and she and the crew bought him breakfast, replenished his supplies, trucked him back up to the Glacier trailhead for his return across the range, home. "You'll all come to Cora," he said, "and I'll see to it that you won't forget it. I owe you all a good time. Couldn't be happier to have found you."

And then years passed, and finally on an afternoon in early September, Gussie drove down from Union Pass, navigated the muddy crossroads until she came to the Green River, followed it south out of the range, sped on to Cora, turned north again toward the range, passed through Jack's gate. His ranch settled in the willow folds, among the cloudy trees. There he was at the doorway, waving her to a stop, and two tall young men followed him out. His boys. They all greeted her, took up her suitcase, settled her in a guest cabin, left her there to wash the dusty road from her hands. The cabin was a cold space. She could see brief lines of sunset between a few of the logs. The floor creaked. The lantern smoked. Dudes paid good money for this. And who wouldn't? At the window, she watched the sunset fade to white and disappear.

At the dinner table, long after the dishes had been cleared, she sat with Jack and Virgil and Jason. They drank down through another bottle of heavy red wine.

"Glad to finally see you face-to-face again," Jack said, "though that's not to say that I ain't enjoyed our correspondence over the years. The doings in your part of the territory are pretty much the same as the doings down here, though they seem a lot funnier when you don't know the people involved." He reminded them all of the snowed-in dying man and the coffin sled, the fireman who torched empty cabins, the grizzly at the window, the wedding party too drunk to find the church.

Virgil and Jason were sweet and handsome. Gussie watched them as they listened to Jack. They were rapt. They laughed too hard. They added their own details, none of which was true, none of which she'd included in the first telling in her occasional letters, all of which sent them into their own private fits of laughter, brother to brother. They had Jack's height, his slim hands. They had each other's manner, the serious attention, the humor that could go bone dry, could turn mean. They were Wyoming boys. They could drink. They could ride. They could look straight past anything that bothered them. And they attended to Jack.

In her bed in the guest cabin that night, Gussie listened to Jack's ranch. Horses snuffled in the corrals. From far across the fields, the cattle bellowed. A coyote yipped, and a whole chorus joined in. Something caught a ground squirrel, and after a moment of wrenching squeals the sound cut short. The wind came in gusts, pushing the cabin's door deeper against the jamb. Gussie could pick out each sound and name it, although they were not the same sounds she heard in the DuNoir. She didn't know this place.

And in her own bed in the DuNoir, the years moving on, she heard a car pass far on the highway along the Wind River. DuNoir Creek rushed with rainwater channeled from altitude, shivered the air. And she thought often now of Virgil and Jason, and their handsome faces, and their hands knobby from a life of hard work. For all their travels, for whatever they'd suffered in war, they were home. And they didn't look to travel any more, unless it was to ride up past their back fence line, wind through the foothills, turn from the known trail, seek a new route, track a forgotten lake.

Sometimes the boys would cross Union Pass or circle the range, come up into the DuNoir, stay a day or two with Gussie, maybe ride into the Absarokas to hunt elk. They knew people all over that corner of Wyoming. They could wave hello at nearly every passing vehicle and mean it. They were the Fisher brothers. They married girls from Pinedale. Gussie watched each wedding from a willow-branch rocker on Jack's porch. The wind buffeted all the airy dresses. The windmill flashed, the brilliant metal in the sky.

"I'm glad the boys have a home," Jack said. "They seem happy enough with it."

"And their girls," Gussie said, "they love the boys, easy to see, and they like to be out of Pinedale."

"Who wouldn't like to be out of Pinedale?"

"The girls are going to make this ranch wonderful."

"It's not already wonderful?"

"You and me been lucky with our acquisition of property, no doubt. But to be born to a place must be a whole different thing. I guess you and me couldn't imagine. And to bring a wife to the place where you first drew breath. And to hope for children to run the same trails you used to run as a child, back when you thought the whole world was the miles around your home."

Gussie lay in the winter nights in her cabin in the DuNoir. The darkness was full of wind and ice. The window opposite the bed opened on the long white miles to the Ramshorn. Even on a moonless night the window framed a lovely etching of forest, toothed battlements, the unearthly soar of the final peak. And when the moon shone, the valley was a cloud of altitude, the shadows almost too insubstantial to hold the dream from drifting away. It was not an easy view. It was not cozy. It didn't comfort her—it dazzled her eyes, turned her away, rolled her into colder folds of the sheets. How long would each winter night stretch? How many more hours would she follow Jack's sons through her waking dreams, their own sons and daughters now sparking their own romances? How many times would she wonder if Virgil and Jason would have loved their sister? Anne was a Wyoming girl, no matter how far she'd traveled.

Dawn would come. The snow would sparkle and swirl. Out into the day, she was warm but for her lungs. Slow steps through the drifts, toward the creek. On the coldest days she wore the skins the Sheepeater girl had tanned and sewn for Walker Avary. She wore the hat that tickled fur across her brow. She came down through the willows to the open snow where the creek lay buried. She thought she could hear the water travel in its icy tunnel, far from the sun, making its way across the valley floor, looking to burst free into the wilder flow of the Wind River, to take its way toward farther ranges. She held still a long while. It might have been her own blood she heard. She knew she was a strange sight, this small figure clad in fur, a Sheepeater long after the last had departed. She knew that if she walked straight out for even an hour, she would come to a place where no one would ever find her. She stood there, closed her eyes, listened to water and blood. In the skins, she would remain warm as long as she needed to remain warm. However long she had stood there, whatever trick of time, the sun had gone mute in a batting of gray, and large flakes angled on a silent breeze, and the snow stung her eyes and brought tears. She heard an engine, the sound trapped between valley and cloud. She turned, came up from the creek. At her gate, two figures emerged from a car, struggled through the snow. She continued toward her cabin—her prints were already lost, and she pushed through the even white. She felt her skin soothed by the fur. The two figures, man and girl, waved at her, high open gestures, their black mittens, their neon jackets. She approached from the past. They descended from the future. Hayden and Laurel.

♦ ♦ ♦

Gussie didn't want to hear how Jack and Hayden and Laurel would lay out the years, the miles, and what part they'd give to her. She backed away, ducked in through the tent flaps, lowered herself onto the edge of her cot, just breathed for a minute, waiting for her shoulder to settle back into a dull throb. Then she felt around on the floor again, found the gear sack, found the matches. With slow moves, after a few failed attempts, she lit a match and raised the flame to the candle lantern suspended overhead. The wick sparked, and then the small light spread through the tent.

The space was a jumble—clothes strewn across the other cots, sleeping bags in wads, the first aid kit open, scissors exposed, bandages, aspirin, iodine. Nothing, it seemed, that could save a person if something real happened.

Gussie found her bird book beside her binoculars. She rested the book on her lap, studied the cover, the crowding of odd birds— great blue heron, Wilson's phalarope, meadowlark, gilded flicker, ruby-throated hummingbird. What possible swamp or field or shore would find this small gathering so calmly posed? None seemed ready to fly. None even seemed to be entirely alert. But they were beautifully rendered. The delicate texture of feather. The stretch of the wing. The glance to the side.

She tipped the book up, let it fall open. Here were the plovers—the snowy plover with its scoop of a nest on the beach or on the salt flat; the killdeer with its nest in pasture or gravel or beside the road, and the pale brown spotted eggs; the mountain plover with its olive eggs on the plateau or in dry grassland. She leafed forward, found the page with the photograph slipped in as a bookmark, the photograph of Anne, the slick image laid against the dark wings and rusty chest of the aplomado falcon, a tough, beautiful little hunter, *Falco femoralis*. "Aplomado," Gussie said, and she thought her way back to winter in the DuNoir.

Laurel had waited a month before giving Gussie the photograph. On a bleak, bright day, when the temperature wouldn't rise above zero, when ice built a thick layer around the edges of the panes, when Hayden had risked the trek to town to pick up the mail, a touch of cabin fever pushing him into the cold, Laurel had sat with Gussie at the table, at the view, passed the photograph across, said, "This is for you. You haven't asked. I thought you'd ask."

Gussie took the photograph from Laurel's hand, laid it on the table, pressed it flat with her palm. The girl waited, looked away. Outside, the afternoon blazed with cold white light, and a mob of black rosy finches dove in through the bare aspens, fought at the feeder. Seeds and fluff angled off with the wind. Gussie rapped her knuckles on the glass, and the finches fled to the willows, disappeared into the shock of red and orange branches.

"They'll be back," Gussie said. "They need a minute to remember that I'm not a threat. This spot's been a refuge for more than forty years—a black rosy finch refuge. You'll keep the feeders full, won't you, Laurel? You'll fill them when I'm gone, or you'll see that whoever lives here has an eye out for finches? I give them thistle and canary seed."

"Are you going somewhere?"

"Not today, I hope. But soon enough, or too soon, depending on your way of thinking. My heart will go before I do. Damn heart."

"Just take care of yourself."

"There's a limit," Gussie said.

"I guess so." Laurel patted Gussie on the back of her hand. "I'll help you if you need any help. I know how to care for people."

"Oh, yes, sweetheart. Your mother . . ."

"And I take care of Grand Anne when she needs it. She doesn't need it much. Don't you want to know about her?"

"Of course I do."

"You don't seem to."

"I just wonder . . ." She slid her hand off the photo, squinted at it in the mix of window light and dimness. "I want her to be what I hope she will be."

"This is where she lives," Laurel said, and she pinched the corner of the photo, held it toward clearer light. "This is her."

In the photograph, Anne's hair was piled loosely on her head, a silvery cloud above her squinting eyes and half smile. The years had thinned her face, but she had not hardened. Shadow found the soft hollows. Beyond her, apple trees spread their mossy limbs, and the apples were heavy. Past the sunlit orchard, a dark forest rose.

Laurel told Gussie of Grand Anne, her house built into the corner of an old orchard. Each apple tree a different variety. Some of the fruit was green or yellow, with thin skin and a taste that was almost not a taste at all, just a crisp sweet, and others were red and tart, for pie or applejack. Deer came into the orchard at night, tasted the fallen apples, never more than a bite or two from each—there was always another apple a step away.

Dawn with fog thick in the trees. Grand Anne had left at the first hint of light, taken her Labrador down along Papermill Creek, a mile walk every morning, Bubba in and out of the water, his yellow fur soaked to gold. Laurel emerged onto the porch, watched the fog flow down from the hill, heard the drops of moisture caught in the forest eaves, pattering on the black soil. Then Bubba came bounding in through the scrim of the fog, and Grand Anne came along, heavy with damp but moving steadily.

Laurel and Anne ate their oatmeal as the fog cleared, and the sun dried the leaves, started the ground steaming. They had a full day planned—out to Johnson's for oysters, to Toby's for corn and tomatoes, a care package for Susanna, who'd come down with something, walk Bubba on Limantour Beach, see if the dead sea lion had been pulled back out by the tide, look for cinnamon teals in Olema Marsh—but, still, they sat at the table, at the view, and watched the hummingbirds squabble at the feeders, the acorn woodpeckers test the bark of the apple trunks. They waited too long. From the cold ocean beyond the hill, a dark storm advanced, and the rain fell in heavy, straight lines, a roar on the roof that swallowed all sound beyond, the apples bobbing on the branch. Anne seemed to sleep for a minute, taken in by the steady wash, soothed, drifting. Then she sat up, ready.

"I think we're inside for a long while," Anne said. "As long as we get some food to Susanna before dark, the rest of the day can slide away."

For the first time Anne told Laurel of Wyoming and Gussie. Laurel didn't ask any questions that day, just followed her Grand Anne on roads that were barely roads as the cold rain washed away the orchard, the woods, all of Point Reyes. Laurel listened to Anne as the Red Desert rolled through summer, Crooks Mountain rose into the parched wind. Across the empty sky, an airplane flew, its buzz trailing far behind. And then Augusta Locke swung up onto the wagon and flicked the reins, started the team into a prancing walk, a gradual acceleration north. And Gussie talked to the rock crew as if she'd known them all her life, and the darkness came down until there was nothing but voices and the jumping firelight, and then Anne lay with Gussie beyond the voices, and the light was a faint dance on the wagon walls, and then the beautiful slowing of Gussie's breath, and Anne laid her hand on Gussie's brow and tried to guess her dreams, must have been wild places she journeyed, the twitching of her eyes, the sounds she swallowed. Anne knew that Gussie hadn't chosen Wyoming, that the air would always feel dry in her lungs, that for all her pure skill against the land she would never awake at dawn and look out and understand exactly how the shadows stretched and jumped across the gullies and outwash and the steep cuts of the buttes. And Anne would never understand the fog in Point Reyes, the ferns, the way the winter tide tore at the sand, the huge soft driftwood logs in the lagoons, though she'd spent most of her life trying. On her bed, on the sofa, across the table, on the floor, Anne laid out her sketches, watercolors, oils, pastels—the shorebirds at the margin, the bay laurel arching into the canopy, the tule elk in the whip of winter on Tomales Point. Anne followed Laurel among the images, was at the girl's shoulder when she found the Red Desert and lifted it into better light. Laurel saw the figure in the nearby sage, on the noon-bright red of the soil. Gussie was small, shaded by the brim of her hat, her hands loose at her sides, hands that were clearly ready to do something, unlikely to remain still for another moment. Gussie—slim in her dark trousers, steady on the plant of her boots.

"Remember what you can of your mother," Anne said.

"Is your mother dead too?" Laurel said.

"I don't know. I don't know where she is. She wouldn't want to see me."

"Why?"

"I hurt her. I left her."

"Does it matter now?"

"I'm sure it does."

"Why don't you find her?"

"We aren't hardly related anymore. It's been too long. I hope she did alright."

"I could find her. It couldn't be that difficult."

"You don't need to do that."

"It would make you happy."

"I can't promise that it would."

"I want to go away. I want to leave this place and forget about things. Is that bad?"

"No, it's not bad," Anne said. "You go where you need to go."

Laurel went silent, finished with the story. Gussie reached across the table for Laurel, held her hand. The finches rushed through the view, didn't pause at the feeder. And there came Hayden, the roar and smoke of the snowmobile. He shut it down, extracted himself from the machine, wallowed through the snow. "I'm old," Gussie said, before Hayden could reach the door. "I'll need to think about things, think if there's something I should do. I'm slow. But I'm glad you told me. She's still Anne. Still Anne Fisher."

◆ ◆ ◆

Gussie looked up. Jack Fisher had pushed the tent flaps aside, and he stepped inside. As he sat beside her on the cot, she passed the photograph to him. "This is your daughter," she said.

He angled the photograph up into the candlelight, took a good look, ran a finger along Anne's jaw, across her shoulder. "Anne Fisher," he said. "She looks like you, Gussie."

"That's kind of you."

"I'm not being kind. If I was a kind person, I would've known somehow that there was a child that needed caring for. I would've found you sooner. I stopped looking once I got a mile past Greeley."

"How could you have known?"

"I was only looking out for myself."

"But you went to Greeley. You asked after me. Hell, you even remembered my name."

"How could I not remember your name? After what we shared?"

"I'm sure you forgot that as soon as you got off the train in the East."

"I didn't forget, Augusta. What type of man do you think I am?"

"You're a good man."

"Yes."

"And responsible."

"Yes."

"A good father."

"Not to our daughter."

"That's not your fault."

"I was not a gentleman. I left you."

"I knew you were going to leave. I was not exactly a proper lady. And then I became worse."

"No way I can apologize enough."

"All forgiven before it happened."

"It's a big punishment, though, to never tell me about my own blood. Why, Gussie?"

"You have your own life."

"A man can always do with more life."

"I didn't know where she'd gone off to."

"A person can be found."

"I let her go."

"She went on her own. Like you did, if I got the story right. A loss for all involved."

"She can't be my daughter. She's everything I'm not. What would you say if you saw her?"

"I've seen her." He held the photo up to the light again, held it where Gussie couldn't help but look squarely into it. "She's not an exact replica," he said, "but she's close enough. She's more you than me."

"She left."

"You left."

He lowered the photograph. She took it from his hand, ready to slide it back into the book, but she paused. She looked for the hundredth time at the apple trees, tried to discern the individual apples, to match the trees to the apples Laurel had brought to the DuNoir. The abundance of such an orchard was amazing to her, apples scattered for the passing deer.

"I've had some of these apples," she said, moving her finger across the branches. "Laurel picked them, or Anne picked them—you know, I don't know who."

"Tasted good?"

"Sure. They were a treat."

"I could use a good apple."

She looked up at him. He was ready to laugh. He was a first-rate fellow, always had been. She started to reach for him, and her shoulder popped, and she remembered the pain. Then she laughed, fell against his side, he threw his arm around her shoulders, more pain, but she laughed harder. "I'm bruised," she said, barely able to get the words out. He laughed then too, tried to rub her damaged shoulder, but she yowled, ducked from beneath the weight of his hand, folded smaller against his side. And he leaned down to her, kissed the top of her head.

"What the hell?" Laurel said. "Sounded like someone was crying or getting killed." She and Hayden stood in the drape of the tent flaps.

Hayden shone a flashlight on the cot. "Do I need to get the bourbon or make some coffee?"

"Apple brandy?" Gussie said, laughing, and again she lost control, twisting against Jack, and he tried to straighten them both up, tried to catch his breath, but he tipped, the cot tipped, and with a crack Gussie and Jack were piled on the floor, broken cot tangled, Jack holding his knee, Gussie holding her shoulder, their laughter confused, gasping.

Laurel came in over them. She was trying to be serious. "Up," she said, taking them each by the hand. "Sit up. You're brittle. Let me see what you've done to yourselves."

West Torrey Creek

The next morning, they left Bomber Lake behind, the water smooth and turquoise in the early light. The basin carried the trail sounds along—horses, leather, stone. They headed generally south toward Spider Peak, turned the corner of the valley, crossed north into the West Torrey Creek drainage, glaciers tucked into shadows far up the cliffs. Past an unnamed lake at 10,359 feet, through the narrows between The Guardian and Torrey Peak. They stretched out along the valley floor toward Upper Ross Lake. Fresh rockfalls had scarred the western cliffs. Laurel was out ahead, leading the packhorse. In the middle ground, Hayden rode along, reins loose, shading his eyes against the heights. Laurel stood tall in her stirrups, looked back, shouted, her voice pure and sharp. "Come along, people."

Gussie took up the rear, behind Jack. Laurel had strapped Gussie's arm across her belly to keep her shoulder immobile. "Could be separated now," the girl had said. The jolt of each hoof fall centered in the bruise, but Gussie just kept her eyes forward, her free hand on the reins.

Jack had the worst of it—he'd punctured his leg below the knee. Although the wound had been fairly bloodless, he'd fainted twice before Laurel could get it properly cleaned and bandaged. He barely rested the foot of his damaged leg in the stirrup—the slightest pressure sent a shock up to his hip.

"If you put us together," Gussie said, "we might make a whole person. Is your heart working okay? I've been meaning to leave mine behind one of these days."

"We're not that bad," Jack said. "Between us, we're just missing an arm and a leg. I've seen a lot worse, and on men not a quarter as old as us. My only lasting pain will be that dear Laurel didn't get her week in Bomber Basin. That would've meant something to her one day, I'm sure."

"Whatever sense she has, good or bad, she must've got from her dear departed mother. If it was up to you or me or Hayden, we'd spend our week in the sun by Bomber Lake, and maybe we would've healed enough in that time to make this ride tolerable."

"She don't want us sitting still, I guess."

"She knows what she knows, and she knows what she don't know, and she's scared that what she don't know could kill us."

"Something's going to kill us," he said. "Could be this as easy as anything else."

"Don't say that."

"You got plans?"

They rode on past Upper Ross Lake, came to the huge long expanse of Ross Lake. It was hemmed tight by stone. They passed along the narrow eastern shore. Almost to the north end of the lake, they came to the crossing where West Torrey Creek flowed from the lake and disappeared over a waterfall. The horses were spooked by the logs in the fast water, the boulders. But they made it through, climbed up past the end of the lake, onto the Ross Lake Trail, which seemed like a highway after the scratched-out trails they'd been following all day.

"That could've been it for us," Jack said.

"What could've been what?" Gussie said.

"Swept over the falls. Stuck under a rock. Never found."

"That would've been worse for us than for anyone else, I guess."

"I don't know. Someone would have to recover the bodies. That water is damn cold."

"Can a person even get down into those falls?"

"I'd lay my bet on a fella with a rope, a wetsuit, and an oxygen tank."

"Why are we talking about this?"

"Because we could've been swept away."

"We weren't."

"Just dealing with possibilities, not even probabilities."

"Okay. So, someday soon, possibly, we'll get swept over the edge of something."

"That's the spirit."

"There aren't any more creek crossings before we loop back to the trailhead."

"That's okay."

"What's okay?"

"We have clear riding for a while."

They turned from the Ross Lake Trail onto the Whiskey Mountain Trail, started down toward Gussie's truck at the Glacier trailhead.

"I thought we might've lost you back there," Gussie said.

"How?" Jack said.

"I thought you might cut onto the Simpson Lake Trail."

"And?"

"You would've gone back to your own side of the range."

"And have Laurel yell at me? She's got me locked in with this side of the family now. Who knows if I'll ever see my boys again?"

They came around the flank of Whiskey Mountain. The view opened. That view hadn't changed since Gussie first saw it, since she first entered the upper country with Walker Avary. There was still nothing but open miles—down from the range, across the Wind River, into the badlands and beyond. She was too high up to see road or fence—there was nothing to take a person in a particular direction, nothing to bar passage except for the folds of the land. She knew her way through.

"We're going on to Point Reyes, aren't we?" Gussie said.

"Yes, we are," Jack Fisher said, "to see Anne."

The author wishes to express his gratitude to Bob Lowney, Paul Davis, Trish Johnson, Bruce and Sally Adams, Jan and John Zimpel, Jennifer Korman, Mike Henry, Andrea Dupree, Walt Domes, Chuck Verrill, and Paul Slovak.

FOR THE BEST IN PAPERBACKS, LOOK FOR THE

In every corner of the world, on every subject under the sun, Penguin represents quality and variety—the very best in publishing today.

For complete information about books available from Penguin—including Penguin Classics and Puffins—and how to order them, write to us at the appropriate address below. Please note that for copyright reasons the selection of books varies from country to country.

In the United States: Please write to *Penguin Group (USA), P.O. Box 12289 Dept. B, Newark, New Jersey 07101-5289* or call 1-800-788-6262.

In the United Kingdom: Please write to *Dept. EP, Penguin Books Ltd, Bath Road, Harmondsworth, West Drayton, Middlesex UB7 0DA.*

In Canada: Please write to *Penguin Books Canada Ltd, 90 Eglinton Avenue East, Suite 700, Toronto, Ontario M4P 2Y3.*

In Australia: Please write to *Penguin Books Australia Ltd, P.O. Box 257, Ringwood, Victoria 3134.*

In New Zealand: Please write to *Penguin Books (NZ) Ltd, Private Bag 102902, North Shore Mail Centre, Auckland 10.*

In India: Please write to *Penguin Books India Pvt Ltd, 11 Panchsheel Shopping Centre, Panchsheel Park, New Delhi 110 017.*

In the Netherlands: Please write to *Penguin Books Netherlands bv, Postbus 3507, NL-1001 AH Amsterdam.*

In Germany: Please write to *Penguin Books Deutschland GmbH, Metzlerstrasse 26, 60594 Frankfurt am Main.*

In Spain: Please write to *Penguin Books S. A., Bravo Murillo 19, 1° B, 28015 Madrid.*

In Italy: Please write to *Penguin Italia s.r.l., Via Benedetto Croce 2, 20094 Corsico, Milano.*

In France: Please write to *Penguin France, Le Carré Wilson, 62 rue Benjamin Baillaud, 31500 Toulouse.*

In Japan: Please write to *Penguin Books Japan Ltd, Kaneko Building, 2-3-25 Koraku, Bunkyo-Ku, Tokyo 112.*

In South Africa: Please write to *Penguin Books South Africa (Pty) Ltd, Private Bag X14, Parkview, 2122 Johannesburg.*